GREENWOOD
AND ARCHER

GREENWOOD AND ARCHER

Marlene Banks

MOODY PUBLISHERS
CHICAGO

Published in association with the literary agency of **Hartline
Literary Agency, LLC., 123 Queenston Drive, Pittsburgh,
PA 15235.**

Interior and cover design: Design Corps (http://designcorps.us)
Cover image: Multiple iStockimages and getimages
Author photo: Butler Prestige Photography

Library of Congress Cataloging-in-Publication Data

Banks, Marlene.
    Greenwood and Archer / Marlene Banks.
      p. cm.
    ISBN 978-0-8024-0621-7
    1. African Americans—Oklahoma—Fiction.
    2. Oklahoma—History—20th century—Fiction.
    3. Tulsa (Okla.)—Race relations—Fiction. I. Title.
    PS3602.A6427G74 2012
    813'.6—dc23

                                        2012016645

1 3 5 7 9 10 8 6 4 2

Printed in the United States of America

As always, first I dedicate this novel with highest praise
to Almighty God and my Savior Jesus, The Christ

And in loving memory and honor
of my grandparents:

Ora B. Banks and Rachel Singleton Banks

George Franklin and Mary Ethel Bowe Franklin Brockett

In late May and early June, 1921, a race riot erupted in the Greenwood District of Tulsa, Oklahoma. An estimated three hundred men, women, and children lost their lives, and churches, schools, stores, movie theaters, a hospital, and libraries were among the six hundred businesses destroyed, besides over a thousand homes. These events were depicted in the author's *Son of a Preacherman*.

The events in *Greenwood and Archer* take place after *Son of a Preacherman*, continuing the stories of members of the Matthias and Freeman families, as well as other Tulsa characters.

GREENWOOD DISTRICT
TULSA, OKLAHOMA
JUNE 3, 1921

The scent of smoke lingered in the air even two days after the horrendous riot. Dazed, many people still wandered around, trying to locate loved ones. It was a time of disbelief that such atrocities happened in their community. Being black in Tulsa had never meant first-class citizenship, but until now it never caused such violent victimization. Murder and mayhem had swept through the successful Negro community of Greenwood District with a deadly and destructive fury.

"Why we gotta wear badges?" a black man protested.

"Cause that's the new law," the irritated police officer snapped.

"It ain't right. After all we been through you is tellin' us we gotta identify who we is? I always been a free, law-abiding citizen, but when they come in our neighborhood terrorizing us and now tell us we under martial law, it ain't right!"

"Go on and have your employer get you a badge or stay off the streets. That's the new rule. Now go ahead, boy, before I throw you in jail!"

"I ain't no boy, I'm a man just like you," he grumbled walking away.

AFRICAN METHODIST EPISCOPAL CHURCH

New laws were being put into effect in Tulsa after the riot, not for protecting the victims but to subdue any thought of retaliation against white citizens.

"Curfew! What gives them the right to issue a curfew only on Negroes?" Pastor Scoggins demanded from in front of the pulpit.

"It's not right!" Reverend Matthias agreed.

"Is it just in the city, or does the county have a curfew too?" Reverend Metcalf asked, troubled.

"They told me my taxis have to be off the street by eight at night," L. D. Johnson said. "That shorts my money to make a decent living. I make a lot of my big fares after dark, and they know it."

"They don't care about you making a living. They want us to all go broke," H. T. Wilson declared.

"What is the NAACP doing about this?" Reverend Matthias asked, turning to Ethan Freeman.

"It's just in the township limits so far, but I think they'll soon change it to include the counties," Ethan said.

"This is the last straw," Reverend R. A. Whitaker declared as he stood up. "I'm sick of them harassing us when we're the injured party." The preacher stepped out into the aisle. "They burned down Mt. Zion Baptist Church because we dared to prepare to protect ourselves and fight back. They murdered innocent human beings and destroyed blocks of valuable property. Then they try to blame us for the riot. I'm sick of their twisting the facts."

"Enough is enough," Mr. French said from the rear of the church. The house was full for this covert meeting. The law was cracking down on every move made in Greenwood District. Police patrolled the area, stopping and questioning its citizens at random. What should have been police protection for the residents of Greenwood District became police persecution.

"I can't find my sister," Georgia Logan said. "They took her out of the house, I'm told, and then burned the house down. I can't find where they took her. She's sick and in a wheelchair."

"We'll help search the hospital and the Red Cross with you," an older woman volunteered.

"I already did and she's not there." Tears pooled in Georgia's eyes.

"Maybe someone took her in," Mrs. French suggested.

"I need help feeding the survivors and finding them shelter," Reverend Metcalf announced.

"You can use this church if you need to, Reverend," Pastor Scoggins offered.

Clara Hydecker started crying. "They murdered my poor Sam for nothing! What are we going to do? My husband is dead, we have no home and no food, and everything we owned was burned with our house. I have no money and I have four children to feed!"

A young man called out, "Yeah, what are we going to do? The law isn't on our side. What are we going to do?"

Billy Ray Matthias stood up. "We're going to find food and feed as many people as we can. Then we'll set up temporary shelter as best we can, tents if we have to for the time being. Then we organize a rebuilding plan. What we don't do is give up. We don't accept defeat, because that is exactly what they want."

"Yeah, we can rebuild this neighborhood even better than before if we try," Vic Brown shouted.

"Easy for you to say since your house ain't burned to the ground," Manny Griswold muttered.

Billy Ray walked to the front of the sanctuary, his imposing figure matched only by what he said. "The people of Greenwood District cannot give up. We have to get to work helping each other and rebuilding what was destroyed, but before we worry about any of that . . . we need to pray."

CHAPTER ONE

EAGLES POINTE COUNTY, OKLAHOMA
SEPTEMBER 1922

The race riot of May 31 and June 1, 1921, had turned a once thriving entrepreneurial community into a bloody battlefield. Hatred and terror reigned throughout the evening and into the wee hours of the night. To the beleaguered residents of Greenwood District, morning's dawn unveiled the full horror of lost lives and property destroyed.

Thirteen months after the racially motivated riot, Greenwood District still evidenced the assault on its citizens and destruction to its infrastructure. The rebuilding process was under way but would never fully heal the scars of that fateful evening. Gradual development was being made to restore demolished businesses and homes. It was not an easy task, but one that would be completed. The spirit of Greenwood would not tolerate eradication by those consumed with violent intent.

Prayers were continually being offered for the people and the neighborhood from Christ-loving citizens of Tulsa, black and white, and across the country as well. Greenwood District would not remain a hollowed-out shell of a community but be raised from the dead by the hand and will of God.

The county beyond the city limits had not suffered much of the murderous invasions and fiery attacks. Ranchers in Eagles

Pointe were busier than ever employing people from Greenwood and providing for the many displaced city dwellers. The most disheartening factor was that after all the wreckage, things had not improved and Tulsa's caste system was still firmly in place.

Amos Grapnel's beady eyes darted around Cordell Freeman's ranch as he was leaning against the large weathered barn. Grapnel's short stature and chubby frame sported a protruding belly and balding head. He sporadically rocked back on his heels to show off the fancy boots he'd recently purchased in Texas. Tom Eberly, a frail gray-haired man who accompanied him, stood slightly bent over leaning on his walking stick as he watched Cord lift a bale of hay. Grapnel pulled out a pipe. "You ought to give it some real thought, boy," he said reaching for the tobacco pouch in his back pocket.

"Told you, I'm not interested in sellin'," Cord said, hauling the bale toward the barn.

"Why not? Offering you more than twice what you paid. Can't beat that for profit."

"Don't care about profit. I'm doing good right here and I don't wanna sell my place, Mr. Grapnel."

"Don't be so quick to turn up your nose at a lot of money, boy. You could get another place if you want with what you'll make, or . . . you could sit on your bank account and move back home with your folks." Grapnel grinned slyly.

"I done told you I'm not interested," was Cord's irritated response.

"Plain pigheaded," Grapnel grumbled, "just like your father."

"We might as well go," Eberly said, shifting his weight impatiently.

"Why are you so attached to this place anyway?" Grapnel continued. "It's not your family's land. You're all alone out here except for those hired workers you got from town. Don't have no family around here to keep you company. I'd think you'd be glad to be rid of this place seeing you lived here with that no-good wife that hung herself."

Cord's head jerked up. Lightning fast he dropped the bale and charged. Before Grapnel could react, Cord had him by throat. "I'll kill you for talkin' that way about my wife," he shouted, clamping tightly on the man's throat. Grapnel's eyes bugged as he desperately groped at Cord's hand to get free.

Eberly straightened up as best he could hollering, "Let 'em go! You'll choke the life outta him!" He whacked Cord across the back with his cane twice. "Turn him loose!"

The blows didn't faze Cord. He was crazed with fury. "You come on my land talkin' against my wife, you lowdown snake! I'll kill you, so help me, I'll kill you!"

Grapnel's color was starting to drain. Eberly looked over at Grapnel's car trying to gauge how fast he could make it to the vehicle and retrieve his friend's pistol. The sound of fast-moving hooves drew his attention and he turned all the way around.

"Cord, let him go," a frantic female screamed from on top of an impressive palomino. "Let him go, Cord!"

A large muscular man ahead of her had already dismounted from a huge brown stallion and was hurrying toward the choking man. Eberly stumbled backward seeing the powerfully built black male rushing toward them. "Stay out of this," Cord yelled, trying to maintain his grip when the man grabbed his hands, prying them loose from Grapnel's neck.

"Cord, please let him go," the woman pleaded, bolting toward him after she jumped down from her horse.

"They'll kill you for sure if you do this," the man warned looking Cord in the eyes. "Is that what you want . . . to die for killing this devil?"

Cord stopped applying pressure but he still had hold of Grapnel. "He should die, him and all his rotten kind. They killed those people in town and the law did nothin' about it! Not one drop of justice to those murdering dogs. He was part of it, you said so yourself. He tried to kill you, didn't he? So why shouldn't he die?"

"You're right, he was part of it and the law did nothing to him or the rest of them but believe me the Lord will do something. He'll have His justice for all the evil done in this world."

"Ain't waitin' on the Lord. This polecat needs dealing with

now. He belittled my wife and I won't put up with him or nobody else talkin' like that about her."

"Make him turn Amos loose," Eberly demanded raising his cane in the air again. "He gotta breathe."

Cord's sister, Benny, reached her brother and gently put her hand on his shoulder. "Cord, please, please don't do this. Let him go. Billy Ray's right; Jesus will have justice for all the wrongs done to our people, but not this way. They will answer to God, and if we wait it out, justice will be done. There's been too much killing already; please, no more."

"I oughta snap his nasty neck."

"Don't let this man goad you into tangling with the law, 'cause you'll lose. That's all they need is for you to get arrested for killing him then they'll gladly see you in the electric chair. I couldn't stand losing my big brother and neither could Momma. Please, please let him go." Tears filled her eyes.

Cord released Grapnel, dumping him on the ground. Grapnel gasped for air, loudly coughing and holding his throat. Eberly limped over to his friend. Cord looked down at his foe with loathing. "I should finish you off," he threatened. "I don't care nothin' 'bout dyin' in no electric chair. I'd be with Savannah if I did." He looked at his sister. "But for your sake, just for you and Momma, I won't."

"Thank the Lord." Benny sighed, laying her head on his shoulder. "We love you, Cord, and we need you here with us." She resented her brother's devotion to his deceased wife but had learned not to show it.

Billy Ray put his hand on Cord's back. "You made the right decision, the wise one."

"He ought to be jailed for attackin' a white man," Eberly insisted, pointing his stick at Cord.

"Shut up, old man. Take your no 'count friend and get off my land!"

"Won't forget this, boy. You wait and see, the law'll handle your crazy black hide."

Billy Ray lifted the still coughing victim off the ground. Grapnel couldn't speak but his expression, a mix of fear and rage did. He jerked away. Billy Ray knew his hateful nemesis would never let this matter drop. Still, he tried to brush the dirt from Grapnel's clothes as the incensed man rejected his assistance. "I'm trying to help clean you off," Billy Ray pointed out.

"Get your big black hands off me, boy," Grapnel croaked snatching himself free, though barely able to stand. "I'd as soon see you dead than have you touch me, you big ape." He walked shakily toward his vehicle with Eberly limping beside him.

"Shoulda let me choke the life out him," Cord grumbled squinting from the noonday sun.

"Don't think I didn't want to, but I couldn't," Billy Ray said, watching the ornery pair depart. Memories of the harrowing riot and his almost fatal encounter with Amos Grapnel and Moose Kegel came vividly back to his mind. He immediately prayed, *Lord, heal my soul and fix my heart because if You don't, what I do to that man won't be pretty. Remove my hatred, Jesus.*

"Why was he here?" Benny asked.

"Wants me to sell this place to Eberly."

"What for? Why does Eberly want this ranch at his age and in his condition?"

"Same reason the rest of them wantin' to buy up all of Greenwood, I reckon. Eberly said something about leavin' an inheritance for his grandkids."

"What did you tell him?" Billy Ray asked.

"That I wouldn't sell."

"I take it he got mad and said what?" Benny wanted to know.

"Opened his foul mouth against Savannah, that's what." Cord's jaw tightened.

Benny shot Billy Ray a telling look. "What does she have to do with you selling your ranch?"

"Nothing, he was being nasty is all."

"You know he's going to cause trouble over this," Billy Ray predicted.

"I'm telling Ethan in case you need his help," Benny said.

"I'll tell him myself. He's comin' here later." Cord walked over to the bale of hay he'd dropped. "What brought you two over?"

"Divine intervention I'd say." Billy Ray chuckled.

"Momma's cooking steaks on the pit tomorrow. She wants you come by and eat with us."

"Tell her thanks for askin', but I can't."

"Why not? You love beef on the pit. You love Momma's rhubarb apple pie too." Benny smiled.

"Sounds good, but I got a lot to do around here."

"Stop making excuses and come over. You never accept our invites to visit. Why can't you let bygones be bygones? Daddy'll be so happy to see you."

"Did he say that?" Cord dropped the bale inside the barn door and headed for another. Billy Ray fell in step behind him.

"Well, not in so many words but I know he misses you and . . ."

"Let it rest, Benny. It's all right; I'm doing fine here on my own. I don't hold no ill feelings toward Dad anymore, but what happened can't be undone. Truth of the matter is I don't think it was all my fault. I feel bad about what I did, don't get me wrong. I should have never disrespected him that way no matter what he said, but he's never owned up to his wrong in the matter so that's it. Leave it alone."

"You know how stubborn Daddy is."

"Yeah, well so am I."

"Daddy still loves you, Cord, and he wants you to be part of our family like always. He said so."

"You can't go back, Benny. That's the hard thing about making bad mistakes. You're stuck with the consequences."

"God gave us the ability and right to repent for our mistakes. To turn away from our misdeeds and ask forgiveness and to forgive people who hurt us."

"I already asked Dad and God to forgive me, and I forgave Dad so let it go at that. Things may never be like they used to be between us. You need to accept that," Cord said firmly.

"But . . ."

"Benny, your brother said let it go so you should respect that," Billy Ray advised.

Benny sighed in frustration. "All right, I'll leave it be."

CHAPTER TWO

TULSA, OKLAHOMA

Tulsa's chief of police, Jake Gilbert, massaged his temples. Listening to Amos's overblown description of the assault prompted him to look down at the aspirin on his desk. Grabbing them up when Grapnel finished his exaggerated narrative, Gilbert threw them in his mouth, swallowing water from a glass in front of him.

"Tom can verify every word I told you," Grapnel said, tight-lipped. Tom Eberly sat beside him, head bobbing in agreement. Gilbert swallowed the pills and closed his eyes sitting back massaging his temples more vigorously than before.

The two men exchanged impatient glances before Grapnel grunted, "Spit it out. What do you plan on doin' about that Freeman boy trying to choke me to death?"

"You were on his property, right?" Gilbert asked. He didn't bother to open his eyes.

"That's right; what of it?"

"Nothin'. Just getting the facts straight."

"Stop stallin', Jake, and send somebody out there to arrest that crazy darkie."

"Don't come in here tellin' me what to do," the chief growled. He sat up and made himself open his eyes. "Listen, Amos, I got a headache the size of Texas. I ain't doin' nothin' till it's gone, so come back tomorrow and we'll see what's what."

"Tomorrow?"

"That's right, the day after today."

"Don't give me any wisecracks. You mean to tell me you're gonna let that colored get away with what he did to me?"

"I didn't say that. I *said* come back tomorrow. Go out to the desk and make an official complaint report."

Grapnel stood on his feet. "Was a time a white man didn't have to file no official reports to get action from the law against them people. You're on thin ice around here, so I would think you'd want to prove yourself worthy."

"And what's that supposed to mean?"

"It means you don't act like you know how you got where you are *or* who put you there *and* who can get you out. Kowtowin' to coloreds from up north don't look good. Neither does lettin' them have their way and ignoring the rights of decent white folks. Don't think any of this has gone unnoticed."

"You're outta line talkin' like that. You and your friends better back off me."

"That's not what you were saying when they indicted you for neglect of duty."

"I was exonerated of any wrongdoing or negligence, remember?"

"Thanks to us."

The chief rose from his seat staring Grapnel in the eyes. "Who do you think you are comin' in here talkin' to me this way?"

"It's not just me. Everybody's taking a real interest in how this police department's bein' run lately."

"Listen here, Amos, run your real estate business and leave enforcin' the law to me. I don't step in your territory, so don't you tread on mine. That goes for you and that so-called everybody you're referring to."

"I wouldn't be stupid enough to make enemies with the wrong people if I were you. In case you haven't noticed, them Greenwood coloreds can't hardly help themselves since they've been put in their place. Sure ain't gonna be able to help you if you turn your back on your own kind. Better act like you know you're a white man and stop caterin' to those government people snoo-pin' round here . . . and stay clear of them high-minded Negroes from that NAACP."

"I don't cater to no-blasted-body and you or nobody else tells me what to do! Now get out of my office!"

Eberly scuffled up out of his chair grabbing his cane. "Come on, let's go."

Grapnel was staring the chief down. "Don't be a fool. Those people aren't worth it." He started toward the door. "You know, I'm surprised at you. You used to have as little tolerance for them as any of us. You've changed, Jake, what happened? Getting soft in your old age?"

"I'm giving you fair warning, Amos; walk a straight line in Tulsa. Don't even spit on the curb and let me catch you, 'cause I'll run your trouble-making hide in, so help me."

"You'll regret going up against me. I promise you won't like me when I'm crossed. So I'm giving you one more chance to redeem yourself. Are you gonna do something about Cordell Freeman or not?"

"I'll look into it tomorrow like I said. Make sure you fill out the complaint with the desk sergeant. Once that's done I'll see what's to be done—in my time not yours."

"I'll fill out your dadblasted complaint. Just make sure you take care of that black boy."

CHAPTER THREE

GREENWOOD DISTRICT IN TULSA

Elizabeth Whitehead was a beautiful woman, elegant and gracefully poised. An enticing figure enhanced her stylishly conservative apparel. Her big round eyes were highlighted by their unusual hazel color. Elizabeth's face, with its smooth, light-complexioned skin and delicate features was perfection itself. Her mannerisms were a paradox tottering between homespun earthiness and learned sophistication.

Elizabeth's constant movements around the room distracted Ethan. He couldn't keep his eyes off the cute little sway of her hips when she walked. He was enchanted by her smile and delighted at her laughter, which sounded like music to his ears. When she said his name in her soft, warm voice, he heard angels singing in chorus to his soul.

The most disturbing thing was her touch. When she casually brushed against him or touched his arm he felt a surge of excitement beyond anything he'd ever experienced. Ethan had witnessed these foolish emotions, the silly inclinations in other men. He'd laughed at their bumbling around like lost puppies because of some woman. He shook his head in sympathy more than once about men who forsook reason and sanity behind loving a woman. Determined not to be consumed by romantic sentimentality Ethan swore off the pitfalls of head-over-heels love. A calm, compatible friendship had always been enough for him.

Now since he'd met Elizabeth, he was reconsidering these views. His head was down trying to concentrate on the document in front of him so she wouldn't catch him staring at her. He managed to steal lingering glances when she wasn't looking. Elizabeth finally stopped arranging the books and closed the glass case door sitting down at the desk on the other side of the room from him. Looking around she said, "I think this will make an excellent outer office for your secretary."

"You've done a great job fixing this place up. I appreciate all your hard work."

"My pleasure. And since you're giving me free office space for an undetermined amount of time, it's the least I could do."

"After all the NAACP has done for the people of Greenwood, office space is an underpayment," Ethan told her sincerely.

"We haven't done half what we could if these judges and politicians would stop tying our hands," Elizabeth said. "I'm so disappointed those indictments brought about no real justice."

"They weren't supposed to bring justice," Ethan reminded her. "They were phony attempts to quiet the public outcries against city officials. How else can anyone explain the ridiculous conclusion that we caused our own neighborhood to be burned to the ground?"

"Exactly. I can't believe the grand jury found that fault lay with the Negro community." Elizabeth sighed.

"Welcome to the face of Negro life in Tulsa," Ethan said with a grim smile. "We're at the mercy of white authority and disposition, which usually isn't too friendly. We have no rights as far as they're concerned. They hate the fact Negroes are living comfortably, especially if they happen not to be."

"I don't understand how everything is so blatantly segregated here and the people just accept it."

"Things are like this all over the country, not just in Oklahoma. Negroes have no political power, so what can we do?"

"Fight for the right to be a legitimate part of Tulsa's economic, political, and social system. Become instruments of change." Elizabeth looked up with sparkling eyes ablaze. It warmed

Ethan's heart. She always took on such an excited air when she talked about injustice and politics. "We will never be given full rights if we don't demand them. We have to insist on equality and be willing to fight for it."

Ethan nodded toward the big storefront window to the street. "You see all that flattened space from burned down buildings? How do people fight that kind of hatred when the law doesn't do its part? A lot of innocent people died last year—men, women, and even children. One hundred and eight thriving businesses were destroyed. Beautiful homes were set on fire, and hundreds more people were assaulted, with many dead or left for dead. All that open violence went on for over sixteen hours and not one white man has ever been properly prosecuted for any of the crimes. Not for murder, looting, or destroying property."

Elizabeth's bright eyes lost their luster as her face saddened. "We tried as hard as we could but the discriminatory laws in this state blocked our efforts for more arrests and adequate prosecutions. Here and everywhere in this nation our people are being grossly violated with either sanctioning or disregard by the governing authority."

"Exactly my point. And those of us who live here have even less power than the NAACP or federal government."

"I suppose you're right," Elizabeth admitted. "I just get so frustrated seeing us treated like second-class citizens or less."

"Me too. I've worked as hard as I know how; fighting through legal means but it's not enough."

"Don't underestimate your work. I've read some of your cases, and you're brilliant. You and Mr. Vaughn made a formidable legal team. We even heard of your work in Chicago."

Ethan appreciated the affirmation. Then he said, "A lot of people around here think it's the devil causing so much trouble."

Elizabeth made a dismissive expression. "They're free to think what they want but I don't believe in religious excuses for man's social ills, do you?"

Ethan cocked an eye. "Well, to be truthful I'm starting to have more confidence in Jesus than in our legal system."

"I can't believe an intelligent man like you would relegate everything to religious superstition. That's one thing that's holding us back, all this religious dependency. Why fight for rights? Just wait till you die and get to heaven and *de Lawd* will make it better."

"Whoa, Bet, don't you believe in God?"

She smiled at Ethan. "I grew up in a very religious home. My grandfather was a fire-and-brimstone Louisiana preacher for decades before he moved to Chicago. My parents practically lived at church and dragged us kids there all the time. All that dedication to Jesus and what did it get them? They continually struggled to survive to the very end of their lives. As far as I could see, no loving God ever helped them in the least."

"So you don't believe in God?"

"I . . . I'm not sure He exists. I know I don't think He's this loving, caring, superior being like I was taught to believe, if He exists at all. At the very least He's not what I was taught He is by my family."

"Then you think God is what?"

"I haven't quite figured that out yet but He's certainly not the Savior of our people, or my soul like my father always said."

"Look at it this way," Ethan suggested. "You came from a Chicago tenement yet you've made great strides in your life. Who enabled you to do that? You went to law school and carved out a notable reputation as an attorney in spite of being Negro, poor, and female? How do you think that happened? You don't think God had something to do with it?"

"It happened because I worked hard pouring everything I could into learning the law. After I graduated and passed my examinations I used that knowledge to help my people's cause. It was torture getting in and through law school being a colored female. You have no idea what I had to do and put up with to get where I am. You can believe this; my decision to be a lawyer was thwarted at every turn including other Negroes! I fought against all kinds of hindrances and I did it by myself—not with any divine help from above, thank you very much."

"But don't you give God any credit for getting you through? Who gave you your interest in law? Who gave you your tenacity to stick it out? And for that matter, where did your intelligence and ability come from in the first place?"

"I didn't realize you were so caught up in religion," Elizabeth replied.

"I'm not caught up in religion, per se, but I'm very interested in this Jesus my mother's always loved so much. I realize more than ever how the Lord has been my family's strength for as long as I can remember. I've strayed from what I was taught, no doubt about that, but I think it's time I get a handle on what I believe."

Benny leaned against Billy Ray's shoulder as they sat companionably together on the wooden porch swing. He put his arm around her and kissed her forehead. "Don't look so miserable. You tried, that's all you could do. They'll patch things up in time."

"I thought after Savannah's death things would get back to normal but they're both so stubborn. They need each other but neither one wants to give in first."

"Your father went to Cord when he first found out about Savannah's suicide, didn't he?"

"Yeah, but Mom said he wasn't very comforting to Cord. He just gave his condolences like he would somebody he hardly knew and left."

"Who could comfort your brother back then? He was a wreck and understandably so."

"Daddy could have tried harder."

"Guess he didn't want to be a hypocrite about it."

Benny straightened up and folded her arms across her chest. "Why do men always take up for each other even when they're wrong?"

"I don't want to argue, sweetie; let's talk about something else. Your father and brother will find their way back to each other in God's time. You can't force it."

"I suppose so." Benny was silent for a moment. "It's just that

Cord is so pitiful and I know he's still hurting. He reminds me of myself not so long ago. When your world crumbles around you and your hopes for the future disappear so horribly like his did, it's too much to handle alone."

"Exactly, and that's why he needs Jesus. No matter how much in love people are they should never wrap *all* their hopes and dreams around each other. Christ has to be first."

"Of course, that's true but it helps to have someone right here on earth to help get you through." Her face softened. "Like the way you helped me. I was every bit as miserable as Cord when I met you. If it weren't for your persistence, where would I be?"

"It wasn't me, it was the Lord who brought you through."

"Well, He used you in my life to do it." Benny was wistful. "Dad and Cord used to be close. I think he could help him get past this obsessive mourning over Savannah if—"

"Benny," Billy Ray cautioned.

"I'm not going to say anything unkind about her, but Cord is my brother and I'm worried about him. She's dead and gone and he's alive, but she's still tormenting him from the grave."

"I've talked to your brother a few times about his grief and it's not her that's tormenting him," Billy Ray told her. "It's his own guilt that's weighing him down. He's not facing his remorse or anger very well. He thinks if he mourns her death hard enough and fights to keep her reputation untarnished then it'll make up for his mistakes."

"What mistakes? Savannah was unfaithful to him."

"I'm not at liberty to give you details of what we talked about. That's for him to discuss if and when he wants."

Benny looked at Billy Ray curiously. "All right. I want you to know how much I appreciate you taking time with him and being there for him. I think it's really made a difference. He'd be worse than he is if he didn't have you and Ethan to help him through this."

"We all need help sometimes."

"He wasn't very sympathetic when you were in trouble but you didn't hold that against him. It's one of many reasons why

I love you."

Billy Ray kissed Benny on the head again. "There's nothing wrong with your brother that more Christ in his life can't fix."

"You're very good at showing people God's light and how we can overcome problems through Christ. It's a gift you have, don't you think?"

He cut her a suspicious look. "Huh?"

"A gift as strong as your musical talent."

"Maybe."

"Don't you think there's some special way you're supposed to use these gifts?"

His suspicious look became more defined. "What are you getting at?"

"Have you ever considered preaching?"

Billy Ray chuckled. "You've got to be kidding; me a preacher?"

"It's not so far-fetched. After all, you are the son of a preacher."

"I'm definitely the least likely of my father's sons to ever preach the Word of God. Besides, the Lord is supposed to call a person to preach"

"You don't think you're called?"

"Not at all."

"Why not? You preach all the time whether you know it or not."

"You are well aware of the not-so-reputable aspects of my past. I'm hardly qualified for the pastorate," Billy Ray reminded her.

"How many times have you told me we're not called to be perfect for the kingdom? It's you who taught me I'm made perfect by Christ's shed blood and not my actions. So why are you any different?"

Billy Ray smiled. "You're a good student."

"You're a great teacher."

He kissed Benny with an undeniable longing, conscious of his need to subdue his desires. When she finally pulled away, he asked, "How long are you going to wear my ring and keep me hanging? Put me out of my misery and let's set a date."

Benny tensed. "I thought we agreed not to rush into anything."

"We're not rushing. We've been engaged for over eight months."

"That's not so long."

"It is for me. I'm hoping it is for you too."

She turned her head. "We have a lifetime together. There's no hurry is there?"

He pulled her tight to him. "I want us to be together, Benny, fully together like a man and woman are meant to be."

"I want that too but I—I want to make sure I'm ready."

He smiled. "You'll be an aging spinster if you wait much longer."

She smiled back, smacking his shoulder. "I'm not that old."

"Seriously, why are you stalling? You do love me, don't you?"

"Yes, of course, I love you. I love you more than I ever thought I could ever love again."

"Then what's the holdup?"

"There is no holdup. Marriage is a very serious step. I'm just taking time before we . . . so we know we're not making a mistake."

"A mistake? You have doubts about us getting married?"

Benny looked up at him mentally flailing for words. "I don't think so, but . . . I'm not a hundred percent sure."

Billy Ray stood up walking to the edge of the porch with his hand in his pocket. "I thought you knew for sure like I do. How long have you felt this way?"

"A few months."

"Why didn't you tell me?" he asked sounding hurt.

"I thought it was a phase and would pass."

He wrapped an arm around a wooden pillar. "You want to call it off?"

"No," she blurted out quickly. "I adore you, Billy Ray. I do love you and I want to be your wife. I really do."

His head dropped. "I'm missing something here. You have doubts enough not to want to set a date, but you love me and want to marry me. It doesn't make sense. What's going on with you, Benny?"

"I'm not sure. I'm confused." She got up and walked over to

him.

He turned to face her and gently pulled her into his embrace. As he kissed her with an overwhelming intensity, he could feel her surrender as she returned his kiss with passion. Releasing his hold, he looked into her eyes. "Are you still confused?"

"No, not when you're holding me or kissing me I'm not. Everything is so clear then."

"Then marry me. Marry me this month."

"This month? It's too soon to plan a decent ceremony in a few weeks."

"We agreed we didn't want a big affair, so that doesn't matter."

Benny moved away, wringing her hands. "Why are you rushing me?"

"It's not rushing if you really want to be with me."

"You are rushing. Stop rushing me to set a date."

Billy Ray went to the porch glider and snatched up his hat. "Okay, I won't rush you. That's a promise you can count on. But I want you to know one thing. I won't wait forever, Miss Freeman." He stomped off the porch to his vehicle without another word and started the motor. Benny watched him drive away, but she couldn't bring herself to call out the words she knew would bring him back.

CHAPTER FOUR

Daniel Patrick Dooley strolled up Commerce Avenue taking in the dry night air. There hadn't been a drop of rain all month. He was trying to empty his mind of important matters so he could rest peacefully for a change. He was overdue for enjoying a night free from business and all it required to get the agency off the ground and financially sound.

Dooley was trying to relax, but it wasn't coming easy. He hadn't known much peace since the riot. His secret had been exposed, and once-friendly white associates were now vowed enemies eyeing him as a target. Most Greenwood residents were surface friendly but some were bitter and distrustful, scrutinizing him, not convinced of his Negro blood or kindred spirit.

His peace was also hampered by relentless flashbacks from the riot. They dulled a little with the passing of time but were always there, images of dead bodies and burning buildings haunting his waking and sleeping hours. He could sometimes still hear screams of victims, the rat-a-tat-tat of machine gun fire used to mow down innocent citizens.

He stopped walking in front of his small building that also housed his modest flat on the second floor. It was one of the newly erected replacement structures put up after the riot to replace buildings that had been destroyed. Dooley stared at the plate glass window with the painted words D.P. DOOLEY AGENCY, QUALIFIED DETECTION & PROTECTION OF PERSONS AND PROPERTY.

He looked up at the black velvet sky generously sprinkled with glittering stars. "They say You're up there," he said doubtfully, "but I wonder if You really are. Why do You let all this evil go on? Why do good decent people who believe in You suffer so much?" Dooley's head, crowned with a thick crop of wavy reddish-brown hair, dropped in an agonized slump. "Why did You let them get away with what they did?" he demanded, shaking his fist in the air.

A cheerfully chatting couple with a big dog turned the corner walking toward him. Dooley quickly got his key out from his pocket to unlock the door. He hurried inside wiping his face with his shirtsleeve because he didn't dare risk anyone seeing the tears on his face.

Cord was glad when his brother, Ethan, and his colleague Elizabeth arrived, even happier when he saw a plate of home-cooked food from their mother. The steak, fried potatoes, string beans, and apple-rhubarb pie was just what his empty belly needed.

He invited his guests to the kitchen and started eating. Cord told Ethan in detail about the incident with Amos Grapnel and how he'd spent the day waiting for the police to come get him. Strangely none had come. Ethan admitted he already knew about the incident from Benny.

Cord was amused, sitting across from Ethan observing his occasional starry-eyed glint. He suspected weeks earlier his younger brother was infatuated with the attractive NAACP lawyer. The attraction was understandable. Elizabeth Whitehead was a lovely creature, so poised and intelligent yet warm and friendly. She sat in the kitchen smiling as if posing for a photograph. Cord had to force himself not to stare at her. "You should have come to the folks' house and had dinner with us," Ethan said watching Cord eat hungrily.

Cord glanced Elizabeth's way and then looked at his brother, embarrassed. "Benny asked me to but I begged off."

"The folks are having a big dinner with the preacher and his family next week after church. Why don't you come then? Mom would be happy if you did."

"I'll think about it."

"That's a no, right?"

"I said I'd think about it," he fired back.

Ethan shrugged, "Okay, have it your way. I won't mention it again."

Cord looked up from his plate, shooting another glance Elizabeth's way and saw that she was watching him closely. "Look, I promise to give it some thought, okay?"

"Your mother was kind enough to invite me. I'd be relieved if you were there. Ethan gets so caught up talking politics and law with your father and leaves me at loose ends. It would be nice to have someone else I'm acquainted with to talk to."

"Benny's there," Cord answered never looking beyond his plate.

"She's occupied with her intended . . . that is except tonight she wasn't. Oddly enough he wasn't there but she wasn't around much either. She ate and went to her room with a headache."

Cord asked Ethan, "What's wrong with Benny and where's Billy Ray? I thought those two were inseparable."

"I'm not sure but I think they had a falling out. It'll blow over, whatever it is. Billy Ray's too far gone on her to stay away long."

CHAPTER FIVE

LUNENBURG COUNTY, VIRGINIA
SEPTEMBER 1890

Hooded men holding torches surrounded the trembling woman. Her face was swollen from the blows that had nearly rendered her unconscious, and the little boy nearby was sobbing, desperately trying to break free of the hooded man holding him.

"Where is he?" The man who bellowed this demand was waving a Bible.

"I don't know," the woman insisted weakly.

"Leave my momma alone!" The boy screamed, kicking and thrashing at his restrainer. Just then the sound of racing hooves approached.

Daniel Patrick Dooley swung his leg off his horse so quickly he looked airborne. He grabbed his shotgun and charged toward the men, demanding an explanation. "Why are you cowards on me property? Let me boy go," he warned, aiming his gun.

"Poppa, they hurt Momma," the boy told him, twisting harder to get loose.

"I said to let him go." Daniel raised the shotgun at the man holding his son.

The leader of the group nodded, and the man holding the child released him. The boy shot off toward his father.

Daniel looked around. "Where's Lucy? Where's me wife?"

"They hurt Momma and they won't let her get up." The boy cried and clung to his father.

"Danny, get away or they'll hurt you," Lucy called out.

The circle slowly opened and he saw his beloved on the ground. The torchlight illuminated the area and Daniel saw her battered face. "You filthy pigs!" He started toward her but the circle closed in fast.

"Go away, Danny, take DP and get out of here," Lucy begged.

"We don't cotton to no white men marryin' up with Negras round these parts," one man announced.

"We told you to leave. Warned you plenty but you stayed anyhow. Any decent white man wouldn't have no colored wife no matter how good he thought she looked," another hooded man spoke out. "It's one thing to get your pleasure with 'em but ya don't marry one."

"Aw, he's not one of us, he's one of them foreigners and a Catholic," another said.

"Get away from my wife or I'll shoot! I'm warning you. Leave her be—I mean what I say!"

"You ain't the only one kin shoot round here," a short, hooded man said. He brandished his pistol.

Danny looked at the men, accepting the reality that he was outnumbered and most likely outgunned. His heart was aching to get to Lucy. He wanted DP safe and he wanted his wife spared any further suffering. He didn't think he could successfully do either but he had to try. He prayed for help and strength. He had to make an effort to protect his family, and he was fearful of the price he would have to pay. "Leave my wife and boy be. It's me you want. Do what you will with me, but don't hurt them. Let them be," he begged, fully understanding the sacrifice he was making.

"Danny, no," Lucy wailed.

The Bible holder stepped out of the circle and faced him. "You that attached to this Negra and her mixed-breed boy?"

"He's me son," Danny declared standing erect and incensed, "and she's me wife. They're me family and a blessing from the Good Lord."

"Blessing from the Good Lord . . . I doubt that 'cause race mixin' is against God's ways. It's an abomination far as I'm concerned. Tell you what, we'll let them be if you put the shotgun down and agree to be the example to any more of your disgraceful race-mixin' kind."

Danny shuffled in place, fear squeezing every inch of his chest and head. "Before the Good Lord, you'll leave them be?"

"As God is my witness, no harm will come to them," the man holding the Bible solemnly promised.

"Example how? What do you want from me?"

"We aims to hang you," the man answered without hesitation. Daniel's body stiffened as he gripped his shotgun tighter. He looked at each man in the circle, but no one spoke.

"Poppa." DP whined, uncertain what was happening, but he could sense his father's desperate tension.

"If you want them to live, then give up and put that gun down. We'll leave the woman and boy to grieve your dead body when it's over. You got my word on it," the Bible holder told him. "You might get one of us with that thing, but we'll get you and them too if you shoot."

Daniel slowly lowered the shotgun. "Be needing time to pray and speak to me family before you—" The circle widened as he placed the gun on the ground and pried the boy's grasp from around his leg. DP ran to Lucy. Daniel followed slowly. He stooped and lifted her to her feet. Tears fell when he saw her condition up close.

"Danny, this ain't happenin'. Tell me it ain't happenin'."

"Shhh . . . calm down, Lucy, it's going to be all right. You and DP won't be hurt any more. You'll be safe, me lass."

"Nooo Danny, not without you we won't," she sobbed.

"Don't you see, me love, I have no choice if I'm to keep you from any more harm. The Good Lord will look after you and the boy. I know He will."

"Don't leave me, Danny, please don't leave me alone." Lucy looked up at one of the hooded spectators pleading, "Please, we'll go away right now, mister. We promise to be gone by sunup. Just don't hurt my man, please! He's a good, God-fearin' man. He don't deserve to die like a dog . . . please, sweet Jesus, please!"

No one responded.

"I beg you not to do this, you can't, it's not right," she wailed falling to her knees. "Please, in the name of Jesus, don't do this to him!"

Daniel lifted her to her feet again. "Don't Lucy, it won't do any good. They mean to go through with it. Me fate is sealed. I'm not afraid to die if I know you will live and take care of our boy. I'd die a thousand deaths to protect you and our son." He looked down at the crying child and dropped to one knee. "You be a big boy, me lad. Be brave and take care of your mother. Promise me."

"I will, Poppa, I promise," DP sniffled. He didn't know the horror that was to happen but he could tell something bad was going on. His mother couldn't be comforted, so neither could he. His father seemed to be saying goodbye and hugged him so tight it took his breath away.

"I want you and the lad spared having to watch," Danny told Lucy. "Take him in the house."

"Danny, I can't leave you. I won't."

"Do as I say," Danny snapped. He ran his shaking hand through his bushy red hair. He took a deep breath. "Please, Lucy, for me, take DP in the house and stay there . . . no matter what you hear don't come out and don't let him see . . . please. I don't want my boy's memory of me to be . . . please, just do as I say." He wrapped his arms around her. She latched on, sobbing. He whispered gently in her ear, "I love you, me darling. Me heart belonged to you since the first time I met you in that little church in the meadow. I love you more than life itself. Don't weep, me lass, I'm going to be with Jesus. Have faith in what the Bible tells us. I'll be well with the Lord." Then he kissed Lucy, fighting back his own tears. He didn't want to let go of his beloved knowing he would never hold or see her again in this life. One of the hooded men pulled him loose from their clinging embrace and tugged him away.

"Danny," she screamed rushing behind him but two other men blocked her way pushing her back roughly.

"Take your hands off her," Daniel demanded. "Lucy, take the boy in the house now! Remember, the Good Lord will keep you. It's all right, me lass, I'm goin' meet Jesus!"

"I love you, Daniel Patrick Dooley! I'll love you forever no matter what they do to me," she wept as they pulled him toward the mammoth oak tree. "They can't change what I feel for you, no one can!"

Lucy fell to her knees praying, when she was pushed inside the little farmhouse. DP never before heard his mother cry so hard and pray so frantically to this Jesus she always talked about. "Pray to the Lord for a miracle," she told him.

"Why are they bein' mean to us, Momma? Why did they hurt you? Are they gonna hurt Poppa too?"

"I can't explain some folks' hatefulness, but pray hard right now for Jesus to save your father."

"Will Jesus help Poppa?" he asked in his childlike innocence.

"Yes, baby, Jesus will help him 'cause ain't nobody else can," she wept.

DP put his hands together and squeezed his eyes shut tight, "Dear Lord Jesus, please, please, please help my poppa. Make those mean men go away and leave us alone." Everything was so pitiful and urgent and that scared him and he began to cry again as he prayed.

It seemed a long time to DP when his mother got up from her knees in a panic after hearing the hooded men's boisterous voices getting louder, but it wasn't. "Stay here," she told him as she rushed to the door and ran out toward the men on horses. Before she reached them she let out a loud wail, "Dear God, no, Danny, no!" The men were circling the tree on horseback talking among themselves, ignoring her screams. When she reached her husband's hanging body it was still swinging, his neck twisted to the side, face ashen and in frozen distress. "Jesus, oh, Jesus why didn't you save him," she cried hysterically.

"Cause what you two done is a sin against God," a man responded as he raised his Bible in the air.

DP couldn't stand hearing his mother's loud piercing agony. He didn't like to disobey her but he had promised his father to be brave and look after her. He ran out the house toward her, but when he saw his father swinging from the same oak tree he often played in he stopped cold and stared in shock. His father's long slim limbs dangled in the night darkness with the glow of many torches lighting up the scene. He couldn't fully understand what he was seeing but he knew he didn't want to look anymore and turned away. "Poppa . . . oh, Poppa . . . " Then he heard the gunshot that made him jump. That was immediately followed by another thunderous blast. When the little boy turned back around, to his horror his mother was on the ground and now one of the hooded men was pointing a rifle at him.

"No, you fool," the leader of the group yelled. "Put those guns away! I gave my word they would be left alone and I meant it!"

"What difference does it make what you told that Catholic potato-picker? She called us cowards. She don't sass no white men like that and live. Let her be with her man if she wants to so bad . . . and the kid too."

Another hooded man agreed. "She deserves to die talkin' to white men that way."

"Bah, I gave my word and you dishonored it. I ought to shoot *you* for what you did! Leave that boy alone!" Three men rode out of the group to the house and used their torches to set it on fire.

"We done what we came to do. The message will be clear we don't tolerate no race mixin' in Lunenburg County, Virginia. It's over, so let's ride outta here." The men followed their leader and left, not bothering to look back.

"You hurt my momma and poppa," DP wailed, kneeling at his mother's side. He could not know he was watching the life ooze slowly out of her.

"Momma, wake up," the child pleaded. "Momma!" Lucy opened her eyes weakly and tried to speak, but they closed with her unable to make a sound. DP spotted his father's shotgun leaning against the same big oak tree from which his lifeless body hung. The boy ran for it and struggled to handle the heavy weapon. He looked at the body and said, "I'm sorry, Poppa, I'm trying to take care of momma. Jesus, where are You? Why didn't You help my poppa and momma?" he whimpered. "Why don't You help me? I promised I'd take care of momma. Help me take care of my momma and get my poppa down from this tree."

A few minutes later he stood up and nervously touched his father's legs. He somehow knew his father was dead. He fell back down crying and crawled to his mother, taking her head in his lap. He gazed in misery from his father's suspended body to the burning farmhouse and back to his unresponsive mother. He cried until exhausted, he fell to sleep.

It was daylight when Wilbur and Annie Mae Hunter, Lucy's parents, came to drop off a few chickens they had raised. To their horror they found their grandson sleeping next to his mother's bloody corpse, his father's body hanging from the oak tree, and the farmhouse burned to the ground.

Dooley was sweating profusely when his eyes popped open. The dream felt as real as the actual experience. After all these years his mind still wandered back to that night in vividly dramatic detail. Jesus did not come and save his family. The Deliverer had not delivered his parents out the hands of those hooded fiends—and that was the last time Dooley prayed.

Since the riot the memories had been coming more often, tampering with his sleep and causing him more grief than ever. The impetus for what he did had always been the tragedy of that dreadful night. Some told him he was making a mistake to quit his government job, move permanently to Greenwood, and open his own agency, but the decision had felt right at the time. Now something must be wrong, very wrong, because he hadn't been plagued with the memory of his parents' deaths this much in years. Why must the past so insistently mar his attempt to settle down and have a bit of normalcy in life?

CHAPTER SIX

Dunbar Elementary, Lincoln Junior High, and Booker T. Washington High Schools formed a cul-de-sac at the end of Lincoln Square. Leading into the dead end were the YMCA and Osborne Monroe's roller skating rink. During the riot, both establishments went up in flames, as did Dunbar and Lincoln. The high school was mercifully spared for some unknown reason.

The newly built replacement school, Lincoln Primary and Prep, merged both elementary and junior high students into one building. Lincoln Square's name was changed to School House Square. The area looked picture perfect now. No signs of the flaming destruction that ravished most of that section including the Dreamland Theater and Poke's Hardware and Feed Store.

Benny was teaching again, at Lincoln Primary and Prep. She was doing what she loved to do, teaching the joy of music to eager young minds. The children exited her classroom with their usual energetic racket and she didn't notice the door hadn't shut all the way when the last eighth graders had walked out, nor did she notice the dapper man standing inside the doorway quietly staring at her with hat in hand. He watched, not daring to move or make a sound to distract her as she erased the musical notes from the blackboard. She started to write the assignment for the next class. Loud laughter from the hallway drew her attention toward the door and she saw him. Benny's heart raced erratically and her mouth went dry.

Her knees buckled as she flopped clumsily into the chair.

The man smiled uneasily and walked in front of the desk. "How are you, Benny? You're looking well." He spoke in a cautiously melodious voice.

She didn't answer.

He kept smiling in that indomitable way that could warm any girl's heart and still stabbed at Benny's. Still distinguished as ever, he was well-dressed in a suit that appeared tailor-made. His shiny black hair was freshly cut and his mustache shaped perfectly to his fine-looking face. He'd gained a few pounds, which only added to his manliness. "Well? Aren't you glad to see me after all this time?" Standing confidently erect, his narrow dark eyes searched hers.

Why couldn't you be stooped over and haggard? Why do you still have to look so good? "What are you doing here?" she finally got out with effort.

"I came looking for you. I've been worried about you ever since the news of the riot made it to Paris. Glad to know you weren't hurt. Aren't you going to ask how I am?"

Benny stood up from the chair, facing him with open contempt. "I don't care how you are. Why are you here?"

His confident smile faded. "I'm performing at the Oklahoma City Music Hall in a few weeks."

"I see."

"Life must be treating you well. You look good, Benny."

"You already said that. What did you come here for, Jordan? You have to know I never wanted to set eyes on you again . . . ever."

"Since I got back to the States I thought about coming to see you but couldn't muster up the courage. When I was booked to perform in Oklahoma . . . I thought maybe this was fate giving me a helping hand, so I decided to take a chance and look you up. How have you been?"

"How did you think I would be after you almost ruined my life?" She hadn't meant to say it out loud although it was in her heart.

He looked down. "I never meant to hurt you, Benny. I hope you believe me."

"How did you know I was here?" She started gathering up papers with nervous energy.

"It wasn't hard to find out what you were doing. You Freemans are well known around here, especially your brother Ethan. I just wanted to see for myself that you were safe . . . after the riot."

"The riot was more than a year ago and yes, I made it through safely, which is more than I can say for a lot of dead and injured souls."

"It must be hard . . . to rebuild I mean after all that trouble. Greenwood looks so different than I remember. It's like Europe is since the war."

"It was a war of sorts. At least it felt like war as I imagine it." Benny's mind returned to the present. "Now that you see I'm safe, I'd rather not waste time with small talk. I have another class coming, so please leave."

"You still hate me, don't you?"

She stopped and looked up at him. "I don't despise you like I used to, but I don't want to see you or be in your company. It's too painful. I put you and whatever deceitfully disgusting relationship we had behind me. I want to keep it there."

"All right, I respect your wishes. I'll be touring the country for nine months. It started in Chicago last month. We'll be leaving Oklahoma, going east to—"

" 'We'?"

"I started a band in Paris and they're with me."

"Oh,"

"And my wife."

Benny stiffened. "You're married?"

"For six months now."

"Congratulations," she muttered. She stared out the window and fought the emotional clanging in her head.

"Do you mean that?"

Her eyes snapped back to his. Her face constricted and fist clenched. "You have the nerve to ask me if I mean it? Do you forget I know what you are? I have the scars on my life to show lessons learned on the illustrious musical genius, Jordan Franks. You dare waltz in here like nothing's happened and expect me to engage in pleasant chitchat! Your ego is as obnoxious as ever. No, I don't mean it and no, I'm not glad to see you! I don't care how you're doing and I want you out of this classroom now!"

"Why are you so angry?"

"You really have to ask after what you did to me? Are you that stupid, completely narcissistic, or just insane?"

He cracked a half smile. "Does it bother you I married someone else?"

She slammed her fists on the desk hard. "Don't for one second think I want anything to do with you! I cringe at the very thought that you ever touched me, and now seeing you sickens me all the more! You're revolting, and I can't believe that I ever thought I loved you!" Benny sat back down. She felt shaky but held her head high. "Apparently you've wormed your slimy way into some other poor woman's heart. She has my sympathy. I suppose she comes from a well-to-do family since I was told you habitually seek to surround yourself with people of means, women from families with money . . . you lousy leech."

"That's not fair."

"How can you be so heartless and destroy another woman like you almost did me? You're a selfish, lying, depraved opportunist. Get out of here and never come near me again!"

"Calm down—people will hear."

"And that would be scandalous, now wouldn't it?"

"I was hoping you'd gotten over it by now, but . . ."

"Gotten over it! What do you mean? Gotten over it like I had a bad cough? Do you have any idea what you put me through? You almost destroyed me, Jordan. Will you ever own up to what you really are?"

"You make me sound like the devil. I'm not evil."

"How you live is a disgrace and the way you used me was vile. You broke my heart. No, you broke my spirit. You intentionally deceived me about the very basis of our relationship. It shattered any semblance of confidence I had as a woman."

"I know I misled you in a way, but I did love you and I did want to marry you."

"You must be stark raving mad. You mean you wanted to marry me to hide your filthy secret. That and latch on to my family's money."

"That's not true. I cared very much about you."

"You don't care about anyone but yourself. Now get out of my sight before I have you arrested for trespassing."

"I thought you would be more forgiving after all you've been through."

Two students walked into the room. "As you can well see I'm not; so goodbye," she said in a low tone with clenched teeth.

Jordan glanced at the children. They chattered as they took their seats, uninterested in what the two adults were doing. He looked back at Benny, noticing her engagement ring. "Who's the lucky guy?"

"None of your business."

He leaned forward and said in a low voice, "I'm staying at the Stradford Hotel for a week before heading to Oklahoma City. We really should talk before I leave. I'm in room 306. Hope to see you before I leave."

"I have no inclination to ever lay eyes on you again, but if I did I would never go to a man's hotel room alone."

"Then where can we meet?"

"I told you I never want to see you again." Benny gritted her teeth still keeping her voice low.

"All right, good day, Miss Freeman. It was nice seeing you again even if you don't return the sentiment." He was smirking as he walked away.

More students were entering the room, so Benny couldn't vent her fury by throwing a book at Jordan as he left.

"Class, I want you to get your pencils and music books out," she said. "Copy the homework assignment and behave until I get back."

She hurried out of the classroom to the large closet at the end of the hall where supplies were kept. Her hands shook as she unlocked the door with the key on a long chain hanging around her neck. Once inside the dark secluded room full of stacked shelves, books, and boxes she locked the door. Without pulling the chain to the uncovered lightbulb hanging from the ceiling, she slid to the floor and wept.

CHAPTER SEVEN

Ada Crump didn't want to be in love. She fought the attraction for nearly two years before giving in to her unthinkable yearnings. Finally she collapsed under pressure when he risked everything to protect her during the riot. It was a shameful secret she would never reveal. Practically the whole district was destroyed, people were being injured and even killed, and yet she was basking in the loving arms of a man as he confessed his longing for her.

And her lover was not just a private citizen. It was Jake Gilbert, Tulsa's chief of police. He was a man willing to be exposed for what undoubtedly would be considered racial betrayal just to make sure she and her property were not harmed.

After the riot he was accused of negligence of duty because he could not be reached for over four hours during the conflict. He never told the truth about his whereabouts. The white population assumed he was hiding out not to be associated with the attacks, hoping to avoid taking any real action to stop them. Negroes thought he was covertly orchestrating some of the violence or deliberately turning his back so he wouldn't have to take action against many of his participating friends. They were all wrong on all counts. Although the indictment and subsequent departmental suspension fizzled under the unjust conclusions of Tulsa's legal maneuverings, what took place that night between him and Ada caused their budding relationship to grow stronger.

At first she told herself it was fear that drove her into the arms of Jake Gilbert. She had been so frightened alone at home where she could see the smoke and hear the distant noises of the riot. That evening of fear, however, did not explain why she continued in their taboo liaison long after the riot's end.

Ada was in love with Jake whether she liked it or not and she didn't. It was crazy to want a man who for years seemingly mistreated her race, making their lives harder. She couldn't explain her feelings for him when she knew he was the same chief of police who, seven years before, had taken no legal action against Moose Kegel for his unwarranted attack on her husband. Shame hovered over her for longing to be in his arms when he stood for everything she hated about Tulsa.

She was thinking on this as she finished scrubbing Kate Boswell's grimy kitchen floor, glad the chore was done. Ada was a short woman in her late thirties, thick around the hips with a more than ample bosom and small waist. A broken ankle when she was a child caused her to develop an unintentional sashay when she walked, a trait men found appealing. By most accounts, Ada was endowed with an attractive figure and eye-catching saunter that put her high on the list of desirability. Her pretty round face with its soft brown eyes and her crop of thick dark hair were indicative of her mixed Kiowa and Negro ancestry.

Her mind floated back to the encounter with Jake the night of the riot. Widowed for years, she was hungry for affection. She had crumbled under his kiss but his kiss was like nectar . . . nectar she craved. Her mind flashed back to her Grandma Nelly and how she warned the girls in the family not to "keep company with no man, colored or white that ain't talkin' marriage." Ada could visualize the look of unadulterated repugnance on Grandma Nelly's sun-toughened skin.

Marriage! It was ridiculous to think Jake Gilbert would ever marry her. Their relationship was not only clandestine but society would consider it sacrilege. Ada was not certain she didn't see it that way herself. She regularly admonished herself for wanting him so much, for melting at his touch and yielding to his kisses.

His kisses . . . oh, what they did to her. Her heart raced as sensation coursed through her body.

"It's about time you finished." A sharp voice cut across her sensual thoughts. "I declare you're getting slower and slower, Ada, standing around daydreaming like a schoolgirl. What's gotten into you lately? Is the dining table set like I asked?"

Ada looked at the thinly built, pinched-faced blonde standing in the doorway. "It's all set," she assured Mrs. Boswell.

"Good, I want everything to be perfect tonight when Jake gets here." She clasped her hands together and smiled. "I think—I think he's going to pop the question."

Ada's eyes widened. "You think . . . What?"

"You heard me. I think Jake's going to ask me to marry him."

Ada didn't respond as she picked up the wash bucket and moved toward the back door.

The woman could tell she was disturbed by the news. "Don't you want me to remarry?" she asked, grinning. "I've been alone for five years since Bob died and I'm not getting any younger, you know. If I want a husband—and I do—I better act now before my last chance is gone. Nobody's looked twice at me in years except Jake."

"If you say so, Miss Kate," Ada said. She set the bucket down outside the back door.

"I know what you're thinking," Kate huffed.

Oh no, you don't.

"You think he's not good enough for me. He's not my intellectual or social equal."

"I don't think nothin' of the kind. Ain't my business no how," Ada replied, expertly hiding her feelings.

"You're right; it's not your business but I was the one who brought it up to you. Well, I know he's not refined but he can be very tender and kind when he wants. He was so good to Bob when he was ill and since he died, Jake's been extremely kind to me. I wouldn't have gotten through it if he hadn't been there for me. He's an important person in Tulsa, in a way, and ambitious, believe it or not. He's done well for himself considering his humble beginnings. I know people who can help Jake move higher than a mere chief of police. Who knows, he might have a political career ahead of him." She looked off dreamily. "He could even become mayor one day." Rubbing her hands together she continued, "I think we'll get along splendidly as husband and wife and . . . well, to tell you the truth . . . he's rather ruggedly handsome and makes my temperature rise if you know what I mean." Kate blushed lightly.

Ada shut the back door more firmly than necessary. "Yes ma'am," she mumbled. The thought of Jake touching Kate Boswell angered her more then she would admit to herself, but she definitely couldn't show a hint of it to her employer. Had he made love to this skinny, high-and-mighty snob? The question circled her mind repeatedly.

Kathleen Mastermann Boswell hailed from wealth and power, being the daughter of a well-to-do businessman. Her privileged lifestyle continued when she met and married Robert Boswell, an older gentleman employed by Mastermann Enterprises and vying for a cushy position at the top of the company. Robert got his high-ranking promotion and pampered his spoiled wife with his hefty earnings until his death.

Years of being alone had given Kate a strong desire to remarry. Yet even with her prominent family name and inherited wealth the men of Tulsa shunned the willful widow. Though not a beauty, she wasn't unattractive, but her inability to curb her snobbery was etched into her features.

Jake Gilbert had been widowed years before his friend Robert took ill. He took seriously his promise to look after his friend's wife. "You think I'm being silly again, don't you?" Kate pouted.

"No ma'am." Ada walked out the kitchen to the dining room.

Kate trailed behind her. "He does have eyes for me. I know he does. After all these years he's always been there for me whenever I need him. That counts for something doesn't it?"

"Yes, ma'am."

"He's never remarried either. Could it be he's wanted me all along?" Kate asked, eyes twinkling. Ada stopped in her tracks and looked over at her but didn't answer.

Kate stepped in front of her. "You think I'm fantasizing again, don't you?"

"Well, Miss Kate, there was that rascal from Louisiana you fell for so hard and he almost took you for a whole bunch of money."

Kate's thin lips pursed. "I knew you were going to bring him up. And just who was it that got me out of that dilemma? Jake Gilbert, that's who. He came to my rescue like— like a knight in shining armor." Kate's eyes dazed off dreamily.

Ada hid her agitation and asked, "Did Chief Gilbert ever come out and say he was courting you? Did he bring up marriage or even try to take any liberties with you?"

Kate's face scrunched up. "How dare you pry into my personal affairs? You're getting beside yourself."

"I'm just asking to see if you're thinking clearly or not."

"I don't need your meddling in my affairs. Of course I'm thinking clearly. Jake's a gentleman and he's in love with me. I should have seen it years ago. So tonight I plan to let him know in no uncertain terms that for me it's acceptable for him to pursue romance."

"He was Mr. Robert's closest friend. He might not want to *pursue* romance."

"I've already figured that out. I'm sure the reason he's never made a move is because of his loyalty to dear Bob, so I'm going to let him know he shouldn't let that hinder our happiness."

Ada didn't answer and went into the parlor.

Kate followed. "Why are you acting like this? I don't understand. You act like you don't want me to marry Jake. My marriage to him won't change your employment here, if that's what's troubling you; you'll keep your job. I'll always feel a special fondness toward you, Ada. When I become Mrs. Jaffice Gilbert, nothing's going to change." She smiled brightly at her housekeeper. "I simply must cut some of my heirloom roses for this table. That's what it needs, some fragrant roses to give it a more romantic feel."

"Yes ma'am, your roses sure would look pretty," Ada murmured, thinking how things would change drastically for her if Kate Boswell married Jake.

CHAPTER EIGHT

HOPEWELL ASYLUM
TULSA, OKLAHOMA

Cord covered the motionless female with the fallen lap blanket. He was accustomed to her blank stare. He noticed with concern the sagging posture of her thinning shoulders. "You're losing more weight," he told her. "You have to eat when they bring your meals and I'm not here. Don't want you to waste away to nothin'."

He pulled a chair in front of her and sat down. The room was dark and dreary with its faded drapes and dingy white walls. A faint smell of urine lingered in the air. "Sorry I haven't been here in a while. Got a lot going on at the ranch. Had to hire another hand, it's so busy." *I need the money since it costs so much to keep you here.* He got up and opened the curtains and both barred windows. "That's better, some fresh air will do you good." He looked sadly at her empty expression. "How 'bout we take you outside so you can get more fresh air and some sun?"

The looks always annoyed Cord when he walked Scarlett by the nurse's station in the Colored Ward. He knew what they whispered about her and what they probably thought about him. Their disapproving stares made him more determined to ensure she received the best care he could afford. He held on to Scarlett as she mechanically moved with him into the garden. They stopped at his favorite spot between the giant magnolia and sycamore trees. Opening the Bible he'd taken from her desk drawer, he glanced down at it mainly to occupy his mind. He hadn't much wanted to hear sermons or read anything about Jesus since his life had fallen apart and the riot took place. He was wondering more and more if what he had believed all of his life was just foolishness.

The day was mildly warm for this time of year. The fragrance of the wild roses and colorful hyacinths enhanced the garden's atmosphere. Visits to the asylum were peaceful times for Cord. He looked forward to getting away from daily chores at the ranch, but more importantly, the visits brought some relief from pangs of guilt and loneliness.

Being around Scarlett made him feel needed, and somehow closer to Savannah. Cord could confide anything he wanted to this woman and she remained unresponsive. Scarlett's inability to actively participate in life had a complicated psychiatric name he'd forgotten, but for him it was refuge. The doctor explained that Scarlett's condition was a subconsciously imposed protection to shield her from the horrors of the attack she had experienced. Her mind simply shut down. She took no part in fundamentals of social interactions though no physical reasons prevented her from doing so. Resorting to near immobility unless coaxed and existing in an aphasic state was her way of surviving the terror . . . then and now. Dr. Poole was of the opinion she didn't want to come back for more complicated reasons than just the brutal rape she had endured.

They had been sitting in the garden for an hour. Cord had the Bible and was reading through the book of Hosea. It bothered him so much he put the book down on the wooden seat beside him and thought about God commanding Hosea to marry a prostitute. The idea was ridiculous to him but he couldn't help but ponder its significance to his own life and why that particular piece of Scripture jumped out at him.

"Cord, Cord Freeman!" A female voice sang out from the gazebo some distance away.

Straining to see, he leaned forward but couldn't make out the individual until she approached him and he recognized Elizabeth Whitehead, who looked stunning as ever in a soft beige and brown dress. Her movements were fluid with the dress's willowy skirt floating daintily in the warm breeze. He felt a jolting sensation as she came nearer. Something about Elizabeth reminded him of Savannah, although they were very different types of women.

"Hello," she said warmly. "Fancy meeting you in this place." She shot a look Scarlett's direction.

"I come here whenever I find time," he said, suddenly self-conscious. "I like to check on Scarlett because she has no one else to look after her. No family or close friends who care about what happens to her."

"You care because you are very . . . close?" Elizabeth asked, cocking an inquisitive eye.

"Not at all," he answered, flicking a look at Scarlett's blank expression. "She was my wife's close friend. *They* were very close at one time so I look after her as a tribute to her."

"How commendable. Your wife was fortunate to have such a devoted husband."

His face turned abruptly cold. "My wife would still be alive if it wasn't for me. So she wasn't fortunate at all."

"Why do you say that? Ethan said she took her own life."

"It was my fault she did."

"I'm sure that's not true. Why would you think you're responsible?"

"Look, Miss Whitehead . . ."

"I thought you said you would call me Bet."

"You're right, I did. Bet, I don't want to talk about my wife's death if you don't mind."

"That's funny, because it was you who brought it up so I assumed you did want to talk about it." She smiled sweetly and sat on the bench close beside him.

Cord was both agitated and pleasantly taken aback. She

was too lovely and charming to be cross with, so he took a deep breath. "Sorry, I shouldn't have mentioned it."

"I think you mentioned it because you're still grieving deeply for her."

"I guess I am."

"You need to talk it out. Stop bottling up your feelings and express your loss."

"Who do I talk to about it? Nobody I'm close to cared for Savannah enough to understand what she meant to me."

"You can talk to me if you like. I don't have any preconceived notions about your wife . . . except maybe the unflattering things I heard from Ethan but that doesn't matter. I don't hold much store with strict moral judgments. There's always another side to anyone's behavior if we examine it close enough. The human mind has more than one dimension, and people are very complex beings."

"What are you, a psychiatrist too? Do you work here?"

"No, I'm not a psychiatrist and I don't work here, but I'd like to be your friend." Bet laid her hand on his, looking into his eyes.

He felt awkward. Not because of her probing into his feelings but her obvious feminine airs that he thought should be directed at Ethan. He shifted uncomfortably. "Yeah, well, I'm not much for spilling my guts out all over the place. That's for womenfolk."

"You should try it. You'd be surprised how liberating it is. Everyone has feelings, men as well as women."

"What's your business here?"

"I'm representing a client about ill treatment in the Negro ward. They keep our people in this separate old dilapidated building on this side of the grounds while the white patients are treated in a beautiful up-to-date facility. The NAACP is trying to get them to allot more of its patient funding for redoing this building so they get better care with modern treatment like the other patients, and also for them to employ some Negro doctors and nurses for that ward," Bet explained. "I had a meeting with two of the hospital's administrators."

Cord smiled. "I bet that went over big. You sound just like my brother. You two make a perfect pair."

"Not true; we don't think alike about everything." She looked down at the Bible.

"That's surprising. I thought you were exactly alike on everything. At least that's the impression he gave me."

"Ethan talks to you about me?"

"Often."

Bet blushed. "That's a surprise. I had no idea. We don't see eye to eye about religion."

"Oh." Cord shrugged. "I'm not so sure even what I think about religion anymore. My life is such a wreck it's like God's fed up with me or something."

"If there is a God, you mean."

Cord stared. "You mean you don't believe in God? Not in Jesus?"

"I used to, but I don't think I do anymore. I believe religion was designed to dazzle the minds of the poor, uneducated masses. Make them content with having nothing and never succeeding in society. The prosperous have no need for God and they know it."

"Wow, I never thought of it that way."

She pointed to the Bible. "That book is full of silly stories and teachings that hold our people down."

"What does Ethan say about your philosophy?"

"Well, I haven't exactly told him all of what I think . . . not yet, that is. Just a little, and to be truthful he wasn't too receptive. I'm trying to ease him into seeing things my way. He's such a nice guy and I'd hate for us to have a falling out because of different religious views."

A prickly looking nurse came outside with a tray. She handed it to Cord, rolled her eyes at Bet, and walked away without saying a word. Cord seemed unbothered but Bet frowned.

"I guess my name is mud around here," she said, "but how unprofessional of her to behave in that manner. It's her job to feed the patients, not just hand you a tray and walk away."

"I always feed Scarlett when I'm here. They know that." He set the tray on the small table next to the Bible.

"She still could have made the offer out of courtesy. She would have if you were white."

"Probably so, but I've learned not to let every little thing white folks do bother me. Around here you'd be mad all the time if you do."

"Don't be so accepting of your less-than-equal status," Bet admonished. "That's what they count on."

He shook his head as he tucked the cloth napkin in Scarlett's collar. "There you go, sounding like my brother."

Bet watched with interest as Cord fed Scarlett with loving care. She was impressed by his calming words and gentleness toward the unfocused young woman. He whispered to Bet a brief explanation of what had happened to Scarlett. "I think I remember reading the report about her in the riot files. It was ghastly to read, let alone live through. The poor dear must be traumatized."

"She's had a hard life all around I think." He looked at Bet, and then took a deep breath. "You know this is my fault too . . . what happened to her."

"How?"

"I ran into her going to town and left her on the road to make it on her own. I saw the smoke and knew something was wrong, but I didn't care what happened to her. I had my own problems and that's all I was concerned about. She asked me to stay with her but I wouldn't."

"How is that being responsible for what those men did to her?"

"If she had stayed with me or I was with her it might not have happened."

"You're wrong. They would have hurt both of you; maybe killed you."

"She wouldn't have gone into town if I took her with me like she asked."

"Look, Cord, you can't take on all the guilt for what happened that night. It's not good for you."

"I'm not asking for sympathy; just speakin' the truth, owning up to my part in it."

"And your part in your wife's suicide?"

"All right, I'll tell you. I found out my wife was stepping out on me. It had been rumored for a long time but I didn't want to believe it . . . wouldn't believe it. Savannah liked a lot of attention; always did. I knew that, but I kept telling myself she was playful but faithful. She just liked having fun but she wouldn't do anything really wrong." The words began to flow. "I thought folks didn't understand her but I did. I thought I could give her what she wanted and keep her happy. I was wrong; people knew how she was and I was the fool. Long and short of it, I couldn't keep her happy." Cord's eyes were as sad as his words. He noticed Bet was taking in everything he said, her eyes glued on his as he continued. "I thought Savannah needed me and that would keep her in line. Anyway, when I found out she was carrying on with this guy I blew my top and things got ugly. I threw her out and told her I never wanted to see her again. It was over and I was divorcing her, cutting her off without a penny." He searched Bet's eyes, expecting condemnation.

"Is that it? That's your great sin?"

"Yeah."

"Cord, your reaction was human, not to say amazing that you didn't do more in that circumstance. Some men would have lost control altogether. You were betrayed by this woman you loved."

"How I treated her caused her to end her life. That's unforgivable."

"It was her choice and her betrayal that drove her to that decision."

"No matter. My reaction drove her to it."

"Ethan said she hanged herself at her lover's house after she stabbed him. Is that true?"

Cord winced. "Yeah."

"That she found him with some other woman . . ." She looked at Scarlett. "A friend of hers that this man had been carrying on with as well as with Savannah?"

"I think so, yeah."

"The same friend who told you about the affair?"

"Yeah, yeah, yeah. What's your point?"

"My point is, your wife was an unfaithful murderess. The man she took up with was a womanizing cad and the informant friend manipulated the situation and you as a pawn for her purpose. I don't understand how you're the bad guy in this. You were a victim on all sides from what I see."

Cord saw Scarlett turn her head and looked directly at Bet without the blank stare. Understanding of what she was saying shone clearly in her eyes.

Cord was shocked. "Scarlett," he said.

She blinked twice and turned back to staring into nothingness. He waved his hand in front of her face but got no further response.

"Was she the one who told you about your wife's affair?" Bet asked.

"Yeah."

"I thought so." Bet was silent for a moment. Then she asked, "How can you take blame for what happened to her? Sometimes we get back what we put out."

Cord didn't like that statement—he hadn't expected cold logic from this delicate beauty sitting next to him. His mind kept replaying Scarlett's brief animation. He put another spoonful of food to her mouth, but she didn't respond. Her jaws were stubbornly clamped shut yet her eyes were still blank. Was she showing anger, unhappiness, or . . . something else? If so, it was the first hint of cognition he'd seen her display since the tragedy. He was unsure if the reaction was a positive development or not. "Can we drop the subject? I think it's upsetting Scarlett."

CHAPTER NINE

GREENWOOD AFRICAN METHODIST CHURCH

Five moods were reflected among the five men who sat around the large mahogany table.

The covert assembly resembled a band of plotting thieves, though they were respected clergymen. At the head of the table was the host church's minister, Reverend Michael Metcalf. Metcalf was a fiftyish, short, stocky, light-skinned Negro. The letters following his name reflected his earned college and seminary degrees. Along with being senior pastor of Greenwood District's African Methodist Episcopal Church he was regional administrative pastorate for the African Methodist denomination. Michael Metcalf was a devout Christian and strong Methodist voice although many considered him to be somewhat unorthodox. This particular church had stood unharmed from looting or vandalism during the hateful conflict, and four blocks surrounding the sacred edifice even remained untouched. It was this church's bell that tolled the next day declaring life after death, giving hope to a battered people that their Savior had not deserted them.

Bishop Harlan Darlington sat opposite Reverend Metcalf at the table's end, a quiet and conservative man whose stylish attire enhanced his handsomeness. The bishop and his family displayed a lifestyle of strict adherence to godly principles, and was ill at ease at this clandestine gathering. He was an upstanding man of God and pastored Tulsa's only Reformed Episcopal Church. The ornate building housing Bishop Darlington's congregation was a magnificent structure that commanded attention due to its size and old-world Saxon-style embellishments. The congregation included many of the elite citizens of Tulsa's white population.

Father Alvarez Montoya sat stiffly. He was priest at the small Holy Sepulcher Church in Grease County outside southern Tulsa. Holy Sepulcher was the only Catholic church in that region of Oklahoma and primarily served Mexican parishioners. Father Montoya wasn't clear on the purpose of this meeting and tugged nervously at his collar.

Across from him was Rabbi Snellenberg. At seventy, he was the oldest in the room. His unbounded energy was as lively as his thick, unmanageable, curly hair. He took it upon himself to allay the worries of the other men. David Snellenberg was used to operating in secret and had always been an outcast. His piano and music store business, situated at the dividing line between white and black Tulsa, had also been burned to the ground during the riot. At the rear of the building was his private self-designed synagogue; David and his wife, Alma, lived upstairs. Though they lost their home, place of worship, and livelihood in one tragic night, the rabbi was able to encourage the other victims in Greenwood. He worked tirelessly, as did Alma, to ease the suffering of his beloved neighbors. It was perfectly in character for him to be peeping over his horn-rimmed glasses and speaking hope-filled words to the others.

The final clergyman at the table was Roman Matthias, pastor of the Bethel Baptist Church in Eagles Pointe County. The rabbi was telling him, "They've done about everything they can to me, short of taking my life."

"Why do you stay?" Father Montoya asked sympathetically in his thick Spanish accent.

"Because this is where I belong. I'm supposed to be here. That's why I came twenty-five years ago, and I refuse to be run away from where God sent me."

"I'm not so sure He sent you to this unforgiving territory," Bishop Darlington said.

"I am," the rabbi responded.

"How do you do it?" Reverend Matthias asked, looking bewildered. "How do you stay so cheerful with all the maltreatment?"

"My people have always known hardship, rejection, and trouble just like yours. Being Jewish and believing in Jesus as Messiah has meant everyone, including my fellow Jews, despise me. Even family members ridiculed me and turned their backs. I decided a long time ago I was going to enjoy my life no matter what. It's the best way I know to get even." The old man grinned.

"Does it work?" Bishop Darlington asked.

"Depends on what you expect. It works to confound those who hate me, and it lifts up my God. I've been able to find peace in the midst of a great deal of trouble, a peace I can't explain other than that it comes from God, so I'd say, yes, it works well."

"I can see that it does, old friend," Reverend Metcalf said then cleared his throat. "Gentlemen, we're here to discuss the idea that came to my spirit about starting an event uniting our congregations in worship and fellowship. More so, forming a godly association that lifts up our Lord and Savior, Christ Jesus, and crosses doctrinally different denominational lines."

"And race lines," Pastor Matthias interjected.

"Yes, especially racial discriminations and all the other differences dividing the Lord's people. We will be the example of the Scripture that says there is one God, one faith, and one Lord."

"A lot of people around here aren't going to like this," Bishop Darlington said.

"Is that our primary concern, or is pleasing God what's important?" Reverend Metcalf asked.

"Doing what the Lord wants is first with me," Reverend Matthias responded quickly.

"And also it is with me," Father Montoya agreed.

"God is my first and final guide in all things," the rabbi added.

Bishop Darlington twisted his mouth. "You don't understand, because my members are different than yours. They're very demanding and they have rules that forbid certain things. Mixing the races is at the top of the list. Not that I approve of it, of course, but what can I do? These are powerful people with a lot of money and influence and—"

Reverend Metcalf pointed at the bishop with a stern expression. "You must show them God's way, and if they don't want to follow the Lord, then they should leave the church."

The bishop was startled. "The place would be empty in no time. Everyone would leave." He wiped his forehead with his handkerchief.

"Then so be it," Reverend Matthias told him.

"Easy for you to say, but ours is a highly organized and established denomination. I have higher-ups to answer to."

Rabbi Snellingberg cocked an eye. "The only higher up you should worry about is Yahweh, our God," he replied. "It seems you have a decision to make. Do you follow the Lord or the people with the money who you think run the church? Who really is the head of that temple of God—your wealthy parishioners or the God of all grace?"

"More important," Reverend Metcalf added, "who is the head of *your* life; people with money? your position? or Christ Jesus?"

"Why, Christ Jesus, of course."

"Then the choice should be simple. I chose you to join us because I know your true heart, Harlan. I've known you for years and I understand your uncomfortable position. I watched your reaction to the riot and saw you work diligently to help the suffering as much as you could . . . but you did it secretly most of the time," he said gently. "I know you don't want to alienate your members but it's time you stop pacifying those so-called saints and show them what Christ in their lives and heart really looks like. You've told me many times how you want to do just that. This can be your first step. Are you willing to take it?" He was silent a moment, then went on. "No one at this table will condemn you if you decide not to join us. We understand the difficulty of your decision. You can get up and leave this meeting if you must. I will still be your friend because I know your heart."

"The only condemnation will be from your spirit, not from us, my friend," Father Montoya said.

A prolonged silence ensued as Bishop Darlington looked from one man to the other. He shifted in his seat and bit his lip several times as his mind raced. One by one the men bowed their heads and fell into prayer. The bishop bowed his last but made a more sincere entreaty than he had ever before. When he lifted his head the others were looking at him. He took a deep breath. "You are right; it's time I take a stand for what I really believe. I will do what the Lord guides me to do and accept the consequences."

"Put yourself in God's hands and the consequences will work themselves out for the good if you believe what God says," the rabbi assured.

Reverend Metcalf nodded, satisfied. "I believe each of us will encounter problems but ultimately accomplish something valuable for God's kingdom by coming together like this. Our churches will benefit and so will all of Tulsa by our example, even if it's met with a lot of resistance. I think we can do this, gentlemen. I believe this is the will of God and a calling for change among His people; now let's start making a plan of action."

CHAPTER TEN

Ella Freeman was worried. Benny had come home from work distraught and locked herself in her room. She'd been troubled by what Ella thought was a lover's quarrel but this seemed even more serious. She hadn't seen such a distressed expression on Benny's face for a long time, not since . . . Ella pounded on the door several times before her daughter unlocked it. "Honey, please tell me what's wrong," she pleaded once inside the room.

"I just need to be alone." Benny crawled back in bed.

"Is it Billy Ray?" her mother probed cautiously.

"I don't want to talk about it."

"You need to talk it out."

"Mom, just go away and let me handle this, okay?"

"Staying locked away in here in bed is not handling anything. You're hiding from your problems."

"Then I'm hiding, so let me be."

"You know that never helps. It adds to your misery and makes things worse."

Benny rolled over and turned her back to her mother. "Will you please go away?"

"Is this why Josephine told me Billy Ray's so miserable too?"

Benny rolled back facing her mother. "She told you that?"

"That and that he said he can't face a future without you in it."

Benny's hard stare softened. "I feel the same way about him."

"Then what's the problem?"

"He's impatient and mad at me for delaying our wedding."

Ella sat on the edge of the bed. "Your father and I have also wondered why you're waiting."

"I'm not sure what to do; I mean if this is right or not. I don't trust my judgment anymore, Mom. Not after—"

"After Jordan Franks."

Benny's face changed at the mention of his name. She sat up and pulled her knees to her chest, putting her arms around them. "I saw him today," she said weakly.

"You saw Billy Ray?"

"No, Jordan."

Ella's eyes widened with alarm. "Jordan? How could you when—"

"He's in Tulsa."

"I thought he went to live in Europe somewhere."

"Paris, but he's performing here for a while. So he says." Benny gazed out the window. "He came to the school this morning."

"He had the nerve to go there?"

"He's married, Mom."

"He told you that? Married to who? What self-respecting woman would have him?"

"I don't know, and I don't care about who the woman is. I just hated seeing him again. It feels like all that humiliation is back." Benny's eyes filled with tears. "Just when I thought I was past it, here he comes dredging it all up again. He's the reason I can't fully commit to Billy Ray. Jordan's still ruining my life. Billy Ray's already mad because I'm stalling; now this." She began to sob. "What do I do, Mom? I can't stand Jordan being in the same hemisphere as me, let alone in Tulsa. It makes me sick just to know he's here."

Ella put her arms around her daughter. "I'm so sorry this happened. I can't believe that man had the nerve to show his face after what he did to you but he did. Honey, don't let this throw you back into the unhappy person you've worked so hard to not be anymore. What happened between you and him is done and over. You can't change it, but you can keep it behind you. You have a new life now and a good future with a wonderful man. Don't mess that up because of that deceitful scum," she pleaded. "That would be letting him have too much influence over your life. He can't ruin your life unless you let him. Believe me, the last thing you want is for Jordan Franks to have any place in your life other than being part of a dreadful mistake in your past."

"So what do I do?"

"You patch things up with your charming husband-to-be and forget Jordan exists."

"It's not that simple."

"It can be if you use that stubborn streak you have and work at it."

The Dutch Oven was the first restaurant to reestablish itself after the riot. Burned to the ground, its owner, Sylvester "Spike" Green, was relentless in his quest to rebuild an even bigger and better eatery. Spike was a driven entrepreneur from his youth, whose business grew as did his family; he and his wife had ten children. Destruction of the restaurant only stoked his money-making fires and he succeeded rebuilding faster than most but with one key flaw. He ignored the fact that his success was contingent on the businesses around him. He relied on customers who ran and patronized other businesses, plus the Greenwood District residents. Seventy-five percent of his clientele were hotel guests, shoppers, workers, or business people in the area. Greenwood was not yet the thriving metropolitan neighborhood it had once been. The new Dutch Oven Restaurant was a modern showplace with a decoratively colonial theme and the latest in food service trade equipment. Business was slow, but the godly proprietor had been blessed with enough residual funds from insurance money to provide him with ample capital until Greenwood's business district was once again a bustling hub of commerce.

The restaurant was nearly empty after the meager lunch crowd had thinned out. Billy Ray was happy to meet there with his old pal after so many years. Mark Coleman looked spectacular. "Paris really agrees with you, Monkey. I hardly recognize you," Billy Ray said eating his roast chicken and cornbread stuffing. His friend had filled out from the spindly and shy youth he had once been to a handsome, confident man-about-town.

"You have no idea what a great place Paris is. I can't say enough about how glad I am I took the chance and moved there. Life is so unencumbered in Paris. Don't have to put up with all the prejudice like we do here."

"So I've heard."

"Hearing about it is one thing, but living in the freedom of it is indescribable. Who would have thought me, Monkey himself, would be playing my horn at a swanky Paris nightclub frequented by Parisian socialites and American millionaires?"

"Yeah, who woulda thought?" Billy Ray chuckled. "They really like the jazz sound that much?"

"Sure do; they're crazy for it."

"I wonder why."

"Cause it's unencumbered sound and raw like the people there. They're totally uninhibited in Paris, and all over France for that matter, not like Americans. Their women are wild as can be and it's not considered bad behavior. Everybody just does what they feel."

"Sounds like Sodom and Gomorrah to me."

Monkey smirked. "Ever the preacher's son, I see. I bet ole Preacher Roman's real proud of his younger born offspring."

"It has nothing to do with my father. I made my own choice to follow Christ and live life His way. That's the only way to have real freedom in this world."

"I beg to differ. Parisians value freedom like I've never known in this country—freedom for everyone, freedom of expression, and freedom to live as you please. They welcome us with open arms. Negroes and anyone else who comes there are considered friends. Our people can be what we never have been in this country. In France we're respected equals, members of a creative society that doesn't care about our skin color but marvels at our talent and judges us by our character."

"Sounds too good to be true."

"Believe me, it is true. And the women? ooh, la la! " Monkey grinned.

"You have changed. Women used to scare you to death."

"Not anymore, my friend. When I left Morehouse and moved to Paris I walked into a whole new world and a new man emerged."

"So I see. No more calling you Monkey, eh?"

"I'm still the same ole reliable fellow I use to be. Even Paris recognizes me as the musician called Monkey, but my days of shying away from the ladies are long gone. Paris has brought a boldness out in me."

"I can't get over the change," Billy Ray repeated, eating a forkful of stuffing.

"Speaking of change, tell me about this fantastic female who's got Billy Ray Matthias of all people willing to settle down." A raucous group entered the restaurant. Monkey smiled. "Here's some of my fellow musicians now. Come over here and meet the best piano player this side of the ocean," he called to them. "This man can rag a song better than anybody you've ever heard." The five men and woman gathered around their table, all smiles. "This is my good friend and college roommate, William Ray Matthias, known to us who personally witnessed his musical feats as Billy Ray."

"So you're the infamous Billy Ray," a superbly well-dressed gentleman said, giving Billy Ray the once-over while extending his hand. "Good to finally meet you. Monkey raves about your playing often."

"He always was prone to exaggeration." Billy Ray was embarrassed in front of the professional musicians.

"I was not exaggerating. Instead of wasting his time in chemistry labs he should have been sharpening his musical skills. The man's a genius. Hears a tune once and practically memorizes it and then improvises like nobody's business."

"You're a chemist?" a medium-height, dark-skinned man asked.

"A pharmacist. I studied pharmacology, and music was my second major."

"Ah, brilliant as well as talented," said a short Caucasian man in his French accent.

Monkey pointed to the larger round table next to them. "Sit."

The sophisticated, best-dressed man was the last to sit, first seating the delicate woman who clung to his arm. Not a wrinkle marred his impeccable clothes, nor could a speck of dust be found on his shoes. His hair was freshly cut and his nails were manicured to perfection on his rather languid hands. Billy Ray watched the group, but his eyes kept darting to this striking individual. He seemed to be the leader and a very confident one.

The woman with him was not especially pretty but she too was well-dressed. She was ultrafeminine in appearance and movements. Her attention-grabbing frock revealed a sense of chic styling and plenty of money. Even her handbag looked costlier than those most women carried for everyday use. She dripped with extravagant jewelry and spoke in hushed tones, almost whispering in her companion's ear. Billy Ray was fascinated by a black woman speaking such fluent French. It was clear this woman was used to the finer things in life. Her makeup was the kind only wealthy women could afford and she used it heavily on her fair brown skin. He observed a sizeable diamond and wedding band on her finger and wondered if the man was her husband. Something was off about those two . . . especially him. Maybe they were illicit lovers.

Spike's daughter left their table amused but somewhat frustrated after taking the complicated orders from the musicians who had to be reminded several times they were not in Paris and crepes were not on the menu. Pancakes were the closest they could expect. "We're not at Zelly's. Give the girl a break," Monkey chuckled. He looked at Billy Ray smiling. "You should come to Paris. I guarantee you'll never want to live here again. The food is fabulous."

"You won't have to worry about the French burning you out of your home, either," the oldest man in the group said seriously.

"Or hanging you from a tree," the handsome ebony man with the slicked down hair added.

"Let me make proper introductions," Monkey said. He started pointing around the table. "This is Zack Bowden, our wild drummer man; Renée Simone, our French horn and saxophone player; and this is Bottoms Jackson, who does bass, violin, and cello. Jaws here is a jazzed-up trumpet player who will play all night if you let him. His real name is Packer Nelson. The lovely lady, Maida, is our French canary with one of the sweetest voices in all Paris. And that lucky devil sitting next to her is her husband and our esteemed leader, Jordan Franks."

Billy Ray almost choked on his food. He wasn't sure this was the same man he had once seen perform and who had been engaged to Benny, but he assumed he was. "Nice to meet you all," Billy Ray muttered, once he realized he was gawking.

"Jordan is well known in these United Sates, unlike the rest of us nobodies until we hit the Paris café scene. Jordan had already made a name for himself right here in the states, hadn't you?"

Jordan smiled faintly. "I had a little success."

"I've heard of you," Billy Ray said hoping he'd hid his feelings. "Heard you and your choir give a very good performance once."

"Nice to know my name hasn't completely faded into oblivion," Jordan responded smiling. He put his arm on the back of Maida's chair.

The conversation continued, but Billy Ray wasn't listening. His mind was on Benny and what this man's presence in Tulsa could do to her. He was confused that Jordan Franks was married after what he was told about him. Somehow, though, it made perfect sense for the prominent musician to guard his reputation by having a wife. Billy Ray wanted to jam his fist into Jordan's face for hurting Benny and daring to involve another unsuspecting female in his sordid lifestyle, but even more so for coming to Tulsa.

"Why don't you come to the hotel and play for us?" Jordan suggested.

Billy Ray's mind snapped back to the conversation. An urge

to get away overtook him. "Oh, um, yeah, maybe I can later." He stood up and said to Monkey, "Have to go. I have something really important to take care of or I would stay."

Monkey looked disappointed. "But we just started catching up. You haven't told me about that future Mrs. Matthias yet."

"You have a week here, right?"

"That's right."

"We have plenty of time. I'll stop by the hotel tomorrow and we can continue where we left off." Billy Ray slid his chair under the table and tossed some cash on top. "The meal's on me." Glancing at the staring faces he said, "Nice meeting you all," then walked quickly toward the exit.

"Till tomorrow," Monkey called out. Before opening the door Billy Ray looked back at his friend with a half-smile, but Jordan's face was in his peripheral range and his actual visual target. He hurried out the door.

When he was gone, Maida said to Monkey with a twinkle in her eyes, "Your friend, he is big and very handsome."

"He's definitely one of a kind, I can tell," Jordan commented. "I think it's fascinating that he can play as well as you say with those large hands."

Maida snickered and said something quietly in French.

CHAPTER ELEVEN

Giuseppe Alonzo Carissi was in his usual tailored pinstripe suit, expensive hat, and specially designed spats when he stepped out of the flashy white vehicle in front of Murphy's Tavern. He usually carried a custom-made cane, which was for show, not need, a fashion statement of sorts, one his grandfather started as a young boy in Sicily.

His grandfather, Guido, was a feared man in their mountain village, who wielded his cane like a lethal weapon. He had been and was still Giuseppe's idol. The cane was partially responsible for Giuseppe's newspaper-inspired moniker, Gentleman Gi. He was seldom seen without his hollow cane in which he kept several expensive cigars. A twist of the handle brought a sharp knife flicking out the end of the fashionable cane. In public Gentleman Gi mostly wore suits accompanied by perfectly starched Italian shirts, and ties with his eighteen-karat gold chain watch. His shoes were always spit clean polished, his hair cut to near perfection. Giuseppe strutted around like royalty, although he'd been born in the poor village of Ragusa. He had been brought to the United States when he was ten and lived in a Chicago tenement with other struggling immigrants.

He was a self-made American success, who worked hard to acquire not only wealth and reputation, but an aura of class and dignity. That his cultural ways were an imitation of others and not inborn was something he kept hidden, and no one who knew otherwise dared criticize. He had an uncanny business sense, resulting in some dubious enterprises in Chicago, and now expanded to Tulsa. He was rumored to be connected with organized crime, part of the Carissi family, but did not flash his connections.

Giuseppe's arrival in Tulsa was exciting to the members of the White Glove Society. Someone had invited him to their meeting, but Bigger Stanwyck, presiding from the podium, was not so thrilled they had snagged the attention of a well-known, reputed criminal. Others were starstruck, enjoying the buzz of how Gentleman Gi could put Tulsa on the map and make it as big as Chicago . . . or maybe bigger.

When the celebrity gangster entered the tavern the crowd immediately quieted. Four men trailed Gi to the podium where Bigger was perched to call order and start the meeting. Bigger's presence normally generated enthusiasm with the members but tonight they didn't want to hear his blowhard grandstanding and empty pep talks. They wanted to hear the big shot from Chicago, who was rumored to be ready to set up in their city. They wanted the thrill of hearing Gentleman Gi say they were not only good enough to be considered but that the White Gloves would be in some kind of partnership with the Carissi family. This was thought to be a coup of enormous proportions.

Benny was worn out though she'd spent most of her day in her room and half of that in bed. Billy Ray became worried when he learned she left school because of illness and had not returned to work. When he saw her, his alarm escalated. A drastic change had taken place in a short time. "How are you feeling?" he asked, trying not to show his apprehension.

Benny looked up at him. "I'm glad you came to see me. I thought you might never come back after our quarrel. You were so mad I thought—"

Billy Ray took her in his arms and held her tight. "Forget about my stupid impatience. I'm sorry I got angry. I don't want to rush you into anything. Forgive me."

Her eyes were closed in his strong embrace. For the first time since he'd left she felt comfort. "I was so afraid you hated me . . ."

"That's nonsense, I could never hate you."

"I'm not so sure you'll feel that way after I—"

He let her go and looked hard at her. "What's wrong, Benny?"

"I—I just don't know how to say this." She looked around the parlor and walked away from him toward the window. "This is difficult to get out. I want you to believe it's the hardest thing I ever had to do."

His nerves knotted in his stomach. "What?"

"I have to be fair to you. The way I am . . . it's not fair to you . . . and I . . ."

"Benny, do you love me?"

She spun around quickly. "Yes, of course I love you."

He sighed relieved. "Okay, then, whatever it is I can stand it."

Her eyes dropped. "I love you but I can't marry you." Her tone was low and sullen.

"What do you mean, you can't marry me?"

"I'm breaking off our engagement. You're free to pursue another woman who's ready to get married right away." Benny pulled the brilliantly sparkling diamond ring from her finger and held it out for him to take. "Here. I'm not worthy to wear this." The shock and hurt on Billy Ray's face was painful for her to watch. She waited, but he never reached for the ring. She set it down on the lamp table and started toward the door.

Billy Ray grabbed her and spun her around. "You're just ending things like that with no explanation?"

"I told you—"

"You've told me nothing! Why can't you be honest with me?"

"I am being honest," she whispered, fighting back tears. "I'm not ready to be your wife and you want to be married now and rightfully so. I have no right to ask you to wait until I feel ready to . . . to . . ."

"You're lying. There's more to this than our little tiff over a wedding date."

"I am not lying. What are you insinuating?"

"Look at you; you look like you've been through the riot again. Are you physically ill?"

She looked away and didn't answer.

Billy Ray stared at her. "Just as I thought; I was afraid my temper had upset you, but now I see it's something more."

"Can't you see I'm torn up about what I have to do?"

"You don't have to break it off with me Benny. Why are you really doing this?"

"You said . . ."

"I apologized for what I said. I was being demanding. You should have known I'd get over it."

"Even so, you were right. I have no right to expect you to wait indefinitely."

"I'll wait a lifetime if that's what it'll take to make you happy."

Benny started weeping. "It's no good; it's just no good for either of us. I'm so mixed up, and I don't know if I'll ever be fit to be anyone's wife."

He took her by the shoulders. "What are you talking about? You're a wonderful woman. You'll make a great wife."

Shaking her head side to side, "I can't—I can't." She sobbed harder.

"You can't what?"

"Be a wife to anyone."

"Why?"

"Because I'm not woman enough!" She pulled away. "Don't you see? I'll never make you happy!"

"That's crazy, why do you think that? Of course you'll—"

"It's over. Accept it and go on to a woman who will be everything you want. It's over between us, Billy Ray." She made it to the door with her hand on the knob.

"Does Jordan Franks' being in Tulsa have anything to do with this decision?"

Benny turned, shocked. "How did you find out he was here?"

"Unfortunately, I met him today."

"You met Jordan?" She started trembling.

"You knew he was here, didn't you?"

"All right, yes, I knew, but not until yesterday when he came to the school."

"Benny, don't let his being here interfere with us."

"I don't want to talk about Jordan."

"We have to talk about him. He's the reason you won't marry me, isn't he?"

"I said I don't want to—"

"Stop avoiding the truth and face what's eating away at you."

"Please, just leave me alone. I can't take this." Benny snatched the parlor door open and hurried out of the room.

Billy Ray sank into a chair and prayed aloud. "You said she was mine, Lord, so help me get through to her. I love Benny, and I can't take seeing her so upset. Help me not hate this man who hurt her so badly. Give me strength so I won't do what I want to do to him. Help me, Jesus, because if You don't I won't be able to control myself."

"If I weren't trying to follow Jesus I'd tell you to go right ahead and do whatever it is you want to do to that no-good Jordan Franks. I try not to hate but he's made it almost impossible for me to forgive him," Ella said as she entered the parlor.

"But that's just what we have to do, Miss Ella, forgive him for what he did to Benny and pray for his deliverance."

"Easy to say, but not so easy to do, I'm afraid." She sat down on a beige velvet settee.

"I agree, but as hard as it is for us it's so much harder for Benny."

"I thought she'd gotten over him; at least that's what she told me. She even said once that she forgave him."

"She thinks she has, but she hasn't forgiven him as much as she needs to. Forgiveness comes in degrees, in stages, like most things when God deals with us. She reached a certain point of forgiveness, but she's got a long way to go before she can forgive enough and live with what happened. Then she can stand up to what he did so it won't affect us."

Ella smiled. "You're such a mature man, a godly man.

Sometimes I forget who's the preacher, you or your father."

"It's definitely my father. The Lord blessed me to be able to do some things well but preaching the gospel to a congregation of people is not one of them."

"I wouldn't be so sure about that."

"Glad to see you're here, young man." Earl Freeman walked through the doorway. "Maybe Benny will stop moping around like a sick calf now."

"Hello, Mr. Earl. Afraid it'll take more than a visit from me to help Benny."

"What the heck is wrong with that gal, now?" Earl was exasperated. "She's got more moods than a body can keep track of. I thought maybe you two had a little sweethearts' falling out."

Ella lifted troubled eyes to her husband. "Jordan Franks is in Tulsa, Earl."

"Jordan Franks is here? What'd he show up for?"

"Who knows? Does it matter? The point is he's here and it's tearing Benny up. She acting like she did before."

"And she just called off our engagement," Billy Ray interjected nodding toward to the ring on the table.

Ella was stunned. "She did what? I didn't realize she'd gone that far."

Earl pounded the piano top. "That lowdown snake. Ain't but one fate fittin' for a no-good belly crawler like him. You cut off his head!"

CHAPTER TWELVE

Chief Gilbert leaned against the wooden fence shaking his head. "Dang it, Cord, why'd you have to go chokin' on Amos of all people?"

"I told you he came here trying to force me to sell, and when I wouldn't he got mad and spoke ill of my wife. Then I got mad."

"You know he wants you arrested."

"I figured as much. What I don't understand is since when do you come inquirin' 'bout matters like this? Why didn't you send one of your officers to arrest me?"

The chief looked over at the four corralled horses behind them grazing lazily. "Who said I'm arrestin' anybody?"

"Ain't that what you here for?"

"I ain't rightly sure yet. You see, Amos is raisin' a stink over this so I gotta have a darn good reason not to arrest you, seein' he's got a witness an' all."

"You sayin' you don't intend on arresting me?"

"Can't stomach that man; he's a big mouth, cocky, know-it-all. Glad you did choke him. Would do worse myself if I weren't chief of police and could get away with it."

Cord grinned. "I can't believe you're Tulsa's Chief Gilbert talkin' like this."

Gilbert's expression changed. "I'm still chief of Tulsa's police department and don't you or nobody else forget it." Jake looked around to see if anybody was within earshot. "But I never wanted what took place in Greenwood District to happen. Wish I coulda stopped it somehow. It makes me sick to think about the folks who lost their lives and property, and for what? Way I see it, you folks done been through enough. I'm tired of white on one side and colored on another. It ain't right."

Cord looked skeptically at Gilbert. "You sure have changed your tune. The Jake Gilbert I've always known had nothin' for Negroes like the rest of white folks round here and never let a chance go by to prove it."

"Bah, I ain't ever cared much one way or the other 'bout white or colored. You break the law in this town, you're mine no matter what color you are. Had to act a certain way cause folks expected it of me if I wanted to move up in the department," Jake reminded him. "That's just how it was. Maybe now things might be changin'."

"Don't appear like the law's changing, or folks either. I don't see much regret or guilt being rightfully placed for what happened by neither."

"Maybe not, but God don't take to cold-blooded murderin' folks no matter what color they are."

"You sayin' you got religion now? Is that what this is about?" Cord asked curiously.

"Something wrong with tryin' to get right before you meet your Maker?"

"No nothin' wrong with it. It's just I never thought you—"

"Yeah, well, everybody gotta come face-to-face with the Lord one day, don't they? Either down here or after they die and I'd as soon get right before I pass on."

"Amen to that."

"You know my brother's a preacher in Arkansas?"

"You don't say." Cord was surprised.

The chief rubbed his chin. "So what do I do about this charge of assault? That was the least I could downgrade it to cause he wanted worse. He's hoppin' mad."

"I don't know what you can do, but I'm shocked and glad you're on my side."

"I'll have to think of something fast to shut ole Amos's trap."

When he held her in his arms the madding world faded, and problems seemed less daunting. His happiness was tied into a tidy brown package named Ada. He hadn't felt like this in decades. The thrill of romance had dulled early in his marriage to Helen; years before her passing she was stricken with a debilitating illness. Jake kept his distance physically and eventually withdrew emotionally knowing she lived in constant pain. He remained faithful but relationally remote and still had pangs of guilt about it to this day. He wanted to do more and be a better husband but just couldn't stand watching her suffer. As much as he cared for his wife he couldn't help her, and it tore him up inside. Her death was bittersweet because she was gone, but at least her agony was over.

Now he and Ada were spooning like youthful lovebirds. "Ada, you make me crazy for you." He was squeezing her tighter.

"Oh, Jake," she sighed, then suddenly she straightened up stiffening. "Is this how you carried on with Miss Kate night before last?"

He frowned. "You should know better. I told you before that Kate is just a friend, the wife of an old friend, to be exact. I don't have any designs on that woman."

"Have you told her that?" Ada folded her arms across her chest.

"No, why should I? She knows we're just friends." He reached to embrace Ada again but she jerked away. "What's wrong, sugar? Why you acting standoffish all a sudden?"

"You made love to her, didn't you?"

"To who? Kate?"

"Yeah, to Kate, you know good an' well I'm talkin' 'bout her. You took her to bed and spent the night with her, didn't you?"

"For cryin' out loud, no, I did no such thing. Why would you think that when you know how I feel about you?"

"Cause she said you was gonna marry her. She told me so."

"She's nuts! I don't want to marry her."

"She wants to marry you."

"No, she doesn't."

"She does too. That cozy little dinner for two the other night wasn't just being friendly. Candlelight and roses on the table ain't fo' friendly folks and you know it."

"Are you're telling me Kate is under the impression I would marry her?"

"That's exactly what I'm sayin'."

"Well, she's wrong."

Ada cocked an eye. "Why not marry her? She comes from a rich family and knows all the right people. You could be somebody real important in Tulsa if you married her. And she's got that big fancy house."

"Yeah, the house you keep clean. Look, Ada, you know how I feel. I'm crazy about you."

"Humph."

"Can't you see I love you?"

"But only in secret." Ada spoke sadly. "You say you love me, but nobody knows you do. We can't be together out in the open like other people."

Gilbert took her in his arms. "I know this is hard for you. It's rough on me too, but I don't know what else to do. You know how people are around here. Both our lives would be a nightmare if the truth about us got out."

"It don't seem right that two people can't be happy without worryin' 'bout folks tryin' to hurt them on account of it."

"It's not right, but that's how it is. It happens to be one of the rules of this life."

"Whose rules? God don't like race hatin'. God's rules are the only ones that count."

"I enforce the law of this city, so I don't agree with that. Men make rules to help regulate society, and most times they should be obeyed," Jake said. "I remember years ago hearing that the Bible teaches people to obey the laws of the land."

"Only when those laws don't go against the Lord's laws. God

always comes first, then people's laws." Ada's face got somber.

"What's wrong?"

"We ain't got no hope for happiness together in the future. What's the point if we have to hide and sneak around for the rest of our days? I don't think the Lord approves of us slippin' round seein' each other like this. It ain't right, and I'm tired of feeling wicked about us being together."

"I don't like it any better than you but you know our situation. I'd marry you right now if I could . . . but I can't. What else can we do?"

"We can either be brave and stop hidin' how we feel or go our separate ways."

CHAPTER THIRTEEN

The formal dining room at the Freeman ranch was crowded with family and guests. Ethan was in an exceptionally cheerful mood. Bet looked more beautiful than ever, and he had plans to step up his romantic pursuit of her this very day. Since he'd been a child, Sundays had always been his favorite day of the week. This particular Sunday was going to be superb.

Ella was elated that her elder son had come even if his younger brother did have to drag him there. Cord was uneasy being around his father but was braving the awkwardness well. Earl was pleased Cord had come, but was coolly cordial.

Talk flowed as freely as the plentiful food. Bet was impressed with all the home-cooked fare. "Mrs. Freeman," she said to her hostess, "I've never seen so much food on a table when there wasn't a holiday celebration."

Ella smiled as she set down a bowl of sweet potato pudding. "This *is* a celebration, dear. The Lord's Day of worship is always a celebration in our house. Our family gathers together with friends sometimes to give thanks to God and fellowship. We like to keep His day holy."

"Yes ma'am," Bet said, lowering her head uncomfortably.

"What church do you attend since you've been in Tulsa?" Josephine Matthias asked.

"I don't go to church," Bet answered softly.

"You don't go to church? Why not, young lady?" Roman asked.

"Well, I . . . I'm not sure I believe in God anymore," was her uncomfortable reply.

Ella shot a look Ethan's way just as he sank slightly down in his chair. "You don't believe in the Lord Jesus?" she asked.

"Why in tarnation, with all your education, don't you believe in the Good Lord?" Earl asked.

"That's precisely why, Mr. Freeman. I'm educated enough to know better. My intellect has helped me weigh out everything, including what I was told as a child as well as what I saw for myself as an adult. Intelligent analysis led me to conclude God doesn't exist. At least not the God I heard preached about all the time," she insisted. "If He does exist, He's not what people think. There is no benevolent deliverer who takes care of His children from what I've seen. Take the riot for instance; most of those people from what I heard believed in God. They were churchgoing citizens who I'm sure prayed for help but were killed, beaten, and burned out anyway. Where was your God then?"

"Young lady, that's blasphemous." The preacher's voice was shrill.

"Calm down, Roman," Josephine cautioned.

Cord looked at the lovely Bet, surprised at her courage to make a challenge of faith among the company of an ordained minister and his family. "Oh boy," he whispered to Ethan. "This is going to get ugly."

"Did you hear what she said?" Roman said, shaking his head.

Ella spoke up. "We all heard what she said, and though I strongly disagree I respect her right to give her opinion."

"That's what happens when women go steppin' into menfolk's shoes," Earl muttered.

Bet sat up straighter. "I beg your pardon, sir?"

"Women becoming lawyers . . . oughta be married and having babies, takin' care of a husband like a woman's spose to do."

"This may come as a shock to you, Mr. Freeman, but I may never marry." Bet flashed her charming smile behind that statement.

Ethan's surprised look did not go unnoticed by his mother or brother.

Bet looked around but was undeterred from speaking her mind. "Women have been denied a chance to make decisions about their lives for far too long. All we could look forward to was getting tied to some man and stuck with a brood of babies. Well, it's time men accept that we want to vote and have careers and own businesses like they do. We deserve more than dirty laundry, a houseful of babies, and catering to men."

Roman's mouth flew open. "Are you one of those ungodly suffragette women?" he asked.

Napoleon Matthias looked at Bet with interest as he waited for her answer. Ella lifted an eyebrow before sitting down next to Earl. Ethan shook his head, and his father leaned back and tapped his foot under the table. Phoebe, Napoleon's wife, smirked a bit. She was glad the accomplished beauty was under so much condemnation. Cord was relieved that he wasn't the focus of attention, but he felt sorry for Bet.

"Why don't we just have a nice meal and forget all this unpleasant conversation?" Josephine suggested.

"Talking about the Lord Jesus should never be unpleasant," Roman responded staring at Bet.

"Since you inquired, Reverend Matthias, yes I am a supporter of equality for women. I champion equal rights for all oppressed people. That includes not just Negroes but all racial minorities . . . and females."

"It's against God what you fanatical females say." The preacher kept his voice low with an effort. "It's almost blasphemy!"

"Roman, please," his wife whispered.

"He's right," Earl chimed in. "Ain't natural, just ain't natural."

"Everybody calm down. This is Sunday dinner and I will not allow it to turn into a political or religious debate. Pastor, will you bless the food?" Ella's eyes went to two empty chairs at the elongated table. Her mind drifted off to Benny and Billy Ray, hoping he was succeeding at changing her daughter's mind.

Voices from the dining room made their way to the veranda behind the house, where Benny sat forlornly in a thatched rocker,

Billy Ray standing next to her. He looked down at her sad eyes that used to be bright brown and full of life. They were red from too much crying and puffy from not enough sleep. Her hair was parted in the middle and carelessly knotted in the back. It pained Billy Ray to see her so depressed. It hurt Benny to see Billy Ray so solemn and wounded, especially when she knew it was her fault. On impulse, his hand stroked her head several times. She didn't complain or push him away. Her eyes closed and for one brief moment she reveled in his touch. "I won't give up on you," he said calmly.

Her eyes shot open. "Why did you insist on coming out here when you know . . ."

"What I know is that God said you're to be my wife. What I know is that I love you more than life itself although heaven knows why since you're the most uncooperative woman I've ever met." He smiled at her gently. "What I know is that you love me but you keep fighting it because of your experience with Jordan Franks. You can't let go of the past, and now you're killing our future on account of it. What I know is that I have done all I can and that this problem is between you and the Lord from here on out. If you want peace about Jordan Franks once and for all you better give it to God and listen to what He says in your spirit. Follow the Holy Spirit's guidance. Learn to forgive to the point of really letting Franks off the hook."

"I can't just ignore what happened. You don't understand how—"

"You can do all things through Christ which strengtheneth you. Isn't that what you say in church? Then say it now and live it. Scripture isn't meant for Sunday recitations and impressing the preacher. It's meant to get into our souls and strengthen us so we can fight when we have to. If you believe what you spout, then call it up when you need it. That's what I do."

Benny rolled her eyes. "You make it sound so simple."

"If Jesus is in you, you can do it. Might be hard but it's possible. Remember, all things are possible with God."

Benny rolled her eyes again. "You're preaching at me again."

"I'm not preaching, just putting what the Scriptures say to action. We're supposed to apply the Word to our lives, aren't we?"

Benny looked up at him. "If through Christ I can forgive Jordan, then through Christ you can face up to your calling. Apply that," she retorted.

He raised his eyebrow. "Don't change the subject, and stop running from your own problems."

"I will when you stop running from your calling and accept your destiny."

"You're part of my destiny and I'm part of yours."

Benny breathed out hard. "Why are you badgering me when our engagement is off?"

"No, it's not."

"I gave you your ring back."

He went in his pocket and took out the ring. "And I'm putting it back where it belongs." Taking her hand, Billy Ray slipped the ring onto her finger. "Now don't take it off again or I might not be as understanding next time."

"I can't."

"You can't what, wear the ring?"

"I can't accept this ring. It's not right."

"Why, Benny? Tell me what's wrong? What's going on in that pretty head of yours?"

She took a long loud breath. "I suppose I owe you the truth or I'll never be rid of you."

"Do you really want to be rid of me?"

Benny looked at him wide-eyed. "No," she answered softly, voice trembling. "But it's the right thing to do; the only thing for your sake."

"Let me decide what's best for my sake."

"All right then, you decide. Do you want to spend the rest of your life with a woman who's not able to be a real wife?"

"What do you mean not able to be a wife? What are you talking about?"

"I'm talking about me. Me, I can't be a real wife to you because . . . because I can't bear the thought of our being any closer than we are. Together, I mean." The tears that were in her eyes spilled onto her cheeks.

Billy Ray stooped down in front of her. "Are you talking about making love?"

She looked away from him. "I can't," she whimpered.

"I don't understand." Billy Ray was confused.

"I can't be with you that way. I know I can't." Her whisper was almost inaudible.

"Of course you can. We love each other and when we're married—"

"Being married won't change it. I can't and I don't think I ever will."

"Are you telling me there's something wrong with you?"

"Yes, I'm not like other women." She swallowed before continuing. "I haven't been since—"

"Since Jordan Franks?"

"Yes!"

Billy Ray hugged Benny as she sobbed in his shoulder. "Don't cry, honey, we'll handle this together. I won't pressure you, I promise. As long as we're together we can get through anything. God's gotten us through much worse than this; my being in jail and us making it through the riot. So I'm sure He'll work this out too."

"What's wrong with me? Why am I such a mess?"

"You're such a sweet mess to me." He lifted her chin. "So this is why you've been stalling about getting married?"

"Uh-huh."

"What makes you think you . . . can't?"

"I just know I can't. The thought of it scares me to death. That's not normal, I know it's isn't."

"Did you feel this way when you were engaged before? To Jordan, I mean?"

"No, and that's what I can't figure out. I couldn't wait until we were to be married. I was so anxious to be his wife and be with him. The thought disgusts me now. How could I have wanted someone like him and not a wonderful, virile man like you? I don't understand what's wrong with me." Her sobs grew more intense.

"I don't either, but there must be a reason, so we'll find it. You'll get over this and we'll be married."

She looked up into his face through teary eyes. "What if I don't get over it? What if I'm a pathetic, frigid female for the rest of my life, then what?"

"Then I'll marry you anyway. You're my wife, Benny, for better or for worse. I made up my mind before I put this ring on your finger that you were. This problem doesn't change that."

"You're the oddest person I've ever known; the sweetest and the most peculiar, but the most wonderful human being in the world."

Billy Ray's face took on a serious look. "I don't know about the most wonderful but I have always felt odd . . . always out of sync with my peers and the world around me."

"You are wonderful, loving, loyal, and steadfast. You're a godly man and wise beyond your years. How did I get so blessed to have you in my life?" Benny said tearfully.

"I don't know if it's so much of a blessing, but you're stuck with me." He smiled.

"I love you so much. I want you to believe that no matter what happens."

"I believe it, and my love for you is strong enough to weather even this storm, so don't worry." He was glad when she finally smiled too. "Now let's go inside and have dinner with the folks. They've probably started without us."

"I look a mess. I need to go fix up first."

In the dining room the once cheerful conversation had dulled to strained cordiality. Billy Ray waited for Benny to spruce up, and when they joined the others and sat down to eat they could feel the tension. Benny immediately assumed they were the reason for the frosty atmosphere, but Billy Ray wasn't so sure.

"I thought you would never come inside," Ella said, pleased to see her daughter looking better than she had in many days and wearing her engagement ring again. "Come eat before the food gets ice cold."

"Sorry to straggle in late, but we had an important matter to discuss," Billy Ray explained.

"I hope it was about setting a wedding date," Earl said.

"Not yet, sir, but soon."

"Said that months ago, what's the hold—" Ella's pointed-toe shoe in his shin cut Earl's comment short.

"I'd marry her tomorrow if she'd agree," Billy Ray assured him.

All eyes landed on Benny. She shifted in her seat uneasily. "There's no rush. We'll be married soon enough." She tried to sound casual.

"Better not wait too long, honey," Phoebe said leaning forward, grinning over at Benny. "The women are crazy about Billy Ray. You should see how that BeBe Morris acts in church when she sees him. It's shameful she's so obvious."

"She acts that way around any unmarried man, not just Billy Ray," Ella said, passing the roast turkey to Cord.

"That's my point. Benny should hurry and marry him so he's not so available."

"He's not available, he's spoken for," Josephine insisted.

"Till a man says 'I do' he's still fair game to a desperate woman like BeBe."

Bet couldn't hide her annoyance with Phoebe's comments. Phoebe looked straight back at her and added, "Unless they're like those suffragette women who hate all men and criticize the sacred institution of marriage."

"Phoebe, that's not nice," Josephine scolded.

"Don't worry, Mrs. Matthias," Bet said. "I can stand criticism from an unfulfilled female burdened with nothing more than mundane house chores and no real purpose in life."

Phoebe's eyes narrowed vindictively. "I've got plenty of purpose in my life."

"Washing diapers and your husband's dirty unmentionables is not purpose, it's menial labor," Bet countered.

Earl smacked his cloth napkin down on the table. "That's indecent talk for the supper table, missy."

"You're wrong, Bet," Ella interjected. "Being a wife and mother is one of the hardest jobs in the world. Raising your children, running a household, and being a wife is not easy or menial. It's harder than you know unless you do it, and it's very important. You sacrifice your dreams and what you want to help everybody else reach theirs and you dare not have any outside interests that pull you away from your laborious duties. If you do, you're accused of neglecting your family, and that includes when everyone's grown." Ella jutted her chin a bit, scanning the faces at the table. Cord dropped his head avoiding her gaze. Benny rolled her eyes, insulted. Ethan looked surprised at what his mother had said. Earl ignored his wife's commentary and looked at Bet, ready to continue his condemnation. Josephine was nodding her head in agreement while Roman managed to continue eating as he shot disapproving looks Bet's way.

Ella went on. "You live all your days expected to be there for everyone else and keep their lives moving smoothly. That's more than enough purpose, if you ask me. It's a hard job to be a wife and mother, often with very little thanks. You have no idea what it takes. Your work is never done because until you die you're supposed to be right there for your family in whatever way they need you. God help folks' opinions of you if you're not."

Phoebe was satisfied, but not enough to keep from giving Napoleon a nasty glare and adding, "That's right, we have to cater to everyone else and see to their happiness and comfort while neglecting our own. That's a sacrificial purpose if ever there was one."

"It sounds more like a life sentence than a purpose," Bet remarked.

"No, it's not a sentence. True, it's sacrificial and sometimes real hard, but I love my life as a wife and mother. I always have," Josephine said.

"I love my life and my family too. I've been very blessed," Ella said. "My point wasn't that I was so unhappy. I was trying to show the importance of being a wife and mother and running a household as compared to having a professional career. I believe running a good home for your family is the backbone of our society. Mothers are responsible for the upbringing of the generations to come and wives are the ones who help the husbands do what they're supposed do. We all have necessary roles in the family and each is equally important. There are no menial jobs whether it's a common chore or not. It has value because it's a necessary part of everyday life."

Bet smirked. "Funny, I thought you were lamenting the drudgery of being a housewife. It sounds to me like housewives are unappreciated, overworked, and unsatisfied with routine chores."

"What you need is a husband to settle you down," Roman said.

"A husband isn't the answer to everything a woman needs," Bet countered.

"You suffragettes are tearing our country's structure apart with your devilish nonsense. God did not intend for women to carry on like men. It's sin."

"That's right," Earl added.

"She doesn't believe in God, remember?" Phoebe said.

Benny looked at Bet, shocked. "You don't believe in God?"

"Let's not go into that again," Ethan said, defending his guest. "Bet has the right to her own opinion without everyone ganging up on her."

"We ain't gangin' up on nobody," Earl protested.

Ella looked at Bet. "I'm sorry. You're our guest and we really don't mean to be unkind."

"Somebody needs to talk some sense into her," Roman grumbled.

"Rome, hush," Josephine snapped. Her husband looked over at her, shocked, but didn't respond.

"Instead of criticizing so much maybe you folks should try to see things from her point of view," Cord said. "She's a smart woman, so there must be something to what she's saying or—"

"Aw, there's nothin' to the claptrap those troublemaking suffragettes spout. It's womenfolk rebelling, is all," Earl growled.

"That's your opinion, but that doesn't make it right," Cord said cutting off his hostility.

"You *would* defend her, wouldn't you? You can't see past a pretty face or shapely ankle."

"Earl," Ella cautioned quietly.

Billy Ray spoke up immediately. "Mr. Earl, Cord's right. Even if you don't agree with something you should try to understand what the other person is saying. Everybody has opinions and a right to them."

"That's right," Benny chimed in.

"Bah, you young people got no respect, is all."

"I respect you and always have," Cord said firmly, "but respect should be earned and returned in like."

Earl's fist slammed down, rattling dishes. "I'll be doggoned if I have to put up with being attacked at my own table!"

"Earl, don't—"

"Leave it be, Ella! I'm sorry, Reverend, but I'm sick of tiptoeing around my own house because these young folk are upset! I run this place and I'm not backing down to nobody 'bout what I say and what I believe! There'll be no mollycoddling anymore with nobody." He looked at Benny. "You get it together and marry this young fella befo' he gets sick of waiting and goes a lookin' elsewhere, missy. Get yourself a husband and stop mopping around here like a sick calf." His eyes shifted to Ethan. "And if you get you a wife, I sure hope it's not some woman like this one here who talks against the Good Lord. You were brought up to respect God and you shouldn't associate with anyone who doesn't. What are you thinking bringing someone like this in here?"

"Earl!" Ella gasped.

"Quiet, woman," Earl snapped. Ethan opened his mouth to speak but seeing his father's inflamed expression decided to shut it. Bet dropped her fork, straightened her back, and pursed her lips defiantly. Phoebe was smiling, and Napoleon's eyes were looking from one disgruntled face to the other.

Billy Ray glanced at Benny. She looked upset again but this time it was from anger. "Mr. Earl, I'm committed to Benny whether we're married or not. I will not be looking for another wife and I'm not pressuring her. I can wait if I have to."

"That's what you say now. Tell me that a year from now. I was young once too, you know. A fella gets tired of going home aching."

A snort escaped from Phoebe.

"Earl, please . . . " Ella said, her embarrassment apparent.

"Daddy, how could you be so crass? Stay out of our affairs," Benny said with quivering humiliation.

"Don't sass me, young lady. Get married and put that man out his misery." Immediately Earl faced Cord. "I'm surprised at your brother being so gullible about a pretty woman, but not you. You take up for any ole kind of trash if it looks good and riles your nature." Gasps circled the table again. Roman nodded in agreement this time. Earl pointed at Bet. "She's a Delilah and you're as dumb as Samson and you know what happened to him, don't you?"

Cord sprang to his feet. "That's it, I don't have to sit here and listen to your narrow-minded opinions."

Bet rose from her seat too. "Mrs. Freeman, I apologize for disturbing your lovely meal. I think it's best I leave."

"Dad didn't mean what he said," Ethan told Bet. "He just gets excitable sometimes."

"I meant every word I said and then some!"

"As well he should," Roman said in support.

Cord left the table. At the dining room doorway he turned. "I knew I shouldn't have come. Sorry, Mom." He walked out.

Ethan was distressed as he stood up and faced Bet. "I'll see you home."

"No, you stay with your family," she said dryly. "I'll ask your brother to take me home." She hurried away.

Ella was in tears. "Look what you've done," she said to Earl.

"Excuse me." Benny jumped up, making her exit too.

Billy Ray got up as well. "Pardon me," he said rushing from the room after her.

Napoleon leaned over close to Phoebe's ear. "Look at him; always the knight in shining armor rescuing the damsel in distress." Ella caught his remark and frowned. Phoebe frowned too. *Well, at least he defends the woman he loves*, she thought enviously.

CHAPTER FOURTEEN

The Gurley Arms was home to Bet since she had arrived in Tulsa with the second wave of legal liaisons from the NAACP. Being one of the first rebuilt commercial structures, the fashionable building was the second tallest in the district, standing six stories high. Before it was torched, it had been a traveler's hotel, but for the time being it was home for many dislocated Greenwood residents. Its stylish new design held its own with that of any elite hotel in Memphis, Chicago, or New York City.

Gus Mills was the oldest doorman at the Gurley. He was an affable gentleman at seventy who enjoyed greeting people in his neatly pressed, red-and-black uniform with his amazingly youthful, ebony skin and neatly cut wooly white hair. He always exchanged a few pleasant words with Miss Whitehead when she left or entered the lobby, but not this evening. She looked flustered as she sped by him without speaking; the oldest Freeman son was in tow. Gus found it strange to see Cord since it was usually the younger Freeman, Ethan, trailing behind the breathtaking beauty. He was even more surprised when Cord got on the elevator with her. He knew Bet was a big city girl, but no respectable single woman took a man to her suite of rooms without suitable explanation.

Bet fell into the King George divan in her sitting room fighting tears. She had sustained a brave front as long as she could. The flashing Gurley Arms sign threw light on that side of the building. Her collapse into sobbing emotion left Cord standing by the window twirling his hat not knowing what to say or do.

"Don't cry," he uttered ineptly. "My father's a mean ole cuss sometimes and everybody knows it. You can't take his insults seriously."

"It was worse than insulting; it was vicious what he said."

"Don't let him get to you. He's a master at getting to folks." Cord gazed out the window remembering his own anger. "I shouldn't let him get to me either," he mumbled.

"It wasn't just your father. That preacher and that Phoebe woman . . . all of them ganged up on me. They hate me."

"Nobody hates you. They don't understand you, is all. Try not to feel so slighted by what they say. They're just plain country folks. They're not used to hearing this newfangled educated talk of yours. It's just as insulting to them. They're reminded of how unworldly and behind the times they are and it riles 'em up."

"You must think I'm awful too."

"No, I don't. What my father said was nothing but his old-time stubborn ideas." Cord moved in front of Bet taking her by the hands standing her up to face him. "You have nothing to be ashamed of. He's the one who acted badly. You have a right to think how you want. Look Bet, you're a beautiful, smart lady and any man would be proud to be in your company."

She sniffled and looked into his eyes. "Do you mean that?"

"Sure, I do."

"Then you don't think I'm some shameless femme fatale?" she asked softly.

"No, you're the prettiest thing I've seen around here in a long time," he said, half hypnotized by her disturbing allure. "Ethan's a fortunate man."

"Ethan?" Her eyes fluttered.

"You know, him being your beau and all."

"My beau? Cord, I thought you understood. Ethan and I are not romantically involved."

Cord looked around the immaculate room with its flowered wallpaper and lace curtains hoping for somewhere safe to land his eyes. Bet's pointed stare was unsettling. "Then what are you?"

"We're just friends and legal associates, nothing more."

"Wait a minute . . ."

She moved closer against him. "I'm extremely fond of Ethan as a friend and colleague but that's the extent of it. Didn't I make that clear before?"

The smell of her perfume and the softness of her body was too much to resist. "I really don't think he sees it that way," Cord stammered.

"Ethan already has a mistress whether he's aware of it or not . . . the law is his lady. Fighting for causes is what he really loves. I want a man who concentrates more on me, a man who isn't hung up on religion. I want a lover devoted to me. The man for me is not occupied with the affairs of the world more than with making me happy . . . I want a man like you, Cord." She wrapped her arms around his neck and kissed him slowly.

Cord hadn't known the delight of being kissed that way since Savannah. His body ached with a longing he'd repressed for a long time. He yearned for Bet with an uncontrollable craving he'd corralled—until now. His lips devoured hers. "We can't," he groaned.

"Of course, we can," she countered. "We're both adults."

"I know, but—"

"No buts." Bet shushed him with her finger on his lips. "Let's just be together tonight and comfort each other and be happy for just a little while."

"This isn't right," Cord managed to say. "What about Ethan?"

"Forget about your brother. He's not here. You are. And I am." She snuggled her body even more closely to his. "Cord, you're the kind of man a woman like me needs. You're strong and rugged and you make me completely weak inside."

She continued to whisper in his ear until he no longer wanted to resist. He scooped her up and carried her to the bedroom.

Billy Ray looked out on the ridge at the setting sun's palette of colors and held Benny's hand tenderly. She was no longer crying but still somewhat melancholy. Her head leaned against him as they watched the herd of bison in the ravine below, huddling close together for safety, preparing for darkness. "I guess we better start back toward the house," he said gently.

"I don't want to go back. Your sister-in-law and my father make me sick. Who asked for her opinion? What's worse is I can't believe my own father would humiliate me like that in front of people. And the way he treated Bet was an outrage."

"I've got a feeling she's used to being criticized, though perhaps not so harshly."

"Well, I'm not used to being embarrassed like that. Maybe I should be but I'm not."

"It's okay, sweetie; he's had his say for now. I doubt if he'll say anything else to us tonight," Billy Ray assured her. They walked companionably down the hill together.

Cord and Bet lay close together, pleased and exhausted, though Cord's physical satisfaction was mingled with guilt.

The soft knocking on the door came twice but they hadn't heard it. The third knocking was followed by the unlocked door being gently opened. "Bet, it's me; are you in here?" Ethan called as he let himself inside the room. "I was worried about you and wanted to apologize for my father's—"

The bedroom was straight through at the tail of the unit and its door wide open. Ethan stared at his brother's startled face as he tried to process what he was seeing; Cord in bed with the woman he adored! Bet sat up, covering herself with the sheet. She looked trapped, not remorseful. Ethan slowly took in the painful sight with numbing despair. He couldn't move.

"I'm sorry, Ethan. Sorry you found out this way," was Bet's softly spoken apology.

"Why her?" Ethan asked in a struggling voice. He looked directly at Cord. "Why her?" he repeated.

"Why not?" Bet replied glibly.

Cord was surprised by her response but he had no idea what to say.

Bet was perfectly tranquil when she told Ethan, "Let's see this as it is. We're all freethinking adults. Cord and I knew what we wanted and that was each other."

Ethan's heart sank as the hurtful words hit full force. His jaw clenched. "I've been at my folks' place all this time arguing, *defending you to everyone*, but once again my father is right. You are shameless, and Cord, my own flesh and blood brother—you're a treacherous snake."

Cord's voice was like gravel in his throat, "Ethan, I didn't mean to—"

"You didn't mean to what? Kick me in the teeth sullying the only woman I ever considered marrying? Dad was right. You can't see any farther than a pretty face. If a woman is beautiful, then reason doesn't count with you. You forget common sense. Blast decency because you don't care a lick about family or anyone else. Look how you let that cheap tart you married come between you and Dad. Well, forget you, big brother." His eyes shifted to Bet. "And forget you too! You deserve each other!" Ethan swiftly made an exit.

CHAPTER FIFTEEN

E zra Cottonwood tilted his salt-and-pepper head toward the lamp, scrutinizing the contracts closely one last time. He reached out his age-spotted hand; bony fingers faintly quivering to pick up the pen.

Billy Ray sat squeezing the arm of his chair and prayed silently. He needed reassurance this was the right decision, the godly choice following guidance from the Holy Spirit and not his own foolish desires like his father had accused. "You sure this is what you want to do, son?" the old man asked, pen poised over the documents, sensing Billy Ray's apprehension.

"Yes sir, I think I'm supposed to do this."

"Are you certain or do you just think so? We can hold off till you're sure if you've got a mind to."

Billy Ray paused, petitioning the Lord one more time for clarity, then answered, "Um, yeah, I'm certain."

"Good, a man ought to be positive when making important decisions like this." Ezra smoothly signed his name to both copies of the document.

Billy Ray leaned forward when the papers were pushed in front of him. He wrote his name with more trepidation then he expected. When he had purchased the pharmacy with his brother he hadn't been nearly as nervous. Everyone said it was a smart move and would be a profitable undertaking. He had trained to be a pharmacist even if it was at his family's urging. Buying the

Fountain Pharmacy was the next logical step. This was different. He didn't have his family's sanction on this venture. He was sure they would not approve or support, emotionally or financially. He was completely on his own operating under what he believed was a pull from God.

This path was slightly questionable in his own mind but definitely not well received by his relatives. Still, he vowed to be obedient to God and follow the guidance of what the Holy Spirit put in him. His comfort was in knowing he was doing what God led him to do and having Benny's approval and encouragement. This would affect her life as well when they married. Even with her support, he was acutely aware he would have to walk this journey fully trusting Jesus. That was okay because what mattered most was being in the will of God. Now more than ever he had to trust the guidance of God's voice in his spirit. Doubting whispers surfaced relentlessly but he confronted those distracting fears when they reared their skepticism. Everything and everybody was saying no but he would not be deterred because God was saying YES! Billy Ray placed the pen down. "I guess it's pretty much final now," he said. "I want to thank you for this opportunity, Mr. Cottonwood."

"Take your papers to your lawyer and we can close this deal in no time. I'll be waiting to hear from him."

"I'll take them to Ethan straightaway when I leave here."

"You know, son, I can't rightly say why I'm doing this. It's the strangest thing. I woke up one morning hard pressed to sell this property after I'd been holding on to it for years. It was like a fire was lit up under me. That was mine and Adelaide's first homestead when we came to Tulsa, a real sentimental piece of land. It's been sittin' unoccupied for almost eight years after our tenant passed on. I always said I would keep it for my grandchildren's inheritance. But for some reason that morning I knew I was supposed to sell it. Then as if you were reading my mind that very day you asked me about my plans for it. I knew right then I was supposed to sell it to you."

Billy Ray smiled and sat back, relaxed. "It was God," he told

Ezra, but saying it more to himself. This was his much-needed confirmation.

"Yeah, well I ain't much on religious stuff, sonny. I leave that sort of thing to Adelaide but I have to admit it must be God working something fierce in me to make me sell this property and for this amount of money." Ezra shook his head again mumbling, "It sure is peculiar how it all happened, mighty peculiar."

Billy Ray replied, "The Lord never ceases to amaze when He moves in my life, sir."

Phoebe was noticeably on edge when Napoleon came home from work at the hospital. She pulled him into his study, hushing him so the children wouldn't come swooping down the steps to greet him as they usually did.

"What's going on?" he wanted to know.

Phoebe closed the door and put her hand on her hip. Napoleon was pleased since she seemed to have gotten a little shapelier in the last couple of months. "We're having another baby," she blurted out.

"What do you mean?"

"What do you think it means? I'm expecting again." Phoebe sat down on the leather chair across from the desk.

"But I thought you said you were . . ."

"I have been. I don't know what went wrong." She looked at her husband's shocked expression. "Like it or not, we're having another baby."

Napoleon frowned. "Another baby is not what I wanted to hear."

"What *you* wanted to hear! Well, that's too bad. You should have thought about that before. I'm not thrilled about it either."

"You were supposed to take care of things."

"I did! This isn't my fault!"

"Keep your voice down."

"How can you blame me when it's you always wanting and impatient?"

"Mommy, is Daddy home?" Cleo asked from outside the study door.

"Go play and wait till we come out, honey," Phoebe called back. "Daddy and Mommy are having an important discussion."

"They're discussing," Julius's little voice said in an attempted whisper.

"Let's go outside on the swings," Dottie suggested.

"Mommy, can we go outside and play?" Cleo asked.

"Yes, you can go out, but stay in the yard."

"Okay," Cleo agreed. Three pairs of small feet moved away from the door.

Phoebe turned and glared at Napoleon. She was hurt and angry by his reaction. He looked back at her frustrated, but knew her well enough to know he shouldn't speak another word about how he was feeling.

CHAPTER SIXTEEN

Even from behind he knew her as though he'd seen her just yesterday. "Bet, is that you?"

Bet turned around in front of the post office stunned at seeing him. "Jerome?"

"I knew that was your luscious frame I was seeing. I'd know you anywhere; and the name's Jordan, remember?"

"Sorry, I forgot the change." Bet looked away for a second and forced a smile as she looked back at him.

He smoothed over the awkwardness and said, "You're as dazzling as ever."

"And you're still the outrageous flatterer." She looked him over. "And still impeccably dressed," she added, thinking he was probably as penniless as ever from frivolous spending.

"Don't tell me you live in Tulsa."

"Only temporarily while I handle some cases from the race riot."

"So you did become a lawyer after all."

"Yes," Bet replied shortly.

"I knew you would. Nothing could stop a determined little minx like you."

She rolled her eyes. "I work for the NAACP. We're still trying to resolve some legal matters for the Greenwood riot victims."

"Lucky riot victims to have you on their side."

"What are you doing in Tulsa? I heard you were the toast of the Paris nightclub set."

"My band and I are on tour in the States. I'm in Tulsa for a while longer, then we head to Oklahoma City to perform at the Negro Music Hall. Come have breakfast with me. It's been a lot of years, and I want to catch up on everything you've been doing since we last saw each other."

"I . . . I don't think that would be a good idea, Jordan, do you?"

His smile faded as his eyes shifted. "You still resent me for what happened, don't you?"

"At this point I try to forget what happened so I don't spend time placing blame. It's a waste, since you've never felt any shame for what you did. You've always justified it, and I admit I was guilty too."

"I never could figure out why you did it. You were smart, and you weren't going to fail the test. Why take a risk and cheat on the exam?"

"Bad judgment would be my short answer. You know how it was and still is. I was an enigma there, a colored woman wanting to be an attorney. Everywhere I went I heard I couldn't or shouldn't try."

"But you were a good student," Jordan reiterated. "You didn't have to take that chance to pass."

"I could pass well enough, but I always had to do better than just pass or do average. I had to excel and be twice as good. I admit it was a foolishly risky decision but it didn't seem that way at the time." Bet paused, remembering those difficult days. "I was desperate to do well, great even. That's the only way I would possibly be taken seriously or respected in this profession. I had to excel over the top. Then I could demand acknowledgment as a serious student of law and someday an attorney. Mediocrity wasn't enough. But you of all people should know that. You had to do more and be more to get the success you have in the music world haven't you?"

"Indeed I did. And still do. I understood your predicament; that's why I helped you."

"You helped me for money, a hefty price I might add," she corrected. "Later you used it against me. I don't call that help."

"You always looked at it the wrong way. It was beneficial for both of us at the time," Jordan reminded her. "You did well, didn't you?"

"Let's not talk about it anymore. It's over with, in the past, and can't be changed." Bet looked around sighing. "I have to attend to an important matter so I have to go, Jordan. I probably won't be seeing you again, so enjoy your stay in Tulsa."

Bet walked rapidly down Federal Avenue. Though she felt his unnerving stare following her, she never looked back. As a naive college student she had learned the best way to deal with Jerome Franklin was stay as far away from him as possible. Her world had been forever changed the day she had met him. It was a change that stripped her innocence and molded her character in ways she was not fully at peace with even now.

Bet turned the corner onto Archer Street where she could casually glance up Federal. To her relief he was gone She could not be bothered with his brand of devious drama now, especially with the strenuous situation between her, Cord, and Ethan. Nonetheless she couldn't help wonder about the current victim in Jerome—Jordan's—life.

The French woman who hired him for a profitable and surprisingly easy job initially intrigued Dooley. Her secretiveness was amusing at first, but once he'd done his fast investigation he wasn't so relaxed about it.

The investigation itself was straightforward enough, but the information revealed was messy. Dooley wanted no further dealings with her from here on out. He'd earned his fee, and once he'd delivered the report to his client he'd be done with the distasteful matter.

She sat gracefully in the chair across from him and read his report expressionlessly. He was surprised she hadn't shown more emotion. Her French accent was a little hard to understand at times but not so thick that it was difficult to converse with her.

"Are you sure you understand all of what it says?" Dooley repeated.

"*Oui*, monsieur, I understand," she replied.

"I assume this is very distressing news for you."

"*Oui*." Her one word answer was dispassionate.

"Then this concludes our transaction to your satisfaction?"

"*Oui*." She pulled out cash and placed it on his desk.

"No, madame, you've already paid me more than enough."

"Monsieur," she said in a soft voice. "You were very . . . swift to this. No one must know . . . no one . . . ever." Her thick accent couldn't cover the seriousness in her tone. She stuffed the envelope into her ornate European purse.

Dooley looked at the money on the edge of the desk. He certainly needed it because his savings were dwindling and business was not taking off fast. "All right, I understand. This is to ensure my silence but you don't have to do this. Confidentiality goes with my services automatically when—"

The woman stood up. "*Bonjour*, Monsieur Dooley. That is all." She spoke abruptly and left.

Dooley watched her departure aware that the name she'd given him, Leticia Moutranée, was not her own; it was actually the name of her Creole grandmother from New Orleans. What *Madame* didn't know was that Dooley had investigated her as well. He knew she was born Maida Moutranée and now was Mrs. Maida Franks, the well-to-do bride of Jordan Franks, a.k.a. Jerome Franklin. Her husband had been the subject of the requested investigation.

CHAPTER SEVENTEEN

Gentleman Gi tried to make friendly with Tulsa's police chief but was rudely snubbed and sent away. Monetary entice-ment usually worked, so Gi decided he'd resort to more under-handed methods of managing the long arm of Tulsa's law. He knew exactly how to make it known in Tulsa or anywhere else to stay clear of him and his operations.

He went back to his newly purchased prairie mansion, steam-ing with indignation. "How dare that back country copper talk to Giuseppe Carissi like that! Before I'm finished with him he'll curse the day he was born!"

"What you going to do to him, boss?" his right-hand man, Tonio asked.

"First, I'm going to do my homework on Chief of Police Jaffice Gilbert. I'll get the dirt on him and put him where he belongs—under my feet. He'll wish he *had* accepted my *dirty money*." Gi slammed his cane down. "There's more than one way to handle a two-bit, pencil-pushing, hillbilly copper. Come on, I want to go to the colored section. It's called Greenwood District."

"What for?"

"Don't ask me questions, just do what I say!"

Dooley was cool and calm although surprised. Sitting in front of him was the infamous Gentleman Gi. He was not the least bit impressed by the debonair attire and flashy cane. He knew the depths of low this sophisticated-looking fiend could crawl. Years ago he'd been in Chicago when Gi was making a name for himself. Dooley had heard disturbing reports but never did he think he'd actually meet the notorious gangster.

Now he appeared before him, flanked by a couple of husky brutes. "What can I do for you Mr. Carissi?" Dooley asked.

"First, before I answer, let me ask you a few questions. You no longer work for the FBI, is that correct?"

"That's correct."

"You have no further allegiance to the US government or its law-enforcing arm?"

"I'm a private citizen in private practice. My only allegiance is paying my bills and servicing my clients."

"Do you have a family, Mr. Dooley?"

"I'm not married and I have no children. Why do you ask?" Dooley was getting impatient. Years of experience dealing with unsavory characters taught him to look people straight in the eyes, showing he wasn't intimidated by them and helping him recognize the truth behind the words they spoke.

"I like to know the people I hire and what . . . *ahem* . . . what complications might arise."

"I'm not the least bit complicated."

"Good. We understand each other. I want to hire you to investigate someone."

"Who?"

"Let me preface the answer with a small incentive." Gi snapped his fingers. "Tonio!" The bodyguard on the right pulled out a thick stack of cash.

Eureka! Today's my lucky day! Money and more money! Dooley inwardly whooped, but kept all expression from his face.

"This is in addition to whatever fee you choose to charge for your service, of course." Tonio placed the money on the desk in front of Dooley.

"Who do you want investigated?" Dooley asked. "The pope?" He chuckled slightly but Gi's raised eyebrows indicated he wasn't amused by the sacrilegious remark. The stack looked like all one hundred dollar bills. This was more like murder money to Dooley. He sat back, looking straight into his client's eyes. "I'm strictly legit. I don't do anything illegal."

"Of course you don't, Mr. Dooley. My request is not outside the law but it *is* highly confidential. It requires the utmost secrecy."

It's always about secrets. "Private investigation is founded on a client's right to confidentiality and their trust in my discretion. I'm as discreet as they come," Dooley said with ease.

"Indeed," Giuseppe replied. "But let me categorically make clear any violation of confidentiality could have fatal consequences."

Dooley's skin reddened. "Are you threatening me? Because if you are—"

"Nah, I don't need to. I'm merely reminding you where I stand so there's no question about my intentions or your loyalty."

"I have no loyalty to you," Dooley told him. "I don't know you and I don't know what you're asking me to do. I have no intentions committing to vague requests for any amount of money."

Giuseppe grinned. "Then you are the right man for this job. What I heard about you is accurate. You're not afraid of me in the least, are you?"

"No, I'm not; why should I be?"

"Why do you, a white man, have your business in the colored section of town?"

Dooley paused for a moment then answered. "My mother was colored." He folded his arms with a measured glare following that announcement.

"I thought it odd but, that explains it adequately. Strangely enough, you're even better for this job on account of that. The person I want investigated, I'm told, is not liked by the coloreds."

"And who would this be?"

"Your chief of police. Jake Gilbert."

Dooley tried to hide his shock but impulsively unfolded his arms and sat up. "Why do you want him investigated? What exactly are you looking for?"

"I'm looking for a chink in his armor. I want to know Gilbert's dirty little secrets; all the back-alley, under-the-table things in his life and his career. The secrets he keeps well hidden, the ones that could destroy his reputation and cost him everything; in particular his position as chief of police. I need to know the ins and outs of Jaffice Gilbert, professionally and personally, to destroy him."

Dooley swallowed hard and looked at the stolid men on each side of the gangster. Their sinister smiles made Dooley edgy. "Not that I care about Gilbert, but could you tell me why you want him investigated?"

Gentleman Gi smirked. "Oh, come now, I'm sure a man with your professional shrewdness and background can ascertain a logical reason without my spelling it out."

Dooley leaned forward. "I could, but I'd rather you spell it out anyway." His voice edged with sarcasm.

"For your sake, I won't take issue with your impudence since we have not previously had dealings. So let me give you some friendly advice, Mr. Dooley. I picked you because I was assured by a reliable source that you were both trustworthy and more than capable to do this job. For the record, I already knew about your mongrel bloodline."

Dooley leaped from his seat and glared at Giuseppe. The bodyguards automatically shifted, eyes on Dooley, ready to spring, hands reaching inside their jackets. Gentleman Gi called off his thugs, gestering in a halting motion. The men relaxed. "Sit down, my good man; I simply wanted to see if you would be truthful about what you are."

"Don't you ever call me a mongrel again."

"Come now, I'm sure you've been called worse. Don't be so sensitive. I'm not one of those people who put all coloreds in the same basket. I know some of your kind, especially those fortunate enough to have white blood in their veins, are as intelligent and productive as the rest of us." Dooley's face showed his anger, as did his tight-lipped silence. Gi was not put off. "Let's take care of business and settle this. That money is for your guaranteed silence. What are your fees?"

"I didn't agree to take the job." Dooley sat back down.

"But you will."

"You're sure of that, are you?"

"Quite sure, I hope, for your sake." Gi flashed another insidious smile.

"All right, we have a deal. I'll be your bloodhound for now but the cost is double this tip you gave me."

Giuseppe nodded and the man on the left pulled a bigger stack of cash out. "This is more than you ask, and rest assured there will be no more coming." He rose, holding his cane like a British nobleman. His suit was the finest quality material Dooley had ever laid his eyes on, and styled to fit a squire in an English county, though the gangster looked woefully out of place in Tulsa, Oklahoma.

Dooley observed that the gangster's olive complexion was darker than his own skin color. "How should I contact you with my findings?" he asked.

"Don't worry, I'll keep in touch. My lodgings are now at my new home on Plains Road on the western tip of the city."

"The old Mastermann mansion?"

"You're familiar with the place?"

"Familiar with the lawyer who used to live there."

"I wouldn't know him. My dealings were mostly with a real estate agent in Chicago. I think he did say a lawyer was the owner. Where is he now?"

"Washington, D.C."

The burly guards opened the door, and looked around. Tonio nodded that the street was safe for his boss. "I'll be in touch Mr. Dooley," Gentleman Gi said. "I expect to hear something worth the substantial salary you've been paid."

Once he was gone Dooley stood up and shook his fist in the air. "You two-bit Sicilian hoodlum. I'll give you substantial all right. When I'm done, you'll eat those fancy clothes and that stupid cane. You'll wish you never messed with this mongrel . . . Gentleman Gi." He jammed his arms into his sport coat. *So he wants to take down Chief Gilbert? Well, we'll just see about that.*

CHAPTER EIGHTEEN

The grounds surrounding the main building of the Hopewell Asylum abounded in greenery and well-kept gardens. But it was not this side of the facility Bet visited; she made her way to the colored ward, where buttercups and hyacinths could be found growing determinedly in the midst of weeds.

Bet sat in front of Scarlett and stared intently into her vacant eyes. Just who was this disreputable woman who held so much of Cord's attention? Bet held a comb and brush in one hand and waved her other hand in front of Scarlett's face.

"Are you in there?" she asked unkindly.

Scarlett made no indication she heard.

Bet began unbraiding Scarlett's hair. She acknowledged to herself her jealousy where Scarlett was concerned. Cord was so dedicated to the withdrawn mental patient, giving her his time and none to Bet.

Their single act of passion pushed him away instead of drawing him into her life as she wanted. Cord hadn't come to visit her again and purposely avoided her when she went to the ranch to see him. They had one short conversation when they ran into each other in Greenwood, and Cord had infuriated Bet by telling her their lovemaking was a sin. Then he apologized for taking advantage of her, and she had almost laughed in his face. Was he really that naïve? She decided his innocence was as much a part of his charm as his muscular physique.

The seduction had been easy enough, but now over two weeks had passed since that afternoon, and things were a mess. Ethan had run off to Washington, D.C., apparently to help his friend Maynard, but she knew the real reason he fled Tulsa. And Cord was hiding out on his ranch, and if things couldn't get worse that Jerome or Jordan or whatever he was calling himself these days had to show up in Tulsa.

Bet stroked Scarlett's hair anxiously thinking of all this. "You have such pretty hair," she murmured, still thinking of Cord. "He's such a wonderful man," she mused aloud. "He's so strong, yet he's gentle and loving. I thought I would near faint when he kissed me. Then when we made love . . . *oh*. He really knows how to make a woman feel beautiful." She thought she felt Scarlett's body tense but dismissed the notion. "I've got to have him again."

She parted Scarlett's hair down the middle and continued speaking softly. "You're a lucky lady to have him look after you like he does." Bet began to rebraid Scarlett's thick hair. "Cord is the kind of man I could get real needy around . . . you know what I mean?" Bet turned to smile at Scarlett, and to her astonishment the woman was frowning. Her habitually blank expression had turned antagonistic. Suddenly Scarlett leaped up, smacking the brush out of Bet's hand. She slapped Bet's face before knocking her to the ground; she pounced on top of her and pulled her hair.

"Get off me!" Bet screamed, scrambling to get free. "You're crazy!"

They rolled into a cluster of rosebushes. Bet's screams intensified as thorns pricked her flesh.

Cord approached for a routine visit with Scarlett and couldn't believe his eyes when he saw the two women scuffling on the ground. "Scarlett, what the—" He grabbed her and pulled her off Bet.

"She's insane!" Bet shrieked. She rolled away from the prickly bushes and covered her scraped legs with her skirt.

Cord was holding on to Scarlett, who resumed her motionless posture and empty stare. "Scarlett, answer me. Why were you fighting Bet?" he demanded before releasing her. She didn't answer. Helping Bet off the ground he asked, "Are you all right?"

"No, I am not all right! I was attacked by that . . . that crazy woman! Bet straightened her clothes and smoothed her straggling hair.

"What happened? What did you do to get her so upset?"

"What did *I* do? She flew at me like a wild woman for no reason! I'm the one upset!"

"She never moves much on her own, let alone acts like this. Something had to stir her up."

"I was brushing her hair, that's all; just brushing and plaiting her hair. Look at my legs—and my arm."

Cord looked at Scarlett, then back at Bet. "Did you say something to set her off?"

"No! I told you I was brushing her hair! She's dangerous, can't you get that through your head? She's a menace to society! She could have killed me!"

"Calm down. I don't think it would have gotten to that."

"Why are you taking her side?" Bet's eyes filled with tears. "You care more about her than you do me, and after we—you know. I don't believe this. You blame me for the trouble between you and Ethan, don't you?" She trembled, determined not to cry in front of him.

Cord embraced Bet to comfort her. When he looked at Scarlett he was surprised to see her watching them with a nasty expression on her face. It confused him. "Scarlett, what's happening with you? Are you okay?"

"She's evil," Bet said.

Cord walked over and took Scarlett's hand. "Scarlett, it's okay. This is Cord, talk to me." He hugged her close.

"I need you more than she does," Scarlett said quietly in his ear.

He pulled back, shocked. "What did you say?" When he looked in her eyes the hollowness was still there so he thought he must have imagined her speaking so clearly.

"I look a wreck," Bet complained. "Cord, we need to talk."

"I have to tend to Scarlett. Her doctor needs to know about

this. He warned me about something like this happening. This is some kind of development in her condition. He'll probably want to talk to you too."

"I don't give two figs about her development, and I'm not talking to any doctor looking like this. Do you see what condition I'm in? I should file a suit against her and against this institution."

"I find it strange that the only time she reacts to anything is when you're around."

Bet walked in front of Cord. "I don't want to talk about her anymore; I want to talk about us. Why are you avoiding me after what happened between us?"

Cord looked over at Scarlett. He saw the hurt and fiery determination on Bet's face. He was cornered and embarrassed. "Do we have to do this here and right now?" He groaned weakly.

"This is the only place I've gotten a chance to see you, so why not?"

"Tell me something, Bet; why are you here?"

She hesitated, startled by the question. "Why . . . I came to do a good deed and check on Scarlett."

"To check on her or on me?"

She stomped her foot. "How dare you insinuate such a thing? I was already here, so I simply thought I'd pay Scarlett a visit. I came to see her *after* I had a meeting with my client, or did you forget about that?"

"Yeah, I did, sorry."

"Let me tell you one thing, Cordell Freeman, you're not so wonderful I would come all the way out here just to spy on you. I never dreamed you'd be so arrogant as to think such a thing." Bet snatched up her purse from the garden table and marched off.

Cord was glad to see her go. He was in no shape to resist her seductive charm. Just seeing her stirred up thoughts of her desirability, so he'd made it a point to avoid her.

Taking Scarlett's hand he led her back inside the hospital and informed the nurses of the incident. They in turn notified her doctor. While they waited for the resident doctor to come for the examination Cord fixed her hair as best he could. He also whispered soothingly to Scarlett and confided his indiscretion with Bet. He unloaded how Ethan wouldn't talk to him when he tried to make amends. At first Scarlett made no visible show of judgment but minutes later she moved her arm and placed her hand gently on his. Her smile was warm. When Cord realized what was happening he said, "You understood what I said, didn't you? You're coming out of it aren't you?" She didn't answer but the sparkle in her eyes said yes.

CHAPTER NINETEEN

The Stradford Hotel stood tall on Greenwood Avenue once again. The hotel, burned during the riot, had been rebuilt and sold, but maintained its locally recognized name. The new hotel was more dazzling in splendor and spacious in size than the original. The once fifty-plus-room brick hotel now donned one hundred elegant rooms and suites. Keeping with its former self-contained guest amenities, it offered an elegant banquet hall. The lobby hosted a barbershop, small drugstore, cleaners, and the Dutch Oven Restaurant.

Benny knew it was a bad idea from the start. She couldn't logically explain to herself why she was going but she had to do something. If she didn't pull herself together she would lose her chance at happiness with the man she loved. Seeing Jordan again was worth the agony if it helped her get over what was tormenting her. She felt trapped inside herself, her mind, and situation.

She lingered outside the hotel room on the third floor rehearsing her words. She'd appeal to whatever slight sense of decency he had. *What if his wife is there, then what? I can't let that stop me. Of course she'll be there, but she should know the kind of man she married anyway.* Taking a deep breath she rapped unnecessarily hard on the door two times. She couldn't explain her sudden aggressive behavior but it brought Jordan quickly to the door.

"Benny! Well, what do you know! I'm surprised to see you standing here, pleasantly surprised that is. Come in." He stepped aside, dressed in a flashy silk blue smoking jacket over what looked like navy silk pajamas.

Benny looked his way but avoided staring. *Look at him all fancied up like the Duke of Wellington, wearing pajamas this time of day . . . a disgrace.*

Jordan held a glass in one hand and picked up a crystal decanter with the other. Standing by another door to the left was a petite, odd-looking female. The woman wore a glamorously ritzy peignoir set Benny thought her mother would love to purchase for the shop. Her jewelry was unnecessarily ostentatious. But what intrigued Benny most were the woman's eyes. They were oddly disengaged, although she was looking straight at Benny. The redness and puffiness indicated she'd been crying, which made Benny feel even less comfortable about her intrusion.

Jordan saw Benny's curious stare and spoke up. "Benny, this is Maida, my wife." He then motioned to the woman and she moved beside him. "Maida, this is the fair Benjamina Freeman . . . the one who got away. Remember, I told you about her," and his chuckle was slightly menacing. He looked Benny over. "Join me in a small libation," he suggested, flinging his hand out with the empty glass in it.

Benny frowned and shook her head. "No, thank you."

"Ah, still the good girl, I see."

She rolled her eyes. "I still don't drink alcohol if that's what you mean."

"What else don't you do still?" he asked. He walked to the mirrored bar in the back of the room and smirked. "I must say I'm impressed. I didn't think you had the nerve to show up."

"Why?" Benny asked, glancing at Maida.

"You were pretty adamant about not wanting to see me again . . . ever . . . and the impropriety of visiting a man's hotel room, as you pointed out."

"I thought about it and since your wife is here, I decided it would be acceptable."

"I see. Well, have a seat. I know this must not be a social call, so tell me the reason you decided to brave my company once more."

"You're right, there is a reason I came." Benny sat down on a luxurious white Queen Anne chaise in front of the small circular window beside a matching writing table. She shot another quick look at Maida. She was still standing staring with a far-off blank expression Benny couldn't read. There was something disturbing about this scenario.

Jordan snapped, "Maida, sit down." She complied immediately, sitting on the bed. Jordan wasn't satisfied though. "Stop staring," he ordered. Maida's eyes dropped to her lap. The interaction was more like a brutish father to a cowering child than a loving husband to his wife. "So what's on your mind, my dear?" he asked, bringing his attention back to Benny.

Jordan's ill treatment of his wife and nonchalant air toward her irritated Benny. By now she was regretting her decision to come. She pulled at her white gloves nervously. "I need to ask you a question."

"What question?"

"I need to know . . . I mean I'd like to know . . . why? I need you to be honest when you answer and tell me why you chose me," she said. She dropped her head, unable to face his smug expression. In a barely audible voice she added, "What was it about me that made me the one you picked?"

His smile faded; he glanced at his wife. "No, I don't think I need to tell you anything."

"You obviously did not want me for conventional reasons," she said and looked up at Maida, whose eyes met hers briefly for the first time.

"Does it matter now?"

Benny crossed her legs at the ankles. "I think it does. I need to know what it was about me that made you think I could live with a sham of a marriage."

"Our marriage would not have been a sham."

"Of course it would have been because you— "

"You never understood, did you? Our relationship was not a

lie. It was good for both of us. I really did have a fond affection for you. Being the way you are made us a perfect match. If you had given me the chance I could have made you understand and we both could have been happy."

Benny shifted in her seat, watching Maida who made no noticeable change in her demeanor. She was confused about what he said and how he could say it in front of his wife and why she didn't react at all. "What do you mean me being the way I am?"

"Do I have to spell it out? A person should have full knowledge of themselves, I always say. Remember I used to tell you that? To be a better than mediocre musician you have to know yourself, know what's inside you, and what your strengths and shortcomings are." He sighed, shaking his head. "You always were so naïve, living that sheltered life on the ranch with everyone in your family doting on you all the time. Still spoiled and unrealistic about life, I see; you haven't come into your own yet have you?"

"I am not spoiled and you know it." Benny was indignant. "My family does not dote on me either."

"Oh yes, they do. That entire Freeman clan thinks you're positively angelic and not to be sullied in the least. They act like you're fine porcelain china that might break at the slightest touch."

"What do mean by that remark? My family loves me as any family should, but I have never been spoiled or treated like you're saying. I don't appreciate your twisted insults."

"Then why are you here, my child?"

"Maybe I shouldn't have come."

"But you did, so it must be important to you."

"It was, but I see with your attitude it's no good. Besides I'd rather not upset your wife."

"Never mind her," Jordan said. "Maida's not upset. She knows all about my um . . . little eccentricities," he said smiling. "I never had to keep anything from her like I did you. She's French, and very accepting of my preferences in life. The French are not puritanical like Americans."

Eccentricity! He calls his appalling behavior mere eccentricity!
Benny was incensed at his constant blasé attitude. She knew he
was lying. She knew Jordan well enough to see he was getting
antsy. His eyes kept darting back and forth between his wife and
her. He was holding back what he really wanted to say. Perhaps
he didn't want his wife to hear. She looked at Maida, who seemed
suddenly anxious too. "Well, I suppose I will have to accept your
view of things." She stood up because something didn't feel right
and it started nagging at her. She knew she should leave. "I thank
you for seeing me," she said moving to the door.

He blocked her exit. "But we haven't solved your problem."

"I have to go," Benny said calmly, trying to hide her nervousness.

He looked at Maida meaningfully, and she got up and word-
lessly retreated into another room. "Why hurry off? We should
talk awhile, get reacquainted." He looked at Benny with a famil-
iarity that alarmed her. What was he thinking? He knew how she
felt about him, so why this phony show of friendliness?

"I have to leave," she said firmly.

"You still find me revolting, don't you?" He ran his fingers
around her collar, moving close to her.

Benny slapped his hand away. "Keep your hands to yourself."

"Ooh, you've developed a little temper since I knew you."

"Get out of my way, Jordan. I have no patience for your games.
Move or you'll regret you didn't."

"Making threats are we? I've always been sort of reckless."
His eyes grew steely cold.

A chill shot through Benny but she stood her ground. "I'm
serious. Get out of my way, you devil."

His hand grabbed her wrist tightly. "I told you before not to
say that. I'm not the devil."

"Let go of—" Before she could say another word he slung her
over onto the bed.

He pounced on top of her and pinned her down. "You think
you're better than me? You think I'm dirt compared to you and
your oil-rich family throwing their weight around, ruining my
life!"

She heard her dress rip in the scuffle. "Stop it!" she screamed.

"Shut up!"

Benny struggled valiantly to get away from Jordan but he held her down, glaring at her with an almost maniacal anger. "I ought to teach you a lesson you won't ever forget for ruining my life!" He grabbed her hands that were trying to claw his face. "You want to know why I chose you. Well, Little Miss Perfect, I picked you because you're so dumb, a total idiot about life. Not only were you ignorant about the world, you were completely in the dark about being a woman. So prim and proper, a stuck-up ice princess, frigid as—"

"Shut up! I won't listen to another word!" Benny cried out and with unnatural strength pushed him off, scratching his face. He bolted off the bed but still blocked the exit.

The door to the other room creaked as Maida opened it and peeked out. Jordan looked at her, his eyes wild. "Shut that door and stay in there till I tell you to come out." The door closed back quickly.

"You're insane!" Benny shrieked moving toward the door Maida had closed. "Help me, Maida," she cried out but Maida never came out.

"You can't take the truth, eh?"

"What would you know about truth? Your whole life has been a lie," she said banging on the door and pulling at the handle.

"The truth is that your rotten family cost me my career and ruined my reputation. I would have made tenure but they tossed me out on account of the big shot Freemans pulling strings. Everything I worked so hard for went down the drain, and it was your fault!"

"It was your own fault for lying and trying to use me! How dare you act like you were done wrong when it was your own sordid ways that ruined your career; not me, not my family, but you!"

"You think you're so good? Well, you're not! You're a cold, unexciting child in a woman's body, and no man will ever put up with your frigid behavior."

"Stop saying that!" Benny yelled moving toward the other door.

Jordan smirked, stepping in front of her. "Tell me, have you and you fiancé tasted the sweet nectar of love yet?"

Benny slapped his face in a blind flash of anger. "How dare you!"

He grabbed her by the shoulders. "I'll take that as a no and it's no surprise to me. Still saving yourself for marriage? Using that religious excuse to escape what you're scared to death of—being a real woman?"

"Let me go!"

"You look down your nose at me, but at least I don't have ice water running through my veins. I'm a warm-blooded mammal. What are you? A frigid female, an ice princess too scared to be with a man!"

"Oh, that's not true! Dear Lord in heaven, please help me!"

"The Lord's not listening, Miss Goody-Two-Shoes. This devil's in charge now, remember?" He threw her back onto the bed but she sprang to her feet quick as lightning.

"I hate you!" she screamed, running to the door. Jordan grabbed at her clothes and snatched her back toward him. Benny grabbed a crystal vase on the table and swung it with all her might, smashing it over his head. His howl was the last thing she heard as she threw the door open and fled down the hall.

Staggering down the hall holding to the wall for support, Benny couldn't catch her breath. Her head was spinning, and she was confused and humiliated by Jordan's insults. Her fears were confirmed. *It can't be true!* She reached the middle of the hallway. No one was around, and she was terrified Jordan would come after her so she pushed the elevator button, frantically looking back toward room 306. She was so afraid she was about to bypass the elevator and go down the stairwell when the elevator doors opened. Three people were inside. The male elevator operator who had bought her up when she first came, another man she didn't recognize, and, to her shock, Billy Ray.

He took one look at her and said, "Benny?" as he was moving toward her.

"Billy Ra . . ." was all she got out before everything went black and she fell into his arms.

Benny could hear voices before she opened her eyes. The room came into focus in a matter of seconds once she did. The first face she saw was Billy Ray's. She moaned, trying to rise up and grab his neck. "You're awake." He grabbed hold of her almost crushing her.

"Oh, Billy Ray," was all she could get out before a flood of tears and choking sobs took over.

He held her for a while comforting her. "It's all right, baby. I'm here now; I'll take care of you." He grimaced, looking at her disheveled appearance, and asked, "What happened? Were you attacked by someone? Should I call the police?"

"No!" She grabbed his arm. "Please don't."

"Why not? What happened?"

"I don't want anyone to know."

"To know what? Look at you, something happened; tell me." He took hold of her arm. "Who did this to you?"

She hesitated before admitting, "Jordan."

"Jordan?" Monkey yelped coming up behind Billy Ray from the other room. He startled Benny and she grabbed on to Billy Ray.

Billy Ray quickly explained, "It's okay, dear, this is my friend Monkey from Paris. This is his room we're in."

"Are you all right, ma'am?" Monkey asked. Benny nodded. "Can I get you anything?" She shook her head. "You said Jordan did this to you, is that right?" Benny nodded again. "Are you talking about Jordan Franks?" Benny nodded once more and burst into tears

The mayor was busy as usual. He didn't have time for this nonsense; a bunch of clerics sitting in his office making foolish requests. There were more pressing issues to contend with like that notorious Gentleman Gi with his criminal element settling in his town. It was bad enough the feds had been snooping around in municipal affairs watching Tulsa and his administration like hawks since the riot. Now this. And whoever heard of such a ridiculous idea—white men, Negroes, Mexicans, and Jews coming together for church? Five men were in his office wasting his time talking about arranging some Christian Unity Day in Tulsa.

"Gentlemen, I know you're respected religious leaders in your communities and your intentions are admirable, but it's just not going to fly in this city."

"Why not?" the rabbi wanted to know.

The mayor scrunched up his face. "Because it's preposterous, that's why."

"Nothing that honors God is preposterous," Reverend Matthias countered.

The mayor glanced his way sucking his teeth. "I have enough trouble in Tulsa. Criminals taking root here like we're running a vacation resort. Who knows, this may become a trend with those racketeering thugs. It's bad enough we had all that bad publicity behind the . . . ah . . . that trouble last year."

Father Montoya blurted out, "You mean the race riot?"

"*I mean* that *small* group of ruffians that attacked Greenwood," the mayor snapped.

"Almost two thousand men is hardly a small group of ruffians," Bishop Darlington replied, folding his hands across his lap.

"There's no proof it was that many people. That's just unsubstantiated hearsay."

"It was calculated by a federal government investigation and report. That's substantial enough isn't it?"

"Well, ah, that may be but—"

"See here, mayor; stop trying to downplay what happened like it was some minor skirmish at a neighborhood taproom. It was cold-blooded murder and mayhem, plain and simple, and you know it." Reverend Matthias's tone was harsh.

"Now wait just a minute here."

"No you wait," Bishop Darlington interjected. "People were killed, and property destroyed, yet you have never once gone to Greenwood to speak to those people to show you think it matters."

"I made my statement to the press, isn't that enough?"

"You mean you tried to save face after newspapers nationwide said it was a disgraceful blight on Tulsa."

"I'm surprised at you, Bishop. I thought you'd be smarter than to involve yourself in something like this."

"I'm smart enough to know I answer to God and not you or anyone else. It's time I act like it and stop allowing my congregation to dictate things to me."

"Not a wise move to alienate your membership."

"God is my boss, not the congregation. I'm making it clear that for me things are changing for the better, and I hope for Tulsa too."

"Have it your way. It's to your ruin, not mine, but I'm sick of hearing about that riot. It was unfortunate, of course, but it's over, so let's all forget it."

"Unfortunate and forget about it?" Reverend Matthias muttered looking at the mayor, offended. "How can you be so cold-hearted to say that so nonchalantly?"

The mayor cleared his throat. "Don't misunderstand. I'm not without sympathy, but we have to move on."

"Moving on is exactly what Unity Day is about," Reverend Metcalf said. "This city's God-fearing believers will show a united front in the name of Jesus."

"Folks don't want race mixing in their churches. You know that." The mayor loosened his tie and unbuttoned his snug suit jacket over his bulging belly.

Bishop Darlington said, "It'll make Tulsa look like we're progressing, trying to make amends. That'll silence the negative publicity."

Rabbi Snellenberg nodded. "Even make us look peaceful, as far as race relations go."

The mayor rubbed his chin, thinking. "Mmm, you might have something there."

"Know this, Señor Mayor, we will have our Unity Day with or without your support. If we cannot have it downtown we will have it in Deep Greenwood or Mexicalitown if we must, or on the line, but we will have it," Father Montoya declared passionately.

"That's right," the rabbi agreed.

The mayor looked at the rabbi. His jubilant smile irritated the mayor more. "You're a Jew. What in tarnation are you doing mixed up in this?"

"I'm a Messianic Jew."

"A what?"

"I believe that Yeshua is the Messiah, Son of God."

"Yawhoa?"

"Yeshua."

"That's Hebrew for Jesus," Father Montoya explained.

"Hebrew, what do you know about Hebrew? You're Catholic; you pray in Latin don't you?"

"Yes, but the original Old Testament Bible was written in Hebrew. I speak Latin but I read a little Hebrew too. The rabbi's kindly teaching me more."

"And he's teaching me the Latin in exchange." The rabbi's grin grew wider.

The mayor fell back in his chair. "Catholic priests reading Hebrew, rabbis believing in Jesus and learning Latin. Baptists, Methodists, and Presbyterians gathering like good old boys at a barn raisin'. Has the whole world gone mad?"

Reverend Metcalf smiled congenially. "Perhaps this is exactly what the world needs to see. All true followers of Christ joined in friendship."

Father Montoya nodded. "Si, Señor Mayor, there is one God and Father of us all, one Lord and Savior, and one baptism of the Holy Spirit. So we who love the Lord Jesus should be one body."

"Christ Jesus is our common bond," Pastor Matthias added.

"Yes, yes, yes that all sounds so religiously wonderful, but I'm telling you the people of this city will not tolerate all this race and religion mixing."

Reverend Metcalf stood up. "With all due respect, mayor, it doesn't matter what the people of this city like or dislike. If it's God's plan it's going to happen regardless to you giving us permission or not. This is not some fanciful idea we just came up with to promote our churches or ourselves. This, sir, is a movement of the Lord, and we are bound by our callings to see it through."

"And we will," Pastor Matthias assured.

CHAPTER TWENTY-ONE

The thunderous pounding on room 306's door caused the adjacent neighbors to peek out from their rooms. Maida cracked the door.

"I want to see Jordan Franks," Billy Ray demanded pushing through, knocking her aside. Jordan was sitting on the bed holding an icepack to his head. Billy Ray saw broken glass on the floor from the vase Benny said she used to fend him off.

Jordan looked at Billy Ray. "Matthias, isn't it? You're Monkey's friend."

Billy Ray pulled him from the bed and landed a hard right to his jaw. "Don't you ever go near my wife again or I'll kill you," he yelled, hurling Jordan back onto the bed. He picked him up again holding him by the collar of his smoking jacket. Through gritted teeth he hissed, "You pay real close attention to what I'm saying, you rotten piece of filth. If you so much as look her way, I promise I'll make you sorry you were ever born."

"What—what are you talking about?" Jordan groaned breathing hard. "I don't know your wife."

"Don't lie to me and try to deny it! You should be in jail for what you did to her!"

"Who are you? Who's your wife?" Jordan struggled to get free of Billy Ray's grip.

"Stay away from Benny! She's my fiancée and you better not go anywhere near her or Lord help me . . ."

He hit him again, harder this time. Jordan sprawled limply across the bed barely conscious. When Billy Ray looked over at Maida, he saw her standing perfectly still, watching wide-eyed, but saying nothing. He thought it strange she didn't cry out for him to stop or for help. Murmurs came from the doorway. He turned all the way around to find people gawking from the doorway. He left, pushing angrily through the small group of spectators.

Dooley didn't trust Jake Gilbert and he knew the feeling was mutual.

When he spotted the police chief approaching, he looked around to make sure no one else was in the vicinity watching. It could be a trap and he needed to be extra careful. He didn't feel safe in this section of the city anymore. Too many people hated him since his work with government intelligence had been revealed. Gilbert may well be one of them for all Dooley knew.

The chief spotted Dooley and walked over to him. He looked annoyed. "What's with meeting in alleys? I thought you gave up pretending to be something you're not when you walked away from your government snooping."

"You know good and well there are folks in this part of town who hate my guts, but that's not the only reason I'm being so careful. This is for your benefit too."

"Meaning what?"

"I just happened to get a visit from the infamous Gentleman Gi."

Gilbert suddenly looked interested. "Carissi came to see you?"

"That's right, and guess what he wanted? To get the goods on you."

Eyebrows furrowed, Jake asked, "What goods?"

"He wants to bring you down, chief. You've somehow upset the gentleman." Dooley was amused at the fear he saw the chief trying to hide.

"He ain't no dang gentleman and I won't have no dealings with that fancy-pants hoodlum."

"Well, he has dealings with you because he offered me a whole lot of money to find out your dirty little secrets," Dooley told him.

"If that's the case, why are you telling me?"

"Cause I don't like him."

"And I suppose you're so all fired-up fond of me."

"Don't kid yourself. You're nowhere on my list of friends either, but I figure you're the lesser of two evils. Our tea-swilling friend thinks he can run Tulsa like he did his territory in Chicago." Dooley's half-smile grew. "I figure he's after you because you won't play his game. Am I right?"

"Something like that," Gilbert mumbled. "I told him I was chief of Tulsa's police department and that I wasn't for sale for no amount of his dirty money." Gilbert frowned. "Said I'd put him and all his thugs behind bars if they made any trouble in my city. Also told him not to get too cozy here cause he ain't welcome and wouldn't be staying."

"Okay, now I see why he's after you." Dooley leaned against the abandoned factory wall.

"So how do you want to handle this?" Gilbert wanted to know.

"The smart thing would be for us to team up against the gentleman gangster from Chicago. I have an idea I think will run him out of town for good."

"He's getting real chummy with the White Glove Society, you know."

"I'll have to use some old contacts and a little remaining government pull I still have, but don't worry about that. I plan on keeping them quiet too."

"They want to lynch you bad. The only thing stopping them from trying is the feds swarming around and your being connected to them."

"I'm not surprised, but if my plan works out like I'm hoping it might rid this city of both problems, Carissi and the White Gloves. Tie them all up in one neat little federal penitentiary package." Dooley straightened up. "Your White Glove cronies aren't too happy with you either from what I hear."

"Blast 'em all. They don't tell me what to do. I run that police department."

"Better watch your back," Dooley warned.

"You too."

"Tell you what. For now I'll help watch yours and you watch mine. For now."

"Seems like we have to, don't it?"

Dooley said seriously, "You're going to have to trust me and I need to be able to trust you, or it's the end for both of us. One slip and everything could be on the line."

"I get it. I'm with you on this. You have my word."

"Oh, and by the way, stay away from Ada for a while."

Gilbert's eyes opened wide. "What?"

"Don't bother pretending. I know about you and Ada Crump."

"Dang it, how'd you find that out? We been so careful."

"You forget; I'm real good at what I do. I keep eyes, ears, and feelers out all over this city. Not much goes on I don't know about. It's an occupational necessity and very handy to have in this business." Dooley grinned again. "Don't worry; your secret's safe with me but lay low for a while . . . for her sake."

The chief took off his hat and scratched his head. "I'll be dog-gone. I thought I was playing things real smart." He chuckled. "You just might be able to get rid of Carissi and shut down those troublesome White Gloves." His hat went back on his head. "So tell me what exactly do you want me to do?"

CHAPTER TWENTY-TWO

The hatchet crushed part of his skull surprisingly easily with the first two blows.

He was surely dead from those but a third, more powerful strike to the neck would make sure. Never again could this man ruin anyone's life with his deceit and vile proclivities. He would damage no more souls and crush no other spirits. It had taken time to accomplish but at last it was done.

Demolition and rebuilding sites were routine in Greenwood District since the riot. The resurgence of Greenwood's splendor kept a steady stream of construction going with its racket and unattractive scaffoldings but it was not a building site that was causing the raucous this particular afternoon. Police and curious onlookers were everywhere. Gawking hotel guests were shooed back to their rooms and instructed not to leave until told.

Chief Gilbert arrived, barking orders. He gagged at the sight of the dead man, admitting it was one of the most gruesome murders he'd seen in his entire law enforcement career. One young officer vomited in the bathroom after one look at the nearly beheaded corpse.

"Get those people away from there, Sergeant Bell!" Gilbert yelled. "And keep 'em back!" he bellowed to another flustered policeman.

He noticed in the crowd of people clamoring to get past the

makeshift barricade, two reporters waving for his attention. Grady Coleman was an *Oklahoma Sun* reporter and Carter Mackey worked for the *Tulsa Tribune*. He'd talk to them when he was ready to make a statement and not before. Grady would be no problem but Carter was a different story. Gilbert was still put off with Carter since his inflammatory reporting had been instrumental in causing the riot. He didn't want to talk to him at all but he knew he wouldn't be able to avoid it. White folks would want all the gory details about this Negro musician who left Arkansas to live in Paris, came back from Paris, ending up just about decapitated in a Greenwood hotel room.

"Where's the wife?" Gilbert asked Lieutenant Booker.

"In the empty room two doors down talking to Detective Woolston."

When the chief got to room 302 the door was cracked open and he peered in curiously. He expected to see an inconsolable, hysterical widow. Instead he found an amazingly composed delicate lady sitting in a chair seemingly no worse for wear than if she'd gotten caught in a rainstorm. She wasn't crying now and didn't appear as if she had been earlier. He stepped inside and she looked up at him but more like through him. *She's not just emotionally unexpressive,* Gilbert thought. *She's emotionally vacant. Maybe she's in shock.*

"Hey, Chief, didn't think I'd see you here," Woolston said, shifting his eyes from the widow to his superior.

"I was at the mayor's office listening to him complain like always, so coming here was my escape. He's having a conniption because this will bring more bad light to the city. This is really some ghastly business."

"It sure is. Have you seen—" Woolston cut an eye at Maida and checked his words.

"Yeah, I went in." The chief looked at Maida. "Are you the victim's wife?"

"*Oui.*"

"You're French?"

"*Oui.*"

"Carry on," the chief told the detective.

"Mrs. Franks is the one who found her husband's body," Woolston informed Gilbert. He tried to silently convey a message to the chief. Gilbert nodded, but was even more bewildered by how calm this woman was considering that she found her husband in that sickening condition.

Woolston picked up his pad. "Now Mrs. Franks, you told me you had gone to the beauty parlor and you were away for over four hours?"

"*Oui*. Yes, that is correct." She looked at the chief instead of at Woolston. "I left at ten o'clock in the morning." Her accent was thick and voice soft.

"And you came back when?" Woolston continued.

"Half past two," she answered.

"How can you be so sure of the exact times?" the chief interrupted.

"J—my husband, he was very, very strict about time."

"What do mean strict?" Woolston asked. "Strict how?"

Maida's eyes dropped and she fiddled with her wedding ring. This uneasiness was her first noticeable reaction.

Woolston looked at Gilbert then back at her. "Mrs. Franks?"

"He would be upset when I was away too long," she whispered. "J had to know exactly where I was and how long I would be away."

Gilbert cocked an eyebrow but didn't speak. Woolston cleared his throat and asked, "Was he always very controlling of your whereabouts?"

"Pardon?"

"Did he try to control you . . . control your movements and what you did all the time?"

"*Oui*. Yes."

"What happened if your husband didn't know where you were or you stayed away too long?"

"I do not understand."

"Ma'am, was your husband violent? Did he ever strike you?"

Her body tensed, then a little composure kicked in but she

gripped the arms of the chair like a vise. "I do not understand," she replied firmly.

"C'mon lady, you understand," Gilbert said brusquely.

"I do not, Monsieur."

Chief Gilbert walked in front her and leaned forward, holding the arms of her chair just next to her hands. He looked directly into her suddenly frightened eyes. "Listen, lady, I'm not swallowing this handy little act about not understanding. You know what he's askin', so spit it out." He straightened up, never removing his steely gaze from her eyes.

"I did nothing," she insisted. "I did nothing wrong. He was all bloody and dead when I returned. Everything was bloody."

"Did he ever strike you?" Woolston asked sternly.

Her shoulders slumped. *"Oui."*

Gilbert moved to the door, indicating he wanted to speak to the detective. Once on the other side with the door closed he said, "Ask her how often he slapped her around. I got a feeling his death may not be exactly unwelcomed to this little Frenchy."

"Me too, and something's not right about her. She's odd all the way around."

"Odd how?"

"First of all, I've never seen a colored French person except for a few Creoles from Louisiana, and they aren't really French far as I'm concerned. This woman said she was actually born in France and lived there all her life, plus she's dressed like a wealthy woman," Woolston said. "The other thing is how calm she's been through all this. Most gals would be in a dead faint after walking into that. Not this one. She's the most unruffled wife of a murder victim I ever encountered. Until I asked that last question she was fine. I don't get it."

"Find out why she took so long at the beauty shop," Gilbert suggested. "Don't take four hours to get hair gussied up."

"Do you think she could have possibly . . . I mean she's such a tiny little thing and seems so dignified."

"Doesn't mean anything," Gilbert answered. "The murder weapon's an axe, and the guy was probably asleep when he bought it. Don't take a whole lot of strength and little women can fool you. Find out about their finances," he suggested. "What was he worth alive and dead. If he was heavily insured, see for how much. Let me know tomorrow morning at headquarters first thing. Gotta go throw these pesky newshounds a bone."

CHAPTER TWENTY-THREE

Kate smiled sociably accepting Gentleman Gi's polite offer. He was pleased to have more suitable company than his musclemen for tea.

"I always like being home for high tea," he said.

"High tea?" Kate repeated.

"Yes, this is my high tea meal. I don't bother with afternoon tea and those dainty little pastries and sweet creams. Low tea fare is for ladies. I like this, more of a man's menu, lamb or beef and potatoes."

"My, you certainly have lovely china," Kate commented, impressed.

"I'm a collector. The full collection will be coming next year after my wife packs up our Chicago house."

"So you're planning to make Tulsa your permanent home?"

"I think so. Chicago is getting too . . . ah . . . crowded, and I prefer more open spaces like around here. New territory to expand my business makes this place very suitable. I know I can get very comfortable in Tulsa once my family is completely relocated here with me, and a few minor details handled."

"Have you sold your Chicago home yet?"

"No, my wife's sentimental, carries on terribly when I mention selling. So we're just closing it up for now. I'll ease her into the idea once she's here."

"That must be an awful added expense."

"Not to worry, my dear. It's not a financial burden at all."

"You said your other china."

"My Royal Albert, Waterford, and Wedgewood."

"Sounds risky and expensive to transport all that valuable china. Is it insured?" Kate asked.

Gentleman Gi was happy to have a guest since he knew no one in Tulsa, but Kate was getting too inquisitive. He decided not to answer. "What do I owe the pleasure of this charming visit, Mrs. Boswell?"

"Please call me Kate. My name's Kathleen but I simply hate it. I was named after my grandmother, and she was a dreadful old witch of a woman. I couldn't stand her, so everyone calls me Kate."

"Indeed." Gi handed her the tea, uninterested in her family history. "What can I do for you, dear lady?"

"Oh, you've got it backward. It's what I can do for you that brings me here. Mark Rhyers, the Realtor who sold you this place, told me he gave you my name to help fix it up before your wife arrives."

Gi thought for a moment then nodded. "Yes, I believe he did tell me about a woman who would tastefully decorate. I have it written down somewhere with your name and address if I remember correctly. He said you were very good at decorating and had excellent taste."

"Mark's a kind friend. He was quite close to my late husband." Kate looked around the huge library. "What do you have in mind? This is a large house and hasn't been properly done since my family moved out."

"This was your family's home?"

"I grew up in this house but my family hasn't lived here since right after I graduated finishing school over twenty-five years ago."

"Then I take it you're familiar with the layout, so that would be a benefit in hiring you. What do you suggest? My wife loves flowers and her gardens. English roses are her favorite."

"Rose gardens don't normally thrive in Tulsa unless you grow the hardy breeds like I have in my own garden. This isn't the best climate for just any type of rose. I had to develop certain species over the years. There's a gorgeous desert rose that blooms beautifully for months on end. I can give you some if you like. Simply everyone comes to me for my roses."

"That's very generous of you. How do you see this place—from a woman's point of view?"

"Well . . ." Kate stood up and started walking around the room. "This was my favorite room in the entire house growing up. My father spent most of his time in the library. I think you would love an English manor look throughout the entire house with splashes of Mediterranean influence since you're Italian."

"Actually, I'm Sicilian, dear lady."

"Pardon me, I consider it all the same."

"Indeed; you would," he replied wryly.

Kate took offense but wasn't going to let that deter her efforts, "Yes, well, a total paint and papering is the first thing. If you ask me it's long overdue. These walls are terribly drab. Then you could use some very nice odd pieces to accent each room. Outside calls for a diverse garden or as close to one as we can manage in this climate; flowers that can survive the drought, wind storms, and twisters."

"Tell me, do you know the people who lived here before?"

"You mean that dreadful Maynard Vaughn and his family."

"You didn't care for them?"

"Absolutely not; no one did. Well, the children, I suppose were all right; folks say they were well-mannered and his wife seemed nice enough from my brief encounters with her. She was kind of shy I thought, but that Maynard Vaughn wasn't shy one bit and nothing but trouble."

"In what way?"

"He's an attorney. Thinks he's so smart because he went to Yale Law School. He only got there because of charity so I was told; comes from very common stock in New York; poor as dirt they say."

His own impoverished childhood coming to mind, Giuseppe

decided at that very moment he did not like this critical woman and her countrified, snobbish ways. He'd rather have teatime alone or with Tonio than be bothered with the likes of her. He sipped his Earl Grey listening to her gossipy ridicule and thinking of how he could get rid of her annoying company. Kate continued to berate Maynard Vaughn when he interjected, "Madam, rising above one's humble beginnings and becoming an attorney is a testament to the man's determination, intelligence, and strength."

Kate was taken aback by the comment. She thought for a moment and responded, "Not for that horrible man, it isn't. You don't know what grief he caused. He was always making legal trouble with the Negroes and Indians; stirring up those people, trying to change the way we do things around here. Nobody wants to change anything but he'd rant and rave in court about unfair treatment of coloreds and giving them equal rights under the Constitution. How the government is mistreating Indians and immorally stole their land. Who ever heard of such a thing, them being equal to respectable white folks? Why the government would never do anything dishonest, would they?"

Giuseppe's expression showed definite disagreement to the statement but he didn't speak.

Kate ran her finger across the fireplace mantel, turning her nose up at the accumulation of dust. "Needless to say Maynard was not well-liked in Tulsa," she said ceasing her aimless circling and finally sitting down.

Giuseppe handed her a small plate with a miniature shepherd's pie on it.

She took it, saying, "Just between us, I heard he was run out of town. Had to leave in a hurry if you get my meaning."

"I don't take idle gossip seriously," he said frowning. "Can't abide it."

Kate sat back stretching her neck indignantly. "This is hardly idle gossip, sir. It came from a very reliable source. The chief of Tulsa's police department is a personal and very dear friend of mine," she boasted.

Giuseppe perked up. "Jaffice Gilbert is a friend of yours?"

"Very close friend."

He grinned. "Ah. Yes, I think you and I should get along quite well. I definitely want to hire you to redecorate."

"Oh, thank you. I have some wonderful ideas. This is just what I need, a project to keep me busy." She looked coyly at the gentleman gangster. "I'm a widow, you know. Life has been so empty without a husband."

"I'm sure."

"But not for long if things go well. Jake, I mean Chief Gilbert will be changing that in the not-so-distant future."

Giuseppe smiled., "Indeed, dear lady. May I say he will be a very fortunate man when he does; very fortunate."

"Benny, tell me the truth why you went to Jordan's hotel room."

"I already told you I had an important question I had to ask. One I needed an answer about!"

"Okay, honey, don't get upset. I just want you to know you can talk to me about anything no matter what." Ella sighed. "There's too much trouble and rage in this house right now. Your father was like a madman after he found out what happened. I've never known him to be so angry and out of control in all our years of marriage."

"Where's Billy Ray? I need to talk to Billy Ray," Benny said.

"He's not here, but he'll be over before long, I'm sure. He loves you so much, honey. I hope you appreciate how devoted he is."

"I know, he's too good for me. I don't deserve him."

"Don't be foolish," her mother admonished. "Of course you do."

"No, I don't." Benny rolled over on her side. "I'm tired. I'd like to rest now, please."

"Okay, I'll let you know when Dr. Cutler gets here." Ella got up to leave.

"I don't want to see him anymore. I'm all right, so send him away."

"But he's coming all the way out here to—"

"Please, send him away. I don't want to see him and I won't let him examine me again."

"Okay, dear, whatever you say; but tell me what's going on. I mean, even before Jordan attacked you . . . what was wrong?"

"I can't talk about it."

"You're just like your father. He never wants to talk things out either. Just keeps stuff bottled up inside then eventually explodes over something having nothing to do with the real problem. Acts like nothing's wrong and thinks it'll go away. That's always his solution to problems except when it comes to this ranch. Then he's the take-charge man." Ella took in a deep breath. "I've prayed my children wouldn't get that trait from him but you have. Every one of you."

"Momma—" Benny tried to cut in, but Ella went on.

"Cord ignores his problems and tries to cover his shame and grief by playing nursemaid to that prostitute. Now Ethan's running from something too; I'm not sure what, but it's troubling him something fierce. Going off to Washington all of a sudden for no good reason. Then there's you who shuts down and closes everybody and everything off to escape your difficulties. Earl goes around angry and roaring like a lion at people because he's still hurt about what happened between him and Cord. Instead of going to his son and making it right he walks around ignoring his feelings and making other people suffer. I felt so bad the way he talked to poor Bet. It's getting to be too much for my nerves. My head aches all the time now from the strain. I just don't know how to help any of my family anymore, especially you."

"Just leave us alone. Have you ever thought of that?" Benny suggested.

Ella stood up, offended. "When I do nothing, you complain I'm not here when you need me and say I don't care." She walked to the door and stopped abruptly. "I may just leave you all alone someday—for good." She slammed the door. Benny heard her mother's words but she was too caught up in her own problems to care.

CHAPTER TWENTY-FOUR

It was too early in the morning to be bored, but Jake Gilbert was. Detective Woolston was more than competent; he was a good lawman, but hearing him recite the reports from yesterday's murder in his monotone was not enough to stave off his coming headache.

This murder was going to be a scandalous mess and it came at an unwelcome time. Enough was already going on. An eccentric gangster trying to take root and coming after him preoccupied his thoughts. Instead of fizzling out since the riot, the White Gloves were getting more powerful. To make matters worse he had to go to Kate's for dinner and set her straight about their relationship and now there was this murder business.

"I've had it with them folks in Greenwood District," the chief complained. "Every time I turn around something's happening over there."

Woolston nodded. "I see your point. I guess all eyes are on it since the riot. Sometimes I still can't believe it happened."

"Even before that there was that crazy gal diving out the window. It's just one thing after another with those people." The chief pushed his chair back against the wide windowsill and threw his sizeable feet up on his desk. "All right, tell me what else you got on this murder."

"You're gonna love this; the list of suspects keeps growing."

"You got his wife and who else?" Gilbert asked.

"To be honest, I don't think that little wisp of a woman could do it but you never know. One thing I've learned is scared or angry people can do amazing things, but listen to this: there was some kind of violent altercation with the murder victim and another man two days before his demise."

"Who?"

"Your old friend, William Ray Matthias." Woolston grinned at the chief's surprise.

The feet came down off the desk. "Him again?"

"Got witnesses who heard him in the room punching the victim. Matthias clobbered the guy good and threatened his life."

"About what?"

"Earl Freeman's daughter, Benny."

"What has she got to do with the dead man?" Gilbert demanded.

"Okay, this is what I was able to put together from people I interviewed at the hotel, including the band members and hotel employees. Benny Freeman was once engaged to Jordan Franks. Something went wrong and it was called off. Apparently Miss Freeman had some kind of emotional breakdown over it. Stopped teaching school and went into seclusion. Enter Matthias who woos the heartbroken lass into getting engaged to him after his episode with the girl committing suicide."

"I still have serious doubts about that but I can't definitely condemn him because of what folks said about that poor girl, especially her own father and a doctor. The DA's office determined she committed suicide and Billy Ray had nothing to do with her death. The books are shut on that one," Chief Gilbert insisted.

"Yeah, well it still seems Matthias can be quite violent because he beat up Franks and threatened his life."

"Matthias is a big guy. Franks wouldn't stand a chance going up against him. So what exactly was his beef with him?"

"That I don't know for sure but it had something to do with the Freeman girl.

"She went to see Franks. The elevator operator confirmed he took her to the third floor. He says when he sees her again she looks like she's been attacked and she fainted right in Matthias's arms. He was coming up with one of the band members getting off the elevator. The band member's name is Monkey something or other."

"Monkey? What kind of name is that?"

"You know musicians. They're all odd," Woolston said confidently.

"This case is odd if you ask me."

"My next questioning will be with Miss Freeman and after her, Matthias." The detective's expression grew thoughtful. "You know, there's something not right with this whole deal."

"Like what?"

"Can't put my finger on it, but I keep getting the feeling people are holding back on telling something important. It's like there's this great secret out there that everyone knows but no one's willing to divulge. The band members for instance, they acted like German spies when I questioned them. Tiptoed around every word they spoke."

"Aw, it's probably nothing; like you said, musicians are all crazy."

"This one French fella went to pieces when I questioned him. He was shaking like a leaf, crying like a woman, and I mean boohooing loud."

"Did you tell them they couldn't leave Tulsa until we say so?"

"That got a few grumbles but I made it clear they were to remain here until the investigation cleared them," Woolston assured.

"What did they say?"

"Asked who was going to pay the hotel bill."

"That is a consideration since they're not permanent residents. We'll make a deal with the hotel. If there's a problem I'll take care of it. I don't want any of them going anywhere outside Tulsa till this is solved."

"Okay."

"Maybe this mess will wrap up faster than we think."

"You mean if Matthias is the guilty one?"

"He just might have gotten away with murder once but I'll be doggoned if he will a second time . . . if he's guilty, that is."

Benny already looked like she'd been in a train wreck, and when Detective Woolston told her Jordan Franks had been murdered she almost passed out. Ella sat next to her nervously holding on to her hand trying to console her. She'd sent Virgie out to get Earl. Woolston would have preferred to question Benny alone, but he saw that wasn't going to happen. The troops were rallying.

He was impressed with the stylish layout of the Freeman house. He knew they were oil rich but he never thought what that really meant for colored people. Their fashionable home put his to shame in size and opulence, yet it felt as homey as his grandmother Gert's little prairie house. He sat in the parlor looking at the grand piano thinking enviously about how well they lived when an anxious looking Billy Ray came barreling into the room. At first sight Woolston was glad. That would save him a trip to the Matthias house. Ella made short introductions.

"Why are you're here?" Billy Ray asked immediately.

"To question Miss Freeman about Jordan Franks. And now you since you're here. He was murdered yesterday." Woolston took notice Billy Ray wasn't shocked at the news. "Didn't you folks hear about it?"

"Out here it takes a while sometimes for news to reach us," Ella said uneasily.

"Why do you need to question Benny? She didn't kill him," Billy Ray asserted.

The detective cocked an eye. "You two are engaged, correct?"

"That's right." Billy Ray sat down beside Benny opposite Ella, "Why are you bothering her?"

The guards are flanking, Woolston, thought. *Must have something to hide.*

"Miss Freeman, what was your relationship to Jordan Franks?" He wasn't going to waste any time. He noticed Benny grip Billy Ray and Ella's hands tighter when the question was asked.

"We—we were once engaged to be married."

"When was this?"

"Almost three years ago," Ella blurted out, irritated. "Why does it matter now?"

"Ma'am, the man was brutally murdered. It was gruesome. I won't go into more detail."

Benny and Ella gasped. Billy Ray's only visible reaction was to put his arms around Benny. His face was coldly unsympathetic. Woolston took his mental snapshot and went on. "Naturally we want to know everything about the victim and everyone who had any ties with him . . . or something against him. He hasn't lived here for over two years, his wife told us. We think it must be an old enemy or some past business that got him killed in such a grisly manner."

"So why are you *here*?" Billy Ray asked again still showing his annoyance.

"You had an altercation with the murder victim it seems, Mr. Matthias."

"Yeah, what of it?"

"You threatened his life, I'm told." Woolston watched Billy Ray's careful reaction. He started to speak and stopped. Benny was looking at Billy Ray surprised. "Is that true?" Woolston pushed harder.

"Yes, it's true but then you already knew that. Enough people saw the whole thing. I threatened him and I hit him too, but I didn't kill him."

"Of course you didn't," Ella said.

The crafty detective immediately returned his attention to Benny. "Why did you go visit Mr. Franks at the hotel?" he asked.

Benny looked terrified at the question. "It doesn't matter," she mumbled.

"I'm afraid it does." Woolston scanned the three faces and took a deep breath, "You visit your ex-lover and—"

"He was not my lover!" Benny's voice was sharp.

"I just meant, since you were engaged to be married."

"How dare you—we were engaged to be married but we were not lovers in the sordid way you're suggesting."

"Didn't mean any insult."

"Then what did you mean? What were you insinuating, detective?"

"Why did you go to your ex-fiancés hotel room?"

"I wanted to ask an important question. To clear up what happened and why."

"Did you get it cleared up?" the detective asked.

"Yes, it is very clear now." She glanced at Billy Ray.

"So why did that cause a fight? Spectators heard Matthias threaten Franks over something he did to you. I'm looking at you and I see you look sick or upset even before I told you about the murder."

Benny sat up straight, letting go of her mother and Billy Ray's hands. "Don't talk to me like I'm a fool, detective. I'm sure you've figured out I was attacked by Jordan in his hotel room. That's why Billy Ray went to his room and did what he did but he did not kill Jordan. I know he didn't."

"Of course he didn't," Ella repeated.

"Peculiar how Matthias associates with people and they turn up dead."

Billy Ray scowled. "Look, detective . . ."

"I mean it wasn't long ago a girl took a dive out a hotel window. And with you right there in the room." Woolston's eyes shifted from one to the other. "Now you're back in a hotel room beating up on a fella and lo and behold he ends up dead too. Head almost whacked clean off."

Ella made a gagging sound.

"I had nothing to do with that!"

"And whoever did, it served him right, the slimy no-good snake." Earl spoke as he entered the parlor. "What's going on around here? Why are you in my home askin' questions about that devil Jordan Franks?"

"Are you Earl Freeman?" Woolston's tone was cool.

"Yes, I'm the head of this house and I want to know why you're botherin' my family. Did I just hear you try to blame this young man for another death?"

Woolston stood up eye to eye with Earl. "A man has been murdered and I'm doing my job, investigating who did it. I don't care what kind of person he was or how you or anyone else in this town felt about him." Woolston scanned the room. Everyone was silent staring at him. "And since you're here, Mr. Freeman I want to question your whereabouts and your relationship to the victim."

"Me?"

"That's right. You obviously hated the man."

"You're dang right I hated him. I could have—" Ella gasped softly. Earl stopped speaking, shooting her a glance.

"Could have what—killed him?"

odney crouched down inside the damaged remains of the *Tulsa Star* newspaper office as two men walked past the window. He looked up at his companion and pulled his arm. "Get down," he whispered. Jack dropped on his haunches, making a face. "That's nobody to worry about; just Mike and Hector going home from work."

"Can't be too careful these days."

"They always leave work and go past around this time of day. What's the big deal? You're mighty jumpy lately."

"You better get jumpy too. Gangsters prowlin' round and some poor guy gets his head lopped off right in a hotel room and nobody knows a thing about it. Somethin' sinister is going on in this city. It's evil."

Jack's eyes rolled. "Don't start with your superstitious mumbo jumbo."

"I'm telling you, evil is in the air all around us."

Jack stood up, chuckling. "Yeah and the headless horseman's ridin' tonight . . . wooo-ooo!"

Rodney got up walking to the door and nervously checked the lock. "Make fun if you want. Tulsa's cursed and has been for over a hundred years. My aunt said an Indian witch doctor put a curse on this land to keep the white man off."

Jack laughed. "Oh really? Well, it didn't work."

Rodney shuffled in place. "Yeah, well maybe it didn't, but

don't forget I was the one who told you somethin' bad was coming right before the riot broke out."

"Okay, so you got one score to your credit. That massacre was evil pure and plain."

"When Dooley gets here I bet he's gonna agree with me. This city is steeped in misery and trouble everywhere you go."

"Well, for what I'm gettin' paid for information that's okay by me; keeps my pockets full."

"Money isn't everything. Some things are better left alone."

"Okay Mr. Doom and Gloom, what dark prediction do you have this time?"

"Never mind; you always make fun and this is serious."

"Serious about what?"

"Not what so much as who."

"All right spit it out, about who?"

"Dooley."

"What about him?"

"Don't know exactly, but there's gonna be a heap of trouble, and he's right in the middle of it. He's about to face two things. One that will challenge his way of thinking and the other might even take his life. Both of them are things he won't find easy to deal with."

"What in the world are you talking about?"

"I told you I don't know for sure. Cassia told me—"

"Cassia? What does she know about Dooley? You're listenin' to that crazy gypsy woman?"

"She's not crazy. She don't know him, but she described Dooley to a T, so I knew it was him she was talking about. She has visions about people."

"She has visions all right, and you have visions when you think about how good she looks. I see how you gape at her all googly-eyed." Jack grinned.

"No, I don't."

"You do too. You could have her for breakfast the way you look at that woman."

"Don't talk disrespectful like that about a lady who has

Cassia's spiritual gifts. She talks to people on the other side."

"Oh great, she's a dark side gypsy at that. That's the devil's business, talking to dead folks and I want no part of it."

"She's a spiritual woman of God. Nothing she does has anything to with the devil."

"Look, I don't know a whole lot about them matters but I do remember my grandfather who was a travelin' preacher saying it was against God to dabble in witchcraft, calling on the dead, and seeking spirits with the stars, all that kind of mumbo jumbo. He said the Bible taught against it. It was a direct order from God to leave that business alone. So don't tell me she's a woman of God when she's talking to dead folks."

"But she wears a crucifix around her neck, talks about Jesus, and reads the Bible."

"That don't make her godly. She ain't read enough Bible to know God said stop that foolishness she's doing." Jack chuckled.

"Says she's a special messenger for God."

"Know what I think? I think you're both nuts and—" Dooley appeared outside at the door turning the handle but it wouldn't open. "Open the door and let him in." Jack told Rodney. "And keep quiet about that gypsy's dumb predictions and crazy visions."

Dooley was intrigued as he talked with his undercover cohorts and they insisted he visit their landlady, Madelle Bridgewater. Rodney and Jack were an odd pair indeed but inseparable most of the time and very good at what they did. They bickered like a married couple but were an unstoppable team. Separately or together they could slip in and out of any place at any time under any circumstance. Rodney's expertise for precise visual recall was unrivaled. He could describe a complete stranger after a half-minute encounter down to the man's tiny mole on the left side of his neck. His detail-oriented brain and knowledge of rare gems made him a once highly regarded money forger and jewel thief. Jack's photographic memory allowed him to scan a document in lickety-split time and recite its contents in exact position. Also at one time his skill to easily pick any lock in existence had criminal organizations paying top dollar for his larcenous talent. The two men now used their abilities for the government after spending time in a federal penitentiary where they became close friends.

Jack Valentine and Rodney Boyce were two men Dooley trusted. He'd worked with them for years and had never been disappointed. He needed their help now more than ever; the stakes were higher than getting information or keeping a shrewd watchful eye. Dooley knew he would never pull off his plan without the help of his reliable associates.

Jack was a dark Negro sporting handsome Ashanti features, dark nappy hair, and a thin, quick moving physique from his West African ancestry. Rodney's Nordic heritage made a complete contrast to his friend. His invading Viking forefathers left their Scandinavian imprint with fair Caucasian skin, muscle-bound body, and thick, untamed blond hair. This odd pair was the best of friends and two of the most resourceful spies in the state of Oklahoma.

Madelle Bridgewater's home was in Eagles Pointe County north of Tulsa. It was a large, seven-bedroom, three-story house built by Madelle's now-deceased husband after he struck oil on a piece of land he owned that had been considered worthless. Timothy Bridgewater had lived in his new home only a few years before he took ill and died. To make ends meet, his widow took in borders, assisted by her unmarried brother who had moved in. Madelle was a medium-brown-skinned woman with pleasant features.

She welcomed Dooley into her home like an old friend. "I hope my unexpected visit is not inconvenient. I can come another time if it is," Dooley said, removing his hat.

"No, not at all. I was expecting you."

"Expecting me?"

"Please come sit down." She ushered him to the drawing room. It was bright and colorful, soft and frilly like its owner. Dooley sat on a light gray chair by the window. A twin chair on the other side of the window was occupied by a large white fluffy cat that gave him a disinterested glance and resumed its nap. "Jack and Rodney told me to expect you to call on me one day soon," she explained with a smile.

Madelle was ultra-feminine. Her frilly, chiffon dress swished as she took a seat. Dooley was truly impressed, as he was partial to dainty ladies.

"Now tell me, what can I do for you Mr. Dooley."

"Just call me Dooley, ma'am."

"All right."

"I'm not sure what you can do to help me, but Jack and Rodney told me you know just about everybody and everything that goes on."

Madelle snickered. "Goodness! They make me sound like an awful busybody."

"No ma'am, they speak very highly of you."

"Please call me Madelle. Ma'am makes me feel ancient."

Dooley was trying to judge her age. She looked younger close up than from a distance. "Okay, what I need is information, and I'm willing to pay for it. But first I need to be sure I'm able to trust you. This is important and lives may be at stake."

Madelle's eyes twinkled. "You sound just like Jack and Rodney. Everything's always so hush-hush and urgent, but I guess in your line of work it has to be. How's the detecting business?"

Dooley smiled. "So you do see and hear a lot."

"Keeping boarders has its advantages in addition to paying bills. Since the riot I've constantly had a full house. People are coming and going all the time. I barely get to change the linen from one roomer before someone's at the door asking about a vacancy."

"I can see why; real nice place you got here."

"Thank you. I try to keep it up but it's hard for a woman with no husband."

"Were you raised in Tulsa?" Dooley asked.

"No, I was born in Atlanta but grew up in Virginia."

"Virginia, huh? I was born there," he said dryly.

"You sound like you didn't like it in Virginia."

"I didn't."

"May I ask why? I loved growing up there."

"Bad memories. A bunch of hooded men killed my parents because they race mixed," he said without hesitation. He was shocked because he never voluntarily told that to anyone other than when he first got the job working for the FBI.

A sincere sadness came across Madelle's face. "How horrible. Bigotry is such an evil, evil thing. Do you ever go back there—to your hometown?"

"Never."

"That's smart of you, I suppose. If something breaks my heart I always avoid it if I can."

"A quality lady like you? Hard to imagine anybody would be cruel enough to break your heart." This verbalized thought surprised him as much as much as the previous one.

"Why Dooley, you sweet man, what a nice thing to say." She beamed at him. Years later Dooley would be asked when he first fell so helplessly in love with Madelle Bridgewater, and he would recall this as being the moment. They spent the next four hours talking. By the time Dooley left her home mutual admiration had burgeoned between them. He was completely enchanted by the lady, and she was quite taken by this unusual man whose life was so deliciously mysterious. He could be the remedy for her dreadfully ordinary existence and she without a doubt would be a valuable fountain of information for him . . . and maybe much more.

CHAPTER TWENTY-SIX

What do you mean we can't see each other no more?" Ada's voice shook.

Unable to look her in the eyes, Gilbert bowed his head.

"It's like you told me, there's nowhere to go with this. I reckon it's best we end it now."

"You're sleepin' with Miss Kate, ain't ya?"

"No!"

"You're lyin'! You been visitin' her mighty regular and now you're droppin' me to be with her! I was just your in-between colored woman!"

He reached for her. "You know that's not true."

"Don't touch me, you lyin' dog!"

"I love you, honey, I do, but . . . we have to be smart about this and end it now. It'll be worse if we keep on—"

"Shut up! I don't wanna hear no more of your lies. I was a fool to ever believe you loved me. It was crazy to think you'd want to marry *me*. I'm such a stupid idiot; just plain stupid."

"No, no you weren't— I mean, no you're not. I'd marry you in a minute if I could, cause I love you."

"Don't say that." Her voice quivered. "You don't love me and you never did." She clasped her hands and began pacing. "This is what I get for sinning against God, actin' like a common strumpet. Serves me right for doing what *I knew* I shouldn't be doing. I deserve to be—" Ada began to sob. "Lord Jesus, forgive me!" She sank to her knees.

"Don't do this," Jake said as he tried to pull her to her feet. The hurt look on her face stabbed at his heart.

"Get your hands off me." She swung at him but he didn't let go.

"I can't stand seeing you like this. Please."

"Lord, I'm so ashamed," she wept, flailing her arms at him. "God's punishing me for what I did; what *we* did." Her grief became more intense.

"No, He's not. I don't believe that," he insisted, finally getting her on her feet. He wiped her wet cheeks.

She wriggled free from his hold. "I never shoulda let you put your filthy white hands all over me. I musta been losin' my mind with fear that night."

"Don't say that—we love each other. You make it sound like we did something dirty and shameful."

"We did. We sinned and don't try to deny it. Can't clean it up to be some grand wonderful love affair cause it weren't. If it was, you wouldn't be tossin' me to the side now. You had your pleasure with me and I let you. Now you want to be rid of me. If you don't confess your sin to the Lord He won't forgive you. So admit it, we sinned."

Gilbert's lips tightened and his face reddened. "I'm not admittin' nothin. I love you whether you believe it or not. That can't be a sin."

Ada was silent for a moment. Then, "I wanted to be with you so bad I lost good sense. I forgot about livin' right in the sight of God. Now I'm paying for it by you wanting to be rid of me so you can take up with Miss Kate. Well, go right ahead." Ada moved to her back door and opened it.

"Ada, don't be this way," Gilbert pleaded. "You know I'm not that kind of man. . ."

"You said your piece so get out and don't bother comin' back. It's over like you said, so just go." She turned her face to hide the tears she felt coming.

Gilbert picked up his hat from the kitchen chair and started out the door. "I need you to believe how sorry, how really sorry I am." Walking out across the back porch he heard the screen door screech closed followed by the back door slamming shut. He knew she was weeping.

Jake drove down the dusty back road where few ever traveled. It was the route he had always taken to Ada's isolated little house on Prairie Flats Road east of the railroad tracks. He drove away, staring straight ahead, willing himself not to blink, but that did not stop the tears from forming in his eyes. Knowing he had ended it for Ada's protection did not dull the ache in his heart.

Detective Woolston could not believe his good fortune. Jordan Franks had kept daily diaries, loads of them. The detective held three books in his hands; he tried to not show his elation as he glanced at Maida. He found dozens more in a steamer trunk that must have been written years ago. This was a detective's investigative dream come true, an inside look at the victim's life from the victim's own pen and perspective. He had a treasure trove of information before him, and he was going to read every word if that was what it took to solve this heinous crime.

Woolston stood next to the trunk, eyes moving across the pages of the first book. Certain words leaped out at him: *Saw her today. She still hates me but it doesn't matter, all is as it should be.* Woolston's curiosity was spiked, but he moved on to another page. *She doesn't think I see but I catch her staring at me sometimes like she hates me or wishes me dead. If she had the nerve I think she would try to do me in, but she doesn't. She's too weak. Like all women she's weak.* Taking the trunk key out of the lock he said to Maida, "I'll have to confiscate these journals for the investigation. There might be important evidence in them."

She blinked a couple of times. "I do not understand."

"It means the police will take possession of these diaries to read for information about your husband," he said slowly.

Maida nodded. "*Oui.* Yes."

"Did he bring this from Paris?" he asked. Maida shook her head. "Then where did it come from?"

"It came this morning. I do not know from where. A man bring it, asking for Jordan. I did not know what else to do. I take it."

"Good move to accept it. Did your husband mention he was expecting a delivery?"

"He did not."

Woolston picked up another book out of the trunk. "Where's the shipping invoice?"

Maida looked puzzled.

"The paper that came with the trunk," he explained.

She took a folded sheet from the table behind her and handed it to him.

"This says from Chicago, Illinois. There's an address but has no name attached to it. This is all he gave you?"

She nodded.

"Okay, let's see what else we have here."

Eager to be done he moved the dairies aside and continued digging in the trunk.

CHAPTER TWENTY-SEVEN

Bet collapsed shaking into Cord's arms as soon as he opened his front door.

"Oh, Cord," she breathed, clinging to him.

"Whoa, calm down." Taken by surprise he put his arms around her.

"Please don't be angry with me," she said softly. "Tell me you're not mad at me."

"I'm not mad at you, but what's wrong?"

"I had nowhere else to go. I had to come. No one else cares about me but you."

He flinched, remembering Savannah saying the exact same words to him on several occasions. "What's wrong?" he asked again.

"Didn't you hear the news, that horrible news? They found him murdered in the hotel room—practically decapitated."

"What?"

"That's what they're saying." She covered her eyes cringing at the thought.

"Who? What are you talking about?"

"Jerome. I mean Jordan—Jordan Franks."

"Jordan Franks?"

"That's right, the musician."

"I know who he is, but I didn't know you knew him."

Bet backed up defensively. "Well, we, um . . . we were at the same college at one time."

Cord's demeanor changed. "That man's lower than a snake's belly far as I'm concerned."

Her eyes widened. "You knew him?"

"Yeah, somewhat; he was close to Benny once."

"Close how?"

"I'd rather not talk about it," he said. "Let's just say you won't see any Freemans cryin' at his funeral."

"But the way he was murdered, it was so ghastly. How can you not feel compassion for any human being dying in that fashion?"

"Whoever did it must have known what it would take to kill a low-bellied snake like Franks, and that's fine with me." Cord's eye showed a darkness that surprised Bet.

"You don't mean that."

"Dog if I don't." He gave her a suspicious look. "You and him were friendly?"

Her body tensed. "No, we weren't friends, at all. I loathed the man after—"

"After what?"

"Nothing, I don't want to talk about him or think about that dreadful murder anymore. I just need to be around you and feel safe."

"Well, since you're here you might as well stay for supper. I warn you though, I'm not much of a cook."

Bet flashed her most congenial smile. "But I'm a very good cook. Let me fix something and serve you."

"You cook?"

"I sure do; why is that such a surprise?"

Cord shrugged. "Don't rightly know, but I thought someone like you didn't fool with women's work."

"Preparing one's own meals is not just women's work. It's a practical skill for survival. Besides I had to cook all the time for my family when I was growing up."

"You're full of surprises. Come on in." Cord opened the door wide for Bet to pass through. Abruptly her jubilant smile faded when she saw Scarlett sitting on the couch.

"What's she doing here?" Bet asked.

"I told you, I'm fixin' supper. Scarlett's getting better. I brought her here to get her away from that place for a spell. I have to take her back later. We can all eat together since you cook—"

Bet spun around. "I'm not cooking anything with her in this house. She's crazy. She might attack me with a knife or frying pan or throw hot grease on me."

"I don't think you need to worry about that."

"You don't think at all; that's your problem. And I thought you wanted to be alone with me. But here she sits, looking nutty as ever."

"Now, wait a minute. You don't have to insult her."

"There you go again taking up for her against me. I've about had it with you and this woman, Cord. You can keep your lunatic *friend*, and for the record I won't be dropping by anymore." Bet faced Scarlett. "There—you happy now? You've got him all to your conniving little mental patient self." She spun around on her heel and let herself out the front door. Cord stood there watching her leave before he looked back at Scarlett. He wondered how much of what Bet said was true. Was Scarlett conniving? Did she want him all to herself, and if she did, how did he feel about that?

Bacon and fried eggs was dinner that evening. Scarlett ate heartily, able to feed herself. She was improving more and more and she smiled often these days. Cord had to get used to her voluntary movements and facial expressions after she'd been aphasic and mentally detached for so long. He talked to her as usual and as usual she gave no verbal response but smiled or frowned at appropriate times, indicating she was listening and comprehending. The doctor had warned of her progressive breakthroughs and the unpredictable sequence in which they might occur.

Cord understood in his head that their relationship would change when her condition improved, but his heart was a different matter. He'd grown attached to her. A completely recovered Scarlett would not need him anymore. She would no longer be his nonjudgmental confidante. Their time together would cease and he'd miss it . . . and her. He was fully aware their relationship was as therapeutic for him as it was for her. The only difference in their situations was that Scarlett was getting better but he wasn't. He still wrestled with heartache, pain, and anger as though the tragedy of Savannah's death and his terrible argument with his father had happened just yesterday. He was pretty much estranged from his family with no companion for comfort. Loneliness crowded in, and resentment was ever crouching at the front door of his spirit urging him to lash out.

In the months past Cord learned how to mask his inner being with everyday living, occupying his mind working hard building the ranch and helping victims of the riot. No one fully knew how he suffered emotional and mental agony . . . no one except Scarlett.

After he stacked the dirty dinner dishes the two of them sat outside on the front porch. The evening sky was striped with colors from the fading sun, and the ranch was peacefully quiet except for the occasional distant lowing of cattle in the west pasture. Cord had his Bible out to read, something he'd been doing recently. The book of Joshua attracted his attention and he started reading aloud as Scarlett moved back and forth in the rocker, contented. When he read about Rahab, Scarlett sat up listening closely. When he finished the sixth chapter, he was tired and took a break.

"Rahab was like me," Scarlett whispered.

Cord looked at her. There was no blank stare or emptiness. She was looking right at him, fully cognizant. "Yeah, but not all of her life. See it says she lived with the people of God from then on, and if I remember my Bible she was even in the lineage of Christ."

Scarlett frowned. "She was like me. How could she be? She was a dirty sinner like me."

"God forgives, Scarlett. He washes our sins away and gives us a new life in Jesus."

Scarlett smiled. "That's what I want."

Cord realized what he'd said and all his Bible knowledge from the past came flooding back. Everything he was taught in Sunday school as a child and what his mother had always told him played out in his head. Sermons and Bible verses paraded through his mind like one of those silent picture shows Savannah had loved so much. He sat silently as he remembered and considered what he must do next. With tears of relief, he spoke. "Lord, forgive me. Please forgive me, Jesus."

Scarlett rose up and walked over to him. "Don't cry. Jesus will forgive you and make it all better." She spoke in a childlike innocence. "You told me He could, remember? You said He can do anything and He saves folks from sin. He can make us brand-new like we never did nothin' wrong. That's what we'll do; we'll get Jesus to make it like we never done nothin' bad."

"You're right, that's what we need. I almost lost sight of it but not anymore." Cord was so choked up he could barely speak any further. "I need Jesus more than ever, and you need Him too, Scarlett."

Scarlett stroked his head, singing a song her mother sang to her when she was a child.

"Pass me not, O gentle Savior, Hear my humble cry; While on others Thou art calling, Do not pass me by. Savior, Savior, hear my humble cry, While on others Thou art calling, Do not pass me by."

Her voice was sweet and soothing. It was all so clear to him at that point what he needed to do. He understood the only One who could move him from under the bondage of anger, guilt, and shame. Cord spoke a sincere prayer, more heartfelt than he had in years. He gave thanks to God for mercy and grace. He asked to be saved, truly redeemed by Christ Jesus. He asked forgiveness and repented for his sins and for denying the power and salvation the Lord offers. The pain started to lift from his heart as the burden transferred from his soul to the Master. He recognized he no longer had to carry the weight of so much tragedy; Christ bore the load for him. He needed to acknowledge, release, and give thanks for it.

Scarlett continued singing while Cord cried out to the Lord.

When Bet reached the Stradford Hotel, Detective Woolston was sitting in the lobby waiting for her. He was amazed at the elegance of this Negro-owned establishment.

Bet had been teary most of the way back, upset over Cord. She didn't want to see or talk to anyone, let alone a nosy police detective. *Why does he want to see me?* she wondered.

Woolston indicated she should take a seat. "What is it you want from me, detective?" she asked curtly.

"I want to talk about you and Jordan Franks." He took in her beauty with mixed feelings, remembering certain diary entries.

"Jordan Franks and I? Why should you talk to me about him?"

Woolston smiled cagily. "You tell me why I need to talk with you."

She stood up. "I don't have time for riddles, detective, so if you'll excuse me, it's been a trying day and I'll say good night."

"I can see you're upset about something, but it's kind of early for bedtime, isn't it?"

"What exactly do you want from me? If it's something legal, then . . ."

"All right, if you want me to be direct, then let's get direct. Exactly what was your relationship with the deceased?" Bet stared at him, but didn't answer. "I asked you a direct question, Attorney Whitehead."

Bet wasn't sure if the condescension she sensed from him was due to her being Negro or a female attorney or both. "Why do you think there was a relationship between us?"

"Jordan Franks was an odd fellow it seems; kept regular journals of all the important people and incidents in his life."

Bet's face paled as she fell back into the chair. "Journals?" she echoed.

The detective leaned forward. "That's right. And you're featured quite prominently in several entries in what I read so far." Woolston sat back and casually scanned the lobby, making another mental note of Bet's extraordinary good looks as he waited for her response. He noticed a couple of guests staring curiously. When Bet did not respond, he asked, "Would you feel better answering my questions in your room?"

"Yes," she said softly and made her way to the elevator.

The detective watched Bet nervously puttering around the room. Tired of the delay, he looked at his watch and said, "Miss Whitehead, my time is valuable."

"I'm sure it is," she replied.

"I want an answer now."

"Very well. I knew Jerome, I mean Jordan, from college in Chicago. He was in his final year of graduate school when I was a freshman coming in for pre-law."

"And—"

"And we were mildly acquainted, that's all."

Woolston shifted in his seat. "What exactly does 'mildly acquainted' mean?"

"What do you think it means? Am I being accused of some illegality? I know you couldn't suspect me of that ghastly murder."

"I haven't ruled anyone out, but your artful dodging is putting you higher on that list every second. Come on, lady, stop playing games and tell me just what your connection was to Jordan Franks. Oh, and since you called him Jerome, I assume you knew him quite well."

"Jerome Franklin was his birth name, as you certainly have learned by now. Jordan Franks is a name he assumed later. He was involved in a scandal of some kind and had to change it to secure a decent teaching position in academia."

"Of course, I'm aware of the name change, so tell me something I don't already know."

Bet sat down and crossed her legs. "Are you married, Detective?"

"Yes, I am."

"Happily?"

"Happily enough not to get involved in anything that could cost my job and my family," Woolston answered. He stood and pulled out a pipe. "Mind if I smoke?"

"Not at all." Bet hoped his icy demeanor was starting to melt. Using her looks to manipulate men or get what she needed usually came easy to her. This ordinary-looking white man should be no match for her if she put her mind to it.

Detective Woolston took a small pouch of tobacco from his pocket, stuffing some into his pipe. "Okay, let's do this fast and painlessly." He started pacing. "You knew Jordan Franks as Jerome Franklin at Chicago Normal College, check?"

"That's right."

"Franks was a real bright fellow it seems." Woolston lit his tobacco and started smoking as he recited what he knew about Franks. "His journals and credentials verify that he earned a teaching degree from Shaw University in Raleigh, then attended Chicago Normal College where he earned his master's in music history while working as a teaching assistant, and then received his doctorate in music theory." He paused before continuing.

"He was cunning and you were a naive young girl who foolishly took up with him. Am I correct?" He drew in smoke and expelled it as he watched her carefully.

"I did not take up with him. We were just friendly, as I already told you."

"You weren't lovers?"

"No!"

"You sure about that?"

"Yes, I'm sure. What kind of idiotic question is that? As if I wouldn't know with whom I'm romantically involved." She rolled her eyes and recrossed her legs in the other direction.

"Okay, so he doesn't get romantically entangled—why? You're a fetching woman, Miss Whitehead. He was single, you were unattached, so what red-blooded man wouldn't want you for a sweetheart?"

Bet smiled. "Why, thank you, detective. I didn't think you noticed."

"Oh, I noticed all right. I'd have to be blind not to notice. Answer the question. Why didn't Jordan Franks chase after you like all the other guys on campus?"

"How would you know what the others did?"

"He wrote about how the men on campus went after you." He sucked in more smoke, puffing it out in small spurts. "Let me speed this along. Franks had other ideas . . . to make you available to the college set; professors and other men who could and would pay good money."

She sat rigidly and her mouth dropped open. "What are you saying?"

"You know exactly what I'm saying. You were for sale to anybody who had the price and Jordan Franks always set it up. From his written accounts you made a lot of money for him and yourself. It kept your tuition paid and you could live well to boot. You two were partners in a sleazy business arrangement. Apparently you had two distinctions while there. You were the only female pre-law student and the campus strumpet . . . *Miss Whitehead*."

"How dare you accuse me of—"

"Don't bother denying it. I told you he kept detailed accounts of things that were meaningful to him and had been doing it for years. He got used to the arrangement until you wanted out and threatened him with something he didn't detail, but he begrudged having to end your partnership. Has a trunkful of books dated by year and location of where he lived. The guy lived an outrageous life and was proud of himself and his dirty deeds." More pungent smoke engulfed Woolston's head.

Bet was thinking he should choke on it. "Jordan Franks was a monster," she said calmly.

"You do have some culpability in this thing. He didn't force you."

"Tell me, detective." Bet stared at nothing for a moment. "Have you ever made a really dreadful mistake?"

"Sure, I've made some bad decisions in my life."

"No, I mean one that could change your life drastically and destroy everything you ever worked for, a choice you couldn't undo. Something so shameful that would follow you for the rest of your days just waiting to be revealed and tear your world apart."

"Can't say as I have."

She saw no sympathy in his eyes. "Then you're a fortunate man. I did and now it's come back to ruin my life like I always feared it would. Jordan held that over me my entire time at college."

"So this thing, it was worse than what you did to keep it quiet?"

"Doing what I did in college robbed me of an innocence I wish I still had. It turned me into someone I hardly recognize anymore. At the time I thought it was my only choice, the smart way out, but I'm not so sure anymore."

"Okay, so Franks was blackmailing you?" Woolston stood by the window aimlessly watching the blinking sign.

"That's right."

"Wanna tell me why?"

"No, I don't, and I never will, so don't pursue it. If he didn't write about it in those infernal journals then I will never tell the police or anyone else. Hopefully that particular episode of my life will be buried with him. If I'm fortunate enough in that respect I refuse to resurrect it under any circumstance."

"Sounds like motive for murder to me."

"As much as I loathed that man I did not kill him. His death is a relief but rest assured, detective, it doesn't completely free me from my past. What I did and what I was forced to do on account of it; and yes, to set the record straight, after a while what I had to do to pay for my education will never leave my mind until I'm in my grave. I've learned to live with the shame and the possibility of being found out, so why would I resort to murder?"

"Perhaps Franks wanted to put the squeeze on you again."

"Prove it. I won't try to defend myself anymore unless you come up with a clear substantial accusation. I warn you, though, if you come after me with any of this or scandalize my name in any way, I'll bury your whole department in legal red tape. And with what I know about the underhanded money dealings, mistreatment of women, and racist injustices in this city, I'll have the federal government and entire country starting with the NAACP perched on your back porch watching every move you and your department make. I'll fight you with every legal resource I know and more if need be."

"I don't take kindly to threats, lady, empty or not."

"Don't think my threats are the least bit empty. You'd be better off spending your time finding the real perpetrator of that horrendous crime instead of digging up damaging information about me." Bet stood up and walked to the door and flung it open. "I think this should conclude your questioning of me. Good evening, Detective Woolston." Her words were polite, the cool smile cordial, but her countenance acidic.

Woolston took up his hat and started for the door. She impressed him although he would never show it. Now he knew why she had a strong reputation as a defense lawyer. He grinned as he left the room. "Your law instructors should be proud of your formidable battles against the powers that be."

"Good day, detective."

"Good day, Miss Whitehead. We'll see each other again, I'm sure."

CHAPTER TWENTY-EIGHT

HOWARD UNIVERSITY
WASHINGTON, D.C.

Ethan couldn't have heard his father right. The telephone lines must be crossed.

Earl repeated the grim news and Ethan knew it was no mistake. A few other words were exchanged and he stammered his goodbye, dazed as he hung up the telephone. Next to him, his old friend Maynard waited for an explanation. He'd heard Ethan's part of the conversation and the look on his friend's face was even more telling. "Is something wrong with your mother?" he finally asked.

"My father said she's not well. They don't know for sure, but the doctor thinks it could be a tumor in her brain. She has to have surgery."

"Oh, I'm sorry to hear that."

"I've got to get back home and be with her."

"Of course you do."

"I can't believe this . . . not Mom. She's the backbone of our family. We need her."

"Don't get ahead of yourself. Didn't you say the doctor only *thinks* it could be a tumor?"

"That's what Dad said."

"Then it's not conclusive. There's hope that it's not a brain tumor. Keep your mind on that." For Ethan's sake Maynard tried to muster up as much optimism as he could without minimizing the seriousness of the situation. He could see the dread on Ethan's face.

Maynard's former colleague was in a poor emotional state when he arrived in the capital. Having a broken heart was not something Ethan Freeman was used to, since he normally didn't lose his head or heart over women. It was also out of the ordinary for him to hold such animosity toward his brother. As a result, the young man's emotions were raw. He had come to Washington to seek guidance from the man who had been his professional adviser, friend, and personal sounding board for years—Maynard Vaughn. Now compounding these problems came more devastating news from the home front.

"I don't know what will become of us if we lose our mother," Ethan moaned.

Maynard's expression showed his reaction. "I don't want to sound unfeeling, but this isn't about you or your other family members. Your mother is the one with the health problem. She's the one you should be thinking about, not what it will mean to the rest of the Freemans if she's not around."

"You're absolutely right," Ethan admitted. "I'm being selfish aren't I?"

"You are, but don't be too hard on yourself for being human. It's a natural reaction for most of us. Just try to stop and think about what your mother must be going through."

Ethan ran his hand across his head. "I can't stand thinking about how scared mom must be."

"Put her into the hands of the One who can help," Maynard encouraged him. "If you really want to help your mother you better talk to Him."

"I haven't exactly been a devout follower, so why would God listen to me now?"

"He'll listen because He's gracious and He loves you in spite of your negligence to Him; and He loves your mother too. She hasn't been negligent has she?"

"I don't think so. Mom loves the Lord and she's always put Him first."

"He'll be glad to hear from you. Believe me, if I can get a second chance, I know you can too if you surrender to Christ."

Ethan raised a brow. "I never heard you talk like this before. You've changed since you moved here."

Maynard got up from his desk and stood by the window looking down at the well-manicured grounds of the university campus. He spoke reflectively. "It's really good for me being here because I see things differently since I left Tulsa. Surviving the riot really opened my eyes to certain things about life, and living here has opened my mind to Jesus. That riot was the worst experience I've lived through, but it showed me without a doubt God is still in control. I also owe a debt of gratitude to Billy Ray for showing me how to really walk with the Lord. He stood firm in his faith when it looked impossible while he was in jail, and during the racial attacks he didn't break either." He paused, then continued thoughtfully. "It's at those moments you either walk earnestly with what you know about the Lord or—everything you claim to believe becomes rubbish. I always thought that just believing was good enough until Billy Ray made a very profound statement to me."

"What statement?"

"That Satan and his demons believe in God too. They know exactly who Jesus is like I claim I did. So there is no real value or power in just believing. There has to be more to it."

Ethan looked taken aback. "I never considered that."

"Neither had I until then but it makes sense. So I've come to realize I spent most of my life's energy fighting the legal and political systems to the neglect of my most important gifts: my relationship with Christ and my family. I should have operated in the Spirit of Christ more in my fight and it would have been more powerful, more lasting."

"But you did a lot of good on your own."

"That's exactly what the enemy of our souls wants us to do: operate on our own and neglect God." He turned, facing Ethan.

"Don't make the same mistakes I did. Don't stuff your life with court battles defending worthy causes just for the world."

"What are you saying? That the work we did—the work I still do—is worthless?"

"Not at all, you're a valuable attorney who champions the underdog. It's a godly endeavor to help the poor and ill-treated. My warning for you is not to get so involved in that one aspect of your life that you sacrifice everything else, especially not your relationship with God. Life is about more than the law and its injustices. A man needs balance, and to get that he needs to put things in their proper order of importance."

"Which is?"

"The right order is God first above all things, family next, then community. Community is the body of Christians, your church, and other believers; after that, everyone else in your circle of influence or associations."

"What about a man's work?" Ethan asked.

Maynard was moving away from the window. "That goes with your community at the end of the list."

Ethan shifted uncomfortably. "This is surprising talk coming from you. You're devoted to the law."

"I know this is different from how I used to think but I know better now, and because I know better I'm living better. So I'm giving you my understanding of life just like I gave you my legal know-how."

"I take it you think my priorities are ill-advised?"

Maynard nodded. "I take partial blame because as your mentor I set a poor example." He looked at Ethan apologetically. "I'm sorry for pulling you into my mistaken way of thinking."

"If I'm wrong in my values, I take full responsibility myself. I won't lay it at your feet or anyone else's. I'm a man and I make my own decisions."

"That's what I always admired about you. You'd take on responsibility like a bull in the rodeo. If my son grows up to be half the man you are I will be very proud."

"It's good to know somebody thinks well of me," Ethan said

with a touch of defeat in his voice.

"You told me about this woman you were enamored with but did you tell *her* how you felt?"

"I was going to, but before I could she took up with Cord."

"Are you still interested in her?"

"I want nothing whatsoever to do with her."

Maynard smiled ruefully. "That doesn't exactly answer my question, but never mind. My advice to you is to forget about her. From the things you told me, she's not the woman for you anyway. Did you have anything else in common besides your legal ambitions?"

"I can't say, but I never felt that way about another woman before."

"You also had never worked around a Negro female attorney. She was a delightful curiosity, an extraordinarily accomplished and beautiful woman who overwhelmed your sensibilities." Maynard tilted his head a bit rubbing his chin. "It's not widely known, but Elizabeth Whitehead has a bit of a reputation in legal circles as an aggressive lady in her professional . . . *ahem* . . . and personal life. She's awe-inspiring in many ways, so I've heard."

"Exactly what have you heard?"

"Listen, specifics really don't matter at this point. You're done with her aren't you?"

"Yeah," Ethan said, "but I doubt if my brother is."

"Cord's no fool."

"How can you say that after the way Savannah made a fool of him?"

"He may have his weaknesses, but he's no fool. Savannah was a lesson I don't think Cord will ever forget. The ones who hurt most usually stick the hardest and I'd say Savannah sticks to him like molasses mixed with honey and glue. He learned hard-core heartache and humiliation from that little lady."

"Dad says he's always been gullible for a pretty woman."

"What man isn't attracted to beauty? I sure was and your mother is a good-looking woman, so I bet Earl went for her at first because she was beautiful. In that respect Cord's like any man including your father, but your mother was a decent God-fearing lady and Savannah wasn't."

"She was a selfish, conniving tramp."

"Whoa, the woman is dead."

"I don't care. She ran around like a trollop and messed up my brother's life. If she had been a decent wife, he wouldn't have ended up in bed with Bet."

"So that was Savannah's fault?"

"I didn't say that."

"You implied it, Attorney Freeman. That's a twisted rationalization if ever I heard one. Savannah's dead, and what your brother did with Bet was a choice he made that cannot be blamed on her; she's been dead for over a year."

"I don't care what you say, that gold-digging harlot made his life a misery."

"He loved her so she made him happy too. Don't forget that." Maynard saw Ethan's agitation but pressed on. "I think there was more to their relationship than just Savannah being pretty. There were plenty of good-looking females in Tulsa for your brother to marry; upstanding ones from good families, but he picked her. If I were a betting man I'd wager money that there was something special she had to offer that went beyond beauty."

Ethan visibly sulked. "Well, I'd sure like to know what it was."

Maynard grinned. "Get a little more experience under your belt with the fairer sex and you might find out. What Savannah did for Cord probably had nothing at all to do with money or morals. Physical attraction is the first draw for many of us, but that alone won't pull us in or keep us there. Has to be more, some psychological, intellectual, or emotional connection, a bonding agent that holds firm during difficulties that could tear you apart."

"You might be right. As lovely as Bet is, I wouldn't touch her now if my life depended on it."

"How are you going to deal with your brother when you get home?"

"Not to deal with him at all is what I want." Ethan sighed squirming uneasily at the thought. "This is a mess. I don't know how I'm going to deal with him. He's still my brother but I don't want to see him right now. I have nothing but hard feelings toward him because he knew how I felt about Bet; he knew." Ethan's fist was clenched tight, pounding the arm of the chair.

"It's perfectly understandable why you resent Cord, but I have a feeling deep down inside you still love your brother. You're hurt and angry and that's okay, but you've got to find a way to forgive him; for your mother's sake now, if for no other reason."

"I don't think I can; don't know how."

"Pray about it. Ask God to help you." Maynard took his suit jacket from a brass coat hanger in the corner by the door. "Come on, let's get lunch. There's a position opening up here some months from now I want to talk to you about. I think you'd be perfect for the job and, well . . . it might be a timely solution to your problem."

CHAPTER TWENTY-NINE

EAGLES POINTE COUNTY, OKLAHOMA

The Matthias family lived at the end of a wide road flanked by a small orchard of prairie crab apples on the east and a rye field to the west. The house was walking distance from church but far enough that people wouldn't take to dropping in on the pastor whenever the inclination hit them. It was a well-made, stately looking clapboard structure a good five miles from Bethel Baptist Church. A few trees circled the yard back and front with a small plot of early blooming wildflowers in the front, and indigenous shrubbery and brambles at the rear.

It was a piece of brooding music that could be heard from the parlor's window because it matched Billy Ray's mood and helped him think. His large hands danced across the piano keys with effortless precision. Absorbing the soothing flow of the opus pushed Benny to the forefront of his mind. The music moved into Beethoven's "Moonlight Sonata" as his loving thoughts overcame his dark mood. Not much was going smoothly in his life at the moment but he knew he loved Benny and no matter how rough things were now, he knew that they would one day be husband and wife. This was the hope he clung to with all his heart.

Billy Ray played on realizing he was once again the focus of his family. They were gathering one by one as they came into the parlor. He figured out quickly this was a calculated move to interrogate him. The question was, what was the reason this time?

He thought he might know but was reserving his guess for more evidence.

The family's large sitting room was not as fancy as the Freemans' but it was well lit and airy, furnished tastefully with colonial pieces. The music swirled around the room, drawing his mind to long ago when he had been a young boy introduced to music by his grandfather. His Grandpa Matthias recognized what Billy Ray wouldn't understand for years: there was a love for music and a God-given gift for playing the piano in him. Memories of long talks while fishing at the big pond on the back section of his grandparents' farm were as vivid as if they happened yesterday.

It was one of those wonderfully lazy country excursions he was thinking about when his sister-in-law, Phoebe, burst into the parlor looking her usual up-to-something disgruntled self. He switched to playing a louder number after seeing her sour expression. Napoleon and Phoebe had come to pick up their rambunctious children who'd spent a few days with the grandparents. Billy Ray was rather glad to see them go. His brother's children were loveable but high-spirited even for children and spoiled to the verge of being bothersome. Roman roared his complaints the whole time they were there, and Josephine was caught in the middle trying to keep peace and play the loving grandmother. It was obvious Phoebe and Napoleon were having problems between them. Billy Ray learned from his parents Napoleon begged them to take the kids for a few days so they could iron out their differences. It didn't seem to have worked. Phoebe was looking as disagreeable as when they dropped the children off. Napoleon followed Phoebe into the parlor like the whipped puppy he was, Billy Ray thought. Roman stomped in a minute later scowling. That's when Billy Ray knew something was up and switched the mood of his piano playing yet again.

"Heard you bought that land after all," Roman said right out over the music. He never was for much dawdling.

"Heard from who?" Billy Ray asked, toning down the volume of his playing.

"Don't matter none from who. Did you buy the land or not?"

"Yeah, I bought it."

"What's wrong with you? I don't understand what's got into you. A man has a good career and business going and you throw it all away for what? A piece of rocky dirt the man couldn't sell to anyone else."

Billy Ray played on determined to cool his annoyance. "It's not rocky dirt; it's good ground. They say he used to grow the best corn in this area on that land." He looked around at the puzzled faces of his family.

"If it's such prime property, why has it been sitting unattended and unsold for years?"

"That had nothing to do with the quality of the dirt. It was personal."

Roman grunted. "Like always, colored folks get worthless land nobody else wants and pay top dollar for the privilege."

Napoleon shook his head. "That was not a smart move. *If* you're marrying Benny you need a stable income to support a wife and family."

"I've already heard your opinion, thank you, and I didn't ask for it. Furthermore it's not *if*, it's *when* I marry Benny." Billy Ray began playing a march.

"Tell me again what you plan on doing with this piece of land." Roman spoke loudly over the music. "And will you stop making that noise and answer me?"

Billy Ray stopped playing and took a deep breath. "I told you, I want to start a home for orphaned or disadvantaged children. Teach them to read and write and teach them all about music. Provide them with a good quality education and decent place to live until they get old enough to fend for themselves. I want to help poor children have a fair chance in life and find what they're good at, what God put in them to do. I'll teach them what I know about Jesus and music."

Napoleon laughed. "You're throwing away a good living to teach poor kids to play the piano and read the Bible?"

"Shut up, Nappy," Billy Ray snapped.

"Don't tell him to shut up," Phoebe feistily rejoined, "You left him hanging about the insurance money, and now you want his support with this harebrained scheme."

"Keep quiet, Phoebe. Nappy got his rightful share of the money and, for the record, I don't expect or need anybody in this family's support. And don't think I don't know it was your big mouth that blabbed to Dad I bought the land. Keep your meddling mouth shut and out of my business," he said.

Josephine nodded in agreement.

"Don't you talk to me that way," Phoebe demanded, then turned to her husband. "Are you going to just stand there and let him speak to me like that?"

Billy Ray smirked. "What's he going to do about it? You can both stay out of my business."

"Well, I won't stay out of your business," Roman interjected. "I'm your father. It's my duty to tell you when you're making a mistake, and son, this is a big mistake. You wasted the insurance money on that land. You had to pay off the bank and then what little was left you squander on some foolish dream."

"Dreams aren't foolish, Dad. God gives us dreams and visions for our lives."

Roman waved his hand at him. "Foolishness. Music is nice but a man has to make a living at something stable. Dreams about being concert pianists and starting schools are silly pipe dreams for a Negro man."

"It's not a pipe dream; it's what I believe the Lord is leading me to do."

"Hah," Phoebe snorted.

"Phoebe, be quiet," Josephine ordered.

"You don't want anyone in your business but as usual you're messing up. Nobody can ever tell you anything because you're hardheaded . . . until disaster strikes," Napoleon said.

"Speaking of disaster," Roman went on, "what's this I hear about you brawling in the hotel and threatening that man that was murdered? Are you going to be accused of killing him now?"

"I don't think so. I had a run in with Jordan Franks but . . ."

"Jordan Franks was Benny's ex-fiancée right?" Napoleon asked, throwing eye signals to Phoebe.

"Yeah, what of it?" Billy Ray answered.

"They say somebody really did a number on him," Phoebe said excitedly. "Had to be a pretty strong man to do that."

Josephine leaped to her feet. "What do you mean by that remark?" she demanded.

Phoebe looked dumbfounded. "Nothing. I didn't mean anything."

"You need to keep your mouth shut about my son," Josephine told her.

"But, Mom."

"Be quiet. I'm tired of your damaging slurs about Billy Ray. All you do is stir up trouble and I'm sick of it." Josephine had one hand on her hip and the other wagging at her daughter-in-law. "You've got the nerve to suggest he killed that man? I won't stand for this kind of insult in our home. Get out."

"Mom," Napoleon said.

"Jo, calm down," Roman said.

"I won't calm down, I mean it. I want her out of this house right now and take your spoiled children with you."

Phoebe looked shocked and wounded. "I didn't mean anything, except—"

"I know exactly what you meant. You made the same kind of snide accusing remarks when he was in trouble over Thelma's suicide. You never pass up a chance to put Billy Ray down. Don't think I can't see it."

"Mom, you're not being fair."

"Don't talk to me about being fair. Is she fair when she accuses your brother of murder? What has Billy Ray ever done to her?" Josephine had both hands on her hips now.

"I didn't say he killed anybody."

"No, you're too underhanded to say it outright; you just make sneaky remarks that suggest it."

"We better leave," Napoleon said standing up reaching for Phoebe's hand.

"It's good to know what you really think of me," Phoebe

complained. "Your precious Billy Ray can do no wrong, I suppose, but I'm a villain for having the guts to say what everybody else ought to be thinking. Well, I don't care."

"Take your wife out of here, Nappy, before I forget I'm a pastor's wife."

Roman stopped gaping long enough to say, "Jo, what's got into you?"

"I'm tired of her ridiculing my son, that's what. This is the final straw. Imagine her even hinting Billy Ray could do such a horrible thing." Josephine glanced over at Phoebe. Phoebe had gotten up but wasn't moving. "I want you out of here and I mean it. You will not be welcomed back in this house until you apologize."

"Mom, don't upset yourself," Billy Ray said calmly. "I know I didn't commit any crime, so whatever she says doesn't matter."

Napoleon took Phoebe's arm pulling her toward the door. "Once again everybody's in an uproar because of you," he told his brother.

Josephine sat back down. "Watch what you say, Nappy, or you won't be welcome here either."

"If I'm not welcome here, you can believe he won't be coming—and neither will your grandchildren." Phoebe left the room shouting, "Kids come on, get your belongings; we're leaving this place!"

Napoleon stood in the doorway looking torn. "Mom, you don't mean what you said."

"Oh, yes I do. I meant every word."

"Just take your family home, son, until things simmer down," Roman advised.

"This is all your fault," Nappy told Billy Ray.

"No, it's your fault for meddling where you shouldn't have," Billy Ray retorted.

"I thought after Thelma's death, you'd learned some sense but I see you're as irresponsible as ever if not more so. Your reckless approach to life is going to do you in for good and when it does I won't be taking your side anymore."

"You never did," Billy Ray threw back.

"I don't care what he does; he's your brother and you better remember that," Roman cautioned.

"We've supported him in all kinds of trouble but he doesn't learn," Napoleon insisted.

"Nappy, get out here!" Phoebe demanded from the foyer. He left immediately without another word.

CHAPTER THIRTY

Earl stood in front of the altar, tears rolling down his face. He fell on his knees and begged, "Dear Lord don't take my Ella from me," he whispered, choking on his anguish. "I don't think I could go on without her." He turned when he heard the squeak of the door and creak in the wooden floor. Billy Ray was standing near the far most pews by the entrance. There was not much light from the stained glass windows, but Earl recognized his tall, husky silhouette.

"Pardon me if I disturbed you," Billy Ray said, moving forward.

Earl wiped his face hastily and scrambled to his feet. "I thought no one was gonna be here."

"I was thinking the same thing, until I saw your horse out front."

"Yeah, felt like a long ride. Need to clear my head."

Billy Ray looked down sympathetically. "Sorry 'bout the bad news. Benny told me about Miss Ella. She's real torn up about it."

"Yeah, well we ain't throwin' in the towel yet. Doctors make mistakes, you know. Nothin's for sure and I'm prayin' for the best."

Billy Ray nodded. "As we all should. I'll keep her close in my prayers . . . her and Benny."

"Yeah, my little girl seems more upset since that polecat got killed. I'd a thought she'd be glad the creep was gone for good."

"She's worried about the scandal. I told her not to worry, but she thinks the dirty details of their breakup are going to circulate again because of the murder."

"So what if they do? She didn't do anything wrong; it was that blasted Jordan Franks who ought to be ashamed."

"I don't think dead men know shame, sir."

Earl sighed and sat down on the pew closest to him. "I reckon so, but it seems like soon as things get to settlin' down more misery crops up worse than before."

"The devil is always busy. We give him too much help sometimes."

"My Ella's a sweet gal and always was. She's a faithful, church-going woman and wife. Why is this happening to her? Sometimes I don't understand the Good Lord. Why does He let His folks suffer so much; like the riot for instance? That was pure evil, and He didn't stop it till the next day. Then He let all them white folks get clean away with killing folks and destroyin' property. Not a one of them demons ever did a day in jail for what they did."

"It seems unfair in our eyes but God has a plan; we just don't know it. He's not the blame for all the bad things that take place, you know," Billy Ray reminded Earl.

"Well, why don't He stop it?"

"Trust the Lord, Mr. Earl, and everything will work out for the best even if we don't see it as such."

Earl's expression was admiring. "You's as much a preacher as your father, ain't you?"

Billy Ray smiled and sat on the row behind Earl. "People have been telling me that but I don't think so. Besides, my father's not too happy with me right now."

"Mad about you not rebuilding the pharmacy and fountain store, huh?"

"Yes, sir."

"Well now, son, he's only trying to look out for your well-being. You's gonna marry my daughter you gotta have a good source of income." Earl grinned. "Benny's used to living a certain way, and she and her mother can sure spend up some money."

"Benny and I have discussed our future, and she's willing to sacrifice so we can open the home for orphans and disadvantaged children."

"Ain't no money in that, is there?"

"It's what God has called me to do. I'm sure of it."

"What about supportin' your wife?"

"I'll earn a living and open the school. There's a small house on the property I just bought, so we can live in that. I don't owe the bank, because I got it at a good price and paid outright for it."

"That's good, I guess, but what about a job?" Billy Ray's future father-in-law wanted to know.

"I'm an experienced pharmacist. I can teach science and chemistry if I have to and give music lessons on the side. Benny said she would keep teaching for a while so we could save money."

"That sounds like a big undertakin' and a sacrifice of how you'll live if you ask me."

"Doing what it takes to accomplish what you have envisioned for years is never a hard sacrifice."

"What about it bein' a sacrifice for my daughter? It's not her dream."

"One of the ways I knew without a doubt Benny was the woman for me is when she told me about her dream of teaching children in a small private school of her own. It's like we were meant for each other, Mr. Earl. God brought us together for that purpose; I know He did."

"Well then, why don't you go 'head and get hitched?"

"We will."

"What's the holdup?"

"Benny needs a little more time."

"Benny needs a stern talkin' to, that's what she needs . . . and a man who won't coddle her like we always did and still do."

Billy Ray stood up. "I'm trying to be patient for her sake. There's a lot going on here, more than meets the eye, but she'll come around." He walked toward the pulpit. "I came to practice a few hymns, if that won't bother you too much."

"Go on, it won't bother me. A little church music may be just what I need. I'll sit here and listen for a while 'fore I head home."

"Sir, I don't want to step out of my place but may I say something to you?"

"Go ahead, son; you're practically family."

"Sir, the Bible says when we pray we should clear up any problems we have with other people. You know, make peace with those we've clashed with, get rid of our ill will toward folks. We have to forgive others, then we can confidently go pray to God because our hearts are in a right condition." Billy Ray saw Earl's expressively stern rejection of what he was saying. "Just felt obliged to remind you of that, sir. I know I have to remind myself often enough."

Earl sat sour faced while Billy Ray climbed the four side steps leading to the platform where the piano and organ sat catty-corner each other in the side pit. By the time Billy Ray sat at the organ and looked over, Earl's expression had softened and he was bowing his head.

Madelle sat her dainty self in Dooley's office looking around inquisitively. Dooley was more than happy to see her but unsure what prompted this unexpected visit. He stumbled about nervously, offering refreshment and a more comfortable chair. It was not like him to be so tense around a woman. She was affecting him in a way he had not felt for years. His chosen line of work and personal background always hindered maintaining a meaningful lasting romance, and it was just as well. He seldom stayed in one place very long, and many women both black and white seemed put off with his lifestyle and his mixed heritage. He had given up hoping to find the right woman who could deal with his work as well as his bloodline.

Madelle stirred in him warmer feelings than he'd encountered in a long while. He chalked it up to her boardinghouse role of congeniality, but something inside whispered it was more. It was that faint whisper, that glimmer of hope he dare not entertain that made him nervous around her. "I've never been in a private investigator's office before," she said, flashing her broad smile. "I never made acquaintance with someone so daring. It's all so wonderfully mysterious and exciting."

"Not merely as exciting as you think, I'm sure. Are you sure you wouldn't like some coffee? I mean tea. I just remembered you prefer tea."

"Nothing for me, thank you, but how sweet of you to remember." Madelle looked at Dooley thinking his somewhat shaggy reddish brown hair was cute on his oddly appealing face. He was handsome, though not in a pretty boy sort of way. His face was interesting and housed the most expressive green eyes she'd ever seen; eyes that said a lot about the heart inside the man. He was slim but solidly built with a hint of muscle, and she noticed he dressed meticulously well for a man without a wife to press and lay out his garments.

"Now tell me, dear lady, what's brought you into town; more precisely, what brought you here?"

"After our talk last week I started doing a little of my own investigating with a few people I know who know other people, if you get my meaning."

Dooley looked alarmed. "Mrs. Bridgewater, I hope I didn't give you the wrong impression. The last thing I want is to put you in any danger. You were only supposed to keep your ears open for the usual boardinghouse gossip and let me know if any interesting information came your way. You should not do anything to solicit information or behave out of the ordinary in any way. I would never forgive myself if you were put in harm's way on my behalf. So please . . ."

Madelle giggled. "You promised to call me Madelle and don't worry, I'm a natural snoop, so it's perfectly ordinary for me to make discreet inquiries. No one suspects a thing." She leaned forward, putting her hand on his. "It's exciting to be part of something so hush-hush. Anyway I think what I learned will be of value to you."

"About what?"

"About those dreadful White Glove people. Apparently they

aren't as happy with this gentleman gangster as they thought they'd be. He's got a heavy hand when it comes to them and Bigger Stanwyck was complaining he'd be trouble and might try to take over and run Tulsa like he did parts of Chicago."

"How in the world did you hear all this?"

"Bigger has a maid who keeps company with one of my roomers. She's a talkative little thing once her boyfriend Lloyd plies her with that moonshine he sneaks in his room. He thinks I don't know but you have to get up pretty early in the morning to get one over on me."

Dooley cocked a questioning eye. "You let your roomers keep company in their private quarters?"

"Oh, heavens no, never; I won't stand for such carryings on. I run a respectable establishment and I will not put up with immoral behavior in my home. They're allowed only to keep company in the sitting room during decent hours."

"I see. Well, this is very helpful information, but I want you to be careful."

Madelle waved her gloved hand. "No need to worry about me. I have more to tell you." Her eye sparkled with excitement. "The White Glove members were on the outs with the police chief because he's changed how he operates. They say it's because his job was threatened after the riot. Everybody knows all eyes have been on Tulsa since then and with this gangster and his mob moving here there'll be federal marshals snooping around. The White Gloves are worried about that because two stills were busted a few months ago and both men got the book thrown at them, maximum federal jail time. So now they want to get back in good graces with Chief Gilbert so he'll run the gangster out of Tulsa."

Dooley grinned. "You don't say! Now that's real good news— real good."

"So I did good?" Madelle asked happily.

"To show my deep appreciation I'd like to take you to dinner and escort you back to your house, if you'd be willing."

Madelle blushed. "Mr. Dooley, I'd be delighted to have dinner with you."

"hief, you look frustrated, what's going on?"

"What ain't goin' on is what you oughta ask. Folks gettin' killed in a messy way, no-good mobsters movin' in and goin' after folks."

"You talking about Giuseppe Carissi? He hasn't been here long enough to make any enemies. Who's he after this quick?"

Gilbert looked at Woolston with narrowed eyes. "Who knows, but mark my words—he's here for some no-good reason. I don't like him tryin' to settle down in my city. Heck, I don't like him period—rum runnin' fancy pants hoodlum. Tulsa's got enough trouble already with federal agents sniffing round like bloodhounds, then jailin' folks for making a little sippin' whiskey. The mayor's on my back like I'm supposed to wave a magic wand and make all the problems disappear. If I can't, then I'm not doin' my job. Well, by golly, he can have this blasted job!"

"Calm down; nobody's blaming you for Tulsa's troubles."

"Oh no? Then what was that indictment charge they tried to hang on me about?"

"That was nothing but the governor and those big shot state folks trying to scramble out from under the gun at the expense of you and the sheriff. Couldn't make it stick because the riot wasn't your fault or the sheriff's and neither are any of these other problems in Tulsa. You can't completely control the criminal element in this town; nobody can."

"Tell that to your double-crossing blowhard mayor."

"He's always been a turncoat. And he's in the pocket of people who got the money. You know that."

"Everybody round here with any pull is in some moneyman's pocket, and folks always thought I was too." Woolston shot him a disbelieving look. "But I'm not and never have been. Oh, I've owed my share of favors all right. I played the good ole boy so I could get what I wanted from the right people but never for money. I wanted respect and position. It wasn't about money."

"I guess I can believe you, seeing that you don't exactly live high off the hog."

"That colored deputy sheriff we ousted had more money and property than me."

"Yeah, everybody knows how he got it too, especially Greenwood District folks." Woolston smirked.

"I'm sick of all this crooked dealing everybody's doing. I just want to be left to do my job the right way." Gilbert caught the baffled look Woolston gave him. "Never mind all that, tell me we got a good solid suspect for that colored killin'."

"I'll give you what I know and you tell me."

"This better be good cause I gotta make some measurable progress on somethin'. Solvin' this murder would get the mayor off my back for a spell."

The office was thick with smoke from Jake Gilbert's pungent Cuban cigar and Detective Woolston's pipe pumping cherrywood tobacco. They sat leisurely puffing and pondering their next move. "Okay, I gave you the information on everybody of interest I questioned and what I learned about them. I figure it most likely narrows down to those last five; so what do you think?" Woolston asked.

Gilbert tipped his chair back and sent a cloud of smoke upward. "Don't think the wife did it, although you're right—she's a might peculiar. Something 'bout her don't sit right with me. Think she might be a little mental maybe; you know, slow-witted. And he did write about her unfavorably in them books of his, didn't he?"

"Yeah, but I don't see her as the one who could axe him to death but I could be wrong. That axe was too heavy for someone like her to swing with such force."

"Hell hath no fury, they say, like the scorn of a woman. When a female's mad enough to kill her man, she finds the strength to do it. Sounds like he was a nightmare of a husband if you ask me, a tyrant and depraved besides."

"True, but I don't put her at the top of my list, do you?"

"Nah, not really."

"What about the musician, the band member he was so cozy with?" Gilbert's eyes rolled. "I don't think there's any doubt Jordan was involved in some kind of disgusting relationship with that Frenchman. You should have seen how that Frenchy carried on when I was questioning the band members. He was a sniveling basket case, cryin' like a woman. Made me sick."

The chief chuckled. "I bet it did. What's with those people? The dead man's wife doesn't even sniffle after she finds her husband in bed with his head practically lopped completely off but the so-called band member falls apart? This whole case is just too bizarre for me."

"Could be he's the killer and only acting all torn up to throw us off track," Woolston suggested.

"Could be, but for what reason? Where's the motive? We got to have motive," Gilbert reminded him.

Woolston looked at the chief. "If they were involved the way we think they were and with Franks having a fairly new bride, who knows; could have been jealousy."

"Possible . . . sickening to think about but possible."

"What about the lawyer? Elizabeth Whitehead's got a real reason to want him dead if you ask me. He had something on her worth blackmailing about and she stooped as low as a woman could to keep whatever it was quiet."

"Do you think she did it?" Gilbert asked curiously.

"Her motives say she's a very likely suspect, but I think not," Woolston responded. "Not that she couldn't, but that she didn't."

"Why?"

"She's too clever to do it in such a sick way. She would have poisoned him or something like that if she wanted him dead. Maybe even shot him from a distance but she wouldn't take an axe to him—that was just vicious. Whitehead is lethal in the courtroom, maybe, but she's pretty cool under pressure."

"If she is guilty we gotta have an airtight case to arrest her. She'd wriggle out of a flimsy arrest in a heartbeat."

Woolston added, "And she'd have that NAACP and everybody else she could get down on us."

"None of that matters if she's guilty. I'd haul her educated self right in here, if I really thought she did it."

"I don't think she's the one."

"Well, then it seems to be down to my old friend William Ray Matthias again." Gilbert was grim.

"He's my choice, to be honest, but I didn't want to influence your decision."

"What about that Freeman gal he's marryin'? She a likely suspect?"

"The Freeman girl also has a strange past with Franks so I thought maybe her and Matthias might have done it together, but definitely not her alone. They say she nearly had a nervous break-down over Jordan Franks when the engagement ended. From his diary I surmised she found out what kind of man he really was and couldn't handle it," Woolston continued. "It's definitely motive for murder and I considered her the prime suspect until I met her; then I threw that thought out the window. She doesn't have what it takes to do something that gory. She's too timid."

"You'd be surprised. Those timid mousy types can be your worst ones. Scared folk kill faster than anyone."

"So who's left other than Matthias?"

Gilbert's eyes narrowed. "I figured it was going to get to him all along. He may have got away with murder once but not twice. So he thinks he can outwit us again. If he's the guilty party I'll show him we won't be made a fool of no more. He's sorely mis-taken if he thinks he is comin' in my town committin' murder twice and getting away with it."

"I have to go along with you. He had a real bad attitude about me questioning the Freeman girl like he was trying to cover up something. And get this—his fiancée didn't know about the fight he had with Franks even though she was the cause of it."

"So you think he's the most likely suspect?" Gilbert asked.

"It's all circumstantial at this point, but he had strong motive and he's definitely capable of committing the crime. He's big and as strong as an ox. From what they say he was ready to do Franks in when he attacked him but too many eyes were on him then. Several witnesses said he was furious, and that after beating Franks up he threatened his life right there in front of everybody, including Franks' wife."

"So I'm thinkin' later when nobody was around he went back and made good on his threat. He might be a real danger to society. And a preacher's son to boot."

"Let's get a search warrant for the house," Chief Gilbert directed. "He might still have the clothes he wore somewhere in there. He had to get soaked in the man's blood if he did it. If we can get the bloody garments or some other concrete physical evidence then it'll be a shoo-in conviction and the preacher's boy will finally get what he deserves." The chief set his cigar in the ashtray. "I intend on being right here when they bring that murderin' bull in."

CHAPTER THIRTY-TWO

Earl watched Cord skillfully work with the mustang he was breaking. He had recognized Cord's gift with God's creatures since his son was a small boy. Now three cautious cowhands took over and Cord finally walked Earl's way.

As Cord got closer he looked at his father but not directly in the eyes. At the fence he stopped and propped his boot on a rung. "Hey there, is something wrong with Mom?"

"Nothing new if that's what you mean. We won't know nothin' for sure till the operation."

Cord's head dropped. "How's she taking it?"

"Ella's a strong woman, but naturally she's scared. Who wouldn't be?" Earl looked straight at his older son. "You ought to come see about your ma. See for yourself how she's doing."

The horse whinnied loud and Cord turned around to see the men struggling with Silver Shadow. He turned back and dropped his head again. "Yeah, well I didn't want any more trouble so I get Benny to keep me informed."

"Your mother needs all her children round her now. You need to come see her regular. Your brother got back a few days ago and he's sticking to her like glue."

"Benny told me."

"Cord, I know we don't see eye to eye 'bout things but we's family and right now we should all be there for your mother. I know you haven't come around cause of me; so I want you to know it's fine with me if you come home to be with her. I don't hold no ill will against you. You're my firstborn, my oldest son." Earl stopped and looked at Cord sadly. "Come see your mother, boy. She needs you."

"It's not just because of you, Dad."

"Then why?"

"You don't know?"

"Know what?"

"I'd rather not say if you don't already know. I thought Ethan would have—"

"Ethan? Ethan has something to do with you not coming at a time like this? What in blazes is wrong between you two?"

"It doesn't matter."

"You're right about that. Whatever it is, forget it. Put aside your differences with your brother and with me. Your mother is the one that matters."

"You're right. I'll be there Sunday to see her. I promise."

"Good. It'll do her good for all of us to be together. I'll get Virgie to come in and whip up somethin' nice for supper. Come in the afternoon and we can all sit around and be a happy family again."

Cord wasn't hopeful about that, but he promised to be there.

Earl untied his horse from the fence. "Cord, I want you to know that I'm sorry for what I said," he told his son. "Sorry for blowin' my stack like I did. I get so riled up sometimes I forget what I'm sayin'. Hope you won't hold it against me."

"Ah, sure, I ah . . . I won't hold it against you. I'm sorry too for how I've acted; sorry about everything. I really am."

"Jes so you know, I think you're shapin' up this place real good. You're a good rancher, Cord; I'm proud of you." That being said Earl climbed on his big bay horse and rode off with no further discussion.

Cord watched his father ride away and though he fought his emotion, tears pushed out and down his cheeks anyway. He walked rapidly toward the barn where he could be alone with his thoughts.

Bet knew Ethan was back days before she saw him. Although he didn't come to the law office while she was there, she suspected he'd been in during the night. Twice items on his desk had been rearranged. Four days into his return, Ethan walked in the door during early afternoon. She was surprised, but relieved to see him.

"Good afternoon," he mumbled.

Bet forced a bright smile. "Hello, Ethan, welcome back. It's good to see you."

"Is it?" he said, then sat down at his desk. "I can't say seeing you is particularly pleasant for me." He avoided looking at her face.

Bet tried not to react. "How's your mother feeling?"

Ethan at last looked over at her face with a questioning stare. "Your father told me she was ill."

"My father came here?"

"He was looking for you this morning. He told me to tell you to be sure to see him today."

"Thank you for relaying the message," he said, noticing how beautiful she looked. The sight of her brought to the surface the pain he'd worked desperately to suppress. Her hair was especially pretty and she was wearing a flattering outfit. Though her appearance was more than pleasing, he was well aware she was equally poisonous. As he knew it would, the memory of her and Cord replayed in his head from the moment he entered the law office.

"Thank you for not telling your family about your brother and me," she said gratefully.

"They'll find out soon enough. No need for me to say anything."

"I doubt if there will be anything worth finding out." She stood up, her clingy skirt falling provocatively around her hips. She walked in front his desk. He couldn't help but detect the faint rosewater scent she always wore. Her hourglass frame was as inviting as ever with those smooth shapely ankles in silk stockings and shiny high heel patent leather shoes. "I think we need to talk, Ethan."

"My mind is on other things. I'm really not in the mood to have a conversation," he replied.

"When will you be in the mood? How long are you going to avoid me, Ethan? You've been back for days and I haven't laid eyes on you."

"What do you want to see me for?" he said nastily. "You have my brother now, so be satisfied."

Bet closed her eyes. "If nothing else, we need to discuss our working arrangements and my continuing to share this office with you."

"I want you out," he shot back without hesitation.

She took two steps backward from the almost staggering verbal blow. "Very well, I'll vacate as soon as I can if you'll give me time to find another office."

"One month. I'll give you one month to leave. That should be enough since Greenwood has a lot of vacant spaces. I'm interviewing to hire a secretary anyway, and by then she'll need this space. I'll settle into Maynard's old office."

"I understand," Bet said quietly in a shaky voice. Blinking back tears, she said, "When your father came by this morning he was very kind to me. He expressed his regret for the nasty things he said to me. He was surprisingly apologetic."

Ethan looked at her surprised, "My father apologized to you?"

"Yes, he did."

"He shouldn't have bothered, since he was right about you and my treacherous brother."

"Ethan, I can't stand your resentment toward me. I want you to know how sorry I am. I feel awful about what happened, and I'd like to apologize to you."

"Don't bother."

"I feel I must for a number of reasons. I was only thinking of myself and what I wanted so badly. I didn't give you or your feelings any real consideration. I won't make excuses for my behavior, but I had no idea how much I would be hurting you. I didn't realize how deeply you cared about me because you never gave me any real indication. I just didn't know."

"You didn't care, would be a more honest way of putting it. Would it have made any difference what I indicated, since you were obviously longing for my brother?"

"I'm not going to try to defend my feelings. All I can say is my attraction to Cord was strong and genuine, but I truly did not want to hurt you. I'm very fond of you; don't you believe me?"

"I don't want to talk about it anymore," Ethan said. He busied himself rifling through papers in his desk.

"Please, Ethan, let me—"

"Let you what?" he snapped. He slammed his desk drawer shut. "Say you're sorry so you can ease your guilty conscious? Let you take pity on poor, idiot Ethan? Or maybe you think if you bat your pretty girl eyelashes long enough I'll change my mind and let you use this office while you sleep with my brother whenever you please? Forget it. I want nothing more to do with you or him. Absolutely nothing, so as soon as you can, I want you to pack your belongings and get out. I expect you to be gone from this office within thirty days. Till then I'll make myself scarce. I can work from my family's townhouse."

"Very well. Thank you for giving me time to relocate. I know I deserve your anger, but you should know there's nothing going on between your brother and me—nothing further that is."

Ethan looked up at her sad eyes and instantly understood. "Cord threw you over?"

"That's right; your brother does not want me. He's made it clear his mind is occupied elsewhere. And I'm sure that makes you very happy."

"You don't expect me to feel sorry for you, do you? I have to hand it to my brother, though. He's more of a louse then I ever suspected. Savannah must have rubbed off on him," he said dryly.

"Ethan please. I really care for Cord. I'm—" Her eyes pooled with tears.

"I don't care about your feelings for my brother; serves you right that he used you."

"I never thought you would be so callous."

"Don't you get it? I'm happy he bedded and discarded you and I'm ecstatic you're hurting because of it. You hurt me, and his treating you so shabbily is your just reward. I doubt if any man before now ever rejected you, so this must be a new experience. Hah, good for you. Join the rejected and brokenhearted club, Bet."

Bet slumped down into her chair. "I see you hate me."

"I don't just hate you. I absolutely distrust and despise you."

The telephone's ring startled Bet. With trembling hands and a slightly quiver in her voice she answered, "Vaughn-Freeman Law Office." She looked over at Ethan and said, "It's Maynard Vaughn for you."

He grimaced and snatched up the phone in front of him. "Afternoon Maynard, how are you today?" He spoke cheerfully looking away from Bet. "Yes. I'm doing better than I have in a while to tell you the truth. Just got some encouraging news as a matter of fact." His smile was deliberately cruel, showing a side of this caring man Bet hadn't seen before.

CHAPTER THIRTY-THREE

Bigger Stanwyck didn't like visitors coming to his house unannounced disturbing mealtime with his family. He wasn't overly fond of the sheriff, Wilbur McKinney, under any circumstance, let alone an unexpected intrusion.

Bigger sat down in his well-worn chair on his mansion's porch, determined not to invite his unwanted guest inside the house. The property's grounds were manicured to perfection. Chirping melodically, birds darted back and forth among the unusual collection of black walnut, soapberry, and Kentucky coffee trees. Exotic ornamental grass sprang up in an intentional design to look as if designed by nature. The mansion's four stories of white paint with four imposing pillars in the front made it the oldest and grandest house in the high-end neighborhood. Huge plantation windows with brown shutters brought the bright light of daytime inside the mammoth structure. Swinging gliders and high-back thatched chairs with ornate cushions lined the porch. McKinney sat on the glider and gently pushed back and forth. "All right now, what's so all-fired important it couldn't wait till later? And this better be good. I was just finishing my supper."

"You got more to worry 'bout than filling your stomach right now. You all got big trouble."

"What trouble and who is this *you all* you're referring to?"

"*You all* is the White Glove Society, as if you don't know. Word's come down Gentleman Gi intends on being appointed leader of the society, and he's calling some kind of unscheduled secret meeting tomorrow."

"What are you talking about? I didn't hear anything about a meeting."

"I said unscheduled and secret, didn't I? You're not supposed to know about it. The purpose is for him to get them to make him head over everything. He's taking over."

"That's ridiculous. How does he think he's going to get away with that?"

"He's paying his way in, that's how."

"Paying how?"

"With money, how else?"

"I mean, how is he distributing the money, you idiot."

"So far he's offered to pay off mortgages, give good-paying jobs to folks, and scholarships for kids to go to college. He's giving out a lot of cash too. Oh, and he's offerin' protection for folks' businesses."

"What kind of protection and from what? If it's protection from street ruffians, it won't do any good because they don't care about the infamous Giuseppe Carissi. If the police can't control them, they won't back down because of some big city gangster."

"Yes, they will. He's organizing some of those hooligans right now. Paying them to work for him and protecting people who make hooch on their property. Guaranteeing that the feds won't get to them or their works."

Bigger pounded his fist on the table next to his chair. "I had a feeling that city slick hoodlum might be trouble, as if we don't have enough of that already."

McKinney let the glider stop moving. He looked over at Bigger's frowning face and asked, "Whatcha gonna do 'bout it?"

Bigger looked back at him and warily asked, "How'd you find out about this?"

"From Jack; he told me to hightail it right over here and warn you."

Bigger's qualms quieted. He trusted Wilbur's brother, Jack McKinney. Information coming from him would be accurate and relayed with good intentions. He looked at the sheriff smugly and told him, "I'm not gonna do anything. I'm leaving the law up to you and your boss. It's your job to keep Tulsa safe from dangerous criminals, and Giuseppe Carissi *is* dangerous."

"Yeah, but what can we do 'ceptin' wait for him to break the law?"

"Exactly. A man like him always breaks the law, already has. I want you and that chief of yours to pounce right on it. From what you just told me he's guilty of racketeering and violating prohibition. Find a way to nail him good. Then we either lock him and his thugs behind bars or make him leave these parts and not return. He left Chicago because it got too hot there when the law was determined to put him away."

McKinney's eyes popped wide. "Are you serious? It'll start a gangland massacre in Tulsa if we lock them up."

"I don't care if it does. I want that power-grabbin' snake outta my hair, you got that?"

The glider stilled. "Yeah, I got it," McKinney muttered.

"I want him out of Tulsa and out of the state of Oklahoma for good; either that or behind bars for a long, long time. I don't care how you do it. I don't even care if it's legal or not. Just get rid of him! War between him and the police don't matter none to me. You're the law," Bigger reminded the sheriff. "You ought to be able to hold your own against a bunch of Chicago hoods. What's wrong with you people?" Bigger scratched at his gray hair. He tried to calm himself down as he rested his eyes on a beautiful cluster of trees.

Wilbur hadn't expected Bigger's angry response to be aimed at him and his fellow law officers. He was anxious, following Bigger's gaze. "What kind of trees are those over there?" he asked knowing full well nothing pleased Bigger more than talking about his precious collection of trees.

A self-proclaimed arborist, Bigger prided himself on procuring unique and well-maintained specimens from every part of the country and some from other nations. The National Arbor Society and each of Tulsa's premier newspapers as well as various gardening periodicals had photographed his elegantly designed landscape and written rave reviews. "That's my little eclectic group, all different colors, shapes, and species. There's hackberry, eastern red cedar, rough dogwood, Chinese pistachio, and sawtooth oak in that group. I have all the information on those trees to keep them healthy in this climate. Their different origins, shapes, and sizes make for an interesting arboretum."

"You don't say," Wilbur murmured not understanding much of what Bigger said.

Bigger looked at the sheriff, realizing he'd been deliberately sidetracked. "Since when do you care about trees?"

"I like trees," Wilbur said halfheartedly.

"Never mind my trees, you imbecile; you wouldn't know a bald cypress from a Japanese maple." Bigger stood up. "I'll be at this so-called surprise meeting, and you can count on that. Be sure an' tell Jake Gilbert I said he better do his job this time, or he won't have one come next year."

da wiped the sweat from her forehead. Vigorously scrubbing clothes on the washboard helped relieve her overwhelming frustration but it gave her back a crick and made her arms ache.

She tried hard not to think about him but she couldn't get him out of her head. She was worn out from crying, tired of feeling let down, and ashamed of being such a fool. She must have lost her mind. How could she ever let herself get involved with him in the first place? Ada hated herself for being so weak she loved a man she never should have looked twice at—an enemy of her race. Worst of all, because of Jake Gilbert, she had sinned.

She must have been bewitched by him. That had to be the way it happened, because she'd known better otherwise. What bothered her most was the fact that she was still under his spell, and wanted him as much as ever in spite of good sense. Her heart ached to hear him again tell her he loved her, and her body yearned for his touch. *This is ridiculous!* She scolded herself forty times a day but the feelings never ceased.

Thank goodness Kate was out shopping for that gangster client of hers who bought Maynard Vaughn's house. Ada was tired of hearing her go on and on about that high-class criminal she was decorating for, and how she was getting paid a lot of money. Lately her chatter had been either about that or her plans to snag Jake for a husband. Well, go right ahead—she could have him! It tore Ada up inside to listen to Kate's romantic fantasies of being Mrs. Jaffice Gilbert. All of her employer's incessant plotting about one thing or another was getting to be too much to take.

Tears mingled with perspiration ran down her cheeks. Her vision was cloudy, and she didn't see Jake come over from around the side of the house. Only when she heard his voice did she realize he was there.

"Hey there, Ada, you seem tired. I hate seeing you working like this, honey," he said in a sad voice.

Ada whirled around, surprised. "Jake," she said.

"How are you?"

"I'm right fine, Chief Gilbert, how are you?" she answered with forced politeness, heart beating hard.

"Are you? You look upset and your eyes are red. Were you crying?"

"No, I ain't cryin'. I'm hot is all. Burning up with this hot water and soap gettin' in my eyes."

"Don't pretend with me, Ada; not with me."

"What do you mean 'pretend'? Who are you to talk about pretending, Chief Gilbert?"

"Stop calling me Chief Gilbert, and I never pretended with you, never."

"Humph, you think I'm a real fool, dontcha?" Ada threw the garment she was holding into the wash bucket. "Well maybe I used to be but I ain't no mo'. I'm done bein' your colored good-time girl."

"Don't talk like that. You were never that to me, and you know it. I love you, and no matter what happens I want you to always remember that. You are the best thing that's happened to me in a long, long time. I mean it."

"Go away, why dontcha? I don't wanna hear no mo' of your sweet talk," Ada said, and she started to sob. "Leave me alone with all them lies, you hear? Cause it ain't gonna do no good. I won't destroy myself on account a you, Chief Gilbert. And I'm gonna keep calling you that because that's who you is to me from now on. Mean ole cantankerous Chief Jake Gilbert."

Jake took Ada in his arms, closing his eyes. He'd yearned desperately to hold her again. Her crying hurt him more deeply than he could handle, and he had to fight back his own tears. "Ada, you don't know how I wish to God things were different for us. I wish this world would change overnight and that I could shout out loud how I feel about you. I'd give anything if I could do that, and know you would be safe afterward."

Ada pushed back. "Well, things *ain't* different and we *can't* tell the world nothing 'bout us. Besides, sin don't know no color. God don't care we was different colors. He was put off cause we sinned against Him. The world can't change that."

"What you think about God means more to you than what we meant to each other?"

"Sho do."

"Okay, I won't argue about it because I've been thinking about God a lot lately myself. Whenever I think of you I think about something or other you said about God." She started wiping her face with her apron. Jake moved her hand away, took out his handkerchief and delicately wiped her face. Impulsively he pulled her to him and kissed her, long and passionately. Ada tried to wiggle loose but in an instant she succumbed to her love for him, kissing back with desire. "I've missed you so much," he whispered.

Suddenly Ada pulled away. "No, no I won't do this no mo'," she said shaking her head. "I won't let you fool me. No, I won't. You get outta here. Why are you here anyhow? Miss Kate ain't home, so why you here?"

"I know she isn't home. I saw her going into Jason's Furniture store; that's why I came by. I knew you'd be here alone and . . . well, I just had to see you."

"No, go away. I don't want to see you. Didn't you say it was over? Why are you here if we's over? If you're done with me, leave me be!"

Jake shuffled anxiously. "I guess you're right. This isn't fair to you. I'm sorry I bothered you. I just miss you so much. I'm sorry. I worry about you, but this is wrong. I won't come here like this again. I promise I won't bother you anymore."

Ada stood trembling, trying to control her tears. Jake walked off toward the front of the house. Ada held it in until she thought he was far enough out of earshot and let herself weep as long as she felt like it.

Kate leaned against the kitchen cabinet looking out her window, not believing the scene playing out before her very eyes. How had she not known about this? Had she missed any signals? Her body tensed as her labored breathing increased and anger swelled.

She had spotted Jake's police car off the road near the house when she came home. Hurrying up the lane into the house, she'd grabbed up the two bottles the milkman had left by the front door. Anxious anticipation stirred in her as she wondered what caused an impromptu visit from Jake and why he parked so far from the house. *Maybe he was working nearby,* she thought dashing to the kitchen putting the milk in the icebox. Glancing out the window she saw Jake and Ada talking. *She must be telling him I'm not home.* Then her breath caught for a second when she saw Jake take out a handkerchief and gingerly wipe Ada's face. *That's an odd thing for him to be doing,* she thought, but didn't think much of it. But when she turned to head out the back door and glanced out the window, her knees buckled. Jake was kissing Ada! This was no hallucination. Jake Gilbert, the chief of Tulsa police, was locked in a passionate kiss with her colored housekeeper!

Kate fell against the sink, staring at them in disbelief. The two of them were deep into the moment clinging to each other like their lives depended on it. She couldn't move her eyes from the pair. Things suddenly made sense now. *They were so familiar with each other—oh, my goodness—they're lovers! Jake and Ada are lovers!* Kate's brain was screaming the harsh reality with merciless pronouncement. She continued to stare out the window, unable to pull herself away. The emotionally charged encounter ended with inaudible but apparent cross words by Ada and Jake walking away. His face was pained. She'd only seen him look so sad twice before: when his long-suffering wife died and when Kate's husband, his closest friend, was buried.

Tears burned in Kate's eyes and trickled down her face. Her

thin lips tightened as the full picture was completed in her mind. Not only were they lovers, they were deeply in love. *This just cannot be; how can this be? Jake loves me! He wants me! How could he do this?* Kate looked at her sobbing maid with loathing. How long has this been going on? *How dare they make a fool of me?*

It was well over an hour later when Ada returned to the house. The sun was about to go down, so Ada went to the sitting room to draw the curtains and found Kate sitting there. "I didn't know you was back," she said, startled and curious about the odd look on her employer's face.

"I just got back," Kate lied calmly.

Ada noticed the pint of bathtub gin and empty glass sitting on the table next to Kate. "Well, I done the washing and got everything else in order for the day. I'll be getting home if there ain't nothin' else for me to do."

Kate turned on the lamp next to her and looked up at Ada, examining her closely. She wanted to see what attracted Jake to this ignorant colored woman. She saw nothing to justify such a breach of decency and common sense. "Sit down," she said brusquely.

"What?"

"I said, sit down," Kate snapped, catching her tone and changing her sour face. "I need to talk to you. Have a seat," she said more congenially.

Ada look at Kate, then sat down in a nearby chair. "Whatcha wanna talk 'bout?" she asked assuming Kate was in one of her moods. It happened sometimes and was overdue since Kate had been abnormally cheerful lately.

"I never wanted to have to tell you this but I can't use you anymore. I can't keep you on because I'm watching my budget."

Ada's eye grew large. "What?"

"I'm letting you go . . . as of today. I'm sorry, but it's necessary, has to be this way."

Ada saw the coldness in Kate's eyes and heard the tightness in her voice. "But why? Ain't I doin' a good job? I been workin' here all these years."

"It has nothing to do with the quality of your work," Kate answered.

Her formal tone irritated Ada. "Then what is it?"

"I told you, I'm cutting down on my expenses."

"I don't believe it. You ain't cutting down on nothin'. You got mo' money than you know what to do with."

"Don't you dare talk back to me!"

"Then don't lie to me. What's the real reason?"

Kate unfolded her hands from her lap. "I don't have to explain myself to the likes of you. Who do you think you are, you common black . . ."

Ada stood up and gazed at her employer for a moment before she said, "Fine, I'll be gettin' my things to leave."

"I'll have your final pay ready in a few minutes."

Kate was standing by the window when Ada came back in. "It's on the table," she said never turning around.

Ada picked up the money and counted it. It was correct to the penny. "I deserve to know why you just up and tossed me out of a job, don't I?"

"I've said all I intend to say on the matter. If you can't accept my decision, I'm sorry, but my mind is made up."

"You telling me you gonna clean this big ole house with no help all by yourself?"

Kate glared at Ada. "I'm telling you that your employment in this household is over. Now get out!"

As Ada snatched up her purse, anger overpowered caution. "I kept this place spotless from top to bottom for eight years, puttin' up with your picky ways, changin' moods, and foolish notions. All that, and you just up and tell me I gotta go for no good reason, not even a thank-you. So I don't have no reason to bite my tongue no more. Miss Kate, you's a selfish, stuck up, miserable, ole bat, and I'm glad to be rid of you!"

"How dare you! How dare you speak that way. You think you can insult me, a white woman, and get away with it! Get out, get out now before I—"

"Before you what?"

Kate folded her arms across her chest. "Before I call Jake Gilbert and have your black hide arrested for talking back and trespassing on my property."

Ada's swift and wordless exit from the parlor gave Kate a small degree of satisfaction but the humiliation and anger were still strong. She looked at her newly fired housekeeper walking down the hall toward the front door and shouted, "And use the back door!"

Ada stopped, standing by the front door for a moment debating within herself, then continued left toward the kitchen. Only for a split second did it enter Ada's mind that Kate might know about her and Jake. She dismissed the thought, telling herself far worse would have happened if she did.

Kate's vindictive smile was short-lived after she heard the back door slam. She fell into the closest chair and released her newest wave of tearful and angry emotions.

CHAPTER THIRTY-FIVE

L oretta Fennimore stood by Dooley's desk, twisting the ends of the scarf she wore around her head. She stared at the detective, unsure if she should continue speaking.

"You obviously came to see me about something important, Mrs. Fennimore. Have a seat and tell me about it." It was early morning, earlier than Dooley had expected someone to visit his office.

"I don't rightly know if I'm doin' the right thing," she said sitting down. "Purdy, that's my husband, he tol' me I oughta come tell somebody but I don't wanna get involved in no killin'."

"What are you talking about? Do you mean the murder at the hotel?"

She untied the flowery-designed silk scarf. It slid down the back of her head and rested on her uniform collar. "I work at the Stradford Hotel," she said, almost whispering.

Dooley waited, but her eyes darted around the room and she hesitated.

"No one else is in the building, so we are in total privacy. You're on your way to work now," he prompted.

"Yeah, I do laundry and sometimes when they need me to I clean rooms."

"Would you like a cup of coffee?"

"No thanks. I have to leave soon or I'll be late. Mr. Judson gets nasty when we late."

"Okay then. Is this concerning the recent homicide at the Stradford?"

Loretta hesitated. "You mean the killin'?"

"That's right."

"Yeah, you could say it has somethin' to do with that. Maybe. In a way, I guess."

More silence. Dooley was annoyed, since he wasn't really yet open for business. He was still in his pajamas, and had still been asleep when Loretta's relentless pounding on the agency door woke him and forced him to come down; now she wasn't saying anything worth hearing. "Mrs. Fennimore, why did you come to see me and at this hour of the morning?"

"I came to tell you what I saw. I came now cause I work all day and when I get done I'm dog-tired is why. I beg your pardon fo' disturbing you so early, but I wanted to come when nobody would see me."

"Why did you come here instead of going to the police?"

Loretta's eyes rolled. "You know them police is crooked and ornery as all get-out. I don't trust not one of 'em. Too many colored haters in that police department. They was in the riot hurtin' folks like the rest of them evil men and the ones that didn't hurt nobody didn't stop those that did. Purdy said I should tell you cause you's one a us even if you do look white. He said you work for the government."

"I used to work for the government."

"You don't no mo'?"

"No, but I'm still in contact with the government if I need to be. Now tell me, what did you see?"

"I was comin' down the hall cause I had to put the clean linen in the closets for the maids. It was late morning and I was on my last batch of laundry fo' I go help strip beds when I sees these mean lookin' white men coming up the hall toward me."

"Who were they?"

"Don't know, never seen 'em befo' but they was all dressed real fancy. They looked at me real mean fo' they went to his door—the dead man's room. They banged on the door hard like they meant business. Somebody opened it. I couldn't see who and they pushed right on in."

"Did you hear anyone speak at all?"

"No."

"Any noise or sounds like a scuffle?"

"Not that I go round listenin' to folks business through the doors, but when I went by I did put my ear close 'cause those men was terrible mean lookin', but I couldn't hear a thing outside of faint muffled voices. Them fancy new doors block noise mo' than them old ones."

"How many men were there?"

"Three."

"Do you know if they came off the elevator, or from the stairwell?"

"Not sure." Loretta stood up and pulled her scarf back over her head, "I gotta go but I feel better now that somebody knows what I saw. You can't tell nobody what I tol' you or at least don't say I tol' it. Not unless you really have to. I don't wanna get caught up in no killin'. Those men might come lookin' fo' me."

"So why did you tell me if you're afraid and I can't say anything?"

"Purdy say I should. I always do what Purdy say do and just in case somethin' happens to me then you'll know."

Dooley walked her to the door. "I won't tell a soul about our conversation unless absolutely necessary, and if I do I will let you know immediately."

"You think they's the ones who done it?" she asked.

"Could very well be, but I wouldn't venture to say until I find out who they are. You go to work and I'll contact you if I have to. Meanwhile, say nothing about this to anyone . . . not even the police unless you absolutely must. I can always reach you at the hotel, right?"

"That's right. I work six days a week. Don't work on the Lord's day if I can help it."

Dooley watched Loretta move rapidly down the street looking around as if she expected to be ambushed any minute. He knew she was scared and his instincts told him she had good reason to be.

"You know, this meetin' in secret business is getting ridiculous," Jake Gilbert complained.

"We have to play this real careful or we might as well put targets on our backs."

Jake twisted his mouth. "Since you're the expert on sneakin' around, I'll have to take your word for it."

Dooley flicked a nasty look. "You've done your share of sneaking around with Ada Crump so don't get self-righteous with me."

"Look, it's over between her and me so drop it."

Dooley glanced around the burned-out remains of the *Tulsa Star* office and found a crate to sit on. "You stopped seeing her?"

"Didn't you tell me that was the safest thing to do for her sake?"

"Yeah, but I didn't think you would actually do it," Dooley said.

"Why not, when *you* told me it was for her safety?" Gilbert replied, a slight edge in his voice.

"Cause I didn't think you'd care that much about her safety."

Jake's eyes narrowed. "You don't have any idea who I care and don't care about, so keep your opinions to yourself. Ada means the world to me. Whether you believe it or not, I'd die to keep that woman safe."

"Funny, for some reason I'm starting to believe you would. Who woulda thought?"

"I didn't come here to talk about my personal life," Gilbert reminded him. "Let's get on with why you wanted to see me."

"Before I tell you that, how's the Jordan Franks murder investigation going?"

"What do you care?" Gilbert asked curiously.

"Just wondering," Dooley said. "After all, it's big news isn't it? It's a gruesome case and *is* the talk of the town. Folks are on edge wondering if some head-chopping maniac is on the loose."

"Don't worry; my department is on the job and it's as good as solved for my satisfaction."

"So you know who did it?"

"Sure do, but we're trying to gather more definite proof before we make an arrest."

"Who is it?"

"Not at liberty to say just yet. Don't want to tip our hand too soon. But I'll tell you this—we may have the guilty party, and if it turns out we do, we're going for everything the law can throw at the culprit: maximum sentence."

"If you say so," Dooley muttered, troubled.

"No matter what people round here think, I know what I'm doing. I do my job, and I make sure everybody else does theirs."

"Don't get defensive; I'm not saying you don't."

"You didn't have to. I get the heat for everything wrong in this town and I'm sick of it. I'm the chief of police, not God. I can't control what folks do or don't do, and I don't make the laws. I just enforce 'em, and I can't keep crime from happenin'. No one can." Jake was red-faced from his outburst.

"People understand that."

"Do they?" Jake wasn't so sure.

"Okay, I have some news that might improve your mood," Dooley announced.

"What news?"

"Interesting news about Giuseppe Carissi and Bigger Stanwyck. I believe they're about to go to war. Gentleman Gi wants to run the White Glove Society and squeeze Bigger out."

"You don't say." The chief took another crate and sat across from Dooley. "I ain't surprised. That Carissi thinks he can come here and be the new big shot. I could see it from the moment he set foot in Oklahoma."

"I don't think Bigger's going to stand for being pushed out."

"I know he won't, and that explains why he wants to meet with me tomorrow. Sent a very polite request for me to come to his house in the afternoon. I figured that was strange him being so polite in askin' cause he don't really like me." Jake Gilbert had no doubt about that. "If he's bein' nice that can mean only one thing; he wants something from me pretty bad."

"You know this plays real good into our hand if Bigger wants you in his camp." Dooley grinned.

Gilbert hesitated. "Yeah, I guess so, but what exactly do you have in mind?"

"This makes our job easier. You play along with Bigger, agree to launch a campaign to rid Tulsa of the gangster element, and I'll feed our gentleman mobster with enough worthless information to satisfy him for a while." Dooley had it all figured out. "Meanwhile, I'm sure they will try to do each other in and we can help them both out. My knowledge of Carissi tells me he won't hesitate to do anything to get what he wants. Bigger had better keep an eye over his shoulder."

"So this business with him and Bigger lets me off the hook with Carissi?"

"Not at all, just maybe it diverts his attention for a little while. Most likely he'll be after both of you. That's what you tell Bigger; that you and Carissi are not friends and you want him out of Tulsa more than he does. Make him believe it."

"That won't be hard since it's true."

"I bet once he finds out you're on Carissi's hate list you two become best pals."

"That's hardly likely but I'd put up with Bigger any day if it gets this so-called Gentleman Gi out of the picture. If it's the last thing I do I'm gonna rid this city of the likes of him. His presence in my town is just too much trouble."

"I'm sure it is, since he's even disturbing your love life."

Jake frowned. "Don't start with that again."

"Don't be so downhearted. It's not forever. Once this mess is over you and Ada can resume your hidden love affair."

"I don't think that will happen."

"Why not? Didn't you explain it to her?"

"Nope, I just ended it. It was for the best for more reasons than one, I suppose." Jake glanced away.

"Sorry, I didn't know. I thought it was just a temporary situation."

"Can I ask you a question?"

"Go ahead," Dooley said.

"How did your parents manage being together? Did the marriage work out for them? I mean, were they happy with all the problems of being racially mixed?" Jake was looking down at the floor and didn't notice the intensity on Dooley's face. "Do you think it was worth all the trouble they had to face?"

"No," was Dooley's curt reply.

Jake looked up at him surprised by his cold tone. "Why not?"

"'Cause it cost both their lives when I was just a kid, thanks to the Klan. Almost cost mine too."

"Oh, that's tragic. I didn't know."

Dooley changed his expression. "You would marry Ada?"

"If I thought it would work out, you bet I would."

"Well, I can only say this; think long and hard before you make a decision like that. It will cause a lot of hardship in your life and hers. Make sure the relationship is strong enough to withstand what you'll have to face. My folks' was. They stood strong, loving each other to the end. That's what hurts most in remembering." Dooley fell silent for a moment. "Out of all that misery they never wavered or showed anything but their love for each other. Unto death."

"'Till death do us part,'" Jake recited reflectively. "It must have been really rough to lose them both like that."

"Yeah, it was wrong for a little boy to have to witness his folks murdered like that. They were decent, God-fearing people, for all the good it did them."

"Do you think God punishes us for the wrong we do?" Jake asked.

"Who knows? God didn't do a thing to help my mother and father when the Klan came a-calling. He didn't stop a lot of the evil I've seen during my life, and I've seen a lot including this riot in Greenwood. So as far as I'm concerned, all this faith in a God that lets so much evil prevail is foolish. What good is having a God when you're just as prone to be a victim as anyone else?"

"Ada has a fierce belief in God."

"What about you?" Dooley enquired.

"Oh I believe, all right, but just not so much like her. I've heard different preachers in my day and got more confused than ever about what's right and what ain't. Ada seems so sure of what she believes, no doubt whatsoever. I sort of envy her that. Everything she does is subject to something about God. She eats, sleeps, and breathes God into almost everything in her life. To me that's overdoing it."

"Is that the real reason you broke it off?"

"Nah, I could handle that good enough. To be honest, it's one of the things I like most about her . . . most of the time. Ada is fiercely devoted and loyal to anyone and anything she loves, even her old hound dog."

"Are you included among those she loves?"

Jake slowly nodded. "At least I was. Sometimes I feel like everything I want most in life is always impossible for me to keep. It can be right there in front of me but unreachable or I can have it but can't hold on to it."

"Like what, for instance?"

"A peaceful, happy life with a good woman for starters, and to know the truth about God. Who is God really? What does He want with us and why?"

Dooley nodded. "Women are pretty easy to handle but this God business is not something I understand myself. Most of my life I haven't had much use for the God I've heard about. Didn't see where it benefitted all the folks who believe in Him. Sure didn't help my folks none but lately I've been wondering if I'm wrong."

"Why is that?"

"I'm not sure, but I know a guy who believes with a fire in him, and this guy is very convincing. He's got something in him I'm curious about."

"What is it?" Jake asked, his curiosity piqued.

"His faith in Jesus."

"Don't you believe in Jesus?"

Dooley shrugged. "Sometimes I think I do and sometimes I don't."

Jake had gotten up and was moving toward the door. "You sound more mixed up than me. Ada believes, she believes too much in all that religious stuff she was taught."

"So does my friend."

"Who's your friend, a preacher?"

"No, but the son of a preacher."

Jake Gilbert looked at Dooley suspiciously and asked, "You ain't talkin' bout that there big fella William Ray Matthias are you?"

"As a matter of fact I am; why?"

"Cause I think he could very well be a murderer."

"He did not throw that girl out that window."

"So *you* say. *Me* . . . I'm not so sure. As a matter of fact I think he might have not only done that but butchered that man in the hotel too."

Dooley jumped to his feet. "Are you crazy? Billy Ray could never do something like that."

"Why, cause his father's a preacher?"

"No, because I've gotten to know him in the past year and he's a good, decent man. He's no cold-blooded killer. You're dead wrong about him."

"So you're friends with Matthias. Okay, if you're so dang sure he's innocent, then who do you think killed that musician in the hotel? Matthias had motive and means. He beats up and threatens the guy less than forty-eight hours before he's found dead. Explain that."

"I can't explain it, but I'd bet all I have he's not guilty."

"You two must be real good friends."

"Are you arrestin' Billy Ray?"

"Shouldn't be telling you since you're friends with the maniac but no, not yet at least. We're gathering evidence. If he's brought in again he won't skirt his just punishment this time. We'll have an airtight case before we make a move."

"So why *are* you telling me?" Dooley moved to the door. "I could warn Billy Ray to leave town."

"You won't, cause what you're gonna do is go lookin' to find evidence to prove him innocent," Jake said opening the door. "And when you do, it will do one of two things: find him guilty as sin or lead us to someone else who's the guilty party. Either way we'll have our killer."

"So you're asking me to help the Tulsa police find who took out Jordan Franks?"

"No, I'm sayin' if you want to keep your friend from the mean arm of the law you should try to get evidence that will clear his name since we got cause to say he's the perpetrator."

"Circumstantial at best, I'll wager."

"When we put those cuffs on Matthias we'll have cold hard facts, you can count on it." Jake walked out the door.

Dooley stood there weighing his options. He hadn't intended to get involved in the Franks murder. It was a police matter and he didn't need any more than was already on his roster but now circumstances were demanding otherwise. Billy Ray was Dooley's friend, and he couldn't stand idly by while he was railroaded for murder by the Tulsa police department. Not with Chief Gilbert after him he couldn't. Dooley knew if Gilbert ever got Billy Ray behind bars again his life would be over. Going out the door he pondered where he should begin looking for the real killer, or killers. Uncovering the identity of the mysterious white men at the hotel was a likely beginning. He considered this while walking along the slowly resurrecting riot-ravaged Greenwood Avenue. When he reached Archer he'd figured out his participation in this investigation was exactly what Jake Gilbert wanted all along.

CHAPTER THIRTY-SIX

Madelle took the pies out of the oven and set them on the windowsill to cool. Their sweet aroma drifted from the open window to the other side of the wide wraparound porch, where she could hear her roomer laughing and talking with his lady friend. He sounded intoxicated as usual.

She put on a pot of water to boil for coffee and sat patiently waiting. Twelve minutes shy of half an hour Lloyd Turner stood in the kitchen doorway grinning. Ollie Cramer was standing behind him, gripping the door to keep her balance. "Umm, somethin' sure smells good Miss Madelle." Lloyd's words slurred while he flashed a crooked smile. "Smells like you done fixed some of that delicious blueberry pie of yours."

"Two blueberry and two apple," Madelle replied.

"I sure is hungry," Ollie whispered to Lloyd.

"Hush woman; Miss Madelle might be having special company fo' supper fo' them pies."

"I'm not having anyone special." Madelle smiled sweetly. "You're welcome to stay for the evening meal, my dear."

"I is? Thank you kindly, Miss Madelle, you sure is a gracious lady always treatin' me so good. You a good cook too, a real good cook." Ollie wobbled forward.

"Thank you, dear, now come help me finish cooking while we talk a spell. Lloyd, why don't you go take a nap. Sober up before supper."

Standing in Bethel Baptist's sanctuary Benny griped his arm, eyes wide in fear. "No, they can't be serious. The police actually think you killed Jordan," she repeated.

"Don't panic."

"What do you mean don't panic? Do you know what this means? They could arrest you; you could go back to jail for a horrible murder you didn't commit. How can I not panic? How can *you* not panic?"

"Panic won't help," Billy Ray asserted calmly.

"What will help?"

"Dooley's investigating on my behalf. Maybe that'll unearth something to get them off me."

"And if he doesn't find anything to help, then what?"

"Then I'll do what I always do—wait on God to work it out."

Benny sucked her teeth. "That's always your answer to everything."

"What else should I do, Benny?"

"Leave Tulsa for good. The police are after you again because they think you got away with killing Thelma. They won't stop until they get you behind bars again and ruin your life. They'll execute you. You have to leave."

"You want me to pack up and run tail like I'm guilty?"

"I want you safe . . . and free."

"Leave my family and you? I haven't been charged yet; why should I run?"

"That's the point isn't it? You leave *before* they arrest you. Get out of this state and go somewhere you can live without fear of police blaming you for every crime committed in its borders. Why do you think Dooley warned you? So you could get away."

"No, he didn't. We talked about that and he said he didn't think I would run. If I did they would know he told me. He put his reputation on the line by letting me know."

"Why would he do that if he didn't want you to clear out?"

"So I could be prepared for the worst. He also needed my side of the story." He sat down on the pew next to Benny, thinking about his options. "They may find the real killer."

"They may not; then what?"

"What about us?" he asked, looking at her sadly.

"There *is* no us if you're in prison or executed." She slid closer. "I have no life without you, Billy Ray. Get away while you can. I'll go wherever you go."

His kiss was charged with anxiety and affection. Benny was fighting fear. They were both resolute that whatever was ahead they would face it together. "I'm not running," he told her after the kiss ended.

Her gusty sigh betrayed her frustration. "This is my fault you're in this fix. If I hadn't gone to see Jordan you wouldn't have fought with him and threatened him. I'm sorry I ever thought talking to him would help."

"I'm not blaming you. What I did was wrong even if I had a strong reason for doing it."

"It wasn't wrong to protect me."

"How I did it was wrong. I lost my temper."

The door creaked open, drawing their attention to the rear of the sanctuary. Ada walked in unaware of their presence until she was midway down the aisle. "Oh, hello, I didn't see you."

"Hi," Benny said with a friendly smile.

"It's been a long time since we ran into each other." Ada returned the smile and glanced at Billy Ray.

"Yes it has; have you met my fiancé, Billy Ray Matthias?"

"Nice to meet you," Billy Ray said, standing up.

"You the preacher's boy, ain't you?"

"Yes, ma'am."

"Nice to make your acquaintance; my name's Ada."

"You haven't been to church in a long time," Benny remarked.

"I know, but that's gonna change. I know where I need to be more than ever now . . . close to Jesus."

"We all do," Billy Ray said pensively.

"I better go." Ada turned to leave.

"Didn't you come here for something?" Benny asked.

Ada turned back around. "Yeah well, I came to talk to God 'bout something real serious but it can wait."

Billy Ray said, "If you want privacy we can leave."

"Oh no, I don't want to chase you away."

"Nonsense, we were leaving soon anyway," Benny insisted as she stood.

Billy Ray took Benny's hand and looked into Ada's eyes. "We'll leave. You look like you should have that talk with God right now."

Ada looked down at the floor. "I—thank you." Watching the couple as they walked to the door, Ada's heart ached for Jake more than ever. "Benny," she called before they stepped out into the sunshine. Benny turned. Her face was glowing more vibrantly than Ada ever remembered seeing her. "You look good . . . and happy. God has blessed you because you're a good and decent woman. I'm happy for you."

"Thank you and yes, I am blessed. I need to remember that no matter what."

After they were gone Ada knelt to pray. Bearing heaviness from a broken heart and a guilty conscience she cried out to the Lord, weeping pitifully.

Bailey Clover paced around the once thriving poolroom. Few customers came his way anymore for more than one reason, and his income was sadly lacking because the riot cost him more than twenty thousand dollars in valuable property burned to the ground. He had no insurance coverage and he couldn't rebuild most of what he owned.

The pool hall had survived the riot with minimal damage. Life had steadily rolled downhill for Bailey since being fired from the Tulsa Police Department prior to the riot. Business conflicts with his police duties got him ousted from the department. Being one of only two Negro law officers in the region Bailey considered himself a privileged person in the eyes of his peers until he was relieved of his duties as deputy sheriff. He had been the eyes and ears of the Tulsa police department keeping them fully informed of all the goings on in Greenwood District. Convinced his role was necessary and unshakeable he played his two-sided hand for years. Taking bribes and shaking down his people for money, Bailey accumulated a tidy little fortune for himself beyond his policemen's salary. All that went up in flames during the riot.

Bailey continued his pacing. He stopped and looked at his reflection with his noticeably receding hairline and wide puppy eyes. "If we don't get more customers soon I'm gonna have to close this joint down," he told Andy, his loyal employee.

"You know folks don't much like you round here no mo', Bailey. They all over at Shockey's. He's raking in the cash since he rebuilt his pool hall."

Bailey was just about to go into one of his vindictive tirades about the competition when Giuseppe Carissi and his two trusty cohorts walked in. Bailey instantly transformed his demeanor. With a welcoming smile, he rushed to greet the dapperly dressed man. "Welcome to Bailey's; I'm the owner, Bailey Clover."

Giuseppe nodded. "I am Giuseppe Carissi."

"Oh, I know who *you* are Mr. Carissi." Bailey's ingratiating smile grew. "Mighty nice to meet you, sir." Bailey extended his hand.

Giuseppe appeared unimpressed with Bailey's and its owner and did not return the gesture. "Indeed."

Embarrassed, Bailey withdrew his hand but this was not his first such encounter. "Won't you have a seat? What can I do for you, Mr. Carissi?"

Giuseppe sat but his goons remained standing. Bailey was torn, being intimidated by these humorless men yet tickled that Carissi was in his establishment.

"I was told you could be of assistance to me. I have a proposition for you that will benefit both of us, if you're interested."

"I'm sure I'd be interested in anything I could do for you, Mr. Carissi."

"Is it true you lost a considerable amount of property during the riot?"

Bailey's jaw tightened. "Yes sir; all I got left that's worth anything is this here place and the house me and my family live in. I lost valuable property cause of them troublemakers. Can't believe my own kind would start so much trouble and cause so much damage and for no good reason. Taking the law in their own hands . . . foolhardy nonsense and look what it caused."

"Well, I might be able to help lessen your financial woes if you do well by me."

"What you want me to do?"

"Nothing you're not already accustomed to doing. I need you to be my eyes and ears in this colored section."

"I can do that."

"So I've been told." Giuseppe didn't like Bailey much. He thought little of disloyal types and he could tell Bailey was loyal only to himself. From his point of view people like this colored ex-cop could be dangerous unless used the right way. Carissi knew the type. Financial gain or improved station was Bailey Clover's only motivation to be straight with a person. The fact that he rose above his race's inferior position to get a post on the police force was admirable, even if he'd been dismissed. In spite of Clover's accomplishments Giuseppe looked at the one-time deputy sheriff with decided disdain. He was treacherous, arrogant enough to want to be where he shouldn't and greedy; all distasteful characteristics. But useful.

"There are certain things I need you to keep an eye on. Certain people, certain situations."

"Who are the people?"

"I have their names written down, along with a list of what I'm most interested in finding out. Do you want the job?"

"Yes, sir. I sure do. Glad to help."

"Good." Carissi held his hand out and one of the goons slid him an envelope. Giuseppe passed the envelope to Bailey. "Here's all the information you need to know, and a small starter's fee. Once you have sufficient information I will compensate you accordingly. Is that agreeable?"

Bailey jaw dropped at the sight of many one hundred dollar

bills in the envelope. "Yes, sir. It's more than agreeable. Thank you, Mr. Carissi."

Giuseppe stood up. "Very well. I will be in touch in a week or so. I can find you here most times?"

"That's right, and if you can't Andy can tell you where to find me or take a message."

"Good enough. I hope you don't disappoint me."

"Oh I won't disappoint you. I promise to come through for you. You can count on me Mr. Carissi." Bailey looked down at the list of names and looked up at the gentleman gangster curiously.

"Is there a problem?" Giuseppe wanted to know.

"Oh, no sir, there's no problem."

"Good, because I don't like problems. Problems make me get ugly, and I don't like getting ugly. Bad things start happening if I have to get ugly." Giuseppe moved to the door. "You sure you don't have anything you want to say to me, any questions?"

"No, sir, no questions and no problems. None at all."

"Good day."

Bailey held his breath until they were out the building. He exhaled long and loud, his heart still pounding. The money was plenty but he wondered if he were in over his head. Another glance at the list and the detailed instructions revived his fear. One name made him curious though, and that would be the easiest and where to start to earn the thousand dollars he was holding.

CHAPTER THIRTY-SEVEN

Ella's weight loss was showing. Her smile was beautiful as always but her eyes revealed emotions she intended to hide. The sight of his once vibrant mother sitting up on the couch looking drawn and weak tore at Cord's heart but he threw on a smile and kissed her affectionately. "You love all this fussing over you, don't you?" he joked.

Ella smiled back. "Why not? For the first time I'm the center of attention around this house and everybody's taking care of me."

"Have we really been so uncaring?" Cord asked. Guilt nipped at his conscience.

Ella reached for his hand and tugged him closer. "No dear, you haven't; but a woman needs more than just her fair share of love and devotion to make her feel satisfied. It's just the way we are. Isn't that right, Scarlett?" The young woman smiled back shyly and nodded. Ella held out her other hand and reached for Scarlett's. "You look lovely, honey, and so well. I'm glad you're doing much better."

"Thanks, Mrs. Freeman."

"Please, just call me Ella. You're a guest in my home."

"Yes, Miss Ella." Scarlett did not quite make eye contact.

Ella looked at Cord, at Scarlett, and then back at Cord. "You have something to tell me?"

Cord looked up, surprised. "What?"

"Is there something you want to tell me?"

Benny had been quietly sitting by the window thinking about her mother's illness and about her fear for Billy Ray. She looked over at her brother when she heard her mother's question.

Cord shuffled, letting go of Ella's hand. "No, got nothing in particular to say except that I love you."

"I love you too, dear, but are you sure?"

"Yeah, I— um, yeah, I'm—"

Ethan entered the parlor and stopped abruptly when he saw his brother. "Hi, Mom, how are you feeling today?" He gently placed a sweet kiss on her forehead.

"Much better now that both my boys are here." Scarlett let go of Ella's hand and backed up. Cord put his arm around her shoulder. Tense greetings were followed by a difficult silence lasting for a couple of minutes. Ethan kept looking at Scarlett while Ella tried to gauge the subdued animosity toward his brother. Ethan was the milder mannered of the two Freeman boys, and she'd never seen him display such coldness toward his brother. Benny watched uncomfortably as the sibling divide became more apparent. "Everyone sit down," Ella said not knowing what else to do.

Benny was watching out the window, and when she heard a car she jumped up. "Billy Ray's here," she said, hurrying to meet him.

Earl had come in and was sitting in a chair next to Ella's couch. Ethan was telling his father, "It's a very good position if I take it."

"Sounds like it would be, except you would have to leave Tulsa."

Ethan's eyes darted toward Cord. "That wouldn't matter. I want to try a new place. I think I've outlasted my welcome in this town."

"That's nonsense; this is your home. Washington, D.C., isn't. You would leave your home for a job?"

"Does a person good to spread out sometimes."

"Is that really what you want?" Ella asked calmly.

"I haven't made up my mind yet but they have officially offered me the job. I got the letter day before yesterday."

"Howard is a prestigious school and having Maynard there would be comfortable for you," Ella said smiling. "I bet there are lots of nice educated women at Howard. Maybe you'll meet a nice girl and finally get married."

"Maybe," Ethan mumbled, cutting Cord a nasty look.

"I don't like it," Earl complained. "You all the way in Washington, D.C. You should be near your family. Maynard Vaughn is a good man and all but he's not family."

"Sometimes family members are your worst enemies," Ethan responded, glaring at Cord this time.

"Ethan, are you going back to see Maynard?" Benny asked walking in the room with Billy Ray.

"He's goin' there to live," Earl said flatly.

"You're moving to Washington, D.C.?"

"Thinking about it. I've been offered a good teaching position at Howard. It would mean a steady salary, a chance to further advance academically and still practice law in our country's capital. I'd be right there at the heart of our political system. It's a great opportunity."

"Sounds perfect for you," Benny said. "We'll miss you."

"I haven't made up my mind quite yet."

"What's to decide? It sounds like a golden opportunity," Billy Ray asked holding a chair out for Benny to sit in.

"It means him leaving Tulsa," Earl snapped.

"Tulsa is his hometown, but Ethan's got what it takes to grow beyond this."

"He don't need to go traipsin' to no Washington, D.C., to *grow* as you call it. He can grow right here in Tulsa or at least in the state of Oklahoma."

"Can I?"

"Sure you can."

Ella sat up taller. "I think it's a wonderful opportunity for you, and if that's what you think you want . . . as much as I will miss you, you should do it."

Surprised, Earl looked at her. "Never thought I'd hear you say that the way you mother these kids."

"Things change, people change. Can't I change too?"

"Too much changing round here for my likes," Earl grumbled.

"Change can be good, Daddy. Well, at least it's good news about the job offer," Benny said. "And we have good news too. Billy Ray and I decided it's time for us to get married."

Ella's face lit up. "I'm so happy. When is the big day?"

"Thanksgiving Day."

"That's an odd choice for a wedding day," Cord commented.

"Not really, it's a fitting holiday for us. We'll be real thankful if everything turns out like we hope," Billy Ray said.

"What things?" Ethan asked.

Benny looked at Billy Ray then glanced toward her mother's direction and said, "Just some plans we have."

"By then you should be better recuperated, Miss Ella. That's a consideration too."

"My Ella's gonna be fit as a fiddle by Thanksgiving," Earl declared.

Ella said, "A Thanksgiving wedding is a nice idea."

"It's going to be a very small ceremony at church with just our families and a few close friends; nothing big and elaborate, just a simple intimate affair."

"Good, cause I heard Morton Dallas complaining about his daughter's big expensive wedding that set him back thirty-five hundred dollars. Can you believe spending that much money on a wedding? You need an oil strike just to get married these days. Keep it small and keep it simple, baby." Earl grinned, satisfied.

"Stop being so cheap," Ella scolded smacking his arm. "Benny's our only daughter and no expense is too much."

"Don't make no sense getting carried away with all that expensive china and caterin' folks, big ole fancy cake with a big-shot college orchestra and choir. He went too far and I'm telling you now I won't be putting out like Morton did. All that unnecessary carryin' on just impressin' a bunch of folks I don't care two beans about. Nope, keep it simple just like you said if I have to pay for it."

Ella rolled her eyes. "Benny, will you go see if Virgie needs any help?" she asked.

"Okay." Benny got up and started out of the room.

"I'll go with you," Billy Ray said joining her at the door.

When they left Earl chuckled. "Them two need to hurry up and get hitched. That boy acts like he can't stand her out of his sight for two minutes."

"They're in love," Ella said dreamily.

"You don't say; well, I know a little something about that, sugar lump." He kissed Ella's cheek adoringly. "I love you to pieces, darlin'."

Cord and Ethan were both taken aback. They had never known their father to behave so romantically in front of people.

Ella grinned happily, then looked at Cord. "Why don't you show Scarlett around the ranch?"

"I will a little later. I want her to be around the family for a while."

"Why?" Earl spoke roughly.

Cord looked at him and then at his mother. He could see Ethan curiously watching out the side of his eye. "So she could get to know everybody since she doesn't have any family of her own," he replied.

"Oh," Earl said less discourteously.

Ella gave him her watch-what-you-say look. She knew Earl didn't like Scarlett's presence the minute he walked into the parlor and saw her. "We're very happy you came," she told Scarlett.

"I'm pleased to be here, thank you." Scarlett spoke quietly, barely lifting her head to see Ella.

"Were you born in this area?" Ella asked.

"No, ma'am. I was born in Albuquerque."

Billy Ray and Benny came back in the parlor arm in arm. Ella noticed how uncharacteristically clingy Benny was toward her beau and wondered why.

"Virgie shooed us out of the kitchen. Said she doesn't need or want us underfoot getting in her way. Dinner will be ready soon," Benny reported before she and Billy Ray sat on the settee, hands still locked together.

"So what plans do you have about supporting my daughter?" Earl asked.

"I have an interview next week to teach chemistry at the high school, sir."

"Oh, you don't say. That's good to hear. Now I can rest comfortable that you'll take good care of my baby girl."

"I plan to take real good care of her," Billy Ray responded lovingly gazing into Benny's eyes.

"You bought a place to live and when you get the job, you'll be set to marry."

"You bought a house?" Cord asked.

"Yeah, Ezra Cottonwood's old place."

"That place will need a lot of work," Cord pointed out.

"I know, but it was affordable, and just what we were looking for. I got it at a steal and don't have to worry about meeting a mortgage."

"When we finish with that whole place it's going to be perfect," Benny added proudly.

"The two things that bond a husband and wife together are raising their children and working toward building their homestead." Ella was daydreaming in her fond memories when she caught Earl frowning Scarlett's direction. She squeezed his hand for a loving warning.

"I wish you the best," Ethan said. "You two certainly deserve some peace and happiness if anyone does."

"We all do," Cord declared

Ethan ignored the remark.

"Cord is right. It has been a rough past couple of years for this family but I feel things are going to turn around now even if I'm not here to witness it."

Earl visibly tensed at his wife's words.

Benny said, "Momma, don't say that."

"We have to face the facts. My chances of surviving this surgery are not great and if I do survive, it may not be a successful cure. This could be the last time we are all together like this as a family."

"The girl is right, Ella, don' say that. You *are* going to come out of this. You have to."

"Why, because you say so? You may make demands on this ranch and folks trip all over themselves to do what Earl Freeman says, and you're the head of this family and we adhere to your rules, but the Good Lord is not subject to any man. He doesn't move because Earl Freeman wants Him to. It's God's will, not yours."

"I know that but I don't believe God is going to take you yet. I just don't and I won't."

"It doesn't matter what you or anyone believes. It's up to God."

Benny started crying.

Billy Ray spoke up. "Nappy says your chances are hopeful. This is a new kind of surgery but it's had great success and he's encouraged about your prognosis. Dr. Peebles is from Johns Hopkins and a renowned surgeon in his field. He's one of the best. You will have him and Nappy both performing the surgery."

"That's right, Ella, you have the best doctors our money can buy. You'll beat this thing," Earl insisted.

"It's not about money. Money can't buy the will or favor of God."

"Dr. Peebles developed improved methods for brain surgery and that improves the patient's chances as well," Billy Ray said.

Ella looked at him unconvinced.

Ethan's voice broke as he said, "Mom, it can't be hopeless. You always taught us the Lord could do anything. He could do what man couldn't. You taught us to always have hope, didn't you?"

"Yes, I did and I'm still hoping. Don't for one minute think I'm not but if the worst happens I'm ready. I'm at peace with Jesus and my fate any way it comes. Don't cry, Benny, it's all right. I'm all right."

Benny continued to cry while Billy Ray consoled her. "Miss Ella, you keep putting your trust in God and praying. It's all we can do sometimes and I figure this is definitely one of those times. I will keep praying for you."

"Thank you. I'm at peace knowing you will be taking care of my daughter." Ella winked. "Although I could go to surgery so much more peacefully if you were already married."

Benny stopped crying abruptly and raised her head looking at her mother.

"Ella, what you sayin'?" Earl asked, confused.

"It would do me a world of good for them to be married before my operation. That way if I die I would have at least seen my baby wed."

Billy Ray looked at Benny. "But—but what about Thanksgiving?" she said feeling trapped.

"You have to face the fact I might not still be here on Thanksgiving."

Benny's face dropped at the prospect. "Is that what you want, is for us to get married before your operation?"

"It would make me happier than you know."

Benny stopped and watched her mother's cagey expression. "I don't believe you, this is blackmail," she finally said. "You're doing this on purpose, aren't you?"

"Why would you use such an ugly word to describe your poor sick mother's request?"

Earl restrained a snicker.

Billy Ray said, "If it would comfort your mother . . ."

"She's manipulating the situation," Benny protested. "Can't you see that?"

"Your mother is sick and she's having a very serious operation. What would be the harm in pushing the ceremony up a bit if that would make her happy?" Billy Ray asked.

Ethan agreed. "If that would please Mom, why not since you were planning to marry soon anyway?"

Ella looked at her daughter with cajoling pitiful eyes.

"Makes good sense to me," Earl chimed in.

Benny wrung her hands as she paced around the room.

"You might regret it if you don't," Cord warned her.

Benny looked from Billy Ray to her mother. The thought of losing her mother was too much to handle. Speeding up the wedding day was almost as terrifying.

Virgie came into the parlor. "Everything is ready, Miss Ella. I set the extra place. You can come have your meal now," she announced.

Ella nodded. "Thank you, Virgie."

Benny said, "All right, you win. We'll get married before your operation."

In the Freeman household dessert was a favorite part of a big meal. The family always looked forward to Ella's delicious sweets but this dinner was different. She didn't have strength to make her tasty pies or delectable bread pudding. Ethan was partial to chocolate cake and apple fritters. Several times during dinner he shook off thinking he may never taste his mother's scrumptious cooking again. Virgie was a gifted cook, but even her skills were no match for his mother's.

White potato pie was one of Earl's favorites along with the sweet bread and corn pudding his wife made like no one else could. Ordinary family meals were made special because his darling Ella made them so. The thought of losing his wife was taking its toll but he refused to accept the dire prognosis, determined to be strong and hopeful.

Cord was partial to apple-rhubarb pie and his mother's sweet potato biscuits. He ate heartily as always but lamented the wasted time during his detachment from the family. Although his mother made sure she stayed in contact with him, things weren't the same after his fallout with his father. Now this situation with Ethan added to the problem. Cord was guilty and knew he had to make it right all the way around. Coming to dinner was just the beginning. He was determined to regain that lost connection to all of them especially in light of Ella's upcoming surgery. That would give her more peace to face the operation.

Though Virgie had prepared a lovely meal, Benny's upset nerves hampered her enjoyment of it. For Ella's sake she was trying to keep from showing her dread of the operation. Added to this was her fear that Billy Ray could be charged for Jordan's murder, and if these weren't enough, now she was apprehensive about speeding up the wedding. She loved Billy Ray with all her heart but the thought of marital intimacy scared her to death. As illogical as she knew that was she couldn't shake the anxiety. *What is wrong with me? Why am I so scared of something I should be looking forward to?*

Everybody had their specially loved Ella dishes, and this was the subject of chatter nearing the end of the meal. Earl tried to hide his irritation at Scarlett's being with the family. Benny wanted to keep her mother happy, so she skillfully kept the conversation light. As Billy Ray watched his future in-laws interact, he concluded that his family and the Freemans weren't very similar when it came to family conflict. Cord was not pleased when he noticed Earl's unfriendly looks shooting Scarlett's way but for his mother's sake tried to ignore it. Scarlett sat quietly picking at her plate not speaking unless spoken to. Ethan played it cool ignoring his brother and directing all his talk to everyone else. Eyes shifted, words were carefully chosen, and tones were pushed up a notch or two to keep things pleasant. Despite the underlying contention it was a collective goal to portray the united family they had once been for Ella's sake. Everyone did their best but the charade was getting tiresome.

"Honey, you look beat. Why don't you go to bed and lie down and rest," Earl suggested.

"That's all I do is rest. I want to be with my family. I can lie down in the parlor. I'll be all right."

Billy Ray and Benny sat at the piano talking to each other in low tones after playing several of Ella's requests. Ella had drifted off to sleep on the couch, her feet in Earl's lap. Ethan sat on the settee examining some papers for his father. As Cord and Scarlett sat in the chair and gazed out on the veranda, Cord took her hand. The look he gave her ended Earl's silence. "You sparkin' with her now?" he asked trying to disguise his disgust at the thought.

Ethan looked up from the papers.

Benny rushed to intervene. "Nobody says sparking anymore, Daddy. That's such an old-fashioned word."

"Well, courtin' then. He knows what I'm talkin' 'bout. Are you courtin' this here woman?"

"No, sir, I'm not sparking with Scarlett and I'm not courtin' her," Cord answered tightly.

"'Pears that way to me. You two is awful cozy actin' over there."

Benny sucked her teeth. "Daddy, don't be rude."

"I ain't bein' rude. I want to know why he brought her here in the first place."

"I brought a guest to dinner. What's wrong with that?" Cord shot back.

"Cause this was for family and she ain't family."

"Billy Ray's not family. I don't hear you complaining about him being here."

Ethan found the dispute more interesting than the papers detailing business matters.

"That's different; he's as good as family. He's marryin' your sister."

"They aren't married, so he's not family yet but it doesn't matter about them. I don't like you insulting Scarlett for no reason. She hasn't done anything wrong."

"Hasn't done anything wrong! She's a common strumpet! I don't understand why you're so dang attached to a woman like that with all the decent ladies there are to pick from. Why do you always go for the lowest of the—"

Cord sprang to his feet. "Don't talk about her like that! She's changed!"

"Likely story; I bet she hasn't change a bit. She's got you snookered just like that tramp wife of yours."

"You don't know Scarlett. You don't know anything about her except what you've heard. You're always judging people you don't know." He couldn't hide his disgust. "You listen to vicious gossip and what other people say but you never try to give folks a chance."

"Since you know that, what you bring her here for?"

"I thought since we were trying to act better toward each other, things would be different."

"Please, Cord sit down," Benny pleaded. "Daddy, please stop; we don't need this quarrelling . . . not tonight."

"Don't worry, Benny; there won't be any more arguing. We're leaving," Cord announced.

"Don't know what you brought her here for anyway," Earl mumbled.

"I thought with Momma being sick you might for once have a gracious heart. Learn to be kind and show a little mercy."

"Mercy? Why? She knew exactly what she was doing."

Scarlett raised her head and looked at Earl. "Jesus forgives me, Mr. Freeman. Why won't you?" She looked back down at the floor.

Billy Ray nodded. "An unforgiving spirit can block your prayers, Mr. Freeman."

Earl shot Billy Ray a nasty look. Turning to Scarlett he said, "What makes you think the Lord done forgave you, missy?"

"I asked Him to. The Bible says if I repent and ask, He would forgive and save me. I did repent with all my heart and asked and He saved me. I'm changed, Mr. Freeman; whether you believe it or not, I'm changed."

"I doubt that," Earl growled stubbornly.

"Daddy, stop being so pigheaded and mean. You need to have forgiveness in your heart when you pray for Momma," Benny reminded him.

"Don't tell me you believe all that claptrap your beau keeps sayin'; that God won't hear my prayers if I don't forgive everybody for everything."

"It's not what I say, sir. It's what Christ said," Billy Ray said gently. "The same degree we forgive comes back to us."

"He doesn't care about that. Dad's too happy standing in judgment of everyone. Come on, we're leaving." Cord took Scarlett's arm.

"You're leaving without telling anyone she's really your wife?"

Ethan blurted out when they reached the door. Startled, Scarlett looked up at Cord. Benny, Earl, and Billy Ray froze in place. Ella stirred, having caught part of what Ethan said.

"What did you say?" she asked looking confused. "Did I hear you say Cord got married?"

Cord looked at Ethan in shock. "How—"

"I happen to be at the courthouse that day and saw you. Charlie Emery told me why you were there."

"You got married?" Benny asked softly.

Earl shook his head. "I don't believe you could be so stupid as to mess up your life twice with that kind of woman."

"Earl, hush!" Ella snapped.

"That's right, we're married, so Scarlett is my wife now whether any of you approve of it or not!"

Billy Ray stood up and walked over to Cord and extended his hand. "Congratulations on your marriage." Cord shook his hand. "May I congratulate the bride with a kiss?"

"Sure."

Benny rushed to Scarlett hugging her. "Oh, honey, I wish I could have been there," she said lovingly.

Scarlett flashed a shy smile.

Ella sat up on the couch holding out her arms. "Come here, dear, and give me a big hug. Congratulations, you're my new daughter-in-law."

Earl looked at his wife like she was crazy. "Daughter-in-law? How can you call her your—"

"Just be quiet if you can't say anything nice, Earl. She's our daughter-in-law whether you like it or not. Haven't you learned anything yet? We made mistakes with Savannah but I won't make the same ones twice."

"Mistakes? What did *we* do wrong?" Earl demanded. "That Jezebel disgraced her husband and all of us with her loose ways."

"We didn't accept her from the start, that's what we did wrong. We never really made her part of the family."

"We did try to make her family," Ethan objected.

"Did we really?" Ella said cocking an eye.

"I did," Benny said.

"What we did was demand Savannah live up to our standards and when she didn't we weren't kind. That's not how family should be. Family should be accepting and understanding."

"So you're saying we should tolerate any ole kind of behavior?" Earl asked.

She frowned at him. "No, not that we tolerate unacceptable behavior but we should try to handle things with a loving hand, not a bullwhip."

"Sometimes a bullwhip is all that works."

"You never gave Savannah a chance," Cord said to his father. "You had her sized up and convicted from the moment we got married. Mom and Benny might have tried a bit but you never approved of her no matter how hard she tried to do things right." He turned to Ethan. "And you were almost as bad, always bringing the latest gossip home to add to the problem."

"That gossip as you call it was usually true. You should know that by now."

"All that is past. We can't change what already happened but we can do better now and fix things for the future." Ella patted Scarlett's hand. "Ethan, you haven't congratulated the newest member of our family."

Ethan shot a stubborn glance at his brother then looked at his mother's disciplining glare. "Congratulations," he muttered.

"Earl."

"Now you're goin' too far, woman! I cannot in good conscience—" Ella's eyes closed and she put her hand to her head slumping down. "What wrong, sugar? You got a pain? What's the matter?" His voice shook.

"I'm all right. All this hostility is just too much for me." She closed her eyes and sighed wearily.

The worried men stared helplessly at Ella, but Benny stood watching her mother for a minute before she exchanged her worry for suspicion.

"Lie back down and don't fret yourself." Earl pulled the sheet up to her neck. "Should I call the doctor?" he asked panicked.

"No, I'll be fine . . . if everybody would be calm and get along." Ella looked at Scarlett. "You haven't welcomed Scarlett to the family. Welcome Scarlett to the family and congratulate your son for getting married, dear. That would make me so happy." Ella's voice trailed off.

"Okay, honey, anything you want." Earl turned to Cord. "Congratulations to you and your wife. I wish you both the best," he said quickly.

"Yes, that's nice, everyone getting along like we should." Ella closed her eyes and smiled as she drifted back to sleep.

Benny looked at Billy Ray's worried face and whispered in his ear, concealing a knowing smile. Billy Ray was relieved. Cord looked at his brother and restrained his anger. Ethan looked back, smirking. Earl was distressed, agitated, and angry but none of that was more important than tending to his wife.

CHAPTER THIRTY-EIGHT

Gentleman Gi was no gentleman in matters of the heart. He exhibited little sympathy for displays of womanly emotion, as he'd decided long ago that female outbursts were a waste of his time and energy. Now he was quickly becoming weary of Kate's tears.

"Dear lady, calm down," Giuseppe advised.

"You have no idea how humiliated I am," Kate told him between sniffles.

"Yes, yes, I'm sure you are but why have you come to me?" *Get to the point, lady.* "What have I to do with this humiliation of yours?"

Kate's crying slowed and she permitted herself a delicate hiccup. "I've thought about this for days now. It took everything I had in me to come to you with this but I don't care anymore. I have no pride left. I'm a completely humiliated woman. You can't possibly understand how mortifying it is to find out the man who has been wooing you, spending his leisure time tending to your concerns and making it known, in very subtle ways of course as any gentleman would, that he has intentions and then to find out—" Her voice broke, but whether from rage or grief Giuseppe could not fathom.

Giuseppe was beyond irritated but he knew she was talking about Jake Gilbert so he indulged her. "Now, now, my dear, what has you so distraught? Tell Giuseppe what happened?" He handed her his handkerchief and tried to sound soothing.

"How am I supposed to go on?" she cried. Kate covered her face with the hanky but not before taking a second look at the exquisite silk and fancy moniker. "To find out that a man like Jake would lower himself . . . how could he?"

"Lower himself? How?" Giuseppe asked more interested.

"In the most degrading way any self-respecting decent white man could. Lying with a dirty colored! Jake Gilbert's been sleeping with that black tramp of a housekeeper I employed!"

The smile that turned up Giuseppe's lips hardly expressed his delight at the news. "You don't say."

"I could die! I could just die!"

"Calm down and sit instead," the gentleman gangster suggested. "Are you sure about this?"

"Yes, I'm sure. I saw them together on my property enthralled like youngsters; practically *in flagrante* on my back lawn."

"Interesting."

"Interesting? It's reprehensible and obnoxious, hardly interesting."

"Point taken, madam. So tell me why have you come to me with this disturbing discovery."

"I've come to ask your help, Mr. Carissi. I know you are a . . . um . . . a businessman with connections and I need Jake persuaded to abandon this shameful behavior."

"Persuade him how?"

Kate looked around, avoiding Giuseppe's direct stare. "Well, I don't know exactly. I mean, I haven't figured out how but I thought you might have an idea since you know more about these things."

"I assure you, romantic troubles are not something I bother with, dear lady. But getting people to see things my way is."

"I imagine you could be very persuasive in your line of work."

Giuseppe kept his expression neutral as he replied, "I suppose I've found myself having to convince a few business associates from time to time."

"I don't care how you do it, Mr. Carissi. All I want is for Jake

Gilbert to be done with that colored trollop and ask me to marry him."

"Are you sure you still want him?"

"I'm not that naïve. I know about men. I also know that for any decent man maintaining his reputation comes first. He never lets outside interests threaten his social position."

"I see."

"Then you'll help me?"

"Why do you still want *this* man? Are you hopelessly in love with him or is there something else?"

Kate took a deep breath. "It's appalling enough to have him involved with that woman but when I realized it was more than mere physical gratification, that he had tender feelings for her it was utterly devastating." She stiffened. "I will not be made a fool of or abide being tossed aside for some colored floozy who scrubbed my floors."

"Ah, you think he is in love with this scrubwoman. Pride: an old friend of mine. I fully understand."

"Does that mean you'll help me?"

"Dear lady, you have helped me more than you know. I am in your debt for your involuntary aid to my cause."

"How did I help you? What cause are you talking about?"

"I mean I will be delighted to come to your assistance."

Kate's sigh of relief was followed by a contented smile.

Amos Grapnel was angry and impatient to exact his revenge on Cord Freeman and also on Chief of Police Jake Gilbert. Gilbert had lied to him for over a month about arresting Cord Freeman. First he insisted Amos hadn't filed a formal complaint. Then after several weeks he reviewed the complaint and it mysteriously got lost. When Amos made out another written complaint Jake continued stalling saying the complaint had to go down the right chain of command and it was the sheriff's job to arrest Freeman. The sheriff told Amos he'd not gotten any kind of written or verbal complaint about Cord until Amos approached him. This was it—the last straw waiting for Jake Gilbert!

The old Mastermann Mansion was starting to take shape with Kate's extensive redecorating project in swing. The furniture in the drawing room was covered with drop cloths. The alabaster walls smelled of fresh paint and the new teardrop chandelier glistened like diamonds from the ornate ceiling. The marble fireplace had been cleaned and polished back to its original Victorian beauty.

Giuseppe's plans were once again interrupted by an unexpected and unwanted visitor. He sat on a dusty white-sheeted chair pondering his guest's request. "Do you understand what you are asking?"

"Of course I understand. I'm not stupid," Amos answered.

Giuseppe disagreed, but this was not the time to insult the man. Amos had just given him more ammunition against the chief of police and an open invitation to take Jake down. "Are all your White Glove brothers in agreement?"

"Not all, but most of us are. Bigger's fighting against it with his measly crew but no need worrying about them. They're a small number in comparison to the rest of us who don't trust Gilbert anymore. He's a danger to our cause and we want him out of that position."

"Good enough. I'll take care of everything. Seems your police chief is not a popular guy. You want him out? Then he goes." The cunning Gentleman Gi smiled as he rose.

"What about Bigger?"

"Either he's with us or against us. If he's not with us then he's an enemy too."

"What you gonna do?"

"Don't concern yourself with the details. Leave it all to me. Rest assured Jake Gilbert will soon no longer be a problem to the White Glove Society."

"But—"

Giuseppe started to the door where his bodyguard was standing. "I'll be in touch when necessary. Good day; Tonio will show you out."

Bailey could hear the girlish laughter when they walked him through the hall from the kitchen. He'd never been in the large imposing mansion before. Any dreams he'd once entertained about bettering himself and owning such a place were destroyed along with his property in the riot.

The man who led him to the cellar didn't smile, speak, or acknowledge him in any way other than pointing for him to go down the steps. Once below, Bailey was dumbstruck after seeing the huge wooden barrels and rows of wine and liquor bottles on racks. He didn't comment but kept following his silent guide through a door that opened to a small room with a desk, table, and a few chairs. Giuseppe sat at the desk donned in a flamboyant set of pajamas and robe. Another man sat across from him appraising Bailey the minute he entered the room. The stranger was tall and slim with dark features and bushy eyebrows. His posture was as stiff as a man who never relaxed.

"Bailey Clover, this is my associate Luke Deville."

"Nice to meet you Mr. Deville." Bailey didn't bother trying to shake hands but he tightened his grip on his hat. The stranger's presence made him more nervous. Deville nodded but said nothing.

"Sit down and tell me what you have for me."

"When I got your summons I come right over, sir. I know you'd be wanting this information fast."

"What information is that?"

"I checked on everybody on that there list you gave me."

"And?"

"I'll start with Loretta the hotel maid. She saw some white men coming in the hotel and going in that room the day of the murder. She went to that half-breed detective early one morning probably telling him 'bout it."

"Who were these men?" Giuseppe asked.

"Don't know yet, still working on that."

"I'd be very appreciative of you finding exactly what she saw and who those men were."

"I'll do my best to find out." He glanced at Deville uncomfortably.

"Is something wrong?" Giuseppe asked.

"No sir, nothin's wrong. Next is I found out Bigger Stanwyck is lining up his powerful friends for something but I'm not sure what or against who."

"Never mind him; he's not going to be a problem much longer. What about your ex-employer?"

"Chief Gilbert is a cautious rascal. He's definitely up to something but he's not confiding in his usual buddies this time. For some reason he's staying to himself a lot, they say. One thing I think will be of interest to you is that he's sent off several telegraphs to the feds this month."

"About what?"

"Can't tell because they have a special code that don't make sense to nobody but other federal agents."

"Then how does a police chief get the code?"

Bailey scratched his head. "Yeah, that's a good question. I never thought of that. Maybe since the riot he got it."

"I doubt it. This is a significant piece of information. I want you to dig deeper into it."

"Yes, sir." Bailey was happy Giuseppe seemed pleased. His eyes shot over to Deville, who had been staring at Bailey steadily the whole time. Bailey could feel the man didn't like him but he wasn't sure why. *Is it my color or something else?*

"What about the detective? Dooley." Giuseppe pronounced the name distastefully. "Have you been keeping a watchful eye on him?"

"Well, I been trying but he's a slippery cuss. Can't get much information on him either. He's cagey, that one. So far I got nothing everybody don't already know. He's a loner, except for maybe keeping company with Madelle."

"And she would be . . .?"

"Lady got a boardinghouse outside Greenwood in the country. Nice gal, pretty dainty little church lady."

"Is she Negro?"

"Course she is."

"And they are seeing each other?"

"Well, I think so because they were having dinner together at the Dutch Oven. Looking mighty taken with each other from what I heard."

"Interesting; not very useful at the moment but good to know."

"If you have any dealings with him watch out. He's a sneaky fellow like I said. Had everybody thinking he was something he weren't for a long time. He can't be trusted," Bailey added.

Deville chuckled. "That's rich coming from you, a lousy snitch."

Offended, Bailey stood up. "I'm not a snitch. Mr. Carissi, that's all I know. If there's nothing else I'll be leaving. When I learn more I'll be sure to let you know."

"Fine; Tonio will show you out."

When Bailey was gone Giuseppe wagged his finger at Deville. "I've warned you about intimidating my informants."

"Informants? They're lousy snitches and I hate snitches. I hate colored snitches even more for ratting out their own kind."

"Yes, yes I know all about your high moral standards against snitching and once again I'm not impressed. You're my highest-paid killer, Luciano. You're as cold-blooded as they come and all for a price. Who are you to criticize that man for making a little extra money giving me information?"

Dooley read the telegram twice. It was a surprise but helped untangle at least two events for him. He kept getting the feeling all the things he was working on were connected some way but he couldn't see how. This good bit of news was just the break he needed; a missing piece to a convoluted puzzle that was getting more complicated all the time.

He grabbed his jacket and started out the front door but quickly ducked back inside. Bailey Clover was outside, trying to look casual. Dooley didn't trust him. He waited until Bailey was out of sight and then went out his back door. It was not mere happenstance the ex-deputy sheriff had been lingering around the vicinity of Dooley's agency lately. Dooley was too good at what he did to not know when he was being watched, especially by an amateur. Bailey seldom knew he was spotted but Dooley knew those eyes anywhere. Once Dooley had seen him clumsily dart behind scaffolding on North Franklin. Another time when he caught a glimpse of Bailey ducking into a burned-out shell of a house he sent him on a wild goose chase for two hours. Then there was the time he drove past Bailey's house on Greenwood and waved at him sitting on the porch after he'd got him off his trail four times that day. It was amusing, but he felt something wasn't right, and it wasn't Bailey Clover's inept attempts. He was under surveillance, and a few of Dooley's many eyes and ears informed him someone was making inquiries about him but he couldn't find out why and for whom.

First thing that morning Dooley was informed that Luke Deville got off the train from Chicago and took a cab straight to the Mastermann Mansion. Dooley knew Deville's reputation as a crackerjack killer. He always got his man and he never got caught. He was in high demand in the world of gangland warfare, but he chose his clients wisely because he was Giuseppe's favorite and loyal executioner as well as a distant relative.

Bigger and Jake had never been fans of each other. They tolerated each other at best. Bigger was an arrogant social climber and businessman with a degree of success in both areas. He saw Jake as an underpaid public servant beneath him on all counts. In turn, Jake was a short-tempered, unsuccessfully ambitious man who considered Bigger a married-for-money blowhard he could not abide.

Bigger scratched at his receding hairline waiting for an answer. He looked around Jake's office thinking the city could at least repaper the dingy peeling walls with all the tax money they sucked up each year. Jake was puffing one of his cigars, knowing Bigger detested the smell. "Okay, Jake, you going to do your job or not?"

"I don't need some lah-dee-dah, tree plantin' opportunist like you comin' in here tellin' me my job."

"I'm not telling you your job. I'm asking if you're going to do your job."

"Same difference. I know my job and I do my job without you or anybody else in this dad-blasted town prodding me!" Jake told him.

"I'm not here to make you look bad or tell you your job. This is your territory, not mine and I respect that." Bigger decided it was time to be tactful.

Jake snatched his cigar from between his teeth. "Oh yeah? Then what you here for?"

"I'm here to continue the conversation we had at my house last week. I was glad we both wanted the same thing—to get rid of Giuseppe Carissi. Things appear to be getting worse as far as he's concerned. I'd like to know what you intend on doing about it."

"You come in here telling me Carissi is about to make some kind of move and I'm supposed to have a solution on the spot? You don't know what, when, or how but I'm supposed to do something about it right away."

"Look, Jake, this man is dangerous in more ways than one. You said so yourself. If we're going to get him out of Tulsa or behind bars we have be smart about it. We gotta plan some kind of strategy."

"We? Since when are you part of law enforcement?"

Bigger stood up. "I thought you were willing to put our personal feelings aside so we could nullify this common foe, but I see you're too bullheaded."

Jake huffed and stuck his cigar back in his mouth. "Sit down. You're right. I don't mind saying I need all the help I can get with this." He debated a moment, then said, "I'm telling you this because I think we're on the same team for getting this gangster element out of Tulsa. We got enough thugs and criminals of our own to deal with. We don't need them coming down from Chicago giving us more grief. I'm getting that Gentleman Gi, Giuseppe Carissi, or whatever he calls himself out of my town if I don't do nothin' else."

"Glad to hear you say that. When you do, it will redeem you with your White Glove Society brothers."

Jake shifted uneasily in his chair. "Yeah, well that gangster is my first concern."

"Agreed."

"Now what I'm about to tell you goes no further than this room. It's strictly hush-hush for now."

"Agreed again."

"Half a dozen crates of guns got stopped and confiscated by the feds on their way into Tulsa."

Bigger's mouth dropped. "Are you sure? How did you find out?"

"Never you mind about that. It's the truth, all right. Government agents were sniffing around for alcohol. Got wind of the trucks coming and thought they'd spring a surprise bust, but they got surprised too. Wasn't alcohol, it was guns, two truckloads of weapons."

"That's incredible. Carissi?"

"What do you think?"

"I think this kettle is about to boil over."

CHAPTER THIRTY-NINE

The crash of a door being kicked open jarred Cord from his sleep, but at first he didn't understand what awakened him. Shaking himself fully awake, he heard footsteps coming toward the bedroom. His eyes darted to Scarlett lying in bed next to him, sleeping deeply from her nightly sedative.

He jumped from the bed and grabbed for his rifle when four white men burst into his bedroom. Immediately someone hit him and snatched the rifle. He began swinging his fists but he was punched again and knocked back onto the bed. Scarlett was awakened and began screaming. *"Oh Lord, no!"*

"Shut up!" the short man ordered.

"What you doing in my house?" Cord yelled. "Get out!"

"Shut up, black boy," an unfamiliar voice said. Something about this one was exceptionally dark and evil. He could make out Amos Grapnel, Oscar Belgrade, and Larry Phipps. Cord knew them for the hateful men they were but the fourth man was a stranger to him.

"Cord, what do they want?" Scarlett asked in panic. Cord couldn't answer her but he figured each one of the men had his own diabolical reason for this violent intrusion.

Amos Grapnel stepped forward. "You thought you could put your greasy black hands around my throat and get away with it?"

"The law may be slack on you coloreds since that riot but we ain't," Larry Phipps declared looking at Cord belligerently. He was a tall, lanky, blond-haired man. Scars from burns he had suffered as a child were still visible on the left side of his face. He was a hate-filled individual and people often attributed his volatile behavior on his disfigurement.

Oscar Belgrade said nothing at first. He was a mean-spirited young man who loathed all the Freemans because of a business matter between his own father and Earl, Cord's father. Oscar looked over at Scarlett and grinned. "We're about to teach your man here what happens when you people choke white folks."

Cord sprang to his feet ready to fight to his death. Phipps took his rifle butt and jammed it into Cord's stomach. He groaned loud and fell back on the bed.

Scarlett put herself over her husband. "Stop it, you're hurting him!"

Grapnel laughed. "That's the point, little lady. He almost choked the life outta me and the law hasn't done anything yet so I'm taking matters into my own hands."

"You had no right coming on my land saying what you said," Cord croaked holding his stomach.

Grapnel's face turned sinister. "I'm sick of you high and mighty Freemans."

"Leave us alone!" Scarlett hollered.

"Scarlett, you done gone and got yourself a husband? Don't you remember me?" Oscar said grinning.

She looked at him trying to think.

"You don't remember me?" He threw his head back laughing. "I sure remember you."

"Shut up," Cord growled. He assumed he'd been one of her clients.

"Freeman, you just love yourself some trashy women, don't you?" Grapnel said. "This here one is worse than your first wife. What is it with you and them low-class females?"

"I said shut your mouth," Cord warned sitting up glaring at Grapnel. "She has nothing to do with this."

Phipps frowned. "You don't tell us to shut up, boy. You don't tell us anything."

The stranger watched with interest but didn't speak or make a move.

Tears rolled down Scarlett's face as she clung to Cord. "Why are you doing this to us?"

Oscar smirked. "Don't cry, little miss. It won't hurt nearly as bad this time. We were all liquored up before but we're sober now."

Scarlett's face lit up in fearful recognition. "You, you were one of them. One of the men who attacked me!"

He grinned. "Glad you finally remembered. My feelings got hurt that you didn't know who I was."

Like a shot, Cord yelped and lunged off the bed, pouncing on Oscar. Three rapid blows were all he got in before a pistol blow to the back of his head stopped him. Another rifle butt in his side caused him to fall over. Grapnel kicked him in the side and added a punch to his head. They snatched Cord off Oscar and commenced to pummel him with blows. Oscar scrambled to his feet.

"Leave him alone!" Scarlett screamed.

Oscar snatched her away as she tried to get to Cord. "You come here, sweet thing. I want to reintroduce myself to you."

"Nooo!" She slapped at Oscar, clawing and struggling to get away from him. He hit her, and tossed her onto the bed. She sprang right up, determined to get free. "Cord, help me," she cried not knowing if he heard her, or was unconscious. "Lord Jesus, help me please!" She begged Oscar, "Please don't do this to me again, please!" Oscar knocked her to the bed again, pawing at her nightgown and grinning as he unbuckled his pants belt.

A gunshot blasted through the air, causing all four men to stop in motion. Earl Freeman stood in the doorway pointing a rifle at the stranger whose long knife he'd pulled out was aimed at Cord. "Drop it, mister, or I'll blow a hole in you right now." Earl moved sideways but kept the rifle aimed. The stranger dropped the knife. "Now step back from my son. Back. Way back over against that wall where I can see you."

Dooley stepped in, pointing his pistol at Oscar. "Get away from her," he ordered. "I'd like nothing better than to pull this trigger." Oscar instantly moved back, his mouth open. Dooley moved farther into the room and helped Scarlett up. She ran to Cord, who was lying limp and barely conscious on the floor.

Larry Phipps lifted his rifle but was shot in the arm and dropped it before he could get it in the air. Billy Ray stood in the doorway scowling at him menacingly. When Billy Ray's eyes met the ominous stranger's, an indescribable feeling came over him.

Grapnel's eyes bugged at first then narrowed. "You again!" he barked. "I'll see you dead yet you big, overgrown—"

"Not today you won't." Jake Gilbert passed through the doorway, his gun also drawn. "All you intruders drop your guns and don't move an inch. These fellas are just itching to shoot somebody and I might not be able to stop them."

Phipps's rifle was on the floor already. Amos didn't move. He could see the other two officers behind the chief.

The police chief put his hand inside Amos's jacket lapel and took a gun from a shoulder holster. "That means you too, Amos. You think I forgot you carry this?" Jake addressed the stranger. "And who are you?"

The man didn't answer.

"That's Lucky Luke Deville," Dooley said.

"Who?"

Deville looked at Dooley contemptuously.

"Luciano Stephanos Deville or Lucky Luke Deville, as he's known in Chicago."

"Chicago? You mean he's the—"

"Yep, he's Gentleman Gi's favorite hired killer. And second cousin on his mother's side." Dooley looked at Deville. "This is small potatoes for you, isn't it? Beating up harmless ranchers and ravishing their wives. That's not your usual kind of job. What are you doing with these yahoos?"

Deville still didn't answer but curled up his lip.

"You know this man?" Earl asked.

"Our paths have crossed a few times."

"Git over there, all of you!" Jake ordered, lining them against the wall next to Deville. The two officers stepped into the bedroom pulling out handcuffs. Earl and Billy Ray went to Cord.

Scarlett had his head in her lap crying.

"Are you all right?" Earl asked touching her hand gently.

She looked up at him, surprised at his genuine concern. She nodded and looked down at her husband's bloody face. Cord's eyes were swollen shut, one already puffing up. "I thought they were going to kill him," she told Earl, giving in to her sobs. "Thank God you came."

"Son, can you hear me?" Earl asked. Cord made a slight nod. "Thank the Good Lord, you're alive."

Chief Gilbert and the officers finished cuffing the hoodlums. "What have we here? Plenty of charges to go around. Breaking into a man's house in the middle of the night, attempted molestation of his wife, threatening folks with firearms and . . . oh yeah . . . destroying property. You practically took that door off the hinges."

"How did you find out?" Amos grumbled when Jake handcuffed him from behind.

"Don't worry about that."

"This is it for you, Jake Gilbert. You might as well kiss your career goodbye. You've sided with these coloreds one time too many. You'll regret interfering in our business and going against your own kind."

The other two policemen looked at Jake curiously.

"You fool; you ain't my kind and you don't scare me, Grapnel."

"Maybe I don't but I bet Giuseppe Carissi will."

The gentleman gangster hurled his posh new vase filled with late season Heirloom Roses across his bedroom. "That does it!" he said menacingly. "That police chief has got to go! He dares to put my cousin in one of those lousy jail cells of his? He's got the gall to arrest Luciano and deny him immediate release! Who does he think he is? No two-bit cop is going to hold my man against my will and get away with it! I don't care if he is head of the police! I'll show him what it means to cross Giuseppe Alonzo Carissi. First my arms shipment gets confiscated by the feds, now this! Gilbert has got to go! He's done!"

Ada wasn't used to sleeping late in the morning. Her schedule was rise and shine at five thirty every day. Being unemployed didn't change that habit. Her hens were extra noisy this morning, and she found their clucking annoying. She knew she was easily irritated in recent days. She was fed up crying over Jake and weary of fuming about Kate firing her. What bothered her most was that she didn't know why her former employer discarded her so abruptly with no real explanation. Ada had exhausted every possible reason from intoxication to insanity but none would satisfy the gnawing suspicion that it was something else. Some more obvious reason that she'd overlooked.

Nothing had turned out right for Ada, but then why should it? She had been deliberately living in sin. Why should the Lord bless her when she was so wicked? "God don't bless no wicked children," she said to herself and sighed. She finished collecting eggs and turned to leave the henhouse. She felt a hand across her mouth and someone taking the basket of eggs out of her hand. She screamed when the hand moved to put the thick burlap sack over her head but a husky voice said, "Shut up or you'll wish you had, lady."

Fear clenched her heart and she couldn't make a sound. She heard two male voices, white men she was sure. She was pushed into a car. As the car drove she found the courage to ask, "Who are you? What do you want with me?"

One man brusquely responded. "Never mind who we are. We know who you are, that's all that matters."

"But I don't have no money!"

"We don't want your money, lady."

"Then what you want with me?"

"We don't want anything from you but cooperation if you want to keep living. It's your boyfriend we're after."

"I'm a widow woman. I don't have no—" Ada stopped when a horrifying thought hit her mind.

"Widow, huh? Well, you're going to lose your boyfriend too."

"Wha—what boyfriend? I don't have no man friend. I told you I'm a widow woman. You got the wrong person."

"Quiet, we don't want to hear anymore. We know who you are and whose colored good-time girl you are."

"I ain't no good-time girl," Ada protested.

"Oh no? What do you call it then?" The one man was laughing.

"Maybe she thinks the chief of police is in love with her," the other man said joining the laughter.

Ada learned what she needed to know: that Jake was the reason for her abduction. "What you gonna do with me?"

"Keep you on ice till your boyfriend comes across. Don't you worry."

"Come across with what?"

"I said shut up, enough with the questions."

Dooley quickly moved south on Archer Street to the new three-story Beyers Building that replaced the two-story Woods Building destroyed in the riot. He lingered in the doorway pretending to look inside the glass door. He gazed at the horizon that had once been hidden by tall buildings. Slowly the corner of Greenwood and Archer was coming back to its former life of prosperous commerce although many buildings had not been replaced yet. Remnants of brick buildings and tall electric poles lined the streets like banners of defiance. It was obvious the community survived and would revive, even surpass its previous splendor.

When Jake reached the corner in front of the Williams Building he looked around, then used his key and went inside. Five minutes later Dooley crossed the street and did the same thing. The two men didn't speak when they met. A silent nod was the greeting as they walked through the building, checking each floor. After they reached the top and started back down they spoke. "I got your message. What's wrong now?" Dooley asked.

"Why'd you bring that Matthias fella with you to Freeman's house the other night? You know he's a suspect to me, even if it ain't official yet."

"I was at the Freeman ranch with Billy Ray when I got the

message they were going after Cord. I took who was available. Besides he's a crackerjack shot, and I told you he didn't kill Jordan Franks."

"I ain't convinced."

"Okay, I just might have something here that will convince you." Dooley took a telegram out of his pocket. "I was going to show this to you after I had more facts, but now is as good a time as any."

Jake took the paper and read it twice before looking at Dooley's cocky face. "This ain't no real proof he didn't do it."

"You want him to be guilty, don't you?"

"I want the killer caught. That's what I want."

"Then this gives you more than enough reason to throw suspicion on someone else if you're trying to get at the truth."

Jake looked down at the paper again. "Yeah, it makes me wonder all right, but I need more than wondering. I need proof."

"You said you need proof to arrest Billy Ray, but you already got your mind made up."

Jake folded the paper. "Get me proof about this, and your boy is off the hook. It's that simple."

"The FBI knows what it's talking about. What more proof do you want?"

"That's pure circumstantial. It won't hold water in court. I got nothing to link them to Franks here and now."

Dooley took the telegram from Jake and put it back in his pocket. "I was trying to avoid this, but it's time you talk to someone who might convince you otherwise."

"Who?"

"You'll find out tomorrow night. Meet me here at 8:00."

"Why so late?"

"Trust me; it's safer."

CHAPTER FORTY

FRIDAY OCTOBER 13, 1922
3:30PM

Maurice Willows Hospital at 324 N. Hartford Street was an indispensable antiseptic hall of healing after the riot. Its small size was enlarged and staff increased with concerned professionals pouring in from across the country including the very diligent Red Cross workers. Since then the hospital had a steady influx of the sick, malnourished, and injured citizens of Greenwood District.

Cord's broken ribs and head concussion landed him a stay at Maurice Willows although it was against his will. And against her husband's wishes Ella was determined to visit her older son at the hospital. "Sit down, honey, you look weak," Earl insisted.

"I'm fine, Earl. Stop fussing. It's Cord who needs looking after." She took Cord's hand. "How do you feel, dear?"

"I'm all right, Mom. You didn't have to come here. I'll be okay." He tried to turn over but it was too painful.

"I wanted to come. I couldn't rest knowing what they almost did to you. What they did do to you is bad enough, but Earl said . . ." her voice trailed off as she looked at Cord's bruised, swollen body. "Never mind, it's over now and when you get out of here you're coming home to recuperate."

"No, that's not necessary. Scarlett can look after me."

"And she will . . . at our house."

Cord looked at Scarlett and then at his father. "That's all right. We'll be fine."

"Your mother's right. You should stay with us for a while after you leave here. You and your wife are more than welcome. We both want you to stay until you're fully back on your feet."

Surprised, Cord looked at Scarlett. "What do you want to do?" he asked.

"I'll do whatever you want us to do," she said softly.

"I won't have a minute's peace if you're not at the ranch with us," Ella threw out quickly.

Cord smiled and shook his head. "Okay, Mom, you win again. We'll come for a short while, just until I'm moving around a little better."

"Good. Now since that's settled, Scarlett can go home with us this evening. She's been here two days without sleeping in a real bed." Ella looked at Scarlett sympathetically. "You must be exhausted. Tonight you go home with us and get some rest. You can come back tomorrow. Cord is in good hands, and we have two men coming to stand guard duty again tonight."

"Thank you, but I need to stay with Cord."

"Why, he'll be fine in here."

"I—I should stay with him."

Cord reached for Scarlett's hand. "It's all right, honey. Go with my folks and get some rest. You look beat and you need to take care of yourself."

"I don't want to leave you," she whispered.

Scarlett looked at Cord for a brief moment with the same frightened stare she had in the sanatorium months before.

"Maybe it'll be better for her if she stays with me."

"I won't hear of it," Earl said, standing up. "That gal needs some sleep in a bed, and she needs a decent meal." He placed his hand on her shoulder looking down at her. "You're family now, and we Freemans take care of our own. Don't you worry. I won't let nobody hurt you again. No woman ought to ever suffer what you went through. You'll be safe in our home. You got my promise. I'll see to it."

Ella tried to stand up but wobbled. She closed her eyes and held her head. "Oh, my, something's wrong." When she opened her eyes, she said, "I—I can't see! Lord help me, I can't see!"

"What's wrong?" Earl asked, taking her hand.

"Earl. I can't see a thing and I feel . . . " Panic shot across her face just before she collapsed.

6:00 P.M.

Benny was frantic when she arrived at Maurice Willows Hospital. She'd been making plans for the modest wedding ceremony when Pastor and Josephine Matthias told her Ella had collapsed at the hospital. The first thing she saw when she entered the waiting room was Ethan's anxious face. "Thank goodness they found you," Ethan said, jumping up to hug his sister.

"Where's Momma? Is she going to be all right? What happened?"

"Sit down."

Benny looked back at the Matthiases and sat shakily in the nearest chair. "What's wrong?"

"It's the tumor. It's growing much faster than they anticipated."

Benny closed her eyes at the discouraging news. "Where's Momma? I want to see my mother."

"You can't now. They're taking tests and prepping her. They told me we'll be able to see her for a few minutes before the emergency surgery."

Her eyes flew open. "Surgery! They aren't supposed to operate yet! It's not scheduled for three weeks! The specialist from Baltimore isn't here, is he?"

"It's too serious now. They can't wait three weeks for Dr. Peebles to come. They said it's too risky to even wait till morning. They have to operate tonight."

"Why?"

"If they don't do it now . . ." Ethan took a breath. "Mom might not make it. She's already lost her vision. The tumor's growing and pressing hard."

Benny broke down in tears. "How could this happen all of a sudden?"

Ethan patted her shoulder as he tried to console his sister, but his own emotions were hard to contain. "It's going to be all right; it's got to be. Billy Ray's brother and another doctor are performing the surgery."

"But they're not the experts on this new surgical procedure." Benny wailed, trying to regain control of her emotions.

"Napoleon is a highly regarded surgeon and he's worked under this Dr. Peebles before. He told us he knows the procedure well and that Dr. Hedley is a specialist in this neurosurgery field. They are both very good doctors. We have to trust them. We have no other choice."

Benny moved her head from Ethan's shoulder. "Where's Daddy?"

"In Cord's room or at the chapel, I guess."

"Why aren't you in there with Cord?" She sniffled, wiping her face.

Ethan frowned, but didn't answer.

Benny snagged his suit jacket sleeve and started tugging him out of the waiting room. "You're going to drop this ridiculous grudge you have against Cord. You both have been secretive about whatever happened between you, but it's time to patch things up. Do you realize we almost lost Cord the other night? He's your brother and you haven't come here to check on him once."

Ethan pulled back. "You told me he was doing all right. That's good enough."

Benny grabbed at his arm again, moving him along. "No, it is not good enough. Now you listen here, Ethan Freeman. Whatever you have against our brother, let it go. We're family and we always stand by one another no matter what. That's how we were raised and you know better than to act like this." She stared at him for a moment. "Momma is in here fighting for her life and Cord was viciously attacked in his own home. He could have been killed by those men the other night. How much more do you need to happen to this family to wake you up? We need God on our side. We need the Lord on our side all the time but tonight more than ever and *you* need God too."

"I know."

Benny's love for her brother rose in her heart and healing tears came to her eyes. "Then behave like you do. Reach out to your brother and forgive him or ask for his forgiveness. Whatever you have to do, but get it done. Our family needs to put our own interests away and come together and ask God to help Mom."

"You're right, sis." Ethan stopped pacing and flashed a big smile at Benny. "You know what, I think Billy Ray is rubbing off on you."

"I sure hope so."

8:15 P. M.
WILLIAMS CONFECTIONARY
GREENWOOD AVE. & ARCHER ST.

Jake was uncharacteristically jumpy, a bad omen for him. He prided himself in being able to handle any situation coming his way but the stakes were considerably higher all of a sudden. He kept looking out for Dooley. It wasn't like him to be late. Something was wrong. He was praying Dooley was not in trouble for a number of reasons, the first being Ada. How did they find out? He was angry with himself for not covering his tracks well enough. He switched on the light and sat on the steps in the stairwell. He pulled an envelope out his shirt pocket. It was lavender-scented and he knew the handwriting. Opening it just to kill time while waiting, he read the note on the feminine stationery.

I would very much enjoy your company for dinner this Sunday at 4:00. It would serve you best to accept my invitation in order to maintain your sterling reputation.

Kind regards,
Kate

Jake blinked at the strange summons. It didn't sound at all like Kate, and the vague remark about maintaining his reputation further befuddled him. He folded the note and stuffed it back in his pocket. He had too much to deal with to waste time with Kate and her foolish romantic fantasies. Dooley's not being there was unnerving him more.

What if Dooley's been setting me up all along? At this point Jake was hard-pressed to trust anyone. When he heard the door unlock he peeped out into the hall. Dooley and a woman were coming his way. He was both relieved and uncertain.

Dooley darted into the stairwell looking worried.

"You're late." Jake dispensed with civilities.

"I think we were followed."

"By who?"

"Maybe Bailey Clover."

"Oh, him."

"Just found out he's on Carissi's payroll."

"Dang it, that gangster's got his tentacles everywhere!"

The woman looked distracted and out of breath. She stared at Jake suspiciously. He'd seen her before but couldn't place where.

Dooley was breathing heavily too. "Let's go into the office and lock the door so you can get your breath, Loretta, and tell the chief what you told me."

The conversation was brief but revealing. Dooley was ready to leave when Jake said, "Not yet. We've got something real important to deal with, something more personal." Jake looked at Loretta. "Would you mind waiting for a few minutes?"

"I done tol' you all what I saw. Can't I go home now?"

Dooley said, "I promise I'll see you safely home in just a bit but give the chief and me a few minutes."

"All right, but hurry, I don't like being in this place at night hidin' and skulkin' round like a thief. I don't want no trouble cause I'm just a washwoman and hotel maid. I ain't tryin' to get hurt 'bout this business." She folded her arms across her chest. "Humph, I wasn't gonna come at all but you was so persuasive." She turned to the chief. "He talked me into it. He even talked Purdy into lettin' me come. Can't many folks talk Purdy into much a nothin'."

"Mrs. Fennimore, your safety is important. Believe me, we need you to stay safe and I aim to see that you do," Jake reassured her.

"All right then, I'll wait a spell while you talk but not too long."

When Dooley and the chief came out of the back room they looked more grim than when they went in. Dooley hurriedly took Loretta's arm and they started toward the hall door. "Let's go out the back," Dooley suggested. "Once I get her home we need to meet a guy who can help us find her."

They walked down a long hall and through another door leading to another long hall. Suddenly they heard voices and the back door shut. They huddled behind an oversized machine and waited.

"Cut the light on," someone hissed.

"Why, you want the world to know we're in here?" another fired back with an irritated whisper.

"There aren't no windows in this room. They can't see from outside. Cut the light on, we need to see where we're going."

"Follow me. I don't need a light. I see the light from the hall under the door. Just follow that."

"I'm not fumbling round here in the dark. Cut the dang light on."

"C'mon, let's just find Dooley and get out of here."

Dooley stood up straight. "Jack?"

"Dooley?" Jack responded in a low voice.

"Hey, Dooley is that you?" Rodney called louder.

Dooley stepped from behind the machine and put on the light. "What are you two doing here?"

Chief Gilbert and Loretta moved into view.

"How'd they get in here?" the chief asked. "Does everybody in Greenwood have a key to this building?"

Dooley chuckled. "Only my most trusted associates."

"We came to warn you. Carissi and his men are headed this way."

"For what?"

"Not sure, but they know you and the chief here are in cahoots and they want him bad. Plus they snatched a woman for some reason but we're not sure why they did that."

Dooley cut a quick look at the chief.

Loretta looked at Dooley alarmed. "Who is this Carissi fella I keep hearin' bout?"

"Gentleman Gi, the Chicago gangster," Rodney answered back. Jack nudged him.

"You mean that criminal fella in the newspaper who moved here from Chicago?"

"Yeah, that's the devil," Chief Gilbert growled.

Loretta's expression showed her quickly elevating level of panic. "What have I got myself into?"

"Let's get you out of here," Dooley said opening the back door. They exited from the back door into the open yard and ducked behind two trucks. When they reached the last truck next to the wire fence they saw a car parked on the street in front of the gate with two white men inside they didn't recognize. They hurried back inside. "Maybe we better go out through the front."

"I'll call for some of my officers to get down here pronto," Gilbert said. He went to the desk and anxiously dialed the telephone.

Dooley said, "You two stay here with Loretta. I want to take a look out front."

8:30 P.M.

Billy Ray had been busy all day making plans too, but not for the marriage ceremony. His day was spent interviewing for jobs and looking for an affordable builder to construct a new house for his bride. It would be a surprise for Benny, a wedding present. What she assumed would at best be a farmhouse renovation will be a brand-new home built on their property.

He was tired from so much driving around and wanted nothing more than his mother's home cooking and his bed for the night. He wondered why all the lights were off when he got home. The foyer light always stayed on until the last person went to bed. He sensed something was off. Making his way inside, he called to his parents and got no response. He turned on the lamp on the table in the foyer and read the note left for him on the table. He rushed out the door, knowing Benny would need him.

Just then something crossed his mind with a powerful nudge. He hurried back into the house knowing that when something dropped in his spirit so forcefully he better act on it.

Billy Ray was driving faster than he realized in the dark on a country dirt road. Preoccupied, he was praying for Ella to survive the operation and for Benny's ability to handle the situation however it turned out. When he reached the border of Greenwood District he raced across the railroad tracks. He was driving recklessly, something he never did. His vehicle sped south.

8:45 P.M.
MAURICE WILLOWS HOSPITAL

The surgery had been in progress for an hour and a half. Earl paced from one end of the waiting room to the other. Benny sat quietly staring out a window, occasionally wiping tears. Ethan was beside her. He took his sister's hand from time to time, reassuring her as well as himself that their mother was going to make it through this ordeal. Cord was there in his wheelchair, Scarlett at his side in quiet support. He was in pain, having refused his medication so he could be clear-headed. Pastor Roman Matthias and Josephine were there with the family to offer prayer and emotional support.

"Wonder what's keeping Billy Ray?" Josephine said.

"He should have gotten the note by now," Roman said.

"I know he'll come as soon as he reads it."

Looking up Benny said, "I hope so. I need him here with me. I'm so scared and he's the only one who always helps me feel everything is going to be okay. I need him with me now more than ever."

Josephine went to her. "It's all right, dear. He'll be here as soon as he gets the message. Try not to cry. Ella's in the Good

Lord's hands, and He sent good doctors."

"That's right, Benny, Mom's a fighter. The doctor said she's strong and has a better than average chance."

"I've been so selfish!" Benny wailed. "All I thought about was myself and what I was going through. I never once considered she was going through something. Never took the time to look at her and see she was really sick."

"I didn't either. I never imagined Mom being this sick," Cord agreed.

Earl stopped pacing and looked at Benny. "Even I didn't see how sick your mother was and she's my wife. How do you think I feel? My own wife and I didn't know she was deathly ill. I thought I was a good husband, but I wasn't if I didn't pay more attention than that."

"We all took her for granted," Ethan said. "We were all selfish, Benny, not just you. I always thought she would be here for us. Isn't that stupid? I always thought in the back of my mind she would be here for me as though she wasn't human and subject to—" He choked on the word.

"I talked with your mother when I learned about her illness, and she's at peace with whatever happens," Roman said. "She's ready to meet Jesus if it's her time."

"I don't want her to meet Jesus. I want her here with us!" Benny cried out.

"Of course you do and we all feel that way," the pastor said calmly.

"Ella's not gonna die," Earl insisted. "Stop all this gloomy talk, cause my wife is gonna make it through this and get well. I don't wanna hear no more 'bout folks dyin'."

"Sure she is, Dad, don't get upset," Cord said.

"I wish Billy Ray would hurry and get here," Benny repeated.

8:55 P.M.

Ada was terrified. This was an unreal nightmare. No one spoke to her other than to issue an order. She had been taken from one place and now they were moving her somewhere else. A couple of times she heard bits and pieces of remote conversation.

Jake's name was mentioned more than once. Her heart pounded with fright when she thought she heard them say they were going to kill him. As angry, hurt, and scared as she was, she couldn't help fearing for his life and praying for his safety along with hers. Lately she'd been praying more earnestly than she had for a long time, and right now she was more desperate than she'd ever been in her life. Ada was terrified about what these men might do to her but just as distressing was the thought of what they might do to Jake. She blamed him for her abduction and she bitterly resented him for ending the relationship; yet she still loved him.

"Cut out that crying! I'm tired of hearing it," one of the men barked.

"Where are you taking me? What do you want with me?"

"We already told you; it's your boyfriend we want not you. You're just leverage."

"I told you I'm a widow and I don't have no boyfriend!"

"Shut up with the lies. We know you're making cozy with the chief of police," the other voice growled.

"That's not so. That man ain't studying me, he's sweet on my employer."

"And who might that be?"

"Miss Kathleen Boswell. At least she was my employer before she fired me."

"We know all about the decorating lady too. She's the one who clued the boss in on you sneaking around with a white man."

"She what? I don't believe it. She couldn't have."

"Who do you think squealed about you and the police chief?"

It all fell together for Ada in one miserable flash. The love affair with Jake Gilbert had caused all the grief she'd been experiencing. Somehow Kate found out, but how? Ada sank down in the backseat of the vehicle, feeling more wretched than ever, fearing her punishment for her sins might be worse than she could have imagined. Her life and Jake's were in jeopardy.

Only God could step in and stop this tragedy but why should He? The tears came in floods now. She just knew it was hopeless.

9:00 P.M.

The automobile veered toward the ditch before Billy Ray could gather his senses. Not paying close enough attention he had instinctively snatched the steering wheel in a quick effort to avoid the stray dog walking in the middle of the road. He rolled over some metal rubbish and blew two tires, sending the car careering down the ditch. It finally bumped to a stop when it hurtled into the exposed roots of an old oak.

Billy Ray sat for a minute and rested, collecting himself. The dog barked at him, then approached the vehicle and whined, as though offering sympathy. He raised his front paws to the window.

"You trying to say you're sorry, ole boy? Yeah, me too; you're not half as sorry as I am." He moved cautiously as he left the car because the ditch was deeper than it had looked. His ankle and shoulder hurt, but nothing seemed to be broken. Looking at his vehicle in the poorly moonlit ditch he shook his head. The front passenger's corner was crushed against the tree trunk, headlight and all. Carefully and painfully climbing up out of the ditch he saw the ragged construction material that caused the blowouts. He looked around at his surroundings. He was just across the county line into the border of Greenwood District, so he started limping up the road with his new furry friend straggling alongside.

CHAPTER FORTY-ONE

9:12 P.M.

The intersection of Greenwood Avenue and Archer Street was getting crowded with automobiles and people just standing around; people who were evidently not locals. The section's business district had long closed. This stretch of Greenwood Avenue was usually empty and quiet with a few strollers passing by or cars rolling through. Tonight there were cars lining Archer Street and Greenwood Avenue on both sides of each street. Dooley knew there was going to be big trouble. Carissi was being bold and letting him know he was coming after them.

"Come with me," he told Jake. "We're going to have to fight our way out of here."

"We's gonna die in this place!" Loretta wailed, grabbing Dooley's arm.

"Not tonight we won't. You stay here with Jack and Rodney. I'll be right back."

When Dooley and Jake returned five minutes later they were lugging a heavy crate. Jack lifted the top up and peeked inside.

"These are brand-spanking new tommy guns. How'd you get these?" he asked with an admiring grin.

"They're part of the confiscated shipment taken from Carissi's trucks."

"But what are you doing with them?" Rodney wondered. "I thought the FBI got all of it."

"I figured we were going to need something equal to what these gangsters are using. Hand guns, shot guns, and rabbit rifles won't stand up against a gang of Chicago hoods and their weapons. Carissi was importing some of the most up-to-date weapons available into Tulsa. So I unofficially helped my FBI buddies with inspection for the report and the reloading. I kept a couple of crates just in case."

"And they let you?" Rodney said, mouth agape.

"Sure, they know what we're up against with Carissi moving in. Naturally they turned their backs so they couldn't be implicated."

"All this going on right under my nose and I didn't know a thing about it," Jake grumbled.

"You know about it now and a good thing you do. Looks like real trouble outside. Come with me and help bring in the ammunition."

Loretta's eyes were closed and her lips moving nervously whispering prayers.

Dooley looked at her feeling a twinge of guilt for bringing her into harm's way. "Don't you worry, Loretta; I'm gonna get you out of this and safely back home to Purdy, so help me."

"It'll take the Good Lord Jesus to get all a us outta this," Loretta said.

Dooley grimaced. He didn't depend on Jesus to help him. He'd learned better long ago. "Yes, ma'am, but it'll take some action in addition to prayin' to Jesus to help us now. Can you handle a gun?"

"Yeah, I shoots Purdy's gun and I hunt rabbit from time to time, but if you mean one of them things, goodness no. I wouldn't know what to do with one of those fancy machine gun things."

Dooley pulled out his ever-present pistol. "Take this and be careful. It's already loaded."

"I'll sure take it, but if the Lord ain't with us, all the guns in the world won't do any good."

"Beg your pardon, ma'am, but I've gotten out of tighter spots than this without God's help. I've survived a lot and God had nothing to do with it," Dooley said with conviction.

"And just what makes you think He didn't?" she asked, lifting a brow.

"I know He didn't because I thought of ways to get out of my jams myself, or something happened in my favor to help me get away. It was good fortune, not God. I was just plain lucky I guess."

"Let me tell you something, Mr. Dooley. What you call good luck, good fortune, or you thinking up ways is all God. Folks love to take credit for what God does."

"Not everybody is so lucky," Dooley retorted.

"I'm a lot older than you, son, and I done seen a lot of suffering in my time. Nothing else but my Lord has kept me to this day and that's why I'm here alive and able to say it." Loretta looked at the doubtful faces around her.

Jake said, "I understand what you're sayin, ma'am, but some folks who loved the Lord ain't alive to say He carried them through because He didn't. They're dead, like my wife."

"And my folks," Dooley added.

"Know what I believe? God carries folks then too. Ushers us right on up outta here."

Jack said, "Well I'm not in the mood for getting ushered nowhere tonight. C'mon Dooley and let's get that ammo before Carissi's men get restless."

Giuseppe's car rolled up to the east side of the Byers Building with three men accompanying him. The proud peacock was disgruntled as he stepped out of his fancy new automobile. The dapper dresser was suitably accessorized—an expensive cigar hung from his mouth, and his tommy gun was tucked under his right arm. The other two cars near the corner had six men total inside. One man from each car got out and walked toward their fearless leader, both sporting similar weapons.

"You sure they're in there?" Giuseppe asked.

"They're there, all right. We got them covered front and back. That black snitch of yours told us he followed that Dooley fella here and actually saw him go inside with some old woman," a chunky dark-haired man told Giuseppe.

"And where is Bailey Clover?"

"He ran tail when he found out we were moving on the building, the coward."

"Just as well; he can't be trusted in my opinion."

"What we doing here? I thought we were busting Lucky Luke outta jail, Boss." The speaker was short and thin with a way too big hat on his head. His eyes darted about all the time. That annoyed Giuseppe about Pauli but he was the most daring man he knew. Pauli could walk into a barrage of shooting bullets and brazenly spew profanity with no hesitation. Many said he was insane but Giuseppe preferred to call him audaciously courageous.

"We'll get Luke soon enough but first I want that double-crossing half-breed and that ignorant hillbilly of a police chief eliminated." Giuseppe pulled the cigar out his mouth.

"Sure, Boss, but that'll bring the feds down on you real hard killing a police chief and ex-FBI agent."

"And I'll buy them off from the top like I always do. It'll just cost a little more, that's all. Federal, state, local, private . . . a cop's a cop in my book and they all have a price." Inside his car Ada Crump remained, blindfolded and terrified.

9:15 P.M.
KATHLEEN BOSWELL'S HOUSE

Kate was scared and regretted what she'd done. How could she have been so foolish as to tell that criminal about Jake and Ada? Now she was afraid of what he might do to Jake . . . *and at her request!*

As she slathered cold cream over her face and neck, she told herself she shouldn't think about it anymore, but she couldn't help thinking about everything. Little else had occupied her mind for the past week. So many thoughts churned through her mind . . . the look that crept across Gentleman Gi's face when he learned about Jake's indiscretion . . . Jake holding Ada in his arms as she longed for him to hold *her*. Their passionate embrace kept replaying in her head. She thought about the warmth of his kisses and how they must have made Ada feel . . . Ada and her insignificant colored self. *How dare she revel in pleasures that should be mine!* She wiped the cold cream off her face with angry swipes, declaring her vengeance out loud. "I'll never forgive that black witch for what she did, never! I won't forgive Jake either and I'll make him pay for humiliating me like that, I will." She looked at her rejuvenated skin with satisfaction and smiled at her reflection. She was feeling better now. Of course Gentleman Gi wouldn't do any real harm to Jake. He'll just put the fear of God in him, and that will be enough to make him more agreeable in seeing things her way when they met on Sunday. She climbed into bed and switched off the lamp anticipating a future with Jake, a rejected and distraught Ada standing outside a window watching. A smudged window.

CHAPTER FORTY-TWO

9:25 P.M.
GREENWOOD AVENUE AND ARCHER STREET

The five of them crouched beneath the plate glass window in the Williams building. Loretta kept Dooley's gun right next to her as she prayed. Jake was impatient and looked out the window every few minutes to see if his men were coming.

"Don't you worry, ma'am, my officers will be here any minute and put a stop to this. You're gonna be okay," he assured the trembling woman.

"Wish they'd hurry and get here," Rodney said.

"Yeah, what's taking them so long?" Jack wondered aloud.

Dooley shot Jake a look.

"What are you thinking?" Jake asked looking visibly worried for the first time.

"Your officers should be here by now, don't you think? Who'd you talk to?"

"Officer Riggs and Sergeant Cavendish, he's the one at the front desk."

"Is he trustworthy?"

"Sure, I think he's a good man."

"Are you certain? Even good men can be bought sometimes."

Jake smacked his hand against his forehead. "Dang it, I didn't think about him being in Carissi's pocket!"

"You never know who you can trust," Dooley said.

"So the police aren't coming?" Jack asked.

"We're going to have to shoot our way out of here?" Rodney's face went pale. "We're outnumbered. How can we make it even with these tommy guns? They have five times as many weapons and men. We're doomed." He looked at Loretta's alarmed expression. "Lady, if you got any pull with God now is sure the time to use it."

"Riggs is a good officer, I know he is," Jake said. "I don't worry that he's on the take. He'll come through for me."

Just then they heard the unmistakable sound of multiple vehicles roaring north up Archer Street. Dooley stuck his head up looking and grinned. A dozen cars loaded with armed men were converging on the intersection with horns honking.

Jack looked out and said, "Whoa, that's not the police. Who are they, more of Carissi's crew?"

Jake rose up and narrowed his eyes then smiled. "No, they're not Carissi's. Like I said Riggs is a good cop. I told him to rush word to Bigger to gather some of the White Gloves that are on his side and get down here for a showdown."

"You mean they're the good guys?" Rodney asked, sounding relieved.

Dooley sighed in relief. "I wouldn't call them the good guys exactly, but for our purpose right now, yeah."

"Thank You, Jesus," Loretta said.

"I'm with you, lady," Rodney said smiling. "Thank God and nobody but God."

Raised voices started flying back and forth but sounded muffled from inside the building.

Dooley saw Bigger Stanwyck hoping off a truck with four men carrying rifles. "What's he going to do?"

Jake looked up. "Blast that stupid blowhard. They can't go up against them gangsters like that. They'll get massacred."

More of the dozen cars were parking on the east side of the Williams Building and the west side of the Byers building. Dooley saw that Carissi's gang east of the Byers building had to go through Bigger's men to get to them. Bigger and Carissi started having words, still a nonviolent standoff at this point.

"Maybe it's time I showed myself and handle this situation," Jake said standing up.

"If you want to get mowed down by one of those gangsters, go right ahead," Dooley replied.

The voices in the street got louder.

"We can't stay in here forever. Somebody's got to go do something before Bigger gets—" The first single shot rang out before the chief could finish his sentence making him duck back down. Several followed. The pandemonium could be heard with yelling and the deadly rat-a-tat of tommy guns.

"You wanted to do something, now's the time. We gotta help them. Take an extra gun and ammo and come on." Dooley crawled to the crate nearby. "You start loading these things, and we'll try to get them to the men."

Rodney looked out the window and saw two men fall to the ground as a little man moved forward spraying gunfire. People were dodging behind vehicles and poles or whatever they could.

Dooley crouched by the front door and hollered back. "Loretta, I know you're a praying woman and though I'm not convinced it's worthwhile, I'd be obliged if you said one for me."

"For all of us, ma'am; I believe there's a God even if He doesn't listen to me most the time," Jake said crawling to the door.

"Get as many guns ready as possible and set them by the door. Rodney, you watch the back end. Jack the front and keep Loretta in the middle. Stay low and you know what to do if Carissi's men get through." Before opening the door Dooley hesitated. "You ready?" he asked Jake.

"Let's go."

Each with one gun aimed to fire and another to pass on to Bigger's men, they moved cautiously but swiftly out the door.

Ada struggled with her bound hands to push herself farther down in the backseat when she heard the first shots. The sound of gunfire terrified her, and the shouting voices increased her fear. She could hear the painful cries as shots found their targets. The men in her car soon abandoned her to join the mayhem.

"Stay down if you don't want to get hit," one of the men said to her. She heard his gun firing even before she heard the door slam. *Lord, Jesus, help me! Stop this madness, please! Don't let them hurt me or kill Jake!* Ada prayed and cried for herself and for Jake who she still helplessly loved.

Harold Campbell was behind his car when he saw Jake and Dooley exit the building. They ran toward him, ducking behind an electric pole where Smitty Evers lay dead, riddled with bullets. Handing Harold a tommy gun and giving the other to Asa Hargrove next to him, Jake said, "There's more inside; if you can get the men to move nearer we can slide them out to you."

"I'm going back and get more. Cover me." Dooley passed off his other gun and ran back toward the front door without waiting for a response. Jake and Asa watched, alert, until Dooley made it safely back inside. Jake motioned to Bigger who was across the street behind a big metal box used by construction crews.

Jake noticed White Glove members battling a gang stronger and meaner than they were. He recognized some of the same bloodthirsty men who had been part of the riots. Now they were back in Greenwood again but not to destroy the colored population; this time it was to run Giuseppe Carissi and his men out of Tulsa.

9:45 P.M.
MAURICE WILLOWS HOSPITAL

Surgery always drained Dr. Napolean Matthias, and this particular procedure was one of the longest and most difficult he ever performed for several reasons. His exhaustion was apparent as he went to the family waiting room to speak to the Freemans.

Earl jumped up. "How's my wife?"

Napoleon hesitated, looking at all the eyes beseeching him for good news. Earl was looking at him like he was about to burst. Benny's eyes were red and Ethan sat frozen as if bracing himself for bad news. Cord was leaning forward in the wheelchair obviously weak and in pain but bearing the discomfort. Scarlett sat beside him gripping his hand, watching him with noticeable devotion. Napoleon glanced at his parents and at Ella's husband and children, and said, "She survived the surgery, I'm happy to say," and was rewarded with relieved sighs and smiles.

"Praise God," his father said.

Earl looked at Napoleon's face. "What's wrong?" he asked seeing Napoleon hesitate.

"We found there was more damage than we anticipated after we got in there. Damage to the parietal lobe was worse than we thought it would be. It was spreading very rapidly for some reason. We think she's had this tumor a lot longer than her symptoms indicated."

"She's complained about bad headaches for years," Ethan said standing up moving next to his father.

"That would be consistent with what we found." Napoleon shifted his eyes from Earl's. "Dr. Headley will come explain things in more detail if you care to wait an hour."

"But you said she survived," Cord said.

"She has. Miss Ella's very strong, thank goodness. Many people would have succumbed on the table."

"Then what's wrong?" Earl repeated.

"There's still a chance she might not make it," Napoleon answered truthfully. "What happens in the next forty-eight to seventy-two hours is crucial. The swelling in her brain needs to stop increasing and hopefully decrease significantly or the skull will not be able to withstand it. If it doesn't I'm afraid . . . "

Benny began to weep.

Cord said, "You're telling us that after all this she could still die."

"I'd be less than candid if I said otherwise, but I think she has a good chance. As I said, she's strong."

"She's gotta make it," Ethan murmured.

"That's not all," Napoleon said solemnly. "The immediate dangers are the swelling and chance of infection, but even if she recovers there's no telling what her condition will be."

"What do you mean?" Josephine asked.

"There are many functions that could be affected by the tumor, the surgery, or the temporary swelling of her parietal and occipital lobes. There seems to be some swelling of her frontal lobe as well."

"I don't know from all this medical talk, son. Spell it out plain so I can understand what's going to happen to my wife," Earl begged.

"Yes, sir. Understand that with the grace of God it's possible Miss Ella could heal and come out of this in fine shape. Better than she's been in years, I'm hoping, but as you know this kind of surgery is mostly uncharted neurological territory. We just don't have a lot of experience with patients who survive such extensive and extremely delicate surgery. We were blessed to have been able to help her as much as we have. Too many people in her situation die without any chance for recovery." Earl's shoulders slumped. "I'm telling you this because I want you to know we did the very best we could for your wife, Mr. Earl. Whatever happens, I need you to believe that."

"I do, son. I know you did all you could."

"We all know you did," Cord said, voice breaking.

"Can you give us some specifics?" requested Earl. "So we can be prepared for what might come?"

"She could be blind for the rest of her life," Napoleon said bluntly. "We have no way of knowing until the swelling goes down. It's pressing the optic nerves right now but that could rectify itself. She could lose motor function." He looked at Earl's confused face. "Be unable to walk or be paralyzed in some other of her limbs. There's also a possibility of her being subject to severe seizures. A loss of cognitive function . . . she may no longer have the ability to think or speak normally," he clarified glancing at Earl.

"I had no idea all this could go wrong," Josephine whispered almost to herself.

"The brain is a very important organ. It affects everything our bodies do. You should know that Miss Ella knew the risks. We discussed it."

"Well, nobody discussed the risks with me," Earl objected. "Neither you or her ever said a word to me about all this."

"She chose not to let her family know because she wanted to spare you all the added worry." He faced Earl directly. "I said nothing because I did as your wife asked. She was adamant that if she died during the operation there was no reason for you to hear all the possible scenarios of what could happen. Only if she survived did I have permission to tell you. Those were her wishes, sir."

"So what happens now?" Ethan wanted to know.

Napoleon put his hand on Earl's shoulder. "We wait."

"It's in the Lord's hands now, so we pray and we wait," Scarlett said softly.

The pastor looked at her in surprise and nodded. "Yes, young lady, you're right. We wait on the Lord to move and until He does, we pray."

10:00 P.M.
GREENWOOD AVENUE AND ARCHER STREET

The ten minutes' reprieve of gunfire was not a reassuring time for the combatants. The streets were splattered with blood, vehicles riddled with bullet holes, as opposing sides regrouped to devise strategies. During the breather, the wounded were pulled to safety and tended to; the bodies of the two dead security guards were dragged out of sight. Greenwood and Archer had become a war zone again.

The streets were smoky but quiet as each side waited for the other to make a move. Bigger Stanwyck found his way inside the Williams Building with a few of his men restocking their ammunition.

"Be careful with those things," Rodney cautioned.

"We know what to do," one of Bigger's cohorts snapped.

Bigger did not relish being in Dooley's company. He wasn't too happy with Jake Gilbert at the moment but he was glad to see the cache of improved weaponry. "Carissi must be desperate to pull something crazy like this against the police," he said.

"And just where are the police?" another White Glove member asked looking at Jake.

Approaching motor sounds could be heard through the shattered glass of the plate window.

Bigger looked up from his position on the floor. "Carissi's bringing in more thugs," he growled then stopped. "No wait . . ."

Dooley peeked out from his cover and said quietly, "That's the police."

Jake moved to the side standing up and looked outside. "It's Sheriff McKinney with some officers."

Four police cars and two wagons were rolling up the street, slowly driving to the construction site before shots were fired. Following that was the succession of rapid gunfire of automatic weapons. McKinney's men were shooting as they leaped from their vehicles. Carissi's men fired back while retreating back to the east side of the Byers building. The men inside the Williams Building went back out carrying more tommies, ready to battle again. This was a new kind of warfare for Tulsa; one fraught with fancy-dressed enemies using fast-shooting weapons.

CHAPTER FORTY-THREE

10:30 P.M.

The gunfight had been quick but intense. More dead men were lying in their own blood on the street. Giuseppe Carissi was like a madman, a vengeful, foul-mouthed maniac having emerged from the dapper, tea-drinking gentleman. His men kept him covered, but he never passed up a chance to shoot off his mouth or his gun.

"You're a dead man, Jake Gilbert!" he roared repeatedly. "You and that mongrel cohort of yours are both dead!"

"Not if we get you first!" Dooley shouted back.

"You're all dead! Do you hear me? Dead!" Giuseppe's eyes were wild with fury. He stepped boldly in the middle of the intersection. "Hey, McKinney, you want to live. Then make a deal and let Luciano Deville out of that jail cell, and you and your men can walk away from here right now."

Sheriff McKinney was in over his head. He had no idea what he was walking into when he'd answered the call to help the chief. He was no gangster, and automatic guns were beyond his ken. He looked at Jake, desperate for direction.

"You can't trust him," Dooley said, reading McKinney's thoughts.

Jake frowned at the sheriff. "No way do we let Deville out. He's a cold-blooded killer, worse than Carissi. They killed four of our officers out there. You wanna let them get away with that and release that murdering hoodlum?"

McKinney was sweating profusely. "We got to do something," he said.

"Not that, we don't," Jake replied unequivocally.

Bigger interjected. "We aren't making any deals with that scum, McKinney, so forget it. We've got to show these hoods we mean business. If we don't, they'll try to take Tulsa over just like they're doing Chicago."

"What difference does it make who takes over what if we're all dead?" McKinney rejoined.

"Don't be such a sniveling coward," Bigger ordered.

Jake stood towering in front of his wavering sheriff. "It's gone too far to turn back now. We're taking this to the end, and when it's over somebody won't be standing."

"He just wants that man let out of jail, right? So let's give him what he wants and deal with him like we want later," McKinney suggested desperately.

Jake and Bigger shot knowing looks at each other.

"Look here McKinney, you get paid to uphold the law and I expect you to do your job, not think about releasin' criminals."

"Well, what about it, sheriff?" Giuseppe yelled. "Do you get wise and release Deville, or die with the rest of 'em?"

"He's insane," Bigger said.

"He's the devil himself," Loretta whispered to Jack.

"What about you, Gilbert, ready to be reasonable? Let Luciano out and make peace."

"Not a chance, Carissi!" Jake yelled, his hatred for the man intensifying.

"You're nothing but a stupid, backwoods copper!" Giuseppe countered bitterly.

The quiet interval following Jake and Giuseppe's angry exchange was used to try to predict the gangster's next move. Something was going to break soon.

Loretta's prayers were accompanied by the sound of shooting outside of the broken window. She did not want to shoot anyone, but she had Dooley's pistol and was ready to defend herself. She had to do whatever necessary to be safe and get home to her beloved Purdy. Keeping busy helped her not panic. She found a first-aid kit and some hard candy; her nurturing spirit helped her administer first aid to their injured men. The color line faded fast in this hour of dire need and common cause. Like soldiers in a foxhole everyone did what they could to help one another and stay alive. She patched up White Glove members, not knowing who they were, and they were grateful for her tenderness.

The policemen outside waited for orders from Sheriff McKinney or Chief Gilbert. Bigger's men stood in ready for a word from him. Just as the the Byers Building clock gonged at ten thirty, a commotion began outside. Giuseppe was standing boldly in the middle of the intersection. The policemen were poised to shoot him down but would not dare without orders. The gangsters were aimed to barrage the police and Bigger's men on the other side of the street with bullets at the slightest hint of their fearless leader's peril.

Giuseppe hollered, "Hey copper! You in there, Gilbert, the big brave chief of police, I got something out here that belongs to you! Come look!"

Jake peeked out the window and groaned. "Ada."

Dooley looked out and pounded his fist. "That rat's using her to draw you out."

Bigger looked at the sobbing colored woman struggling to break free of the cords that bound her and asked, "What's he doing? Who's that woman?"

"Her name's Ada Crump," Jack answered, teeth clenched.

"What's she got to do with you, Gilbert?"

"She's someone he knows." Dooley spoke up quickly.

Jake hesitated, choking down his mixed anger and fear. Resenting the curious faces he spoke low. "I know her real well."

"Oh yeah, so this bum thinks he can get to you by holding your cleaning woman," Bigger chuckled.

"She's an innocent person who shouldn't be caught up in this any more than Loretta here," Dooley replied testily.

"That's a good point now that you mention it. Just why is she here?" Bigger eyed Loretta suspiciously but directed his question to Jake instead of Dooley. He might have to deal with Dooley for the time being but he didn't have to like it or chitchat with him.

"Never mind about her now," Jake said brusquely. "She's not the one being held by Carissi." His head was whirling with the fact Ada was in danger. Danger he had put her in by loving her and not being careful enough. She looked so helpless and frightened he wanted to charge out the door and take down Carissi and every one of his men single-handedly. Good sense took immediate hold, however.

"At least we know where she is now," Dooley pointed out, looking at Jake's reddening face and standing up, blocking him from making an impulsive dash out the door.

"I gotta get her outta this," Jake muttered to himself almost oblivious of his comrades listening to every word.

"What's all this about?" McKinney asked looking at his boss confused. "I thought they just wanted that Deville fella let lose. What's she got to do with Deville?"

"Shut up," Jake growled.

"She seems all right for the moment, probably scared out of her wits, so keep that in mind. Don't make any rash moves," Dooley advised calmly.

Jake continued to stare out the window. One of Giuseppe's men was holding on to Ada roughly. "He's gonna pay for this."

"We've got to be smart how we handle this. If we're not, she's dead and so are all of us." Dooley kept his eyes on Jake's face. He could see and feel the man's rage mounting.

"I want that polecat dead." Jake spoke flatly.

Bigger shuffled gripping his gun tighter. "We all do."

Loretta spoke up. "I beg your pardon, sir, but I don't wish death on no living soul. Mean as folks has been to me and my people I still don't wish death on them. I pray for them to change their wicked ways but not that they die."

"Oh yeah, well what if they don't change?" Jack asked. "What if it's you or them like it is now. Giuseppe Carissi ain't changin' his ways for nobody, so then what?"

"Then I keep praying for the Good Lord to step in and either change that man's heart or help us outta this fix."

"Look out there," Dooley said with a wide sweep of his hands. "Do you think the Good Lord is listening?"

"We got dead folks lyin' in the street, lady. Ain't no time for religion," Bigger scoffed.

"Yes, sir, you's right, ain't no time for religion but it sure is time for Jesus to step in."

Dooley flinched but didn't speak. In the face of such danger it impressed him how such devotion was garnered at a time like this. He was amazed that Loretta's initial panic had somehow been pacified by her trust in Christ, which seemed to be her anchor in life. Recognizing it as the same faith his parents had, in a flash he revisited those horrible memories. "Hope you aren't let down," he murmured.

CHAPTER FORTY-FOUR

10:45 P.M.

T he pastors sensed in their spirits that something was wrong.
Reverend Metcalf had felt an urgent need to initiate strong
prayer against some forceful evil and violence in Greenwood,
and had requested his fellow clergy to join him for prayer at his
church from eleven o'clock to midnight.

Everyone was present except Pastor Matthias, who they hoped
was on his way to the church from the hospital.

"There is something in the air this night, amigo," Father
Montoya said as soon as he reached Butterworth Avenue with
Rabbi Snellenberg.

"I heard there is some kind of commotion up near the railroad
tracks, but no one knew exactly what was happening."

The priest's forehead wrinkled with momentary worry. "It is
God's will to keep this place safe, I think."

"I certainly hope it is, my friend." They continued to the
church.

"But I think we should not wait until we reach the church. We
should pray now and all the way to our destination."

"This is your last chance, Gilbert! Come out here and face me
like a man or leave your lady friend's fate in my hands. What'll
it be?"

"Lady friend? I thought she was your housekeeper," Bigger said watching Jake's face closely. "What's really going on here?"

"Stay out of this. This is between me and him." Jake balled up a fist.

"Don't go out there. He'll kill you and maybe her too." Dooley stepped closer to Jake.

"If he kills me, take him down but I can't leave her at his mercy."

"We can fight them but—"

"He'll kill her! Don't you see, that animal will kill Ada."

"Lord Jesus, please come by here right now," Loretta whispered.

Jake glanced her way and looked back out the window. Ada had been pushed down on her knees, and though her sobbing was almost inaudible, he could see her body shaking. Giuseppe stood beside her, smiling cruelly, as he looked over at the window. He couldn't make out exact images but he knew Jake could see Ada, and Giuseppe relished having the upper hand. Having guns aimed at him by the men on the other side of Greenwood Avenue meant nothing to him. He wasn't fazed by the eyes trained on his every move. He knew they wouldn't shoot first and he knew it would be a bloodbath those Tulsa greenhorns would lose. Giuseppe had been in worse spots in Chicago against seasoned gangsters. These amateurs were no match for him and his guys.

"Don't do it," Dooley said, knowing his advice was offered in vain.

"I don't have a choice," was all Jake said before opening the door.

"Are you insane?" Bigger yelped as Jake went out, stepping onto the street. "You would put your life in the hands of that gangster for some colored cleaning lady?"

Dooley dropped to his knees by the window lifting his tommy gun muttering, "Never can tell how much of a fool a man will be for a woman."

Loretta had reloaded the pistol. She crouched beneath the waist high window's broken glass with her lips moving in quiet prayer but her grip was tight on the weapon. Rodney and Jack were silent, aiming their tommies straight at Giuseppe's flank-ing gunmen.

Giuseppe grinned, seeing the tall chief of police defeated and coming slowly toward him. "Tell your men to back off," he ordered.

Jake froze for a moment, then looked at Ada still on her knees. She had stopped crying when Giuseppe told her Jake was com-ing out.

"Jake, he'll kill you!" Ada cried. "Go back!"

Jake turned to face his men. "Put your guns down," he ordered but no one moved. "I said drop your weapons now!" he commanded. Men lowered their arms and some of the officers relaxed a bit but none of them completely let go of their weapons or took their eyes off the gangsters. He turned back to face his nemesis. "This is between you and me, Carissi; let her go. Tell your men to pull back and let her go."

As much as Giuseppe disliked Jake Gilbert, he had to admire his courage. Without blinking he held up his arm. "Drop your aim, fellas. This is personal now and it's between just us two."

Tonio started to speak. "But Boss what about—"

"Do as I say and nothing more!" Carissi yelled. "No one does anything until I give the order. Here, take her over to the car." He lifted Ada to her feet and Tonio shoved her toward the car.

"You're supposed to let her go," Jake protested.

"Don't worry, cowboy, she won't be hurt if you don't pull any-thing. Move over here," Giuseppe instructed.

Jake moved to the left keeping his eyes pinned on his foe. He could see Ada out of the corner of his eye being pushed inside a vehicle. For two minutes it was eerily quiet at the Greenwood and Archer intersection. No conversation took place between Jake Gilbert and Giuseppe Carissi. Carissi wasn't about to give up Ada. She was his ace, a bargaining chip that had paid off. Jake said, "I'm telling you for the last time to let her go."

"You tell me nothing. You just listen and do as I say. Don't worry about your colored girl. I have morals and I don't hurt women . . . unless I have to." Carissi pointed his tommy gun downward. "Get on your knees, big guy."

"What?"

"You heard me. Get down."

Jake stood motionless.

"I won't tell you again." Giuseppe's eye went dark.

Jake turned around and looked at the side window of the Williams Building. He could barely make out any distinct figures in the dark but he knew they were in there watching as were his officers on the street along with Bigger's White Glove allies. Filled with shame and self-loathing, he went down on his knees.

"Good, you're not as stupid as you look. Now one last chance, are you going to let Luciano out of that jail or do I have to use you to get them to set him free?"

"It won't work. They won't let him go no matter what you do to me. They have my orders not to release Deville for no reason whatsoever. He's a wanted killer in three states."

Giuseppe looked back. "Not even for her?"

Jake froze. "Please, let her go," he repeated his voice low.

"So you'll make a bargain, an exchange of sorts." Giuseppe grinned.

Jake's head dropped.

"Answer me! I'm tired of this game! Luciano goes free and then I release the little lady. Agreed?"

The tension in the silence was palpable. Finally Jake spoke.

"Agreed." The word stuck hard in his throat.

A smile crept across the gangster's face. "Good. Now that I have humiliated you, made you agree to compromise your official authority, and tampered amusingly with your personal life . . ." He laid his tommy gun on the ground and pulled out a pearl-handled pistol. "I'm satisfied your reputation is sufficiently destroyed. So I can get rid of you without you becoming a martyred hero for doing your duty. You die a cowardly traitor to everything you're supposed to stand for!" Carissi pointed the pistol at Jake's head.

Fear caught Jake's breath and he closed his eyes. Asking God for forgiveness and mercy, he heard two successive shots sing out into the night like cannon fire shaking his thoughts. Jake realized he was still conscious. His eyes shot open in time to see a large male dive quickly behind the empty parked ice wagon, a dog running after him. His eye shifted to Giuseppe's changing expression. The gangster's smirk dissipated as his skin went pale and the pistol slid out of his hand to the ground. Jake quickly grabbed the falling pistol and rolled off, crawling for cover. He didn't stop to see Carissi drop to the ground.

Pauli yelped like a madman and came running up. Rapid tommy gunfire started playing a deafening symphony with rifle, shotgun, and police machine guns returning in chorus. Soon everyone was shooting in total pandemonium. The noise was almost ear shattering. Deadly disorder erupted as enraged gangsters shot their way toward their fallen leader and pushed forward some more in a blaze of vengeance. Assuming Jake had been shot, a hyped-up and infuriated Bigger burst from the Williams Building spewing obscenities from his mouth and bullets from his weapon. Dooley looked with mixed emotions when he saw Bigger fall as his body was riddled with a barrage of bullets. Police officers rose up from their stooped and hiding places shooting at the oncoming attackers. It was a nightmarish and bloody confrontation.

"Give 'em everything you got!" Dooley shouted. "If they get in here we're all dead!" With that he crawled toward the door rising up enough to aim and bring down two armed thugs as they advanced near the building.

"This is a massacre!" McKinney screamed, his eye bugging as he pumped bullets from the corner of the broken glass window. Suddenly he yelped as a bullet whizzed by and grazed his extended arm.

Rodney was speechless pointing his tommy gun with his eyes squeezed shut. Jack jumped up cursing and moved his weapon left to right hitting anything and anyone in its path. "Open your dang eyes!" he yelled at his friend. "This ain't no time to get too scared to look!"

"Oh, Jesus!" was all Loretta called out, readying herself for whatever happened next.

"No time for Jesus!" Jack screamed. "Shoot that thing out this window!"

Just then the rear door to the room was kicked open and the two gangsters who were parked at the rear of the building burst in and shot Jack two times in the back. "Lord, help us!" Loretta cried swinging her pistol around fast and shooting one of the men in the chest. "Jack!" Rodney shouted and fired at the other gangster who leaped behind the desk in the back of the room. One of Bigger's men crawled toward the desk. Wedging himself sideways he stood up. The gangster appeared from the other side with tommy gun aimed out to shoot. Bigger's man pointed his weapon down at the desk and sprayed gunfire until the other man dived out from the side catching several bullets.

"Hurry, two men go and guard that back entrance!" Dooley yelled. Two tommy-carrying White Glove members scurried out the rear door toward the back. Rodney and Loretta were hovering over Jack. Rodney kept talking to Jack and crying. Dooley picked up another loaded tommy to cover them, hoping against hope Jack would somehow survive.

CHAPTER FORTY-FIVE

11:00 P.M.

With desperate maneuvering Jake made his way to the car Ada had been shoved into. He stopped for a second when he saw the few bullet holes on the front side of the vehicle. Now brandishing a dead gangster's weapon, he snatched the door open fearing the worst. Ada was lying on the floor, still blindfolded, hands bound. "God please," was his simple but sincere prayer. He reached for her.

"Get away from me!" she screamed trying to thrash around.

"Ada, it's me, Jake." His voice was raspy with emotion. "I won't hurt you, honey."

Her movements stopped but she didn't speak. She was trembling and confused. He removed the blindfold and sat her up, and they listened to the racket not far from them. When he started untying her hands, he said, "Thank God you're all right. I don't think I could stand anything happening to you."

Ada stared, speechless, feeling the slow tingle of reviving circulation as she moved her free arms. She looked into Jake's sorrowful eyes, thankful to be alive and equally grateful that he was also. When she couldn't hold it in any longer, she flung her arms around his neck and wept, telling him how much she loved him.

"Oh, darlin', I never stopped lovin' you, never. I'd die a thousand deaths to keep you safe," he said. In one swift move he scooped her up, exiting the car. "Pray, honey. Pray to Jesus we can make it out of this."

A succession of vehicles came barreling one way toward the shootout. More came up another way surrounding the intersection. Armed local and federal lawmen disembarked ready for action. The shooting was sporadic; more men down than up at this point. The remaining gangsters surrendered without much resistance. With its litter of human bodies, fragments of shattered glass, and bullet damage all around, Greenwood and Archer once again looked more like a battlefield than a city street.

George Barry had been a federal officer for over ten years but never had he seen such a sight on a city street in his career except for the riot. He watched his men search for the living among the fallen. He heard the moans of the injured and he saw the blood-soaked clothes of the fatally wounded. He spotted the chief of police walking toward him by the Williams Building carrying a woman.

Officer Mendel shouted to Barry, "We found this one hiding over here holding this weapon! Should we take him in?"

Barry turned to see Mendel walking beside a male Negro with a scraggly dog following him. "Who is this guy?" Barry asked.

"Says he got into a car wreck and was just walking to town when he got caught up in the shooting," Officer Mendel answered.

"What's your name, boy?"

"His name's William Ray Matthias," Jake said loudly. He stopped and looked at Billy Ray hard. "He's not involved in this mess. He's the son of a preacher. Leave him be."

ONE WEEK LATER
TULSA POLICE HEADQUARTERS
AND ADMINISTRATION BUILDING

"You willing to testify at a hearing?" Jake asked a jittery Bailey Clover.

"Yeah, I reckon so if I have to. Do I?"

"Most likely, you will."

"You know this is gonna put me in a bad position."

"You don't say," Jake responded indifferently.

"It's serious business, rattin' out Carissi."

"You got a conscience now? You never had one before."

"Did you forget Carissi's a cold-blooded killer?"

Sheriff McKinney dismissed his objection. "Carissi's dead."

"But the rest of his gangster family ain't. They might wanna retaliate."

"Then you shouldn't have gotten involved with him," Sheriff McKinney said unsympathetically.

"You don't say no to a man like Giuseppe Carissi," Bailey defended.

"Not if he's paying you a whole lot of money." Dooley tried to control his dislike of the man.

"Okay, tell me again what you know," Jake said.

"I done told you twice already."

"Tell us again; wanna be sure you ain't lying just to cover your sorry self." Jake leaned back.

"It's no lie, Chief. Carissi ordered that musician fella's murder."

"Why?"

"I told you; in Chicago he had a colored maid his family was real fond of. She was with their family for years. This maid had a granddaughter who was the pride of her family because she was the first in the family to go to college. That musician man got hold of her in college and did something to her."

"Did what?" Dooley asked.

"Like I said before, I don't rightly know but whatever it was she had a nervous breakdown and did herself in over it."

"So you want us to believe Giuseppe Carissi had Jordan Franks killed because he's so loyal to his colored maid." Jake's tone was skeptical.

"That's right, but it wasn't because he was loyal to no maid. He had planned to get the guy while he was in Chicago but Franks hightailed it out of town right after the girl's suicide, and Carissi was mad about that. He never saw or heard about

GREENWOOD AND ARCHER

him again until he was spotted in Tulsa."

"Wait a minute; that doesn't make sense. Franks traveled all over the east for years and was in a lot of newspapers because of his musical skills before he moved to France. Carissi could have gotten to him plenty of times if he wanted," Dooley reasoned.

"Do you think Carissi reads colored newspapers and keeps up with colored singing choirs?" Bailey countered nastily.

"Okay, so he spots Jordan Franks in Tulsa and then what?" Jake demanded.

"He didn't spot him. One of his guys did and told him. Then he gives the order to finish what was intended years ago."

"Who did he send?" Dooley asked.

"Lucky Luke, who else?"

"He didn't get here till after the murder."

"That's what they wanted you to think," Bailey said, smiling. "He snuck into town and snuck right out afterwards. Then he came back with a grand entrance wanting to be seen. It was all planned."

Dooley nodded. "I wondered why he was so open about arriving here on the train when he knew he would be spotted and watched."

"Who was with him when he killed Franks?" the sheriff asked.

"I think Tonio was, and the one they call Pauli. He's a real odd one, that Pauli fella, crazier than Lucky Luke if you ask me. They were both there."

"And just how did all this information come to you?" Dooley asked suspiciously.

"I'd rather not say," Bailey muttered, dropping his head.

"Well then, who can corroborate what you're telling us?" Jake asked.

"Folks could be in danger if I tell who told me. Besides I heard a few comments myself that made me suspicious and I fished around with the house staff and found out but I promised not to involve them."

"You mean his hired help just up and confided in you?" McKinney asked.

"Not for free. It cost a pretty penny to get but it wasn't my money, it was Carissi's cash"

"What do you mean his cash? Are you saying he paid you to spy for him and you ended up spying on him instead?"

"That's right. I had to get something to protect myself just in case. He was a gangster, for cryin' out loud. "

"Okay, if your sources can't be used, then who can we get to tell us whether or not this story of yours is true?" Jake asked.

Bailey frowned. "Pauli's all shot up, ain't he? Is he going to make it?"

McKinney answered, "Looks like he will, which is surprising considering the shape he was in."

"They all know what happened and why. They can tell you anything you want to know if they have a good reason, like saving their necks."

"That tall one who was always with Carissi is in jail. The feds want him after we're done with him."

"That's Tonio; get the truth out of him. He can tell you everything I said and more. He was Carissi's right hand from what I could see."

"It's not goin' to be easy. Those men are usually loyal. They don't betray their own," Dooley said looking accusingly at Bailey.

Bailey paused for a moment, then shot a crafty look at the chief of police and sheriff. "This solves that big murder case for you, doesn't it? Makes you look real good, and with you standing up to Carissi and his gang your reputation should be well established. So since I did you a good turn maybe I can be reinstated deputy sheriff again?"

"Reinstate you deputy sheriff? You ought to be glad I don't throw your slimy troublemaking hide behind bars," Jake snorted in reply

When Sheriff McKinney and Bailey Clover left the chief's office, he and Dooley rehashed the details of what they'd been told. Neither trusted Bailey very much but they believed the information because Bailey was scrambling to avoid trouble after his brief but widely known association with the gangster. He was scared for several reasons. He knew the Carissi family was suspicious of him. Lucky Luke Deville didn't like him, and he was well aware of it and terrified. He also feared reprisal from Dooley and from the long unforgiving arm of the law now that Giuseppe Carissi was dead and his surviving cronies were in custody.

"Well, at least this clears Billy Ray," Dooley said cocking an eye. "Right?"

"Yep, with what the hotel lady saw and what Clover says, it's pretty clear he had nothing to do with Jordan Franks's murder. What still bothers me is that no one else at the hotel saw the men but your little lady."

"Don't assume that. Somebody else had to see them come and leave. Several white gangsters coming through the hall of that hotel attracted attention, you can bet on it. I think folks were too scared to say anything after the murder."

"Either that or they were paid not to talk. Whatever took place your friend is no longer a suspect."

"I told you he wasn't capable of doing something like that. He's not the monster you think he is."

"You're probably right. I've been thinking about it since I realized he saved my life. He's the person who shot Carissi, you know."

"I know. He told me about it and he's torn up about killing a man even if it was Carissi."

"So why did he do it? It couldn't have been to save *my* tail. He risked his hide doing what he did."

"Instinct, I guess. He thought no one was going to stop Carissi from blowing your brains out. He saw a gangster getting ready to kill an officer of the law."

"Amazing that after all that happened he would react to keep me alive. I would think he'd be glad to see me dead."

"That's because you don't think like Billy Ray does. I don't either, most people don't. He's a special kind of person. I can't explain it."

"I guess it's cause he's a preacher's son."

"It's more than that. I can't quite put my finger on it. I admire the man, but he's a mystery to me."

"I expected to die last week when I gave the orders not to shoot. I was going to be a target anyway, so I had to at least think about Ada."

"I wouldn't have let it get to that. My gun was trained on Carissi and I was seconds from blasting him myself when Billy Ray took him down. Your orders didn't mean anything to me. I was going to stop him from killing an officer of the law in cold blood."

Jake grimaced. "Should I thank you or dress you down?"

"It's your choice but a thank-you will do."

"How about since there's a deputy sheriff job still open you fill it? This department and Greenwood District could use someone like you in it."

"Are you serious?"

"Very."

"You know they won't like it. You're going to get a lot of heat if you put me on the police force."

"I don't care. I'm on my way out anyway."

"You voluntarily resigning?"

"That's the story I'm sticking to, but truthfully I'm being squeezed out after this term. I'll be looking for new employment courtesy of the mayor and a few other city officials and yeah, some of those White Glove members too."

"Sorry to hear it. I guess it's on account of Ada."

"This has been coming for some time, before the shootout, even before the riot. It was bound to happen eventually. Believe it or not, few people actually caught on to the truth about me and Ada or if they did they're not saying."

"How is she after what she went through?"

"All right, I guess. I've only seen her twice since then. She was pretty shaken up but she's a strong woman. She'll get over it . . . I hope. She'll get over me too, I'm sorry to say."

"Maybe it's for the best." Dooley tried to be consoling.

"That's what I keep telling myself but I don't feel so great about it if it is. I miss her. She was real important to me."

"Life is a lot sweeter with a good woman in it, isn't it?" Dooley said, thinking of Madelle.

"A whole lot sweeter, but that's over for me and I have to accept it."

Jake's downhearted face touched Dooley deeply. "Are you sure about that?" he asked.

"Yeah."

"I'm sorry; I wish things could have worked out for you two."

Jake looked at Dooley unsure. "You mean it?"

"Yeah, I do. I know what my father and mother suffered because they were of different races and it's wrong in every way. They loved each other and were devoted to each other, I'm sure of that. Yet they died because of it. If a man and woman love each other and want to be together they should be able to in peace, no matter what color they are."

"Not in this country they can't, as long as we have antimiscegenation laws on the books," Jake said sourly. "Do you know they even prosecute the person who performs the ceremony?"

"Maybe one day all this will change."

"It won't happen in our lifetime," Jake predicted. "Things would have to change awful fast around here and it won't. Meanwhile there's no hope for Ada and me."

"You could leave Tulsa and move to a state where it's not illegal. My folks got married in spite of what people thought or said and in spite of that law."

"Yeah, and look what happen to them. I wager not one man was charged for killing them either. It was unlawful for the races to mix, but that doesn't justify murder in my book. Tell me, do you ever think they were foolish for getting together knowing what could happen?"

Dooley looked reflective for a moment. "I did for a long time, but not anymore."

"What changed your mind?"

"I realized what they did was because of the deep love they had for each other, it was stronger than their fear. Them marrying was more brave than foolish. I guess I inherited that courage from them but I use it in a different way. Isn't that how change occurs; some brave souls take it all on their shoulders and suffer society's backlash? That's what my folks did to be together, stood against the world." His voice cracked.

Dooley's display of emotion made Jake uncomfortable. He cleared his throat and said, "About God, I think I'm settled on that now. I prayed to Jesus with no hesitation when I thought Carissi was going to shoot me and the Lord was merciful. I prayed again that Ada wuld be alive and unharmed and He blessed me again. I know I should be dead and so should Ada. There was no other way we weren't killed and then survived that hailstorm of gun fire like we did. I asked God to keep Ada safe and she prayed every minute I was carrying her. She kept crying for Jesus to help us."

Dooley's face hardened. "That doesn't necessarily do any good. My parents begged Jesus for help, but He didn't."

"Are you sure?"

"What is that supposed to mean? The Klan murdered them," Dooley reminded Jake.

"The way I see it is maybe now they can be together in a way that doesn't condemn them for it; a life together with God. A life they don't have to be afraid about so they're better off in a way."

"So if you and Ada had died last week you would have been better off?" Dooley's voice had an edge.

"Ada said God didn't bless us being together because we were not married and we sinned. She really believes that."

"Do you?"

"I don't know, but maybe she's right."

"Yeah, maybe what Billy Ray tells me is right too."

"I'd hate to think our being together wasn't right with God cause no matter what, I love her and I know she loves me."

"So where does that leave you and her?"

"Nowhere, like she wants it, and I have no choice but to respect that."

Daniel Patrick Dooley didn't respond. He felt the antimiscegenation law was absurd. In the midst of his jumbled thoughts shone the bright light of Madelle. Theirs was a joyful relationship he wanted very much to grow.

Jake was miserable without Ada in his life. Looking ahead to a future without her destroyed his hope of every being really happy again.

The two men sat quiet for a while; Jake puffing his pungent smelling cigar thinking about Ada; Dooley staring out the window, his mind racing in a combination of unrelated thoughts. They both ended up with their minds in the same place, pondering the jumble of events that culminated into a violent crescendo at the intersection of Greenwood Avenue and Archer Street just one week before.

MAY 30, 1923

I t was a Wednesday afternoon, and instead of the usual bustling pursuits of construction and commerce, Greenwood was out in celebration.

A joyful Decoration Day parade came marching down Greenwood Avenue, made up of veterans of the Great War. White and black soldiers in military uniform marched proudly and in unison with the spirit of national oneness. Most of the Greenwood District was in high emotion because the next day would be the second anniversary of the race riot. Yet hope, healing, and brotherhood were thematic rivals to thoughts of the tragedy.

Tulsa still continued to operate as two distinct entities within one city. The clerics' effort to unify churchgoers was a very small step toward a much larger goal, but it was a positive step nonetheless. Weary of the violence and racism, more of Tulsa's citizens than expected joined in the celebration for Decoration Day and Unity Day, which had grown to Unity Week.

Bishop Harlan Darlington was officiator for the Decoration Day program, which honored all Americans who died in military service. He stepped up to the podium proud to be associated with his friends, other men of God.

"Dear friends and neighbors. It is with great joy I welcome you all to this commemorative celebration of our fallen military. Let us bow our heads in thankful prayer that there are those willing to sacrifice all so we may live richer, safer, and more meaningful lives in this country and around the world," he began.

Loretta and Purdy were at the corner in the back of the crowd near the public phone booth. She looked around watching all the people milling about in a flurry of excitement, but her mind drifted back to the terrible shooting and to her aiming to kill. The memory haunted her sleep at night.

Across the street, Deputy Sheriff Daniel Patrick Dooley stood in the crowd next to Madelle, holding her hand. He wasn't sure what lay ahead, but he anticipated deeper commitment and an emotional steadiness he hadn't experienced since childhood. The torturous dream didn't come much anymore. Now he dreamed of Madelle and their future together, and that suited him just fine.

Looking back he spotted Rodney standing off from the crowd. His sad eyes affected Dooley every time he saw them. Rodney still mourned his fallen friend, Jack, whose death was a loss he found hard to handle.

Kate fingered her expensive pearls, wishing it were time to go home. She wasn't enjoying being around a crowd of both white and black people all watching a parade and listening to speeches together. She hadn't wanted to attend, but her new husband, the chief of police, insisted he had to make an appearance. Jake looked around anxiously, hoping to spot Ada. Kate held on to his arm and smiled up at him sweetly, but Jake didn't love her and doubted if he ever could. He was kind to her but it was hard to manage because he knew she wanted more. His marriage to Kate was his final declaration of true love lost and forever gone. He gave up on any chance to regain any kind of relationship with Ada. He settled for financial ease and security and professional advancement with Kate as his wife.

Ethan sat in his automobile in the distance, taking one last look at his hometown and familiar faces before he left for Washington, D.C. A new life awaited him there where his legal aptitude could take him farther than it ever would in Oklahoma. He hadn't realized he would have such mixed emotions about leaving, but he knew he had made the right decision. Scarlett waved at him, smiling sweetly. Ethan waved back. Cord waved too, happily greeting his younger brother he had finally mended fences with. Ethan grinned and nodded, his antagonism gone. He was glad Cord and Scarlett were together.

The Matthias family huddled together on Carolina Street near Michigan Avenue. Napoleon and Phoebe stood in the middle of the crowd with their children in front of them. Josephine was between them holding her newborn grandson, Alexander Matthias.

Earl sat down next to Ella by the window of their townhouse watching the crowds and parade go by. He took her hand lovingly, kissed it and smiled. She smiled. After a long road she was getting stronger. "Honey, why don't you go out to the parade? You love parades. I'll be fine here alone for a little while," Ella suggested.

"I'm staying right here with you. We can see all the parade we need right from this window."

"But I don't need a nursemaid anymore."

"True, but do you need a husband?" He grinned. "I'll go out for a little while when the kids get here. Why don't you come with me?"

"I'll be a burden with this wheelchair since I can't stand very long."

Earl looked at her with tender love pouring out every inch of him. "Stop saying that. I told you you can never be a burden to me no matter what." A knock came at the door. He stood up and kissed her forehead. He was too grateful to have her alive and getting better. God had been merciful and answered his prayer.

Billy Ray, Benny, and their faithful canine companion they named Caesar left the parade and came to the townhouse. Benny was radiant; marriage suited her well. Life with Billy Ray was everything she'd hoped it would be. Her husband of eight months was every bit the patient loving man she needed. The plaguing inhibitions were finally gone. She felt whole again and loved, which helped her become the warm and eager wife she wanted to be.

Billy Ray was in a good place. His life was sweet with a loving wife, a new home, and a stable teaching job. The new school for underprivileged children was being built. He had funds coming in from many well-to-do donors, and a waiting list of needy children from all over the state. The school was becoming a beautiful building on his property and bigger than he envisioned. Even his parents were involved now, and Nappy offered free medical care for all the children.

Later that evening after the parade and ceremony were over and the crowds had dispersed, Billy Ray and Benny walked the District taking in the night air. The street was quiet, though littered with evidence of festivity. They strolled down Greenwood Avenue passing a few others also winding down from the excitement. Several people stopped and patted the fluffy brown dog walking dutifully between them. The dog scarcely left Billy Ray's side since they had met that fateful night. Caesar became a beloved member of the Matthias household and Billy Ray's constant companion.

"We've been through a lot, but look how God has brought us through," Billy Ray said reflectively to Benny. "We went through it but came out on the other end still standing. In spite of everything God has been good to us, Benny."

"You're preaching to me again," she teased.

"Don't start with that again," he replied, smiling.

"But you are; you do it all the time, you preach at everyone . . . but mostly to me."

"Maybe so." I was just saying that after all the troubles and tragedies we are finally married and happy." He put his arm around her pulling her closer. "Our families are safe and the children's home will be opening soon. We have so much to be grateful for."

Benny smiled and snuggled close to her husband. "Let's go home," she said, and the couple walked slowly, strolling in the evening past Greenwood and Archer.

THE END

AND I STILL RISE

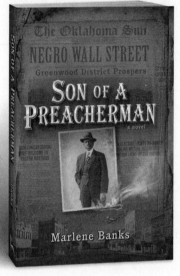

978-0-8024-0618-7

Benjamina Freeman and her family live in one of the most successful African American neighborhoods in the 1920s south —their own wealth a product of hard work, business savvy, and Tulsa's oil boom. Not even strict segregationist policies could hinder development in the Greenwood district.

Billy Ray Matthias, the son of the new pastor in town, is convinced that "Benny" Freeman is the woman God has for him. Benny, on the other hand, is not so sure. But when the infamous Tulsa Race Riot erupts, Billy and Benny find themselves caught in the heat of chaos as their hometown crumbles around them. He vows to keep her safe—will she let him? And will their faith be enough to sustain them amidst deadly acts of hatred?

Also available as an eBook

LIFT EVERY VOICE BOOKS

RUTH'S REDEMPTION

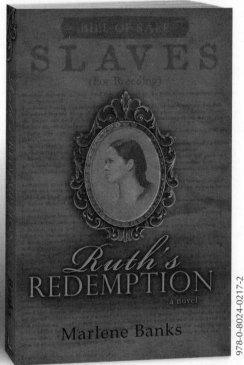

Ruth knows nothing but servitude and brutality since being separated from her mother. Purchased and sold for breeding, her heart is filled with resentment and bitterness. Ruth wants no part of Bo's godly devotion. Yet he's unlike any man she's known. Her experiences with him will leave her changed.

Also available as an ebook

L E V B®
LIFT EVERY VOICE BOOKS

lifteveryvoicebooks.com

Lift Every Voice Books

Lift every voice and sing
Till earth and heaven ring,
Ring with the harmonies of Liberty;
Let our rejoicing rise
High as the listening skies,
Let it resound loud as the rolling sea.
Sing a song full of the faith that the dark past has taught us,
Sing a song full of the hope that the present has brought us,
Facing the rising sun of our new day begun
Let us march on till victory is won.

The Black National Anthem, written by James Weldon Johnson in 1900, captures the essence of Lift Every Voice Books. Lift Every Voice Books is an imprint of Moody Publishers that celebrates a rich culture and great heritage of faith, based on the foundation of eternal truth—God's Word. We endeavor to restore the fabric of the African-American soul and reclaim the indomitable spirit that kept our forefathers true to God in spite of insurmountable odds.

We are Lift Every Voice Books—Christ-centered books and resources for restoring the African-American soul.

For more information on other books and products
written and produced from a biblical perspective, go to
www.lifteveryvoicebooks.com or write to:

Lift Every Voice Books
820 N. LaSalle Boulevard
Chicago, IL 60610
www.lifteveryvoicebooks.com